19 JAN 2017

This book should be returned/renewed by the latest date shown above. Overdue items incur charges which prevent self-service renewals. Please contact the library.

Wandsworth Libraries
24 hour Renewal Hotline
01159 293388
www.wandsworth.gov.uk

Wandsworth

CHARACTER PROFILES

WILL has been a Ranger for several years, having trained with the legendary Ranger Halt. Delivered to Castle Redmont as an orphan, he does not know the true story of his parents. When he was younger he dreamed of becoming a Knight, but now as a Ranger, he cannot imagine doing anything else. Will is known for his loyalty and bravery, and has proven himself in countless battles. As a Ranger, his next mission is always just around the corner.

HALT is a renowned member of the Ranger Corps, known for his mysterious ways and his unstoppable nature. He is a superb archer and uses a massive longbow. Like all Rangers his skill with the bow is uncanny, deadly accurate, and devastatingly swift. Although he rarely shows his emotions, he thinks of Will as his son.

HORACE is a legendary Knight of the Araluen Court, renowned throughout the Kingdom for his courage, strength and loyalty. Like Will and Alyss, he is an orphan, and grew up in the ward of Castle Redmont. He has the deepest respect for the Emperor, and will do whatever it takes to protect him.

EVANLYN (real name is Cassandra) is the Princess Royal of Araluen and King Duncan's only daughter. She created the alias

'Evanlyn' to protect her identity when she was captured by the Skandians. Tall and slim with long blonde hair, she's known for being strong-willed, brave and capable. She is an expert with the sling and is learning how to use a sword. She is good friends with Will, much to the dismay of Alyss.

ALYSS is a former ward mate of Horace and Will. Her beauty, intelligence and calm nature make her a perfect fit for her Diplomatic Service missions for the Kingdom. She is determined to learn how to defend herself, and takes a great interest in the martial arts. She is very fond of Will, having known him for many years, but can't help feeling jealous of his friendship with Evanlyn.

EMPEROR SHIGERU is kind and calm. He believes strongly in helping everyone in society — which has made him the enemy of the Senshi warriors, who wish to keep the class barriers in place. Although small, he is exceedingly fit with a wiry strength.

GEORGE grew up with Will, Horace and Alyss in Castle Redmont. In contrast to the others, he trained as a scribe and attorney and he has a particular interest in the ways of the Nihon-Ja. Because of his knowledge of local matters, he has been sent on this trip with Horace to observe and advise the young warrior on matters of protocol, and to update a dictionary of the Nihon-Jan language that he wrote two years ago.

HAVE YOU READ THEM ALL?

THE RUINS OF GORLAN (BOOK 1)
Will's training as an apprentice is gruelling, but his skills will be needed if he is to prevent the King's assassination.

THE BURNING BRIDGE (BOOK 2)
Will faces his most dangerous mission yet: the King's army has been deceived, and are headed for a brutal ambush.

THE ICEBOUND LAND (BOOK 3)
Will is trapped on a ship headed to the icebound land of Skandia. If he cannot escape, he faces a life of backbreaking slavery.

OAKLEAF BEARERS (BOOK 4)
Evanlyn has been taken captive by a mysterious horseman, and Will's attempts to rescue her lead him to the territory of a fearsome new enemy.

THE SORCERER IN THE NORTH (BOOK 5)
Will is a Ranger at last, but his new land is under threat from the terrifying figure of the Night Warrior.

THE SIEGE OF MACINDAW (BOOK 6)
A renegade knight has captured Castle Macindaw, and someone Will loves is being held hostage.

RANGER'S APPRENTICE

HAVE YOU GOT WHAT IT TAKES TO BE A RANGER?

The Rangers are an elite Special Forces Corps in the medieval Kingdom of Araluen. They are the eyes and ears of the Kingdom, the intelligence gatherers, the scouts and the troubleshooters.

Rangers are expert archers and carry two knives — one for throwing, and one for hunting. They are also highly skilled at tracking, concealment and unseen movement. Their ability to become virtually invisible has led common folk to view them with fear, thinking the Rangers must use black magic.

Occasionally, a young man who is judged to have the qualities of honesty, courage, agility and intelligence will be invited to undertake a five-year apprenticeship — to develop his natural abilities and instruct him in the almost supernatural skills of a Ranger.

If he passes his first year, he is given a bronze medallion in the shape of an oakleaf.

If he graduates, the bronze will be exchanged for the silver oakleaf of an Oakleaf Bearer — a Ranger of the Kingdom of Araluen.

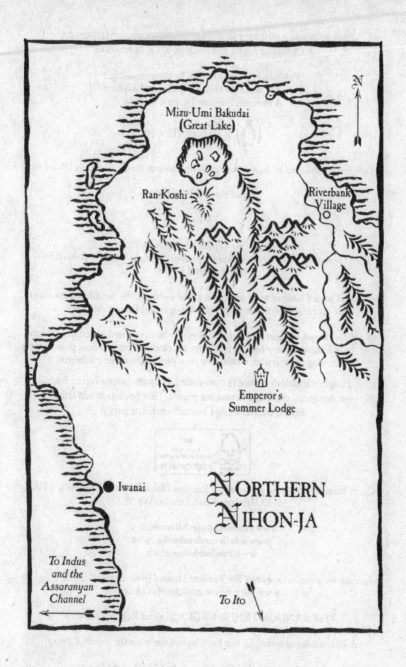

Mizu-Umi Bakudai
(Great Lake)

Ran-Koshi

Riverbank
Village

Emperor's
Summer Lodge

Iwanai

NORTHERN
NIHON-JA

To Indus
and the
Assaranyan
Channel

To Ito

RANGER'S APPRENTICE: THE EMPEROR OF NIHON-JA
A CORGI YEARLING BOOK 978 0 440 86984 9

Published in Great Britain by Corgi Yearling,
an imprint of Random House Children's Publishers UK
A Penguin Random House Company

Penguin
Random House
UK

Originally published in Australia in 2010 by Random House Australia (Pty) Ltd

This edition published 2011

7 9 10 8

Copyright © John Flanagan, 2010
Cover design by Tony Sahara. Cover illustration copyright © Shane Rebenschied
Map by David Elliott

The right of John Flanagan to be identified as the author of this work has been asserted
in accordance with the Copyright, Designs and Patents Act 1988.

Penguin Random House is committed to a sustainable future for
our business, our readers and our planet. This book is made from
Forest Stewardship Council® certified paper.

MIX
Paper from
responsible sources
FSC® C018179

Corgi Yearling Books are published by Random House Children's Publishers UK,
61–63 Uxbridge Road, London W5 5SA

www.**randomhousechildrens**.co.uk
www.**totallyrandombooks**.co.uk
www.**randomhouse**.co.uk

Addresses for companies within The Random House Group Limited can be found at:
www.randomhouse.co.uk/offices.htm

THE RANDOM HOUSE GROUP Limited Reg. No. 954009

A CIP catalogue record for this book is available from the British Library.

Printed and bound in Great Britain by Clays Ltd, St Ives plc

THE
EMPEROR OF
NIHON-JA

BOOK 10

JOHN FLANAGAN

CORGI YEARLING

One

Toscana

'*Avanti!*'

The command rang out over the sun-baked earth of the parade ground and the triple files of men stepped out together. At each stride, their iron-nailed sandals hit the ground in perfect unison, setting up a rhythmic thudding, which was counterpointed by the irregular jingle of weapons and equipment as they occasionally rubbed or clattered together. Already, their marching feet were raising a faint cloud of dust in their wake.

'You'd certainly see them coming from quite a distance,' Halt murmured.

Will looked sidelong at him and grinned. 'Maybe that's the idea.'

General Sapristi, who had organised this demonstration of Toscan military techniques for them, nodded approvingly.

'The young gentleman is correct,' he said.

Halt raised an eyebrow. 'He may be correct, and he is undoubtedly young. But he's no gentleman.'

Sapristi hesitated. Even after ten days in their company, he was still not completely accustomed to the constant stream of cheerful insults that flowed between these two strange Araluans. It was difficult to know when they were serious and when they were speaking in fun. Some of the things they said to each other would be cause for mayhem and bloodshed between Toscans, whose pride was notoriously stronger than their sense of humour. He looked at the younger Ranger and noticed that he seemed to have taken no offence.

'Ah, Signor Halt,' he said uncertainly, 'you are making a joke, yes?'

'He is making a joke, no,' Will said. 'But he likes to think he is making a joke, yes.'

Sapristi decided it might be less confusing to get back to the point that the two Rangers had already raised.

'In any event,' he said, 'we find that the dust raised by our soldiers can often cause enemies to disperse. Very few enemies are willing to face our legions in open battle.'

'They certainly can march nicely,' Halt said mildly.

Sapristi glanced at him, sensing that the demonstration so far had done little to impress the grey-bearded Araluan. He smiled inwardly. That would change in a few minutes, he thought.

'Here's Selethen,' Will said and, as the other two looked down, they could see the distinctively tall form of the Arridi leader climbing the steps of the reviewing platform to join them.

Selethen, representing the Arridi *Emrikir*, was in Toscana

to negotiate a trade and military pact with the Toscan Senate. Over the years, the Toscans and Arridi had clashed intermittently, their countries separated only by the relatively narrow waters of the Constant Sea. Yet each country had items that the other needed. The Arridi had reserves of red gold and iron in their deserts that the Toscans required to finance and equip their large armies. Even more important, Toscans had become inordinately fond of *kafay*, the rich coffee grown by the Arridi.

The desert dwellers, for their part, looked to Toscana for woven cloth — the fine linen and cotton so necessary in the fierce desert heat — and for the excellent grade of olive oil the Toscans produced, which was far superior to their locally grown product. Plus there was a constant need to replenish and bring new breeding stock to their herds of sheep and goats. Animal mortality in the desert was high.

In the past, the two nations had fought over such items. But now, wiser heads prevailed and they had decided that an alliance might be mutually beneficial for trade and for security. The waters of the Constant Sea were infested by corsairs in swift, small galleys. They swooped on merchant ships travelling between the two countries, robbing and sinking them.

Some in the region even looked back regretfully to the time when Skandian wolfships used to visit these waters. The Skandians had raided as well, but never in the numbers that were seen these days. And the presence of the Skandian ships had kept the incidence of local pirates down.

Nowadays, the Skandians were more law abiding. Their Oberjarl, Erak, had discovered that it was far more profitable to hire his ships out to other countries who needed to secure their national waters. As a result, the Skandians had become the de facto naval police in many parts of the world. The Toscans and Arridi, with no significant naval forces of their own, had decided, as part of their agreement, to lease a squadron of wolfships to patrol the waters between their two coastlines.

All of which were the reasons why Halt and Will had spent the past ten days in Toscana. The longstanding enmity between the two countries, accompanied by the inevitable suspicion of the other's intentions, had led both sides to agree to ask a third-party nation to act as arbitrator in the treaty that was being put in place. Araluen was a country trusted by both Arrida and Toscana. In addition, the Araluans had close ties with the Skandian Oberjarl and it was felt that their intervention would be helpful in forming a relationship with the wild northern seamen.

It was logical for Selethen to suggest the inclusion of Halt and Will in the Araluan delegation. He had included Horace in the request as well, but duty had taken Horace elsewhere.

The actual wording and conditions of the treaty were not the concern of the two Rangers. They were simply here to escort the chief Araluan negotiator — Alyss Mainwaring, Will's childhood sweetheart and one of the brighter new members of the Araluan Diplomatic Service.

She was presently locked away with the Arridi and Toscan lawyers, thrashing out the fine details of the agreement.

Selethen dropped gratefully into a seat beside Will. The three companies of Toscan legionnaires — thirty-three to a company, with an overall commander making up the traditional Toscan century of one hundred men — pivoted through a smart right turn below them, changing from a three-abreast formation to an extended eleven-abreast. In spite of the wider formation their lines were still geometrically perfect — straight as a sword blade, Will thought. He was about to voice the thought, then he smiled. The simile wouldn't be accurate so far as Selethen's curved sabre was concerned.

'How are the negotiations progressing?' Halt asked.

Selethen pursed his lips. 'As all such things progress. My chamberlain is asking for a reduction of three-quarters of a per cent on the duty to be charged for *kafay*. Your advocates,' he said, including Sapristi in the conversation, 'are holding out for no more than five-eighths of a per cent. I had to have a break from it all. Sometimes I think they do this because they simply like to argue.'

Sapristi nodded. 'It's always the way. We soldiers risk our lives fighting while the lawyers quibble over fractions of a percentage point. And yet they look upon us as lesser beings.'

'How's Alyss managing?' Will asked.

Selethen turned an approving look on him. 'Your Lady Alyss is proving to be an island of calm and common sense in a sea of dispute. She is very, very patient. Although I sense that she has been tempted to whack my chamberlain over the head with his sheaf of papers on several occasions.' He looked down at the three Toscan companies, now reforming into three files.

'A destra! Doppio di corsa!'

The order was given by the century commander, who

stood in the centre of the parade ground. Instantly, the companies turned right, reformed into three files, then broke into double time, the thud of their sandals and the jingle of equipment sounding louder and more urgent with the increase in pace. The dust rose higher as well.

'General Sapristi,' Selethen asked, indicating the tight formations, 'this precision drilling makes for quite a spectacle. But is there any real benefit to gain from it?'

'Indeed there is, *Wakir*. Our fighting methods depend on discipline and cohesion. The men in each century fight as one unit.'

'Once a battle begins, my men fight largely as individuals,' Selethen said. His voice indicated that he saw little value in this style of co-ordinated, almost machine-like manoeuvring. 'Of course, it's the commander's job to bring his forces into the most advantageous position on the field. But after that, I find it's almost impossible to control them as individuals. Best to let them fight their own way.'

'That's why all this drilling is necessary,' Sapristi replied. 'Our men become accustomed to reacting to orders. It becomes instinctive. We teach them a few vital drills, and practise them over and over. It takes years to train an expert warrior. Constant drilling means we can have a legion ready to fight effectively in less than a year.'

'But they can't possibly learn to be expert swordsmen in so short a time?' Will asked.

Sapristi shook his head. 'They don't have to. Watch and learn, Ranger Will.'

'*Alt!*' The command rang out and the three companies crashed to a stop as one.

'A cloud of dust and a line of statues,' Will mused.

Across the parade ground, a trumpet blared and warriors began to appear from behind the buildings there. They moved quickly to form an extended line of battle — not as disciplined or as rigidly maintained as the century's formation. They were armed with wooden practice swords — long-bladed swords, Will noticed, and round shields. Roughly one-quarter of them carried recurve bows in addition to their swords.

At a command, the 'enemy' began to advance across the parade ground. The line undulated as some sections moved faster than others.

'Tre rige!' shouted the century commander. Halt glanced a question at Sapristi.

'Form three ranks,' the general translated. 'We don't use the common tongue for field commands. No sense in letting the enemy know what you have in mind.'

'None at all,' Halt agreed mildly.

Moving smoothly and without any undue haste, the three companies trotted into position, three ranks deep and thirty-three wide. The ranks were separated from each other by about a metre and a half.

The enemy force halted their advance some sixty metres from the rigid lines of legionnaires.

The wild-looking enemy tribesmen brandished their weapons and, at a shouted command, those among them with bows stepped forward, arrows ready on the string. The observers heard the faint sound of fifty arrows rasping against the bows as they were drawn back to the fullest extent. At the same time, the centurion called his counter order.

'*Tartaruga! Pronto!*'

Ninety-nine man-high, curved shields came round to the front, with a rattle of equipment.

'*Tartaruga* means "tortoise",' Sapristi explained. '*Pronto* means "ready".'

The enemy commander shouted an order and the archers released a ragged volley. As the first arrow sped away, the Toscan centurion bellowed:

'*Azione!*'

'Action,' translated Sapristi.

Instantly, the soldiers reacted. The front rank crouched slightly, so that their shields covered them completely. The second and third rank stepped close. The second rank raised their shields to head height, interlocking them with those of the front rank. The third rank did likewise. The hundred men of the century were now sheltered by a barricade of shields to the front and a roof of shields overhead.

Seconds later, the volley of arrows clattered against them, bouncing off harmlessly.

'Just like a tortoise,' Will observed. 'Who are the enemy?'

'They're all warriors from neighbouring countries and provinces who have elected to join our empire,' Sapristi replied smoothly.

Halt regarded him for a moment. 'Did they elect to join?' he asked. 'Or was the decision made for them?'

'Perhaps we helped a little with the decision-making process,' the Toscan general admitted. 'In any event they are all skilled and experienced warriors and we use them as auxiliaries and scouts. They are extremely useful for demonstrations of this kind. Watch now.'

The attacking force had stopped at the point from which they had fired the volley of arrows. The general pointed to where a group of orderlies were running onto the field, each one carrying a rough outline of a man cut from light wood. There were at least one hundred of them, Will estimated. He watched curiously as the men placed the upright targets in place, thirty metres from the front rank of the legionnaires.

'For the purpose of the demonstration,' Sapristi said, 'we'll assume that the enemy has reached this position in their advance. We don't use real warriors for this part of the exercise. It's too costly, and we need our auxiliaries.'

The orderlies, many of them glancing nervously at the still ranks of legionnaires, ran from the field once their targets were in position.

Will leaned forward eagerly. 'What happens now, General?'

Sapristi allowed himself a small smile.

'Watch and see,' he said.

Two

Nihon-Ja, some months earlier

Horace slid the screen to one side, grimacing slightly as he eased the door open. By now, he had learned to handle these light wood and paper structures carefully. In his first week in Nihon-Ja he had destroyed several sliding panels. He was used to doors that were heavy and needed some effort to get them moving. His hosts were always quick to apologise and to assure him that the workmanship must have been faulty but he knew the real reason was his own clumsiness. Sometimes he felt like a blind bear in a porcelain factory.

Emperor Shigeru looked up at the tall Araluan warrior, noticing the extreme care he took with the door, and smiled in genuine amusement.

'Ah, Or'ss-san,' he said, 'you are most considerate to spare our flimsy door from destruction.'

Horace shook his head. 'Your excellency is too kind.' He

bowed. George — an old acquaintance of Horace's from his days in the Ward at Redmont and his protocol adviser on this journey — had impressed upon him that this was not done out of any sense of self-abasement. The Nihon-Jan bowed to each other routinely, as a mark of mutual respect. In general, the depth of the bow from both sides was the same. However, George had added, it was politic to bow much deeper to the Emperor than you might expect him to bow to you. Horace had no problem with the custom. He found Shigeru to be a fascinating and gracious host, well worthy of deference. In some ways, he reminded Horace of King Duncan — a man for whom Horace had the deepest respect.

The Emperor was a small man, much shorter than Horace. It was difficult to estimate his age. The Nihon-Jan all seemed much younger than they really were. Shigeru's hair was tinged with grey, so Horace guessed that he must be in his fifties. But small as he might be, he was amazingly fit and possessed a deceptive wiry strength. He also had a surprisingly deep voice and a booming laugh when he was amused, which was often.

Shigeru clicked his tongue lightly as a signal that the young man didn't need to hold the position any longer. As Horace straightened up, the Emperor bowed in reply. He liked the muscular young warrior and he had enjoyed having him as a guest.

In training sessions with some of the leading Nihon-Jan warriors, Shigeru had seen that Horace was highly skilled with the weapons of his own country — the sword, longer and heavier than the curved Nihon-Jan *katana*, and the round shield that he used so effectively. Yet the young man showed no sense of arrogance and had been keen to study and compliment the techniques of the Nihon-Jan swordsmen.

That was the purpose of Horace's mission. As a Swordmaster in Araluen, and as a potential Battlemaster, it made sense that Horace should be familiar with as wide a range of fighting techniques as possible. It was for that reason that Duncan had despatched him on this military mission. In addition, Duncan could see that Horace was becoming bored. After the heady excitement of his clash with the Outsiders in company with Will and Halt, it was easy for the young man to become impatient with the humdrum routine of life at Castle Araluen. Much to the chagrin of Duncan's daughter, Cassandra, who enjoyed Horace's company more and more, he had sent him on this fact-finding mission.

'Look at this, Or'ss-san,' Shigeru said, beckoning him forward.

Horace smiled. None of the Nihon-Jan had been able to master the pronunciation of his name. He had become used to being addressed as Or'ss-san. After a few early attempts, Shigeru had cheerfully adopted the simplified version. Now he held out his cupped hands to Horace and the young man leaned forward to look.

There was a perfect yellow flower nestled in the Emperor's palm. Shigeru shook his head.

'See?' he said. 'Here we are, with autumn upon us. This flower should have withered and died weeks ago. But today I found it here in my pebble garden. Is it not a matter for thought and wonder?'

'Indeed it is,' Horace replied. He realised that he had learned a great deal in his time here — and not all of it about military matters. Shigeru, even with the responsibility of ruling a varied and, in some cases, headstrong group of subjects, could still find time to wonder at the small occasions of beauty to be found in nature. Horace sensed that this ability led to the Emperor's enjoying a great deal of inner peace and contributed in no small measure to his ability to face and solve problems in a calm and unflustered way.

Having shown the flower to his guest, the Emperor knelt and returned it to the neatly raked array of black and white pebbles.

'It should remain here,' he said. 'This is where its fate decreed that it should be.'

There were stepping stones through the garden so that the Emperor and his guest could avoid disturbing the symmetry of the raked stones. It was like a stone pond, Horace thought. He was aware that each morning, the Emperor would rake the pebbles into a slightly different pattern. A lesser man might have had servants perform this task, but Shigeru enjoyed doing it himself.

'If everything is done for me,' he had explained to Horace, 'how will I ever learn?'

Now the Emperor rose gracefully to his feet once more.

'I'm afraid your time with us is coming to an end,' he said.

Horace nodded. 'Yes, your excellency. I'll have to return to Iwanai. Our ship is due there at the end of the week.'

'We'll be sorry to lose you,' Shigeru said.

'I'll be sorry to go,' Horace replied.

The Emperor smiled. 'But not sorry to return home?'

Horace had to smile in return. 'No. I'll be glad to get home. I've been away a long time.'

The Emperor gestured for Horace to follow and they left the pebble garden and entered a perfectly cultivated grove of trees. Once they were off the stepping stones, there was room for them to walk side by side.

'I hope your trip has been worthwhile. Have you learned much while you have been with us?' Shigeru asked.

'A great deal, your excellency. I'm not sure that your system would suit Araluen, but it is an interesting one.'

Nihon-Ja drew its warriors from a small, elite upper class, known as the Senshi. They were born to be trained in the art of the sword and began their training from an early age, to the detriment of most other forms of learning. As a result, the Senshi had become an aggressive and war-like sect, with a sense of superiority over the other classes of Nihon-Jan society.

Shigeru was a Senshi, but he was something of an exception. Naturally, he had trained with the *katana* since boyhood and he was a competent, if not an expert, warrior. As Emperor, it was expected that he should learn these skills. But he had wider interests – as Horace had just observed – and a compassionate and inquiring side to his nature. He was genuinely concerned for what were held to be the lower classes: the fishermen, farmers and timber workers who were regarded with contempt by the majority of Senshi.

'I'm not sure that we can maintain it as it is for much longer in this country either,' he told Horace. 'Or that we should.'

The young warrior looked sidelong at him. He knew that Shigeru had been working to improve conditions for the lower classes, and to give them a greater voice in how the country was governed. He had also learned that these initiatives were highly unpopular with a significant number of the Senshi.

'The Senshi will resist any change,' he warned the Emperor and the older man sighed.

'Yes. They will. They like to be in charge. This is why it is forbidden for the common people to carry arms or learn any weapon skills. They far outnumber the Senshi but the Senshi make up for their lack of numbers by their skill with weapons and their ferocity in battle. It's too much to ask untrained fishermen or farmers or timber workers to face such deadly opponents. It has happened in the past, of course, but when the workers did protest, they were cut to pieces.'

'I can imagine,' Horace said.

Shigeru stood a little straighter, held his head a little higher. 'But the Senshi must learn. They must adapt. They cannot continue to treat the people — my people — as inferiors. We need our workers, just as we need our warriors. Without the workers, there would be no food for the Senshi, no timber for their homes, no firewood to heat them or for the forges that create their swords. They must see that everybody contributes and there should be greater equality.'

Horace pursed his lips. He didn't want to reply because he sensed that Shigeru was setting himself an impossible task. With the exception of the Emperor's immediate retainers, the majority of Senshi had shown themselves to be fiercely opposed to any change in the current system — particularly if it gave a greater voice to the lower classes.

Shigeru sensed the young man's hesitation. 'You don't agree?' he asked mildly.

Horace shrugged uncomfortably. 'I agree,' he said. 'But my opinion doesn't matter. The question is, does Lord Arisaka agree?'

Horace had met Arisaka in the first week of his visit. He was the overlord of the Shimonseki clan, one of the largest and fiercest groups of Senshi warriors. He was a powerful and influential man and he made no secret of his opinion that the Senshi should remain the dominant class in Nihon-Ja. He was also a Swordmaster, regarded as one of the finest individual warriors in the country. Horace had heard rumours that Arisaka had killed more than twenty men in duels — and even more in the internecine battles that flared from time to time between the clans.

Shigeru smiled grimly at the mention of the arrogant warlord. 'Arisaka-san may have to learn to agree to his Emperor's wishes. After all, he has sworn an oath to me.'

'Then I'm sure he'll honour that oath,' Horace said, although he had grave doubts about the matter. As ever, Shigeru saw past the words themselves and recognised the concern in Horace's voice.

'But I'm being an impolite host,' he said. 'We have a little time left together and you should enjoy it — not spend it worrying over the internal politics of Nihon-Ja. Perhaps we can ride together to Iwanai? I'll have to be leaving here soon to return to Ito myself.'

They had spent the past week relaxing in the informal atmosphere of the Emperor's summer lodge, at the foot of the mountains. His principal palace and seat of government was a magnificent walled fortress in the city of Ito, a week's ride to the south. Their time at the lodge had been pleasant but, as Shigeru had noted earlier, autumn was forcing its way across the land, with its cold and blustery winds, and the summer lodge was not the most comfortable accommodation in cold weather.

'I'd enjoy that,' Horace said, pleased at the prospect of spending a few more days in Shigeru's company. He wondered at the bond of respect and affection that he felt for the Emperor. Perhaps it had to do with the fact that Horace had grown up as an orphan, and so he was drawn to Shigeru's understated strength, gentle wisdom and unfailing good humour. In some ways, the Emperor reminded him of Halt, although his smooth good manners were a marked contrast to the Ranger's often acerbic nature. He gestured to the carefully cultivated trees around them, their leaves now blazing yellow and orange to herald autumn.

'I should tell George to start making preparations for the trip,' he said. 'I'll leave you to contemplate your trees.'

Shigeru, in his turn, gazed at the patterns of dark trunks and blazing leaves around him. He loved the peace and solitude in this garden, far away from the self-serving politics of the capital.

'Their beauty will be small recompense for the loss of your company,' he said smoothly and Horace grinned at him.

'You know, your excellency, I wish I could say stuff like that.'

Three

Toscana

A command rang across the parade ground and Will
watched the roof of shields disappear as the legionnaires lowered them back to their normal position.

Then, in response to another command, the second and
third ranks took a pace backwards. Each man carried a long
javelin in addition to the short sword he wore on his right side.
Now the men in the rear rank reversed their grip, turned side
on and raised the javelins to the throwing position, right arms
extended back, the javelins balanced over their right shoulders, aiming upwards at an angle of about forty degrees.

'Azione!'

Thirty-three right arms came forward, thirty-three right
legs stepped into the cast and the flight of javelins arced
away towards the wooden targets. They were still on their
way when the second rank repeated the action, sending
another thirty-three projectiles soaring.

There was no individual aim — each man simply cast his weapon at the mass of targets in front of him. Will realised that in a real battle, the optimum distance would be decided by the century commander, who was calling the orders.

The first volley arced up, then pitched down as the heavy iron heads of the javelins overcame the force of the throw. There was a rolling, splintering crash as the javelins hit home. Half of them struck the ground harmlessly. The other half smashed into the light wooden targets, knocking them to the ground. A few seconds later, the second flight arrived, with similar results. Within the space of a few seconds, nearly a third of the hundred targets had been splintered and demolished.

'Interesting,' Halt said softly. Will glanced quickly at him. Halt's face was impassive but Will knew him well. Halt was impressed.

'The first blow is often decisive,' Sapristi told them. 'Warriors who have never fought our legions before are shaken by this sudden devastation.'

'I can imagine,' Selethen said. He was watching keenly and Will guessed that he was imagining those lethal javelins crashing into a company of his light cavalry at full gallop.

'But today, for the sake of demonstration, our "enemy" will be overcome with rage and will go on with the attack,' the general continued.

As he spoke, the wild mass of enemy warriors moved up to the point where the targets had been savaged and splintered. Now they brandished their swords and charged at the wall of shields.

The solid crash as they hit the wall carried clearly to the observers. The front rank swayed a little under the initial impact. Then it steadied and held fast. Looking carefully, Will could see that the second row had closed up and were actually pushing their comrades forward, supporting them against the initial impact of the charge.

The tribesmen's swords flailed in swinging arcs at the big square shields. But for the most part they were ineffective — and they were getting in each other's way. By contrast, the short wooden practice swords of the legionnaires began to flicker in and out like serpents' tongues through narrow gaps in the shield wall, and the observers could hear the shouts of rage and pain from the attackers. The demonstration might be using blunt wooden weapons, but those jabbing impacts would be painful and the legionnaires weren't holding back.

'How can they see?' Will asked. The men in the front rank were crouched low behind the barrier formed by their shields.

'They can't see very well,' Sapristi told him. 'They see an occasional leg or arm or torso through the gaps and they stab out at them. After all, a man hit on the thigh or arm is rendered as ineffective as much as a man stabbed through the chest. Our troops just plough forward, jabbing and stabbing at anything they see on the other side of their shields.'

'That's why your men don't need to be expert swordsmen,' Will said.

The general smiled appreciatively at him. 'That's right. They don't have to learn any advanced techniques of strike and parry and riposte. They just stab and jab with the point of the sword. It's a simple technique to learn and a few centimetres of the point does just as much damage as a wide sweeping blow. Now watch as the second rank add their weight to the advance.'

The perfectly aligned front rank was edging slowly forward, crowding the enemy and forcing them back. Now the second rank suddenly rushed forward, once more adding their weight and impetus to those of the men in front of them, and the extra drive sent the enemy staggering back, buffeted and shoved by the huge shields, jabbed and harassed by the darting short swords. Then, having gained a brief respite, the formation stopped. A long whistle blast rang out and the second rank turned in place so that they stood back-to-back with the front rank. Another signal on the whistle and the front rank pivoted to their left, while the second rank pivoted right. Each pair of men stepped in a small half-circle. Within a few seconds, the front rank had been replaced, all at once, by the fresh men from the second rank. The former front rankers passed back through the third rank, who took their place behind the new front row. The attackers now faced totally fresh opponents, while the former front rank had a chance to recover and redress their losses.

'That's brilliant,' Will said.

Sapristi nodded at him. 'It's drill and co-ordination,' he said. 'Our men don't need to be expert swordmasters. That takes a lifetime of training. They need to be drilled and to work as a team. Even a relatively unskilled warrior can be effective in these conditions. And it doesn't take long to learn.'

'Which is why you can maintain such a large army,' Halt said.

Sapristi switched his gaze to the older Ranger. 'Exactly,' he replied. Most countries maintained a relatively small standing force of expert warriors as the core of their army, calling on less-skilled men at arms to fill out the numbers in time of war. The Toscans, however, needing to maintain order in their spreading empire, had to have a large permanent army on call at all times.

Selethen fingered his chin thoughtfully. His left hand had strayed unconsciously to the hilt of his sabre as he watched. Sapristi glanced at him, pleased to see that the demonstration had had a sobering effect on the Arridi leader. It didn't hurt, Sapristi thought, for Toscana's new ally to appreciate the might of the Toscan legions.

'Let's go and take a look at the results,' Sapristi said. He rose and led the way down from the reviewing platform to the parade ground, where the two forces, the demonstration now complete, had drawn apart. The legionnaires still stood in their measured rows. The attacking force milled about in a loose group.

'We had the practice swords dipped in fresh paint, so we could measure results,' Sapristi told them. He led the way to the enemy group. As they drew closer, Halt and Will could see arms, legs, torsos, necks spattered with red blotches. The marks were testimony to the number of times the legionnaires' wooden swords had found their mark.

The attackers' longer swords had been coated with white paint. Looking now, the Araluans could see only occasional evidence that these swords had struck home. There were criss-cross patterns and random splotches of white on the shields and some of the brass helmets of the legionnaires, but the majority of men in the century were unscathed.

'Very effective,' Selethen told the general. 'Very effective indeed.' Already, his agile mind was at work, figuring ways to counteract a force of heavy infantry such as this.

Halt was obviously having similar thoughts. 'Of course, you've chosen perfect conditions for heavy infantry here,' he said, sweeping an arm around the flat, open parade ground. 'In more constricted country, like forest land, you wouldn't be able to manoeuvre so efficiently.'

Sapristi nodded in acknowledgement. 'True,' he said. 'But we choose our battlefields and let the enemy come to us. If they don't, we simply invade their lands. Sooner or later, they have to face us in battle.'

Will had wandered away from the group and was studying one of the javelins. It was a crude weapon, he saw. The square wooden shaft was only roughly shaped — just a very ordinary, minimally dressed piece of hardwood. The point was equally utilitarian. It was a thick rod of soft iron, about half a metre long, hammered flat at the end and sharpened into a barbed point. A groove had been cut down one side of the shaft and the head had been slotted into it and bound in place with brass wire.

Sapristi saw him looking at it and walked over to join him.

'They're not pretty,' he said. 'But they work. And they're easy and quick to make. In fact, the soldiers can make their own, at a pinch. We can turn out thousands of these in a week. And you've seen how effective they can be.' He indicated the rows of smashed and splintered targets.

'It's bent,' Will said critically, running his hand along the distorted iron head.

'And it can be straightened easily and used again,' the general told him. 'But that's actually an advantage. Imagine one of these hitting an enemy's shield. It penetrates, and the barb holds it in place. Then the head bends, so that the handle is dragging on the ground. Try fighting effectively with nearly two metres of iron and wood dragging from your shield. I assure you, it's not an easy thing to do.'

Will shook his head admiringly. 'It's all very practical, isn't it?'

'It's a logical solution to the problem of creating a large and effective fighting force,' Sapristi told him. 'If you pitted any of these legionnaires in a one-on-one battle against a professional warrior, they would probably lose. But give me a hundred unskilled men to drill for six months and I'll back them against an equal number of warriors who've been training in individual combat skills all their lives.'

'So it's the system that's successful, not the individual?' Will said.

'Exactly,' Sapristi told him. 'And so far, nobody has come up with a way to defeat our system in open battle.'

'How would you do it?' Halt asked Selethen that night. The negotiations had been finalised, agreed, signed and witnessed. There had been an official banquet to celebrate the fact, with speeches and compliments on all sides. Now Selethen and the Araluan party were relaxing in the Araluans' quarters. It would be their last night together as the

Wakir was due to leave early the following morning. Selethen had brought some of the trade gift *kafay* with him and he, Will and Halt were all savouring the brew. Nobody, Will thought, made coffee quite as well as the Arridi.

Alyss sat by the fireplace, smiling at the three of them. She liked coffee, but for Rangers, and apparently the Arridi, coffee drinking was close to a religious experience. She contented herself with a goblet of fresh, citrus-tasting sherbet.

'Simple,' said Selethen. 'Never let them choose the conditions. As Sapristi said, they've never been defeated in open battle. So you need fight a more fluid action against them. Catch them when they're on the move and in file. Hit them on the flanks with quick raids, before they can go into their defensive formation. Or use artillery against them. That rigid formation makes for a very compact target. Hit it with heavy bolts from a mangonel or rocks from catapults and you'd start to punch holes in it. Once it loses cohesion, it's not so formidable.'

Halt was nodding. 'I was thinking the same,' he said. 'Never confront them head-on. If you could get a force of archers behind them without their realising it, their tortoise formation would be vulnerable.

'But of course,' he continued, 'they rely on their enemies' sense of outrage when they invade a country. Very few armies will have the patience to carry out a running battle, harassing and weakening them over a period. Very few leaders would be able to convince their followers that this was the best way. National pride would force most to confront them, to try to force them back across the border.'

'And we saw what happens when you confront them,' Will said. 'Those javelins were effective.' Both the older men nodded.

'Limited range, however,' Selethen said. 'No more than thirty or forty metres.'

'But quite deadly at that range,' Halt said, agreeing with Will.

'It seems to me,' said Alyss cheerfully, 'that the best course to take would be one of negotiation. Negotiate with them rather than fight them. Use diplomacy, not weapons.'

'Spoken like a true diplomat,' Halt said, giving her one of his rare smiles. He was fond of Alyss, and her bond with Will made him even more inclined to like her. She bowed her head in mock modesty. 'But what if diplomacy fails?'

Alyss rose to the challenge without hesitation. 'Then you can always resort to bribery,' she said. 'A little gold in the right hands can accomplish more than a forest of swords.' Her eyes twinkled as she said it.

Selethen shook his head in admiration. 'Your Araluan women would fit in well in my country,' he said. 'Lady Alyss's grasp of the skills of negotiation is first class.'

'I recall you weren't quite so enthusiastic about Princess Evanlyn's negotiating skills,' Halt said.

'I have to admit I met my match there,' he said ruefully. In his previous encounter with Araluans, he had tried to bamboozle Evanlyn in their haggling over a ransom payment for Oberjarl Erak. The princess had remained totally un-bamboozled and had very neatly outwitted him.

Alyss frowned slightly at the mention of Evanlyn's

name. She was not one of the princess's greatest admirers. However, she recovered quickly and smiled again.

'Women are good negotiators,' she said. 'We prefer to leave all the sweaty, unpleasant details of battle to people like your —'

She was interrupted by a discreet knock at the door. Since this was a diplomatic mission, she was in fact the leader of the Araluan party. 'Come in,' she called in reply, then added in a lower voice to the others, 'I wonder what's happened? After all, it's a little late for callers.'

The door opened to admit one of her servants. The man glanced nervously around. He realised he was interrupting a conversation between the head of the mission, two Rangers and the most high-ranking representative of the Arridi party.

'My apologies for interrupting, Lady Alyss,' he began uncertainly.

She reassured him with a wave of her hand. 'It's perfectly all right, Edmund. I assume it's important?'

The servant swallowed nervously. 'You could say so, my lady. The Crown Princess Cassandra has arrived and she wants to see you all.'

Four

Nihon-Ja

The wind had picked up since they had left the Emperor's summer lodge the previous day. Now it was keening through the valley as they rode carefully down the narrow track that angled down one side, and gusting strongly as it was funnelled between the constricting hills that formed the valley. The trees around them seemed to have adopted a permanent lean to one side, so constant was the force of the wind. Horace pulled his sheepskin collar a little higher around his ears and nestled gratefully into its warm depths.

He glanced up. The sky was a brilliant ice blue, but already heavy grey clouds were scudding across it, sending bands of shadow flitting silently across the landscape below. To the south, he could see a dark line of solid cloud. He estimated that it would be upon them by early afternoon and it would probably bring rain with it. He considered suggesting that they might make camp for the day before the rain added its force to the wind. There was no need to rush their journey — the port of Iwanai was within easy riding distance — and he didn't relish the idea of pitching tents in a driving rainstorm. Better to get them up while the party was still dry and shelter inside them through the deteriorating weather.

The trail they were following levelled and widened for a hundred metres or so, so Horace urged his horse alongside that of the Emperor, who was riding immediately before him. Shigeru, huddled deep in his own fur robes, sensed the presence beside him and looked around. He grimaced at the racing clouds overhead and gave a small shrug.

Horace pulled his collar down to speak, feeling the icy bite of the wind on his face as he did so.

'Do you think it will snow?' he called, pitching his voice above the constant battering of the wind.

Shigeru looked at the sky again and shook his head. 'It's a little early in the year. Perhaps in a week or two we'll get a few light falls. Then, in a month, the real snow will begin. But we'll be far away from here by then. Once we're out of the mountains, the weather won't be so severe.' He glanced again at the ominous cloud front.

'Plenty of rain there, however,' he continued cheerfully.

Horace grinned. Very little seemed to faze Shigeru. Many rulers would have spent the morning complaining loudly about the cold and the discomfort, as if their complaints would actually serve to alleviate the situation and as if their attendants should be able to do something about it. Not the Emperor. He accepted the situation, knowing that he could do nothing to change the weather. Best to endure it without making life more difficult for those around him.

'Perhaps we should make camp early,' Horace suggested.

Shigeru was about to reply when a cry from one of their point riders caught their attention.

In addition to a few household servants — and of course Horace and George — Shigeru was travelling with a relatively small screen of bodyguards. Only a dozen Senshi warriors, under the command of Shukin, the Emperor's cousin, had accompanied him to the summer lodge. Again, Horace thought, it was a measure of the man himself. Shigeru had little cause to fear attack. He was popular with the common people. They knew he was working to improve their lot and they loved him for it. Previous emperors had not enjoyed such esteem and it had always been necessary for them to surround themselves with large parties of armed men when they travelled through the countryside.

One of the Senshi had been posted well ahead of the group as a point rider. Another three were grouped some ten metres ahead of Horace and the Emperor. The remainder were stationed behind. On this narrow trail, there was no room for outriders on their flank, although they would be deployed once the party reached the valley floor.

The rider who had cried out now held up his hand, bringing the main party to a halt. Horace heard a clatter of hooves and a warning call from behind him. Glancing back, he edged his horse to one side to allow Shukin and four of the guards to edge past him. The Emperor did the same.

'What's the problem?' Shigeru asked Shukin, as the escort leader trotted past. Out of deference to Horace, and to avoid the need for translation, he spoke the common language, not Nihon-Jan.

'I don't know, cousin,' Shukin replied. 'Kaeko-san has seen something. I'll report once I've spoken to him. Please wait here.'

He glanced over his shoulder, reassuring himself that the four men remaining in the rearguard had moved up to form a closer screen, then rode on.

Without conscious thought, Horace's left hand dropped to his scabbard, angling it slightly forward so that, if the need arose for him to draw his sword, he could do so quickly. His trademark round shield was still slung on his back. No need to change that at the moment. He could shrug it round into position in a second or two if required.

Shigeru's horse shifted its feet nervously as the guards rode past. The Emperor patted its neck and spoke soothingly to it and the horse settled. Then the Emperor slumped more comfortably in the saddle, looked at Horace and shrugged.

'I imagine we'll hear what's going on in a moment or two,' he said. His manner indicated that he was sure this was a false alarm, that his guards were being over-cautious. He gazed after Shukin as his cousin reined in beside the Senshi warrior who had been riding point. There was a brief discussion, then both Shigeru and Horace saw Kaeko pointing to something further down the valley, where the trail zigzagged back to accommodate the steep slope of the hillside.

Shukin trotted back to report.

'There's a rider coming. It's one of your household staff, cousin. And he seems in a hurry.'

Shigeru frowned. It would take a lot of bring one of his official staff out in this sort of weather.

George edged his horse up to Horace now. George was a trained scribe and attorney and he had made a comprehensive study of the ways of the Nihon-Jan. This was not his first trip to the country. Because of his knowledge of local matters, he had been sent on this trip with Horace to observe and advise the young warrior on matters of protocol, and to update a dictionary of the Nihon-Jan language that he had written two years ago.

George could be a little stuffy and full of himself at times but he was essentially good-hearted and he had provided excellent advice to Horace on the journey. Horace had been glad to have him along.

'Why are we stopping?' he asked.

Horace jerked a thumb further along the trail. 'There's a rider. A messenger, probably. Best if we wait for him to come to us.'

'A messenger? Who is it? Is Lord Shigeru expecting a message? Do we know what it's about?' George's questions came tumbling out before Horace had a chance to begin answering.

Horace shook his head and smiled at his old childhood companion. 'I don't know. I don't know. And . . . I don't know,' he said. He saw George's shoulders relax as he realised his questions had been unreasonable. 'I imagine we'll find out when he comes up to us.'

'Of course. Silly of me,' George said. He sounded

genuinely aggrieved that he had let his mask of professional calm slip the way it had.

'Don't let it bother you,' Horace said, then he couldn't help parroting one of George's oft-repeated catch cries. 'After all, if you don't ask, you'll never learn.'

George had the grace to allow a thin smile. He never liked being the object of jokes. He felt it undermined his dignity.

'Yes, yes. Quite so, *Sir* Horace.' His slight emphasis on Horace's title was evidence that he felt Horace's sally had been unnecessary.

Horace shrugged to himself. Live with it, George, he thought.

The rattle of galloping hooves was closer now. The rider had reached the sharp elbow turn in the trail and was heading up the last hundred metres or so towards them. A call from Shukin saw the four warriors ahead of the party make room on the trail to let the new arrival through.

He drew level with the Emperor and Shukin and did his best to bow from the saddle. That was odd, thought Horace. He'd been around Shigeru long enough to know that the proper etiquette called for the rider to dismount and then kneel. The message, whatever it is, must be urgent.

George had noticed the breach of normal behaviour as well. 'Something's gone wrong,' he said quietly.

The messenger was speaking rapidly to Shigeru now. He kept his voice low so that those around the Emperor couldn't hear him. Horace saw the Emperor and his cousin both stiffen in their saddles and sit a little straighter. Whatever the message, it had taken them by surprise. And the surprise seemed to be an unpleasant one. Shigeru halted the messenger's flow with a quick word and turned in the saddle to beckon them forward.

Quickly, Horace and George trotted their horses up to join the small group.

'Tell us again,' Shigeru said. 'But speak the common tongue so that Or'ss-san can understand.'

Horace nodded his thanks to Shigeru. Then the messenger spoke again. In spite of his haste in arriving here, he spoke calmly and clearly.

'Lord Shigeru, Or'ss-san and George-san, there has been a revolt in Ito. A revolt against the Emperor.'

Five

Nihon-Ja

Horace frowned, puzzled. George evidently felt the same. He leaned forward to question the messenger.

'But why would the people turn on their Emperor?' he asked. 'They love Lord Shigeru.'

It wasn't idle flattery or the sort of sycophancy that you might expect to hear around a ruler. Both Horace and George had seen ample evidence of Shigeru's popularity as they had travelled north with him from the palace. But Shigeru was shaking his head at them, a look of immense sadness on his normally cheerful features.

'Not the people,' he said bitterly. 'The Senshi. Lord Arisaka has led his clan in a revolt against my rule. They've seized the palace at Ito and killed many of my supporters. The Umaki clan has joined them.'

These were two of the most powerful and influential Senshi clans in the country. Horace and George exchanged horrified glances. Then George addressed the Emperor.

'But, your excellency, these clans have sworn their obedience to you, surely? How can they break that oath?' George knew that among the Senshi class, an oath was inviolable.

Shigeru's lips were drawn together in a tight line and he shook his head, unable to speak for the moment, overcome with emotion. It was Shukin who answered for him.

'They claim the Emperor has violated his own oath by trying to raise up the common people against their betters. They claim he has betrayed his class — the Senshi class — and is no longer worthy to be Emperor.'

'And as a result,' Shigeru added bitterly, 'their oath of loyalty to me is worthless. I am the oath-breaker, not they.'

'But . . .' Horace hesitated, searching for the right words. 'You're not "raising up the common people". You're simply trying to make their lives better, by recognising their value. How can Arisaka get away with such a distortion of the true facts?'

Shigeru met the young man's gaze. He had regained a little control now and spoke evenly.

'Or'ss-san, people will believe half-truths and distortions if they coincide with what they want to believe. If they reflect their fears. The Senshi have an irrational fear that I want to take away their power over the people and Arisaka has traded upon that fear.'

'But Arisaka doesn't believe it himself?' George said.

'Arisaka believes something else,' Shigeru replied. 'When the previous emperor died without an heir, Arisaka believes he should have been chosen as Emperor in my place.'

'He's been busy for months,' Shukin told them, his contempt for the traitor Arisaka all too obvious in his voice, 'sowing fear and dissent among the Senshi, spreading the lie that my cousin is betraying his class and planning to give the common people power over them. His campaign has been successful, it seems.'

'Like all successful lies, it is based on the tiniest grain of truth,' Shigeru said. 'I do want the people to have a greater stake in the way the country is governed. Arisaka has blown that out of all proportion.'

Horace turned to the messenger. He recognised him now as one of the senior advisers he had seen at the Ito palace. 'You said two clans had joined this revolt,' he said. 'What about the others? What about the Emperor's clan?'

'Many of the Emperor's clan are dead already. They tried to resist Arisaka, and his men killed them. They outnumbered them five or six to one. Those who aren't dead are scattered and in hiding.'

'And the others?' George asked. 'The Meishi, the Tokoradi and the Kitotashi? They owe no allegiance to Arisaka.'

'None of them can stand against the Shimonseki on their own. And each is waiting to see what the others will do. So far, all they will say is that *if* what Lord Arisaka says is true, then perhaps his actions are justified.'

George snorted in disgust. 'If and perhaps,' he said. 'The language of procrastination and uncertainty. That's just people looking to justify their own lack of action.'

'Arisaka has the momentum,' Horace said. As a soldier, he understood the value of swift and determined action that presented possible dissidents with a *fait accompli*. 'If they'd resisted at the very beginning, Arisaka might not have got away with it. Now he has control of the palace and the ball is rolling. It's too late to stop him easily.' He looked at Shigeru. 'The question is, your excellency, what are you planning to do about it?'

Shigeru paused thoughtfully and glanced at the messenger. 'Where is Arisaka now?'

'He's heading north from the capital, your excellency. He plans to take you prisoner.'

Shukin and the emperor exchanged a quick glance.

'How far behind you is he, Reito-san?' Shukin asked and the messenger shrugged.

'Probably several days. He didn't set out immediately. But there are some survivors from the royal army not far behind me. They could be here in a few hours.'

'How many of them?' Horace asked quickly. Without any conscious decision on his part, he was beginning to think about the possibility of a quick counterattack, but Reito's next words dispelled the idea.

'Only forty or fifty,' he replied. 'And Arisaka has at least three hundred men with him.'

Horace nodded, chewing his lip thoughtfully. Shigeru's army had been a small one. He ruled by consensus, not force. Which was why, he thought, Arisaka's coup had been so successful.

'All the more reason for us to pause here for a few hours,' Shigeru said, taking charge of the situation. 'Arisaka won't be here for several days. But my soldiers will arrive soon. We should join up with them. And while we're waiting, we can decide on our next move.'

They moved off the track onto a small, level meadow beside it. The men from the escort pitched two pavilions

— one for the command group and one for the rest of the party. They wouldn't be camping overnight so all that was needed was temporary shelter from the weather while they waited for the survivors of Shigeru's army to arrive.

And while the leaders had time to consider the situation and make their plans.

A woven bamboo mat was placed over the damp ground inside one pavilion and a low table and five stools placed on it. Shigeru, Shukin, Reito, Horace and George sat around the table. An orderly placed several pots of green tea and handle-less porcelain cups before them. Horace sipped gratefully at the tea. It wasn't as good as coffee, he thought, but any hot drink in this weather was welcome.

The canvas walls of the pavilion shook in a gust of wind and the first rain rattled against them.

'North,' Shukin was saying. 'We have to head back north.'

'Logical, since Arisaka and his army are in the south,' Horace said. 'But is there any other advantage in the north? Do you have allies there — clans you could raise so that you could face Arisaka?'

Shigeru shook his head. 'There are no Senshi clans in the north,' he said. 'There are the Kikori, that's all. They're not warriors.'

His two countrymen nodded agreement. But Horace wanted more information. 'Who are the Kikori?'

'Timber workers,' George told him. 'They work in among the tall timber in the mountains. Their villages are scattered everywhere.'

'If they're timber workers, they'll be fit and strong and they'll have axes,' Horace said. 'And they'll know how to use them. Could we recruit them as soldiers? Would they fight for you, your excellency?'

Shigeru and Shukin exchanged glances and the Emperor shook his head.

'They would. They are intensely loyal. But I won't ask them to. They're not trained warriors, Or'ss-san. Arisaka's men would massacre them. I can't ask them to fight when they have no hope.'

George leaned forward and touched Horace's sleeve, drawing his attention. He added, in a lowered tone, 'There's another problem, Horace. The Kikori would fight. But they wouldn't believe they had any chance against the Senshi — because they'd believe they have no right to fight them.'

'No right? What do you mean? Of course they —'

'It's a matter of their mindset. They've spent centuries believing they are inferior to the Senshi. Shigeru-san is trying to turn that around but it will take a long time to do it. Just as the Senshi are conditioned to believe they are superior to the other classes, the Kikori believe the Senshi are their superiors. They might go into battle against them. But they'd do it expecting to lose.'

'That's crazy,' Horace said. But he could see the reason in George's statement.

'You're a soldier, Horace. Would you lead an army into battle if the men expected to be beaten? Even worse, if the men thought they had no *right* to win?'

'I suppose not.' Horace's shoulders slumped. For a moment, he thought he had seen a possible course of action, but George was right. An army that believed it was destined to lose would be marching to its death.

'There are the Hasanu,' Shukin was saying thoughtfully. 'And Lord Nimatsu is an honourable man. He wouldn't turn his back on his oath of allegiance.'

'The Hasanu are certainly fighters,' Shigeru said. 'But to the far north, with an enormous mountain range separating us from them. It would take weeks, months even, to reach them. And I have no idea how they would respond. They are strange people.'

'If they are people, in fact,' Reito put in.

Shigeru gave him a look of rebuke. 'Don't believe the old superstitions, Reito,' he said. 'The Hasanu are . . . unusual, shall we say? But I'm convinced they're human.'

'Who are the Hasanu?' Horace whispered to George. 'Are they another clan of warriors?' But George was shaking his head, a puzzled look on his face.

'I've never heard of them. They're not a clan. I'm sure I know all of them.'

Before they could pursue the matter any further, Shukin spoke in an authoritative tone.

'Whether or not we can muster forces for a counterattack against Arisaka, our first course is to make sure the Emperor is safe. We have to head north back into the mountains. We won't ask the Kikori to fight, but they'll be willing to hide us from Arisaka.'

Shigeru was nodding agreement. 'Perhaps not the most gallant course of action,' he said. 'But certainly the wisest. If we can evade Arisaka's men for a month or two, winter will be here and the weather will protect us.'

'There's always the fortress at Ran-Koshi,' Reito suggested and the Emperor and his cousin looked at him quickly.

'Ran-Koshi?' said Shukin. 'I always thought that was a myth.'

Reito shook his head. 'Many people do. But I'm sure it's real. The problem is, how to find it.'

'What is this fortress?' Horace asked.

'Ran-Koshi is a fortress that's spoken of in an old folk tale,' Shigeru told them. 'That's why Shukin doubted its existence. It's said to be high in the mountains, in a hidden valley. Many hundreds of years ago, there was a civil war over the rightful succession to the throne.'

'Not unlike now, in fact,' Shukin said grimly and the Emperor glanced at him.

'Precisely,' he said, then turned back to the two Araluans. 'The eventual winner used Ran-Koshi as his power base. It was said to be an impregnable fortress, with massive walls and a deep moat.'

'Sounds like the sort of place you could use,' Horace said.

Shigeru nodded thoughtfully. 'It would be derelict by now,' he said. 'If it exists at all.'

'If it's there, there is one group of people who will know where it is,' Reito said. 'The Kikori. They've spent generations combing the mountains for groves of trees, then building trails to bring the fallen logs down to the low country. They know every inch of the northern mountains.'

'Then why have they never revealed its location?' Shukin said.

Shigeru inclined his head towards his cousin. 'Why should they?' he replied. 'Over the years, the Kikori have had little reason to love the ruling class of this country. If they knew this secret, I doubt they would have told the Senshi about it. They won't fight the warrior class, but there's no reason why they should do anything to help them.'

'Good point,' Horace said. 'So all we have to do is head north, contact the Kikori, and take shelter in this mythical fortress?'

Shigeru gave him a good-humoured nod. After his first shock at the news of Arisaka's treachery, he had recovered some of his normal spirits.

'Perhaps we should take it one step at a time, Or'ss-san,' he said. 'Our first priority is simply to evade Arisaka, and for that, I agree that we have to head north. But I'm afraid you won't be coming with us.'

Horace opened his mouth to reply, felt George's hand on his arm and stopped.

'We're on a diplomatic mission, Horace,' George said quietly. 'We have no right to interfere in internal matters among the Nihon-Jan.'

That statement brought Horace up short. His first instinct on hearing about Arisaka's rebellion had been to help the Emperor find a way to defeat the treacherous warlord. Now, he realised, he had no right to do any such thing. He sat back, confused. Shigeru saw the conflict on his face and offered Horace a sad little smile.

'George-san is right. This is not your battle. You are observers in our country and, just as I can't ask the Kikori to fight, I can't expect you to risk your lives on my behalf. You should return to your own land.'

'It might be better if Or'ss-san and George-san also avoided Arisaka's men,' Shukin said. 'The Shimonseki may not understand the niceties of diplomatic immunity.'

Shigeru looked at his cousin. Shukin made a good point, he thought. Arisaka's men would have their blood up. They would be arrogant and argumentative, and Horace might well be provoked by them if he encountered them. They would know the young Araluan was a friend of the Emperor and they would know he was a warrior. Better if he avoided contact altogether.

'There is a secondary road to Iwanai a little north of here,' he said. 'It's not as well travelled as the main road. In fact, it's more of a mountain track. But you'd be better to take it, I think. Perhaps you should accompany us that far, then leave us.'

Horace shook his head helplessly. He knew they were right but he hated to desert a friend in danger.

'I don't like it, your excellency,' he said eventually.

'Neither do I, Or'ss-san. But, trust me, it's for the best.'

Six

Nihon-Ja

An hour passed without any sign of the remnants of the Emperor's army. Shukin came to a decision.

'We can't wait any longer, cousin. Every minute we delay lets Arisaka get closer to us.'

'I don't like deserting my men. They fought in my name, after all. It's a poor reward for them if I abandon them,' Shigeru replied.

'Poorer still if they see you taken by Arisaka. Reito-san can ride back and lead them to join us. We can arrange a rendezvous. But right now, you must get on the road again.'

'Reito said that Arisaka's men were several days behind him,' the Emperor pointed out, but Shukin was unconvinced.

'His main army, yes. But in his place, I would have sent out fast scouting parties to search for you. They could be upon us any time. After all, the survivors from the Ito garrison are travelling on foot and bringing their wounded with them. They'll be moving a lot slower than a mounted scouting party.'

Reluctantly, Shigeru agreed. The men from the escort began to dismantle the two pavilions and pack them away. Reito and Shukin put their heads together over a map and agreed on a rendezvous point where Reito should lead the survivors.

'Wait for us here,' Shukin told him, pointing to a village marked on the map. 'We'll make contact with you.' He was all too aware of the possibility that Reito and the rest of Shigeru's men might be followed and captured. Best if they couldn't tell Arisaka exactly where the Emperor had gone to ground. Reito met his gaze, understood, and nodded.

'Look for us in a few days,' he said. Then, bowing hastily to Shigeru, he mounted his horse and rode off down the trail to the south.

The others mounted and turned their horses' heads north, starting back along the trail that had brought them down from the summer lodge. After a few kilometres, they came across another trail that branched off to the west, and led down into the valleys.

Shukin, riding in the lead, reined in his horse and waited while Horace caught up with him. He indicated the new trail.

'We'll take this track. It will lead us to the turn-off for Iwanai, where you'll leave us.'

Horace nodded unhappily. 'I hate to leave,' he said. 'I feel as if I'm deserting you.'

Shukin leaned over and grasped the young warrior's forearm. 'I can't imagine anyone I'd rather have by my side, Or'ss-san,' he said. 'But as the Emperor says, this is not your fight.'

'I know that,' Horace replied. 'But I don't have to like it.'

Shukin smiled grimly. 'Look on the bright side. At least the rain has stopped.'

Then he spurred his horse into a canter and rode to resume his position at the head of the little column.

George moved up to ride beside Horace. He shifted in his saddle, standing in the stirrups to ease his aching backside. George was not an accomplished rider and Shukin had been pushing the pace for the last few hours. The attorney had been bounced and jounced continually in the saddle and he was sure his behind would be black and blue. His thigh muscles were aching and cramped. His discomfort was physical, but he knew that Horace was feeling an acute mental anguish that was just as bad and he wanted to take his friend's mind off it.

'Are we nearly there?' he asked, hiding a smile as he voiced the age-old complaint of children on a journey.

Horace couldn't help grinning in return. 'You didn't sign up for this, did you?' he said. 'You probably thought it would all be polite meetings and formal banquets in the palace at Ito.'

'Too true,' George replied, with some feeling. 'It never occurred to me that we'd spend our time galloping up and down mountains on tracks that a self-respecting goat would avoid. If I'd . . . Look out!' he yelled suddenly and leaned over in the saddle to shove Horace to one side.

Horace heard a savage hiss as something flew past his face, missing him by inches. Then he saw George swaying, a long arrow buried in the upper part of his arm. As he watched, George slid sideways from his saddle and thudded onto the rough, churned-up earth of the track.

Their attackers came out of the trees on either side. The initial volley of arrows had taken down three of the escort, as well as George. Now nine swordsmen charged in at the small party. Horace drew his sword and shrugged his shield round into position, his left arm slipping through the straps and finding the hand grip with the speed of long practice.

It was a well-staged ambush, he thought. The enemy had let the advance party go past, poured in a volley, then charged out of the trees while the small column milled about in confusion.

Three of the attackers converged on the Emperor, who was riding in the middle of the column, a few metres ahead of George and Horace. One grabbed the reins of the Emperor's horse, and as Shigeru drew his sword and struck at him, the man ducked under the horse's neck to avoid the blow. Instantly, the other two were on the Emperor like jackals on a deer. They grabbed his arms and pulled him from the saddle, the sword falling from his hand as he hit the ground. His retainers were caught by surprise, engaged with the other six attackers.

Horace made his decision in a split second. His normal instinct would be to attack on horseback. But he wasn't riding Kicker and he had no idea if this horse had been trained for battle. Besides, the Emperor was on the ground and he'd risk trampling him. He threw a leg over the pommel and dropped to the ground, dashing forward to protect Shigeru.

One of the Senshi had raised his sword in a two-handed grip, aiming a downstroke at the helpless Emperor. Horace's sword was heavier than the *katana* that the Nihon-Jan warriors used. But it was also longer and Shigeru's attacker didn't factor that in. He thought he had just enough time to kill Shigeru and turn to face the onrushing warrior. He felt a moment of surprise when Horace's horizontal stroke took him in the rib cage, exposed as he raised the sword high, and smashed through his lacquered leather armour. Then he felt nothing.

Horace sensed rather than saw the second man swinging a diagonal overhead cut at him from the left. He pivoted in that direction and his shield seemed to move of its own volition, intercepting the razor-sharp blade with a ringing clang. He felt the super-hard steel of the *katana* bite into his shield, sticking for a fraction of a second. As it did, he stepped forward, cramping the man for space, and kicked flat-footed into the side of his knee. The man's leg collapsed under him and he stumbled forward with a shrill cry of pain. A quick thrust cut off his cry and he fell at Horace's feet.

In a fight against multiple enemies, it was fatal to face in one direction for too long. Horace spun one hundred and eighty degrees, shield raised, just in time to block a thrust from the third man — the one who had seized the Emperor's reins. Before Horace could retaliate, the man threw up his arms with a choking cry.

He fell to his knees, shock and surprise on his face. Behind him, Shukin was poised with his sword ready for another stroke. But it was unnecessary. The assassin pitched forward, face down in the wet earth.

Horace looked around quickly. The rear guard had closed up and were taking care of two other Senshi attackers. He heard the crashing sound of someone running through the undergrowth on the downhill side of the track. At least one of their attackers had got away.

Shukin sheathed his sword. Then he helped Shigeru to his feet.

'Are you all right, cousin?' he asked anxiously.

Shigeru brushed his concern aside. 'I'm covered in mud and winded, but otherwise unharmed – thanks to Or'ss-san.' He smiled his gratitude at the young Araluan.

Horace shook his head. 'I'm glad to be of service,' he said, a little formally. Horace was always uncomfortable when people thanked him for doing what he considered to be no more than his job. He sheathed his sword. The senior man from the rear guard had approached and was talking to Shukin in rapid Nihon-Jan.

'Are they Arisaka's men?' Horace asked the Emperor.

Shigeru nodded. 'That's the Shimonseki crest,' he said, indicating a stylised owl emblazoned on the attackers' breastplates, over the heart.

Shukin moved back to join them.

'My corporal counted nine of them,' he said. 'Two got away. My men killed four others, Or'ss-san accounted for two and I finished off the seventh.' He cast a contemptuous glance at the sprawled figures on the track, then grudgingly had to admit that the attack had nearly been successful. 'They were well organised. Two parties of three moved to cut off the advance and rear guards, while the remaining three attacked you, cousin. I don't think they reckoned on Or'ss-san's skill with a sword. That was their main mistake. We lost two men and one was wounded in the volley of arrows they fired.'

His words brought a terrible realisation to Horace.

'Oh god!' he cried. He swung round and ran back along the track to where George had fallen from his saddle. In all the action, he had forgotten about the scribe. His heart surged with relief as he saw the thin figure sitting upright beside the muddy track, painfully nursing his right arm, still impaled by a long, white-feathered arrow. His sleeve was soaked with blood and his face was pale – paler than normal – but he was alive. Horace dropped to one knee beside him.

'George!' he said, the relief evident in his voice. 'Are you all right?'

'No! I am not!' George replied with considerable spirit. 'I have a whacking great arrow stuck through my arm and it hurts like the very dickens! How could anybody be all right in those circumstances?'

Impulsively, Horace went to touch the arrow, but George jerked away, then howled as the abrupt movement sent pain coursing through his arm.

'You saved my life, George,' Horace said gently, remembering how his gangly companion had shoved him away from the arrow aimed at him.

George grimaced. 'Well, if I'd known it was going to hurt like this, I wouldn't have! I would have just let them shoot you! Why do you live this way?' he demanded in a high-pitched voice. 'How can you bear it? This sort of thing is very, very painful. I always suspected that warriors are crazy. Now I know. In future, I . . .'

Whatever it was he planned to do in the future, Horace never discovered. At that moment, shocked by the pain of the wound and weakened by the loss of blood, George's eyes rolled upwards and he slid over onto his side.

Horace looked round to find Shukin studying the wounded scribe.

'Might be a good thing,' the Senshi leader said. 'We'll get that arrow shaft out while he's unconscious.'

George remained unconscious for a few minutes. But it was enough time for Shukin, and the Emperor's healer, to remove the arrow from the wound. They applied a salve to the entry and exit wounds and bound his arm with clean linen. Shukin observed the result with a satisfied look.

'It should heal cleanly,' he said. 'The salve will take care of any infection — although the arrow was new and seemed clean enough. He will have a sore arm for some weeks, though.'

As if on cue, George's eyes fluttered open. He looked around the concerned faces looking down on him, then frowned.

'My arm hurts,' he said. Horace and the others burst into relieved laughter, which did nothing to assuage George's feelings. He regarded them indignantly.

'It may be funny to all you heroic warrior types,' he said. 'I know you all make a habit of just shrugging off this sort of thing. But it hurts.'

Horace gently helped him to his feet and led him to where his horse was waiting patiently.

'Come on,' he said, helping his companion into the saddle. 'We've a way to go yet.'

He was glad that George, normally a garrulous companion, didn't feel like talking as they rode towards the junction with the track to Iwanai. Horace had a lot to think about and he wanted to prepare his words carefully. He knew George would argue with what he had in mind and he knew that George was trained in logic and the ability to express thoughts clearly and precisely.

Eventually, the time came when the Emperor and Shukin reined in their horses and indicated a steep, narrow track leading downhill to the south-west.

'You leave us here,' the Emperor said. 'It's about a day's ride to Iwanai this way. I doubt that you'll run into any more of Arisaka's men on the trail. Take care when you reach the port, however. Stay out of sight as much as you can until you're aboard your ship.'

'One of my men will guide you,' Shukin said.

But Horace shook his head. 'Not one of your Senshi,' he said. 'A servant will be fine. You need all the fighting men you have with you.'

Shukin nodded, acknowledging the wisdom. 'Good point. Very well, one of the servants can guide you.'

Horace sat silently as George made his farewells. The Emperor, he noticed, looked quizzically at him while this was happening, perhaps sensing what Horace had in mind. Eventually, George slapped the reins on his horse's neck and turned his head towards the steep, narrow track.

'Come on, Horace. It's time to go.'

Horace cleared his throat uncomfortably.

'That's the thing, George,' he said. 'I'm staying.'

Seven

Toscana

'Evanlyn? Here? What on earth can she possibly want?' Will asked of no one in particular. He could never think of the princess by her real name. He had met her as Evanlyn and shared so many dangers and adventures with her under that name that she would always be Evanlyn in his mind.

Alyss's immediate reaction was one of suspicion. She's here to barge in between Will and me, she thought peevishly. She knew that Will and the princess had been very close in the past — and remained so — and this made her suspect the worst of Evanlyn. She thought of her by that name as well because it made it easier to dislike her. If she thought of Evanlyn by her real name, Cassandra, she had to acknowledge that she was the Princess Royal of Araluen and afford her the respect due to that rank. As Evanlyn, she was just another girl, trying to get her hooks into Alyss's boyfriend.

After that first knee-jerk reaction, Alyss recognised that she was being unreasonable. Even Evanlyn wouldn't go to so much trouble simply to interpose herself between Will and herself, she realised. There must be some other, more important, reason behind her sudden arrival. Was Evanlyn here to cancel Araluen's agreement to the treaty conditions, and nullify the hard work that Alyss had put into the negotiations over the past five days? Perhaps Araluan policy had changed towards the treaty between Arrida and Toscana? It would be extremely awkward if that were the case — after all, the treaty had been signed and ratified and she had witnessed it on behalf of the Araluan crown.

'Perhaps we should invite her in and ask her,' Halt said mildly, in response to Will's question. He had seen the furrows of concentration on Alyss's face and he had a shrewd idea as to the thoughts that were going through her head. But it wouldn't do to leave the Princess Royal cooling her heels in the anteroom while Alyss got over her pique.

'Of course,' the tall blonde girl said, gathering her thoughts, annoyed with herself for acting in such an unprofessional manner. 'Please show her in, Edmund.'

The attendant, who had been hovering anxiously, aware that he was keeping the princess waiting, nodded gratefully and withdrew, leaving the door open. A few seconds later, he reappeared, standing aside as their visitor entered.

'The Lady Evanlyn, to see you,' he announced.

Halt frowned. The princess only used that name when she travelled unofficially or incognito. Halt knew it reminded her of a time when her life and behaviour weren't constrained by royal protocol and court procedures. He rose now and stepped forward, his hands out to her. As an old friend and adviser, he didn't feel the need to bow to her. After all, if she chose to be incognito, she wouldn't expect any royal treatment.

She smiled when she saw him and took his hands in hers. 'Hello, Halt,' she said. 'It's good to see you.'

'You too, my lady,' Halt told her.

Evanlyn glanced around the room. Her smile faded slightly as Alyss rose to greet her.

'Welcome, your highness,' Alyss said.

Evanlyn waved the title aside impatiently. 'Not on this trip, please, Lady Alyss. I'm not travelling in my official capacity. Evanlyn is good enough.' Her gaze moved on and her smile regained its original warmth as she saw Will.

'Hullo, Will,' she said and he stepped forward to hug her. He knew Alyss wouldn't like it, but he had a genuine affection for Evanlyn and he wasn't going to pretend otherwise. He and Evanlyn had gone through too much together for him not to greet her that way. At the same time, he was wise enough to make the hug a brief one.

'Welcome to Toscana,' he said.

But Evanlyn's gaze had swept on. The room wasn't brightly lit and it was only now that she made out the identity of the fourth person present.

'Seley el'then!' she said, the pleasure evident in her voice. 'How wonderful to see you!' Selethen, noticing her correct pronunciation of his name, made the ritual Arridi greeting, touching his hand to his mouth, brow and mouth again, and bowing slightly.

'Lady Evanlyn. I am delighted to see you again.' He

paused, then added, with a mock frown, 'Unless you have discovered that I owe you money?'

She shook her head, laughing at his sally. Then, realising that the others were standing by, waiting to hear why she had arrived so unexpectedly, she gestured to the chairs and couches around the central table.

'Please. Sit down, everyone. I need to talk to you.'

Selethen hesitated as the others resumed their seats.

'Perhaps I should leave you?' he suggested, sensing that this might well be a private matter for the Araluans. But Evanlyn considered his suggestion for a second or two, then shook her head.

'No need for you to go, Selethen. This is nothing secret.' She noticed the coffee pot on the table and added, 'I'd happily kill for a cup of coffee, however. It's been a long trip.'

'Of course! My apologies!' Alyss leapt to her feet again, irritated that her sense of hospitality had been found wanting. No doubt about it, Evanlyn's sudden appearance had flustered her. She quickly poured Evanlyn a cup and handed it across the table. The princess smiled gratefully, their mutual antipathy forgotten for the moment.

'Thanks, Alyss,' she said. Her omission of the formal 'Lady Alyss' was sign enough that her gratitude was genuine. Alyss nodded acknowledgement and resumed her seat. Evanlyn took a deep draught of the coffee, then looked appreciatively at the cup.

'I take it you supplied this coffee, Selethen?'

He smiled and she drank again, draining most of the remaining beverage. She set the cup down, paused for a second or two to gather her thoughts and plunged in.

'Long story short,' she said. 'Horace has gone missing.'

There were exclamations of surprise around the room. Will was the first to voice the thoughts of all of them.

'Missing?' he said. 'Missing where?'

'Nihon-Ja,' Evanlyn told them. 'My father sent him on a military mission some time ago. He was to present himself at the Emperor's court — he had letters of introduction from my father — and then spend some time studying Nihon-Jan military techniques and weapons.'

'What's happened? How did he go missing?' Will asked.

'To be accurate, I don't know what's happened. Look, let me explain,' she said, hastily cutting off Will's next question. 'Horace was travelling with George —'

'George Carter? George from the Ward? Our George, you mean?' Will interrupted. As he said 'Our George' he made a circling gesture that included himself and Alyss.

Halt raised an eyebrow at him as he saw the impatience on Evanlyn's face. 'Perhaps one of those interjections would have been sufficient,' he said, 'since they all relate to the same person.'

Evanlyn nodded gratefully at him. 'That's right,' she said. '*Your* George. He was there to advise Horace on protocol and to act as an interpreter.'

Halt cocked his head to one side. 'But the common tongue is spoken in Nihon-Ja, surely?'

Evanlyn shrugged. 'Not as widely as in other countries. The Nihon-Jan have kept themselves a little . . . isolated . . . over the centuries. And my father thought it might be a diplomatic touch,' she nodded in Alyss's direction, 'if the Emperor was addressed in his own language.'

Alyss nodded. 'We try to do that wherever possible.'

'I still don't see what Horace would hope to learn from

the Nihon-Jan about weapons and methods,' Will said. 'After all, he's a Swordmaster himself.'

'The Nihon-Jan warriors — they call them Senshi — use a different technique,' Halt interjected. 'And their sword-smiths have perfected a method of making extremely hard blades. Our Ranger weapon makers learned some of their techniques many years ago.'

'Is that why your saxe knives are so incredibly hard?' Alyss asked. It was a well-known fact that saxe knives could put a notch into the blades of normal swords.

'It's a technique where several iron rods are heated and beaten, then folded and twisted together to form a composite whole. Over the years, we've made it a practice to adopt good ideas from anywhere we can find them,' Halt told her.

'Our swordsmiths in Dimascar developed a similar technique for creating extra-hard blades,' Selethen put in.

'You're talking about Dimascarene blades, I assume?' Halt said. 'I've heard of them but never seen one.'

'They're very expensive. Not many people can afford them,' Selethen told him.

Halt nodded thoughtfully, filing the information away for future reference. Then he turned back to Evanlyn. 'I'm sorry, Evanlyn, we're digressing here. Please go on.'

'All right. Just to cover any further interruptions . . .' She looked meaningfully at Will, which he considered to be a little unfair. After all, it had been Halt and Selethen who had prattled on about super-hard sword blades, not him. But his indignation went unnoticed as she continued.

'I take it you're all familiar with the Silasian Council's fast message system?'

They all nodded. The Silasian Council was a cartel of traders based in the eastern part of the Constant Sea. They facilitated trade by instituting a central credit system so that funds could be transferred between countries, without the risk of actually sending money overland or by sea. In addition, they had realised some years prior that fast communications could be as beneficial to trade as efficient money transfers. They had set up a network of carrier pigeon services and express riders to take messages almost from one end of the known world to the other. Distances that might take weeks for a ship or a rider to cover could be traversed in a matter of days. Of course, the service was extremely expensive, but in emergencies, many users felt it was worth the cost.

'We received a message via that service from George several weeks ago,' Evanlyn said. 'It was only brief and he sent it from a port on the Ooghly River in Indus — which is pretty much the eastern limit of the message service. Apparently, there was a rebellion against the Emperor of Nihon-Ja, and Horace got caught up in it. The Emperor's forces are badly outnumbered and he's a fugitive. When last seen, he was heading north into the mountains, to hide out in some legendary fortress. Horace has gone with him.'

Will sat back and whistled slowly. It would be just like Horace, he thought, to get involved in such an idealistic venture.

'And what are you planning to do?' he asked, although he thought he knew the answer already. Evanlyn turned a steady gaze on him.

'I'm going to find Horace,' she said.

Eight

Nihon-Ja

Horace's announcement met with a hail of protests from the others. Most vocal of all was George.

'Horace, you can't stay here! Don't you understand? We have no right to interfere in internal Nihon-Jan politics!'

Horace frowned at his countryman. 'This is a little more serious than just politics, George,' he told him. 'This is a rebellion against the lawful ruler. You can't pass that off as a matter of politics. It's treason for a start.'

George made an apologetic gesture towards the two Nihon-Jan leaders standing close by. He realised that his words could be deemed as undiplomatic.

'My apology, your excellency,' he said hastily. 'I meant no offence.'

Shigeru nodded. 'None taken, George-san. I understand your point of view. Whether this is a case of politics or treason, it's an internal Nihon-Jan matter.'

'That's right,' George said and he turned back to Horace. 'It's not as if Araluen has any sort of formal treaty with the Emperor. You and I were simply here as diplomats. We're granted freedom of movement throughout the country but we have to maintain our neutrality. If we get involved, if we take sides, we'll invalidate those credentials,' he cried. 'Don't you understand? We simply can't afford to do that!'

'As a matter of fact, I do understand,' Horace said. 'But it's a little late to start worrying about what will happen if we take sides. I'm afraid I've already done it.'

George frowned at him, not understanding. 'I don't —'

Horace cut him short. 'While you were having your little nap beside the track back there,' he said, 'I killed two of Arisaka's soldiers. I think he might see that as taking sides, don't you?'

George threw his hands out in a gesture of bewilderment. 'You what? What could have led you to do such an incredibly stupid thing, Horace? Surely you knew better than that! Why? Just tell me why?'

The Emperor coughed politely before Horace could answer and stepped forward to lay a calming hand on George's forearm.

'Perhaps it was because they were trying to kill me at the time,' he said.

George, once again, looked suitably chastened. As an expert on protocol, he wasn't performing so well, he thought. Horace, seeing George momentarily stumped for words, followed up his advantage.

'I just didn't think, George,' he said, with a hint of a smile flickering at the corner of his mouth. 'I should have checked through our credentials to see what I should do if someone tried to kill the Emperor. But, gosh, I just dashed in and stopped them the best I could.'

Shukin began to smile as well. But the Emperor's next words quickly dispelled the expression from his face.

'In fact, Arisaka might well view the act of saving my life as a bigger affront than the killing of his two men,' Shigeru said.

'His excellency is right,' Shukin agreed, all seriousness now. 'That will establish Or'ss-san as his sworn enemy. Arisaka doesn't like to have his plans thwarted.'

George looked from one face to another, desperately trying to see a way out of this predicament.

'But he doesn't have to know about it, surely? We're miles from anywhere, in a remote forest on a mountain! Who's going to tell him?'

'Maybe,' Horace said, 'the ambushers who escaped will mention it. I know I would, in their place.'

George, seeing the ground crumbling under his feet, shook his head in disgusted resignation.

'Oh, great!' he said wearily. 'You let witnesses get away! If you were going to join in, Horace, why didn't you make a complete job of it?'

Horace frowned at him. 'Are you saying that our diplomatic status would be in better shape if I'd killed twice as many of Arisaka's men?' he asked. The logic of George's position seemed to escape him.

'No. No. No,' George said, finally accepting the inevitable. 'Well, I suppose you've made our bed. Now we just have to lie on it.'

A silence fell over the small group. Shukin and the Emperor exchanged awkward glances. Horace looked at them and nodded almost imperceptibly. He sensed what they were thinking.

'I wonder would you excuse us for a moment, your excellency?' he said.

Shigeru inclined his head and Horace gestured for George to ride a few metres away from the group gathered round the Emperor. George followed him, looking mystified.

'What is it now?' he asked as soon as they were out of earshot. 'What else did you do when I was unconscious — because I *was* unconscious, you know. I had a whacking great arrow stuck in my arm!' He added the last with a little heat. Horace's joking reference to his 'little nap' had struck a raw nerve.

Horace made a placating gesture. 'I know. I know. I'm sorry I said what I did. After all, you did save my life.'

George looked a little mollified. There weren't too many people who could claim to have achieved anything like that, he thought. Horace normally didn't need anyone else to save his life. He was pretty skilled at doing it for himself. Now he thought about it, George found himself wondering if even his former wardmate, Will Treaty, famous as he might have become, had ever actually saved Horace's life in such a definite manner.

'Well, yes. All right. But what did you want to talk about?'

'George,' Horace began, then hesitated. 'There's no tactful way to put this, so I'll just come out and say it. You're not staying.'

'Well, of course I am!' George exploded. 'If you're staying, I'm staying with you. I'm your friend. Friends don't run off and desert other friends just because there's a bit of danger! All right, I carried on about my arm hurting. But I'm not afraid, Horace. I'm not some kind of coward who'll go slinking off and leave you to face the danger on your own!'

Horace was nodding as the scribe delivered this impassioned response. George wasn't a coward, he knew. Far from it. But facts were facts and they had to be faced.

'George,' he said calmly, 'you're seriously injured with that arm. But even if you were in perfect health, you wouldn't be up to the journey we're about to undertake.'

'Don't worry about me!' George said, with considerable spirit, regardless of the fact that his voice would carry clearly to the Nihon-Jan warriors a few metres away. 'I'll keep up all right. I won't hold you back!' But he saw Horace shaking his head again and, deep down, George knew that the tall young warrior was right.

'You wouldn't *want* to hold us up,' Horace said. 'And I know you'd try your best. But you're not cut out for this sort of life, George. For starters, you're not a good enough rider.'

'I . . .' George stopped. He knew it was true.

'You're riding the slowest horse in the group,' Horace pointed out. 'If the rest of us have to come down to his pace, you will be slowing us down. It won't be your fault, George. But if Shigeru is going to escape Arisaka, we're going to have to ride fast and live rough. And if we're waiting for your slow horse all the time, we're putting the Emperor's life at risk. Surely you don't want that?'

Horace thought it was more tactful to blame the horse for George's potential to slow the group down. It was true up to a point but George saw through the device. He had a slow, old horse because he was a poor rider and a slow, old horse was all he could handle.

He hung his head miserably. 'I'm just not good enough, am I?' he said in a low voice.

Horace reached over in the saddle and patted his shoulder.

'It's not that you're not good enough,' he said. 'You're just not trained for this sort of life. You're at home in diplomatic meetings, working out complex treaties between countries, and in courtrooms, coming up with a brilliant argument to save somebody's life or property. That's what you're good at. That's what you've trained for. On the other hand, this is what *I've* trained for.' Horace swept his arm around the mountainous countryside that surrounded them as he said the words. George wouldn't meet his gaze. His narrow shoulders rose and fell as he heaved a deep sigh.

'I know,' he said finally.

'Besides, I need you to get word back to Araluen, so they'll know what's become of me. I can't just disappear off the face of the earth without telling people where I've gone.'

George raised his eyes to meet Horace's then. 'You think you're going to die here, don't you?' he said quietly. 'You don't think Shigeru has a chance.'

Horace shook his head. 'George, I never go into any fight thinking I'm going to lose.'

'But you said you can't just disappear off the face of the earth. That doesn't sound like you're too confident.'

Horace grinned at him then. 'That's the trouble with you attorneys,' he said. 'You're too darned literal. Let's just say my disappearance will be a temporary matter.'

George's face was screwed up as his mind moved rapidly. 'If I could get word to Will and Halt,' he said, 'they might come to help you. In fact, they'd surely come to help you.'

'It's a great idea,' Horace said sadly. The thought of having the two Rangers by his side in this affair was an extremely attractive one. 'But it's a pipe dream. It'll take you months to get all the way back to Araluen. By that time, things here will be well and truly settled — one way or another.'

But now George was bubbling over with enthusiasm for his idea.

'No! No! No! I don't have to get all the way back! I only need to get to Indus! From there, I can use the Silasian fast message service. That'll get word to them within a few days!'

Horace looked at his companion with new respect. 'You see?' he said. 'That's what you're good at. Thinking. Coming up with ideas. Let me tell you, if you can get word to Will and Halt, you'll be doing much more good than if you simply stayed here with us.'

'And got in the way?' George said, grinning now. Horace returned the grin.

'Exactly.' He offered his hand to George, who took it and gripped it warmly. Before he released his own grip, Horace added, 'One other thing. I will never forget that you offered to stay here, George. It took a lot more courage for you to offer that than it took me. I appreciate it and, when I get home, I'll be letting people know about it.'

George finally reclaimed his hand and made a small self-deprecating gesture, although Horace's words had warmed his heart.

'Well . . . you know. It wasn't much. I mean . . . we were wardmates, weren't we? That's what wardmates do for each other. They stick together. No big deal.'

'Very big deal,' Horace said firmly. 'And I won't forget it.'

Nine

Toscana

'Then I'm coming with you!' Will said impulsively. Halt smiled to himself at the instant response. He had expected no less of his former apprentice. Horace, after all, was Will's best friend. They had grown up together, fought side by side and saved each other's lives on numerous occasions.

Evanlyn favoured Will with a warm smile as well. 'I was sure you'd say that,' she said. 'My father gave me permission to ask for your help on this mission but I told him there'd be no need to ask. Thanks, Will. I'll feel a lot more confident with you by my side.'

'Of course, I'll come too,' Halt said, then added with a raised eyebrow, 'That's if I'm needed?'

'Lady Pauline said you'd say that,' Evanlyn told him. 'She said you should go with her blessing.'

Will glanced quickly at his mentor, not sure how Halt

would react to the assumption that he needed Lady Pauline's permission to join the expedition. The Halt he knew of old would have come up with some pithy reply to the effect that he was quite capable of making his own decisions, thank you very much. He was a little surprised to see Halt smile fondly at Evanlyn's words.

'Well, that's a relief,' Halt said, without the slightest trace of irony.

Now it was Will's turn to raise an eyebrow — an expression he had studiously copied from Halt over the years. Things had changed, he thought.

Alyss cleared her throat nervously and they turned to look at her. There was a bright spot of colour in each of her cheeks.

'I'd like to come too,' she said. 'Horace is one of my oldest friends. He helped Will rescue me from Castle Macindaw and I owe him for that. Besides, you'll need someone who can speak Nihon-Jan.'

The words were phrased as a suggestion. But her tone left no doubt that they were a firm statement of intent. She wasn't asking permission. She was telling Evanlyn that she wasn't letting her go swanning off to the other side of the world with Will. Not this time.

'Yes, Lady Pauline said you'd say that, too,' Evanlyn said dryly. She wished she could reassure the tall girl that she had no designs on Will, other than friendship. She could see that Alyss could be a valuable friend and ally to her — not just in this case but in the years to come — and she wished there was some way she could break down the barrier between them. Maybe this journey might give her the opportunity.

Halt thought it might be best if he stepped in. 'It sounds like a good idea to me,' he said. 'Alyss is a handy person to have around.'

Alyss remained flushed. She had been prepared to argue the point and hadn't expected Evanlyn to give in so easily. At the back of her mind, a small doubt formed. Maybe she had been judging Evanlyn too harshly. But she forgot the thought as Will asked her a question.

'Do you speak Nihon-Jan? When did you learn?'

She shrugged, feeling her pulse settle back to normal now that there was no longer any question about her accompanying the party.

'I've been studying the language for a year or so,' she replied. 'Mostly using George's translations. I'm not fluent but I can get by.'

Will raised both eyebrows. 'Well, you learn a new thing every day,' he said reflectively.

'In your case, that's no exaggeration,' Halt said, completely straight-faced.

Will pursed his lips in annoyance. He'd have to learn not to give Halt openings like that, he thought. Then another question occurred to his grasshopper mind and he turned to Evanlyn.

'How do we get there? How did you get here, by the way?'

He heard Halt's deep sigh and knew he'd done it again.

'Do you ever,' the older Ranger said with great deliberation, 'manage to ask just one question at a time? Or does it always have to be multiple choice with you?'

Will looked at him in surprise. 'Do I do that?' he asked. 'Are you sure?'

Halt said nothing. He raised his hands in a 'See what I mean?' gesture and appealed to the others in the room. Selethen was amused by the byplay between the two. And, since the enjoyment of this sort of obscure, trivial debate was very much part of the Arridi character, he couldn't help himself. He had to join in.

'Halt,' he said, 'I could be wrong, but I think you were just guilty of the same fault. I'm sure I heard you ask two questions just then.'

'Thank you for pointing that out, Lord Selethen,' Halt said with icy formality.

Will grinned at the *Wakir*, who gravely inclined his head to Halt. Then Will remembered that Evanlyn hadn't answered either of his questions.

'So how did you get here?' he reminded her.

'I used the Skandian duty ship,' she told him.

The treaty between Araluen and Skandia had been in force for some years now and was regularly updated. One of the latest clauses stationed a Skandian wolfship each year at a base on the coast of Araluen, with its crew at the disposal of the Araluan King. Since wolfships were among the fastest craft in the world, it was a valuable addition. In return, King Duncan paid a fee to Skandia and granted favourable trading terms to other wolfships seeking to buy water, firewood and provisions. In reply to other nations like Iberion and Gallica, who complained that Duncan was helping the Skandians to raid their coastlines, the King merely shrugged.

'No system is perfect,' he'd say. 'And besides, they could always pay the Skandians *not* to raid.'

Which was, of course, true.

'I imagine we'll take the wolfship on to Nihon-Ja?' Halt said.

Evanlyn nodded. 'My father has given permission for that. It'll be faster than any commercial vessel we could charter. And besides, Gundar is eager to see Nihon-Ja. He'd be the first Skandian to visit there.'

'Gundar?' Will said. It was a fairly common name among Skandians, he knew, but he couldn't help hoping that it was an old friend. Evanlyn was already nodding.

'Yes. It's Gundar Hardstriker's ship. He's eager to see you and Alyss again and he has a crewman who said nothing would stop him from rescuing the General. I assume he means Horace?'

Will and Alyss exchanged amused glances. 'Yes. That's what Gundar's crew call Horace. Sounds as if Nils is still with him,' Will said.

'He'll be a handy person to have along,' Alyss put in, recalling Nils Ropehander's massive build and ferocious skill with a battleaxe.

'Any Skandian is handy to have around if there's a fight in the offing,' Halt said. Then, changing the subject, he turned to Evanlyn. 'Is there any need for you to present yourself to the Toscan Emperor's court? Do you have any official duties to attend to?'

Evanlyn shook her head. 'Officially, I'm not here. That's why I'm travelling as the Lady Evanlyn. So no, I'm free to come and go.'

'Then I suggest we do go, and as soon as possible. We've already made our official goodbyes. We'll get a good night's sleep and get down to the docks first thing in the morning.'

'You can take my room, Lady Evanlyn. I'll sleep on one of the couches,' Alyss said quickly. But Evanlyn shook her head.

'We'll share the room, Alyss,' she said firmly. 'I don't want any special privileges. We may as well get used to it. A wolfship is too small for all that nonsense.'

Alyss was astute enough to recognise an olive branch when she saw one. She smiled at Evanlyn — a genuine smile for the first time.

'It'll be my pleasure to share with you,' she said.

The others had risen now and Selethen shook hands with them all as he bade them farewell.

'Good luck to you,' he said. Then he added, a little wistfully, 'It sounds like an interesting trip. I'm tempted to join you. Horace is a friend of mine as well. But . . .' He made a graceful hand gesture, dismissing the idea.

Halt nodded. 'You'd be welcome to join us any time, Selethen. But you have your own duties to attend to. We understand.'

Selethen made the Arridi gesture of greeting and farewell, touching his hand to mouth, brow and mouth again.

'Yes,' he said finally. 'I have my duty, and it's a hard mistress. But as I say, I am tempted.'

He smiled at them all and left to return to his own quarters.

They arrived at the docks just after first light. Gundar's wolfship, named *Wolfwill* in Will's honour, was moored alongside the jetty. Will frowned as he caught his first sight of her. He'd seen the ship when she'd been launched. But now there was something different about her.

'Something looks odd,' he said thoughtfully.

Halt was studying the ship too. 'Have they moved the mast?' he asked of no one in particular. 'It seems a little further aft than I remember.'

'And where's the cross-tree?' Will asked. Normally, the square-rigged cross-tree was set seven-eighths of the way up the mast, with the big square sail brailed up on it when in port. *Wolfwill*'s mast was bare, aside from a complicated arrangement of rigging at the masthead, and what looked to be a pair of carefully rolled sails lying fore and aft on the deck at its base.

'All I know,' Evanlyn said, 'is that it's the fastest ship I've ever sailed on. Look, here comes Gundar. You can ask him.'

She pointed to where a familiar figure, huge as all Skandians were, was rolling in his seaman's walk along the jetty towards them.

'Will Treaty!' he bellowed, startling the gulls for a fifty-metre radius into squawking, screeching flight. Will braced himself as the huge figure approached. He knew what was coming but there was little he could do about it.

Sure enough, Gundar swept him off his feet in a breath-draining bear hug. Will could only grunt a greeting as he felt his ribs on the verge of giving way.

'Gorlog's beard, boy, but it's good to see you! I hoped we'd run across each other when Erak assigned us as the duty ship. How have you been? What have you been up to?'

'Le' go an' I'll try . . . tell you,' Will managed to grunt breathlessly. Finally, Gundar set him down. Will staggered as Gundar released him, and his friends were a little alarmed at the groaning intake of breath that was Will's first, reflexive response as his emptied lungs desperately sucked air back in.

Then, sighting Alyss, the huge seafarer seized her hand in one of his enormous fists and planted a smacking, clumsy kiss on it.

'Lady Alyss!' he boomed. 'How can you have grown more beautiful than you were?'

Evanlyn, it has to be admitted, pouted a little at this. Gundar had never commented on her looks and she was aware that alongside the elegant blonde girl, she was a little . . . tomboyish.

Alyss was grinning delightedly at him. 'Ah, Gundar, I see you haven't lost any of your courtly charm. You'd turn a girl's head with that silver tongue of yours.'

He beamed at her, then turned his attention to the grey-bearded, slightly built figure standing behind her.

'And you must be the famous Halt?' he said. 'I expected someone a little larger,' he added, half to himself, as he advanced.

Halt, experienced in the ways of Skandians, retreated at the same pace. 'Yes. I'm Halt,' he said. 'And I need all my ribs intact, thank you very much.'

'Of course you do.' Instead of bear-hugging Halt, Gundar contented himself with a firm, manly handshake. Halt's eyes glazed as he felt his fingers and knuckles crushed inside the island-sized fist. He shook his hand painfully as Gundar finally released it.

'Any friend of Erak's is a friend of mine!' Gundar glanced around curiously. 'But where's that shaggy pony of yours, Will?'

'We left our horses in Araluen,' Will told him.

Since the trip had been intended as a brief, ten-day mission to the Toscan capital, there had been no good reason to bring Tug and Abelard. They had been left in the care of Old Bob, the Ranger Corps horse breeder. Now, Will wasn't sure if he regretted that decision or not. He'd like to have Tug with him, but the sea journey to Nihon-Ja would be a long one, far longer than any Tug had undertaken before. There would be little chance of going ashore to exercise the horses, and he wasn't sure how they would have coped.

Similarly, Ebony, Will's dog, had been left behind with Lady Pauline. Ebony was only half trained and he felt her boisterous behaviour might cause problems with the rather starchy Toscan officials.

Gundar nodded vaguely. He had no idea of the soul searching that had gone on with the two Rangers before they decided to leave their horses behind. He glanced up the quay.

'And who's this Lenny Longshanks?' he said. 'Is he with you?'

The four Araluans turned quickly to look back up the jetty. Striding purposefully towards them, a pack slung over one shoulder, was a tall, slender figure.

'Temptation got too strong,' Selethen told them as he came closer. 'I decided to come with you.'

Ten

Nihon-Ja

After George left them and headed down the back trail towards the port of Iwanai, Shukin picked up the pace.

Now, as they kept their horses in a steady canter along the narrow, muddy mountain track, Horace realised just how much George had been slowing them down and felt a guilty sense of relief that he'd convinced his fellow countryman to go his separate way.

The rest of the party, all of them skilled horsemen, managed easily and the local ponies, somewhat smaller than the battlehorse that Horace was used to, were sturdy and long winded. Best of all, he thought, as his mount slithered, slid and then recovered himself, they were sure-footed beasts, well used to these sloping, rough mountain trails.

One of the escort noticed the stumble and saw Horace

suddenly sit up straight in the saddle before the horse recovered his footing. He rode up close beside him.

'Leave it to the horse, Or'ss-san,' he said quietly. 'He's used to this sort of terrain and he'll manage by himself.'

'So I noticed,' Horace said, between clenched teeth. When the uneven ground gave under his horse's hooves again, he forced himself to remain loose and supple in the saddle, instead of tightening his muscles and bracing himself, and trying to haul the horse's head back up again. The horse grunted as he recovered. Horace had the uncomfortable feeling that it was a grunt of grudging appreciation, as if the horse were saying to him: *That's better. Just sit easily, you big bag of bones, and leave the work to me.*

He reached forward and patted the horse's neck. The animal responded by shaking its head and mane.

They rode on, maintaining a steady canter for half an hour, then letting the horses walk and trot for the next twenty minutes. It was similar to the forced march pace of the Rangers, which Horace had learned from Halt and Will in their travels together. And while at first he begrudged the time spent at the slower pace, he knew that in the long run they would cover more distance in a day this way.

The sun was a milky presence, glowing weakly through the scudding grey clouds that passed over them. When Shukin judged it was pretty well directly overhead, he signalled a halt at a spot where the trail widened and formed a small, level clearing.

'We'll eat and rest for a short time,' he said. 'That'll give us and the horses a chance to recover.'

They unsaddled the horses and rubbed them down. In this weather, it wouldn't do to leave the sweat on them to dry and cool in the chill wind. While this was going on, three of the servants unpacked food from the panniers they carried behind their saddles. By the time the riders had tended to their horses, the food was ready, and the servants had a fire going to make tea.

Horace accepted a plate of pickles, smoked trout and spiced rice rolled into balls, and made his way to a level patch of ground. He hunkered down on a fallen log, groaning slightly as his knees and thighs let him know how hard they had been working. It was pleasant to rest for a few minutes, he thought. He just hoped that the brief stop wouldn't be enough to let his muscles stiffen. If they did, the first half hour on the trail again would be torture. He resolved to get up and walk around the clearing once he had eaten.

The food was good. Light, tasty and with a welcome tang. Horace looked at the size of the helping on his plate. The Nihon-Jan were, on the whole, a small race. He felt he could have happily dealt with a much larger portion of lunch. Then he shrugged philosophically. He always thought that, wherever he was and whatever he was given.

Shukin, having checked that Shigeru needed nothing, had done a quick tour of the temporary camp, ensuring that all the men were eating and none of the horses had developed problems. Then, when he was satisfied, a servant handed him a plate of food and he sank down on the log beside Horace. The Araluan noted glumly that Shukin, used to sitting cross-legged on the ground since childhood, showed no sign of stiffness or discomfort as he sat.

'How far do you plan to go today?' Horace asked him.

Shukin screwed up his face as he considered the

question. 'I had hoped to cross the Sarinaki River,' he said. He indicated the direction they had been travelling in. 'It's another twenty kilometres uphill from here. There's a waterfall with a crossing just above it.'

'We should be able to make that distance,' Horace said. 'We've got another five hours of daylight, at least.'

'Depending on the trail,' Shukin told him. 'It's relatively easy going at the moment but it gets steeper and rougher in a few kilometres. That will slow us down.'

'Hmmm. That could be a problem. And if it rains, the track will get more slippery, I suppose?' Horace asked.

The Senshi lord nodded. 'It certainly won't help. But if we can, I'd like to get across the river before dark.'

That made sense to Horace. Crossing a river just upstream of a high waterfall could be a difficult and dangerous business. And any waterfall in this mountainous terrain would be a high one, he knew.

'The crossing's tricky, is it?' he asked.

Shukin pushed out his bottom lip and made a so-so gesture with his hand. 'It's not the easiest,' he admitted. 'But I have another reason for wanting to get there before dark. The spot commands a view of the country below us. I'd like the chance to see if there's any sign of Arisaka and his men.'

Travelling as they were, surrounded by high, dense trees on either side of the trail, they could gather little knowledge of what was going on behind them. Horace realised that Shukin was feeling the inevitable uncertainty of any leader conducting a retreat from a superior force. He needed to know where their pursuers were — how close they were, whether they were gaining on the small party that travelled with the Emperor. Running blind, as they were, was a recipe for tension and uncertainty. You never knew when armed warriors might burst out of the trees, yelling their battle cries, swords poised to strike.

Just as they had that morning.

'And if we don't make the river?' Horace asked. It was all very well to plan for the best possible circumstances. But the worst possible had to be considered as well.

Shukin shrugged. 'There's a small village not far from the falls. We'll shelter there for the night.'

The rain, which had been absent for almost an hour, began again as he spoke. It was a light, misting rain, deceptive in its intensity. It seemed harmless enough at first but it was constant and unremitting. After ten to fifteen minutes of this, Horace knew, cloaks and trousers would become saturated, so that the water, no longer being absorbed by the weave, would flow off and run down into boot tops. It didn't take long under these conditions for a person to become sodden and miserable.

'Well, if we don't make the falls,' Horace said philosophically, 'at least we'll have somewhere dry to sleep tonight.'

The rain turned the surface of the trail to a slippery, glue-like consistency. The horses lurched and stumbled upwards, occasionally causing Horace's hair to stand on end as he caught glimpses of the dizzying depths below him, when the screen of trees beside the road thinned from time to time.

Even more serious, the thick, sticky mud built up on the horses' hooves, forcing the riders to stop frequently and clear the mess away.

He saw Shukin glancing more frequently at the pale, watery disc that marked the sun's position. The Senshi lord's face was fixed in a frown now. It was midafternoon and Horace, even though he wasn't sure how far they had travelled, knew it was nothing like the distance they would have to cover if they were to cross the river in daylight. Eventually, with a slumping of his shoulders, Shukin seemed to come to the same opinion. He held up his hand to stop the little column and edged his horse back down the slope to where the Emperor sat patiently. Horace urged his own horse closer to join in the discussion.

'We won't get across the river tonight,' Shukin said.

Shigeru pursed his lips in disappointment. 'You're sure?' he asked, then he waved any possible answer aside as he corrected himself. 'Of course you're sure. You wouldn't have said it, otherwise.'

'I'm sorry, cousin,' Shukin said, but Shigeru repeated the dismissive wave of his hand.

'You've done everything possible,' he said. 'I can't blame you for the rain – or for this mud.'

He glanced meaningfully down at the irregular balls of mud that encased his horse's feet. As he did so, one of his servants slipped from his saddle and hurried forward to clean the sticky mass away. Shigeru looked down at the man as he bent over the horse's left forefoot.

'I should send him away and do that myself,' he said ruefully. 'A man should attend to his own horse.' He paused, then allowed himself a weary grin. 'But I'm just too damned tired.'

Horace smiled in return. 'It's good to be the Emperor,' he said and Shigeru regarded him cynically.

'Oh yes indeed. Look at the excellent time I'm having. Warm, comfortable travelling conditions. Plenty of good food and drink and a soft bed at the end of the trail. What more could I ask?'

He and Horace shared the small joke but Shukin lowered his gaze. 'I'm sorry, cousin,' he said bitterly. 'You don't deserve this.'

Shigeru reached over in the saddle and laid a gentle hand on his cousin's shoulder.

'*I'm* sorry, Shukin,' he said. 'I'm not complaining. I know you're doing your best to keep me safe. I'll be grateful for a straw bed in a leaky hut in some small village tonight.'

'Unfortunately, that seems to be what's in store for us,' Shukin agreed. 'A little further up this rise, the road levels out and forks. Left leads to the falls and the crossing. Right leads us to a timber cutters' village. We'll turn right.'

'One thing,' Shigeru added doubtfully. 'Will this rain have any effect on the crossing? What if it causes the river to rise? Should we perhaps try to get there even if it is in the dark?'

But Shukin shook his head without any sign of uncertainty. 'It's not heavy enough for that. The water doesn't build up because it escapes so easily at the falls.'

Shigeru smiled at his cousin, understanding how heavily the responsibility for his Emperor's safety and wellbeing was lying on the Senshi's shoulders.

'Well, my friend, there's no sense in bemoaning what we can't achieve today. Let's get on with what we can achieve and find this village. As Or'ss-san mentioned earlier, at least we'll have somewhere dry to sleep tonight.' He included Horace in the smile.

Shukin nodded and turned to issue a command to the small column. As they moved out, Horace noticed that

Shukin now had a determined set to his shoulders. Not for the first time, Horace reflected on how the Emperor's good-humoured, unselfish response to setbacks could inspire so much more loyalty and effort from his subordinates than blustering and bullying could ever achieve. It was a valuable lesson in leadership, he thought.

It was another difficult two hours on the trail, riding, slithering, sliding and stumbling before they reached level ground once more. Shukin called a brief halt while horses and men caught their breath for a few minutes. He consulted his map, with one of his troops holding a waterproof cape over him. There was barely enough light to see the details on the sheet, Horace thought, but the Senshi warrior folded the map away and pointed down the trail.

'Ten more minutes,' he said.

A little while after, they saw the glimmer of lights through the trees, flickering intermittently as branches, moving in the wind, interposed themselves between them. Then, abruptly, they were in a clearing, at the beginning of a small group of thatched-roof cabins. Warm yellow light glowed through the waxed-paper window panes of the houses and smoke curled from several chimneys. The smell of woodsmoke spoke to Horace of warm rooms and hot food and tea. Suddenly, he was eager to dismount.

As he had the thought, he became aware of movement in his peripheral vision. He looked to the side and saw doors sliding open as dark forms materialised on the wooden porches that fronted the houses.

The villagers were emerging from their homes to welcome the strangers who had arrived among them.

At least, Horace hoped they were planning a welcome.

Eleven

Wolfwill had been sailing east for two days, and Toscana was far behind them. The strangely rigged ship, with a curving triangular sail whose boom was set at a steep angle to the vertical mast, was swooping eagerly over the small waves, with the wind on her beam. The sail had been trimmed right round until its curved, swelling length was almost parallel to the line of the ship itself. The rigging hummed with the wind of their passage and the deck vibrated slightly underneath their feet. It was an exhilarating feeling, putting Will in mind of one of the low-flying seabirds that accompanied the ship for hours each day, planing easily just above the surface of the sea, with hardly any perceptible movement of their wings.

The Araluans and Selethen were gathered in the prow, leaving the main deck clear for the sailors to work the mast and sails. With this wind and this speed, there was no need for rowers, although the ship could mount eight long oars a side, in case the wind should drop.

Even Halt had joined them. Wisely, none of them commented on the fact that this was the first they had seen of him in the past two days. Evanlyn, Alyss and Will knew the delicate nature of Halt's stomach in the opening hours of any sea journey and they had appraised Selethen of the grey-bearded Ranger's touchiness on the subject.

Halt eyed them balefully. They were all being so obvious about not mentioning his sudden reappearance that it was even worse than if they had commented, he thought.

'Oh go on!' he said. 'Somebody say something! I know what you're thinking!'

'It's good to see you up and about, Halt,' Selethen said gravely. Of all of them, he was the most capable of keeping a straight face when he said it.

Halt glared at the others and they quickly chorused their pleasure at seeing him back to his normal self. But he could see the grins they didn't quite manage to hide. He fixed a glare on Alyss.

'I'm surprised at you, Alyss,' he said. 'I expected no better of Will and Evanlyn, of course. Heartless beasts, the pair of them. But you! I thought you had been better trained!'

Which was a particularly barbed comment, seeing how Alyss's mentor had been none other than Lady Pauline, Halt's beloved wife.

Alyss reached a hand out and touched his arm gently.

'Halt, I am sorry! It's not funny, you're right . . . Shut up, Will.' This last was directed at Will as he tried, unsuccessfully, to smother a snigger. 'There is nothing funny about *mal de mer*. It's a serious business.'

Halt was a little taken aback when he heard that. He thought he had nothing more than seasickness. An annoying problem, admittedly, but one that passed within a day or two of being at sea. But Alyss seemed to believe it was something far more exotic. And the more exotic an illness was, the more life-threatening it might be.

'Malldy-mur?' he said with a twinge of anxiety. 'What is this Malldy-mur?'

'It's Gallican,' Alyss told him. She had used the phrase because she knew how much Halt hated the word 'seasick'. If one were wise, the word was never even uttered in Halt's presence. She glanced at the others but they offered no help. None of them would meet her gaze. *You got yourself into this*, they seemed to be saying. *Now you can get yourself out.*

Halt was right, she thought. They were heartless beasts.

'It means . . . "seasick",' she finished weakly.

'I thought you spoke Gallican, Halt,' said Evanlyn.

He drew himself upright with some dignity. 'I do. My Gallican is excellent. But I can't be expected to memorise every obscure phrase in the language. And Alyss's pronunciation leaves a little to be desired.'

The others hastened to agree that no, he certainly couldn't, and yes, her pronunciation certainly did. Halt looked around them, feeling that honour had been suitably restored. It has to be admitted that, in a sneaking way, while he hated the discomfort of seasickness, once he was over it, he enjoyed the attention and sympathy that it created among attractive young women like Evanlyn and Alyss. And he liked the fact that Will tended to walk on eggshells around him when the problem was mentioned. Keeping Will off balance was always desirable.

Things took a downward turn, however, as Gundar, seeing Halt upright for the first time in two days, stumped up the deck to join them.

'Back on your feet then?' he boomed cheerfully, with typical Skandian tact. 'By Gorlog's toenails, with all the heaving and puking you've been doing, I thought you'd turn yourself inside out and puke yourself over the rail!'

At which graphic description, Alyss and Evanlyn blanched and turned away.

'You do paint a pretty picture, Gundar,' Will said and Selethen allowed himself a smile.

'Thank you for your concern,' Halt said icily. Of all people, Skandians seemed the most intolerant of seasickness — or, as he now knew it, malldy-mur. He made a mental note to get Gundar on horseback as soon as they reached Nihon-Ja. Skandians were notoriously bad riders.

'So, did you find Albert?' Gundar went on, unabashed. Even Halt was puzzled by his sudden apparent change of subject.

'Albert?' he asked. Too late, he saw Gundar's grin widening and knew he'd stepped into a trap.

'You seemed to be looking for him. You'd lean over the rail and call, "Al-b-e-e-e-e-e-r-t!" I thought he might be some Araluan sea god.'

The others had to agree that Gundar's drawn-out enunciation of the name sounded very much like the sound of Halt's desperate, heartfelt retching over the side. Halt glared at the sea wolf.

'No. I didn't find him. Maybe I could look for him in your helmet.'

He reached out a hand. But Gundar had heard what happened when Skandians lent their helmets to the grim-faced Ranger while on board ship and he backed away a pace.

'No. I'm pretty sure he's not there,' he said hurriedly.

Selethen, ever the diplomat, thought it might be time to get everybody's minds off Halt's stomach.

'This is an interesting ship, captain,' he said to Gundar. 'I can't remember seeing one quite like it. And I've seen many Skandian wolfships in my time,' he added meaningfully.

Selethen was the *Wakir*, or local ruler, of one of Arrida's coastal provinces. He'd usually seen wolfships while they were engaged in raiding his towns. Gundar was oblivious to the reference. But, as Selethen had suspected, like any Skandian, he was eager to talk about his ship.

'She's a fine ship!' he enthused. 'Built her myself, up on the banks of a river in north Araluen — remember, Will?' He looked to Will for confirmation. Gundar and his crew, having been shipwrecked on the north coast, had been conscripted by Will to assist him in the siege of Castle Macindaw. As a reward for their services, they had been granted permission to stay in Araluen while they built a new ship for the journey home. Will had also been instrumental in making sure that timber, cordage, canvas, tar and other materials were supplied to them at the bare minimum price.

'I remember well enough,' Will agreed. 'But she was square-rigged then. This new sail arrangement is something quite different.'

'Ah yes, the *Heron* sail plan. It's really something,' Gundar agreed. 'We kept the hull and changed the mast, sails and rigging.'

'Why do you call it the *Heron* sail plan?' Alyss asked.

Gundar beamed at her. He had met Alyss at Macindaw as well, and been rewarded by a kiss on his bearded cheek when they were reacquainted in Toscana. Gundar was partial to being kissed by beautiful blondes. But he sensed there was something between this particular one and Will, so he took things no further.

'It's named for the original ship rigged this way. The *Heron*. Not really a ship at all — she was only three-quarters the size of a wolfship. But the mast and sail plan were a brilliant new arrangement. It was the brainchild of a young Skandian lad. A genius, he was.'

'I'd heard he was half-Araluan,' Halt put in dryly.

Gundar eyed him for a moment. Most Skandians these days chose to forget that they had sneered at the design when they had first seen it.

'Maybe he was and maybe he wasn't,' Gundar said, then continued, with a total lack of logic, 'But it was the Skandian half that came up with the design. Everyone knows Araluans know nothing about ships.'

'Really?' Halt said.

Gundar glared at him. 'Well, of course. That's why so many of them start heaving their guts up the minute they step aboard.'

Will saw the conversation heading back into danger. 'So tell us about this design. How does it work?'

'The most important part of it is that it lets us sail into the wind,' Gundar told them.

'Into the wind?' Halt said. 'How can that be possible?'

Gundar puckered his face in a frown. He was reluctant to admit any shortcoming in his ship, but he knew that if he didn't answer truthfully, his audience would see through his boasting eventually.

'Not really *into* the wind,' he admitted. 'We can sail across it, gradually making ground against it. We're able to move at an angle to the wind so we can still make progress when it's on our bow. No square-rigged ship can do that.'

'So that's why you were constantly changing direction yesterday when the wind was against us?' Selethen asked.

'That's right. We move diagonally to the wind. Then after a while, we switch and go the other way, gradually zigzagging in the direction we want. We call it tacking.'

'Why?' Alyss asked and he frowned again. He'd never queried why the manoeuvre he'd described was called tacking. Gundar was an accepting person, with a non-inquiring mind.

'Because . . . that's what it's called,' he said. 'Tacking.'

Wisely, Alyss pursued the matter no further. Will hid a small smile with his hand. He knew Alyss and knew that Gundar's answer was totally inadequate to her inquisitive mind. He thought it best they should move on.

'So how does it actually work?' he asked. Gundar looked at him gratefully. This part he could explain.

'Well, the young Skandian lad who designed it,' he glared quickly at Halt, daring him to challenge the inventor's nationality again, 'had spent a lot of time studying seabirds, particularly the shape of their wings. He thought it might be a good idea to stiffen the front edge of the sail like a bird's wing, and shape the sail itself so it was triangular, not square.

'So he shortened the main mast, then designed that flexible curved boom you see that sits on top. The boom strengthens and supports the leading edge of the sail so that we can face it into the wind. A traditional square-rigged sail would simply flutter and vibrate and lose its shape. But with the boom, the sail forms a smooth curve so that we can redirect the driving force of the wind much more efficiently. The result is, the ship can move at an angle to the direction the wind is blowing from. In effect, we can sail against the wind.'

He paused, seeing a few questioning faces, then amended his statement. 'All right. Across the wind. But it's a huge improvement on the old square sail. That's unusable once the wind is any farther forward than dead abeam.'

'But you've duplicated that thin top boom and the sail,' Evanlyn said. And she was right. On the deck, lying fore and aft, was another boom, with its sail furled around it. It lay on the opposite side of the mast to the boom that was currently in place.

Gundar favoured her with a smile. 'That's the beauty of this design,' he told her. 'As you can see, the sail is currently on the starboard side of the mast, with the wind coming from the port side, so it's blown away from the mast into a perfect curve. When we tack . . .' He glanced quickly at Alyss but she kept her expression blank. 'The wind will be on the starboard side, forcing the sail against the mast, so that the perfect wing shape would be spoiled. So we rig another boom and sail on the port side. Then, when we tack, we lower the starboard sail and raise the port sail. The two are linked by rope through a pulley at the masthead, so that the weight of one coming down actually helps us raise the other one.'

'Ingenious,' Halt said at length.

Gundar Hardstriker smiled modestly. 'Well . . . most of us Skandians are.'

Twelve

Shukin held up a hand and the small party of horse-men drew rein, stopping in the central cleared space among the houses.

The villagers were wary, but with the long-ingrained habit of respect for the Senshi class, they waited silently for the newcomers to state their business.

They edged a little closer, forming a loose circle around the horses. Some of the villagers, Horace noted, were carrying heavy blackwood staffs, while others held axes loosely. But none of the makeshift weapons were being brandished in threatening gestures. They were simply kept close at hand while the villagers waited to see what might happen next.

Shukin, who had been riding a few metres ahead of the group, turned in the saddle.

'Come forward and join me, please, cousin,' he said quietly to Shigeru.

Shigeru urged his horse forward until he and Shukin

were on their own, in the middle of the group of waiting Kikori. It was a courageous move on the part of the Emperor, Horace thought. Up till that moment, he had been safely surrounded by his group of warriors. Now, if trouble started, he was vulnerable to attack from all sides and his escort would not be able to reach him in time to save him.

The rain began to mist down again, pattering softly on the thatched roofs and forming misty haloes around the hanging lanterns under the eaves of the verandahs that fronted the cabins. A cold trickle ran down the back of Horace's collar and he shifted uncomfortably in his saddle. It was only a small movement but even so, a dozen pairs of eyes swung to him instantly. He settled back in his saddle and remained still. Gradually, the wary eyes returned to Shukin and Shigeru.

'Kikori people,' Shukin began. His voice was deep and authoritative. He didn't speak loudly, but such was the timbre of his voice that his words carried clearly to everyone in the clearing. 'Today, a great honour has come to your village.'

He paused, his gaze scanning the waiting timber workers and their families. He felt a twinge of disappointment as he saw the disbelief in their eyes. They were cynical of any Senshi warrior who told them they were about to receive a great honour. Usually such statements were the prelude to a series of demands on their homes, their food, their time and their wellbeing. *Be honoured because you can give us whatever we ask for — after all, we plan to take it anyway.*

Sad to say, it was the way the world had always been between the two classes.

He sought for the words necessary to convince them that he and his men were not seeking to impose themselves on the village. They were asking for hospitality and shelter, yes. But they would pay. They would treat the villagers fairly. Any such reassurance would likely fall on deaf ears, he knew. The Kikori had years of experience of arrogant treatment at the hands of the Senshi and no number of soft words could change that.

As he hesitated, he felt a light touch on his forearm.

'Perhaps I should talk to them, cousin,' said Shigeru.

Shukin hesitated. Even in such humble surroundings, Shigeru should be accorded a certain level of esteem. And that meant that he should be announced properly, with all his titles and honours, so that the people could greet him respectfully.

He drew breath to say something along those lines when he realised that Shigeru was already swinging down from the saddle. The Emperor grinned at the man nearest to him, a heavily muscled, thickset type who had obviously spent his lifetime swinging the massive axe that he held loosely in his right hand. The man's face was set in a stubborn, unsmiling expression. He had the look of a leader about him. He was the one to win over, Shigeru knew.

'Aaaah!' the Emperor said, with deep relief as he rubbed his buttocks. 'That feels so good!'

The timber worker couldn't help a small, surprised smile forming. He was disarmed by Shigeru's ingenuous statement and informal manner. They were far removed from the haughty demeanour of the Senshi that the timber worker had encountered in the past.

Shukin watched anxiously from his saddle, his eyes fixed on that massive axe. He desperately wanted to move his hand closer to the hilt of his sword but he knew that would be a mistake — possibly a fatal one. At the slightest sign of aggression, this tableau could explode into bloodshed.

Shigeru, however, seemed to have no such misgivings. He stepped closer to the man, bowed to him, and held out his hand in greeting.

'What's your name?' he asked.

The timber worker was taken aback. This Senshi was offering to clasp hands in friendship, an unprecedented gesture. And he had bowed first — a totally unexpected sign of politeness. He started to reach for Shigeru's hand, realised that he held the axe in his own right hand and shifted it awkwardly to his left. Then he hesitated, glancing down at his callused hand, still stained with dirt and tree sap from the day's hard work.

Shigeru laughed, a deep booming sound that was genuinely amused.

'Don't worry about me!' he said. 'I'm not such a fragrant flower myself!' And he held up his own palm, dirt and travel stained, for them all to see. 'Just don't crush my tiny fingers in that massive grip of yours!'

A muted ripple of amusement ran through the watching villagers. Horace sensed a certain lessening in the tension. The timber worker grinned in reply and reached forward to clasp Shigeru's hand.

'I am Eiko,' he said.

Shigeru nodded, filing the name away. Horace knew the Emperor could be introduced to another twenty people this night and he would remember all their names after hearing them once. It was a skill that Shigeru had demonstrated on more than one occasion.

Eiko now cocked his head to one side expectantly, wondering if the Senshi would respond with his own name. If he did, it would be a first. Senshi normally proclaimed their names loudly, expecting lower classes to respond with respect and awe. In Eiko's experience, they didn't exchange names in friendship with Kikori axemen.

Shigeru held the pause just long enough to make sure he had everyone's attention. Then he reclaimed his hand, shaking it a little in joking deference to the strength of Eiko's grip.

'Nice to meet you, Eiko. I'm Shigeru Motodato.'

There was an intake of breath from the assembled villagers. Of course they knew the name. There had been rumours that Shigeru was visiting his mountain lodge, not too far away. And they had heard other rumours over the past few years. It was said that this Emperor was a friend of the lower classes, that he spoke easily and freely with farmers, fishermen and woodcutters when he encountered them, refusing to stand on his dignity, and treating them as friends.

'Oh,' Shigeru said, as if adding an afterthought, 'sometimes people refer to me as "the Emperor".'

He turned, grinning at the people around him, and contrived in that movement to allow his outer robe to open, revealing the Motodato crest on the left breast of his tunic — a stylised bunch of three red cherries. It was the royal crest, of course, recognised throughout Nihon-Ja.

Now the whispered intake of breath became a general chorus of respect and each of the villagers bowed their heads and dropped to one knee in deference to the Emperor. They had no doubt that this was he. It was an offence punishable by death for anyone other than the Emperor or his entourage to wear the royal emblem. They couldn't conceive of anyone being foolish enough to do so.

But now Shigeru stepped forward among them. He selected an elderly woman, grey-haired and stooped from a lifetime of hard work, reached down and took her hand, gently assisting her to rise.

'Please! Please! There's no need for such formality! Come on, mother! Up you come! Don't get yourself all muddy just because of me!'

The woman stood, but still kept her head lowered respectfully. Others in the crowd raised their heads as Shigeru reached forward, tipping her chin up with his hand so that their eyes could meet. He saw surprise mingled with respect, then a sudden glow of affection on the lined face.

'That's better! After all, you've worked hard all your life, haven't you?'

'Yes, lord,' she muttered.

'Harder than me, I'll bet. Got any children?'

'Eight, my lord.'

'Eight? My lord!' Shigeru said, cleverly repeating her phrase but changing the inflection to one of awed respect. Laughter ran around the assembled villagers. 'You've definitely been working harder than me!'

'And seventeen grandchildren, my lord,' said the woman, emboldened now by his easy manner. Shigeru whistled in surprise and smacked his forehead.

'Seventeen! I'll bet you spoil 'em, eh?'

'No indeed, Lord Shigeru!' she responded indignantly. 'If they play up on me, they feel the flat of my hand on their bums!'

Her hands flew to her mouth in horror as she realised she'd said 'bums' in front of the Emperor. But Shigeru merely grinned at her.

'Nothing to be ashamed of, mother. We've all got a bum, you know.'

Now the laughter grew louder. Shigeru turned to the crowd and made an upward gesture with his hands. 'Please! Please! No bowing and scraping needed! Stand up, all of you!'

And they did, with a mixture of wonder and amusement at his easygoing, informal approach. They were a canny group, difficult to deceive. And they sensed, as did most people on first meeting Shigeru, that he was genuine. He liked people. He enjoyed meeting with them and laughing with them. There was neither deceit nor conceit about him.

Instinctively, the villagers moved a little closer to their Emperor. But there was no threat in the movement. They simply wanted a better view of this legendary character. It was unknown for someone so exalted to visit a little village like this one — and laugh and joke with the inhabitants.

'This is a beautiful village,' Shigeru was saying, as he looked around the rows of neat, thatched cabins. 'What do you call it?' He selected a young boy for his question — a boy barely in his teens, Horace guessed.

The youngster was tongue-tied for a few seconds. He stared wide eyed at his Emperor, not believing that he had been addressed by such an important personage. A woman standing beside him, probably his mother, Horace thought, nudged him with her elbow and hissed something at him. Thus encouraged, he stammered out an answer.

'We call it *mura*, my lord,' he said. His tone seemed to imply that Shigeru should have known that. There were a few muted giggles from the crowd but Shigeru beamed at him.

'And an excellent name that is!' he said. The villagers laughed out loud once more.

Horace was puzzled until one of the escort edged his horse closer and said in a low voice, '*Mura* is Nihon-Jan for "village".'

'And is there by any chance a hot spring somewhere close to this *mura*?' Shigeru asked.

There were several affirmative murmurs from those around him. It wasn't surprising. There were hot springs throughout these mountains and, wherever possible, the Kikori sited their villages near them. Horace felt a warm glow of pleasure flow through him. Hot springs meant a hot bath. The Nihon-Jan people loved hot baths and Horace had grown to enjoy the custom since he'd been here. After a day of hard riding and sore muscles, the idea of sinking into scalding hot water and soaking away the aches of the day was almost too good to bear thinking about.

Shigeru's gentle hint seemed to help the villagers remember their sense of hospitality. An older man, who had been in the second row of people standing around the Emperor, now stepped forward and bowed deeply.

'My apologies, Lord Shigeru! In the excitement of seeing you, we have forgotten our manners. I am Ayagi, elder of the village. Please, have your men dismount. My people will tend to your horses and we will prepare hot baths and food for you and your men. We would be honoured if you will accept whatever rough hospitality we can offer you. I'm afraid it won't be worthy of an Emperor, but it will be the best we can do!'

Shigeru reached out a hand and laid it on the village elder's shoulder.

'My friend,' he said, 'you might be surprised at what's worthy of an Emperor in these times.'

He turned and signalled for his men to dismount. Some of the villagers stepped forward to take the reins of their horses and lead them away. At Ayagi's bidding, others hurried off to prepare food for their unexpected guests. Horace groaned softly as he swung down from the saddle.

'Take me to that bath and colour me happy,' he said, to nobody in particular.

Thirteen

'Down sail,' Gundar ordered. 'Rig the oars, men.'

While the sail handlers brought the long, curving boom and its flapping sail back to the deck, the designated rowers were unstowing the white-oak sweeps and fitting them into the oarlocks. By the time the sail was furled and wrapped around the boom, the rowers were on their benches. They spat on their hands, rolled their shoulders and stretched their muscles in readiness for the hard pulling that lay ahead.

Wolfwill rocked gently in the waves, a hundred metres off a low, featureless shore. There were no hills or trees in sight. Just bare brown sand and rock that stretched as far as the eye could see. And directly ahead of them, what appeared to be the mouth of a small river was just visible.

'Ready, skirl!' called the lead rower. It was Nils Rope-hander, Will noted without surprise. Nils was one of the bulkiest and strongest in the crew. He was a logical choice as lead rower and he would set a cracking pace for the others.

He was also not the most intelligent or inquiring of men and Will had noted over the years that those qualities, or lack thereof, often were the mark of an excellent rower. With nothing else to distract his mind, such a man could concentrate completely on the necessary sequence and rhythm of the rower's craft: *Up, twist, forward, twist, down, back.*

'So that's it?' Halt said, looking keenly at the gap in the low-lying coastline. 'That's the mouth of the Assaranyan Channel?'

Gundar hesitated. He glanced at the sun and the horizon, then down at the parchment chart he had spread on a small table beside the steerboard.

'According to this Genovesan chart I bought before we left Toscana, that's it,' he said. 'That's assuming that any Genovesan could draw an accurate chart. I've heard their skills lie more in the area of people-killing than map-making.'

'That's true,' Halt said. Genovesa had a long seagoing history but in more recent times the city had become infamous for its highly trained assassins, who worked as hired killers throughout the continent — and occasionally, as Halt and Will had discovered not long ago, in Araluen.

'Genovesans aren't so bad,' Will said. 'So long as you manage to shoot them before they shoot you.'

'Let's go a little closer,' Gundar said. 'Oars! Give way! Slow ahead, Nils!'

'Aye aye, skirl!' Nils bellowed from his position in the bow of the ship. 'Rowers! Ready!'

Sixteen long oars rose as one, swinging smoothly forward as the rowers leaned towards the stern, setting their feet against the stops in front of them.

'Give way!' Nils shouted. The oars dipped into the water and the rowers heaved against their handles, with Nils calling a relaxed cadence for the first few strokes to set the rhythm. Instantly, the wolfship came alive again, cutting through the calm water as the oars propelled her forward, a small bow wave gurgling under her forefoot.

'You're planning to row through?' Halt asked Gundar, glancing at the telltale strip of wool at the masthead. It indicated that the wind was slightly aft of the beam and he'd learned over the past few days that this was one of the ship's best and fastest points of sailing. Gundar noted the glance and shook his head.

'We'd lose too much distance to leeward,' he said briefly. 'This channel's too narrow for that. We'd go forward, of course, but we'd lose distance downwind. Have to make our way back again too soon. Not a problem in the open water where we have plenty of sea room, but awkward in a confined space like this.' He peered carefully at the coastline, now much closer to them.

'Nils!' the skirl called. 'Up oars!'

The oars rose, dripping, from the water. The rowers rested on them, keeping the blades clear of the sea. Accustomed to physical work as they were, none of them was even breathing hard. Slowly, the ship glided to a stop once more, rocking gently in the small waves.

Gundar shaded his eyes, peering at the narrow opening — barely thirty metres wide. He glanced down at the chart and the navigation notes that had come with it, sniffed the breeze, then squinted up at the position of the sun in the sky. Will understood that this was all part of the instinctive navigation system that the Skandians relied on. Some of them, Oberjarl Erak, for example, were masters of the art. It seemed that Gundar was another adept.

But obviously, it never hurt to ask a second opinion. The skirl looked around and sought out Selethen. Of all of them, he had the most knowledge of this part of the world.

'Ever been here before, Selethen?' he asked.

The *Wakir* shook his head. 'I've never been this far east. But I've heard of the Assaranyan Channel, of course. This is where I'd expect it to be. Further north and south, the land becomes more hilly.'

They all followed his gaze along the coastline. He was right. Here, the coast was flat and low lying. On either side, north and south, the brown, dry land rose into low hills.

'What exactly is this Assaranyan Channel, anyway?' Will asked.

Evanlyn, who had studied the route of their journey before she left Araluen, answered. 'It's a channel through the narrowest part of the land mass here. It runs for forty or fifty kilometres, then opens into a natural waterway to the Eastern Ocean.'

'A natural waterway?' Will said. 'Are you saying this part isn't natural?' He gestured towards the unimpressive-looking river mouth ahead of them.

'People believe it was man-made — hundreds, perhaps thousands of years ago. It runs straight through this low-lying area — that's why it was built here.'

'Of course,' Will said. 'And who built it?'

Evanlyn shrugged. 'Nobody knows for sure. We assume the Assaranyans.' Forestalling Will's next question, she went on: 'They were an ancient race, but we know precious little about them.'

'Except they were excellent diggers,' Alyss said dryly.

Evanlyn corrected her, but without any sense of superiority. 'Or they had a lot of time and a lot of slaves.'

Alyss acknowledged the point. 'Perhaps more likely.'

Will said nothing. He stared at the opening to the channel. It seemed so insignificant, he thought. Then he thought of the labour involved in digging a fifty-kilometre channel through this harsh, dry land. The prospect was daunting.

Gundar seemed to come to a decision.

'Well, as my old mam used to say: if it looks like a duck and quacks like a duck and walks like a duck, it's probably a duck.'

'Very wise,' Halt replied. 'And what exactly do your mother's words of wisdom have to do with this situation?'

Gundar shrugged. 'It looks like a channel. It's in the right place for a channel. If I were digging one, this is where I'd dig a channel. So . . .'

'So it's probably the channel?' Selethen said.

Gundar grinned at him. 'Either that, or it's a duck,' he said. Then, cupping his hands round his mouth, he yelled at Nils. 'Let's get moving, Nils! Slow ahead!'

The lead oar nodded. 'Oars! Ready!'

Again there was the squeak of oars in the oarlocks and the involuntary grunt from the rowers as they prepared for the stroke.

'Give way all!'

Wolfwill surged forward again, gathering speed with each successive stroke, then settling to a smooth glide across the water. Gundar, eyes squinted in concentration, leaned on the starboard tiller to line the bow up with the centre of the channel.

They fell silent. The only sound was the creak and groan of the oars in their oarlocks as they swung up and down, back and forth, in unison, and the occasional grunt of exertion from one of the rowers. The sheer immensity of the task undertaken by those ancient people settled a kind of awe upon the travellers as the ship glided smoothly down the dead straight channel.

It had to be man-made, Alyss thought. No natural river was ever so straight. As they moved away from the ocean, the dull brown desert enveloped them on either side and the freshness of the sea breeze, light though it had been, was lost to them. The channel grew wider as they progressed, until it was nearly one hundred metres across. Erosion over the centuries had widened the channel considerably. On either bank, the immediate ground looked soft and treacherous for another twenty metres or so.

Selethen noticed Alyss studying the ground.

'Step in that and you might not come out alive,' he said thoughtfully. 'I'll wager it's quicksand.'

Alyss nodded. She had been thinking the same thing.

The heat beat down on them, folding itself around them like a blanket. The air was heavy with it.

Gundar spoke softly to two of the sailing crew. They hurried aft and slung buckets overside to haul up water. Then they passed along the rowing benches, tossing the cooling water over the hard-working men. A few of the rowers muttered their thanks.

The Skandians, experienced travellers as they were, had all donned long-sleeved linen shirts and had more of the same material fastened round their heads as bandannas to protect them from the sun. In the colder northern waters, Will had often seen them bare chested, seemingly impervious to the cold. But they were a fair-skinned race and years of raiding in the warm waters of the Constant Sea had taught them to respect the burning power of the sun.

The sea water flung on them soaked their shirts, but Will noticed that they dried within a few minutes. He recalled his own experience of the sun's power, in the desert of Arrida some years before, and shuddered at the memory.

Some of the crew busied themselves rigging canvas awnings so that those not engaged in rowing could shelter in their shade. It was a welcome relief to be out of the sun's direct glare. But the air itself was still heavy and oppressive. Will glanced over the stern. There was now no sign of the sparkling blue sea behind them. Only this brown river cutting straight through the equally brown sand.

'How long is the transit?' he asked Gundar. For some reason, he spoke softly. It seemed appropriate in this oppressive stillness.

Gundar considered the question. When he replied, it seemed that he had the same aversion to making too much noise.

'Five, perhaps six hours,' he said. Then he reconsidered. 'Could be more. The men will tire more quickly in this heat.'

Acting on that thought, he gave an order and the relief rowing crew began to change places with the rowers. They did it gradually, a pair of oars at a time, working forward from the stern. That way, the ship maintained its motion through the murky brown water beneath them. As each pair of rowers relinquished their oars to their replacements, they sprawled instantly on the deck in the shade of the awnings. They were tired, but nowhere near exhausted, Will knew. He'd had plenty of experience with Skandian crews in the past. They had an inbred ability to fall sleep almost anywhere, almost immediately. In an hour or so, they'd be rested and ready to replace their companions at the oars again.

'We might even anchor in the channel once it gets dark,' Gundar said. 'There'll be no moon until long past midnight and it could be a good idea to rest in the cool hours.'

Will could understand the wisdom of that. The channel might be straight, but with no reference points to guide them, the brown water would merge with the low brown banks either side. They could possibly veer one side or the other and run aground.

'Not such a good idea,' Halt said quietly. 'We have company.'

Fourteen

Ayagi and his people had been appalled at the news of Arisaka's rebellion against the Emperor. The common people of Nihon-Ja thought of the Emperor as a person whose accession to the throne was guided and consecrated by the gods. To rebel against him was an unthinkable sacrilege.

'We are your people, Lord Shigeru,' the white-haired village elder had said. 'Tell us what you want us to do. We'll stand beside you against Arisaka.'

There had been an indignant rumble of assent from the other villagers. Foremost among them, Horace had noted, had been Eiko, the heavily built worker Shigeru had first shaken hands with. Ayagi might be the village elder, but Eiko was obviously a person of considerable influence among the younger Kikori.

'Thank you, my friends,' Shigeru had replied. 'But at the moment I hope to avoid further bloodshed. All we need is a guide to the village of . . .' He had hesitated and looked to Shukin for the name of the village he had nominated as a rendezvous point with Reito and the survivors of the army.

'Kawagishi,' Shukin had said. 'Riverbank Village.'

Ayagi had bowed. 'We know this village,' he had said. 'My nephew, Mikeru, will show you the way in the morning.'

Shigeru had bowed from his sitting position. 'Thank you, Ayagi. And now let's have no more talk of this unpleasantness with Arisaka. Let's enjoy the evening. Do any of your people have a folk song for us all to sing?'

A hot bath, hot food, dry clothes and a warm, dry bed for the night worked wonders on Horace's tired body.

Shortly after dawn, the Emperor and his party woke, breakfasted and prepared to move out once more. The rain had stopped during the night and the sky had cleared to a brilliant blue. Horace's breath steamed in the cold air as he exhaled. One of the village women had taken his wet, travel-stained clothes during the night and cleaned and dried them. The same service had been performed for the rest of the travellers. Putting on clean clothes, still warm from the fire they had dried in front of, was a distinct luxury.

There was the usual bustle and confusion involved in setting out. The riders inspected their girth straps. Weapons were checked, belts tightened, armour adjusted. As was his habit, Horace had cleaned and sharpened his sword the previous night before he slipped between the warmed bedcovers laid out on the matting floor of his room. He guessed that each of the Senshi had done the same.

As the rest of the party mounted, Shukin held back. He reached into the purse at his belt and produced a handful of golden coins, each stamped with the triple cherry crest.

Ayagi saw the movement and backed away, holding his hands out before him.

'No! No, Lord Shukin! We don't want any payment! It was our pleasure to have the Emperor as our guest!'

Shukin grinned at him. He had expected the reaction but he knew that times were hard in the mountains and the Kikori had little to spare. He had his answer ready for Ayagi's protestation.

'The Emperor, perhaps,' he said. 'But nobody would expect you to provide for a dozen hungry Senshi — or for a massive *gaijin* with the appetite of a black bear!'

He indicated Horace when he said this, grinning to make sure that Horace knew he was joking. Horace shook his head ruefully. He couldn't dispute the fact that he had eaten more than any of the others in the party. Nihon-Jan helpings seemed so small to him and he was famous even in Araluen for his prodigious appetite.

The villagers laughed. Horace had proved to be a figure of great interest and popularity among the Kikori. He was polite and self-effacing and ready to join in singing their folk songs — albeit with more enthusiasm than melody.

Even Ayagi smiled. His sense of hospitality made him reluctant to take the money but he knew that if he didn't, his people would go short. With the gold Shukin was offering, they could buy more supplies at the monthly market held in one of the larger villages.

'Well then,' he said, capitulating with good grace, 'in deference to the *kurokuma* . . .'

He accepted the coins and Horace was given the name by which he would be known among the Nihon-Jan — *Kurokuma*, or Black Bear. At the time, however, he was unaware of it. He was busy fastening a loose strap on the bedroll tied behind his saddle and missed Ayagi's statement.

Shukin bowed gracefully and Ayagi returned the gesture. Then he turned and bowed to the Emperor, with all of the assembled villagers doing the same.

'Thank you, Ayagi-san,' Shigeru said, raising his hand to them all, 'and thank you, Kikori.'

The villagers remained, heads bowed, as the small party rode out of the village.

Mikeru, the elder's nephew, was a keen-faced, slimly built youth of about sixteen. He rode a small, shaggy-haired pony — the kind the Kikori people used as beasts of burden when they gathered wood. He was familiar with the area, of course, and led them on a much shorter route than the one shown on the map Shukin carried. They had been travelling for less than an hour when they reached the ford in the river that Shukin had hoped to cross the night before. They rode across in single file, the horses stepping carefully on the slippery stones beneath their hooves. The water rose shoulder high on the horses and it was icy cold as it soaked through Horace's leggings and boots.

'Glad it's not raining,' he muttered as he rode up the far bank, his horse shaking itself to rid itself of excess water. He wished he could do the same.

'What was that, *Kurokuma*?' asked one of the escort riding near him. The others chuckled at the name.

'Nothing important,' Horace said. Then he looked at them suspiciously. 'What's this *"kurokuma"* business?'

The Senshi looked at him with a completely straight face.

'It's a term of great respect,' he said. Several others, within earshot, nodded confirmation. They too managed to remain straight-faced. It was a skill the Nihon-Jan had perfected.

'Great respect,' one of them echoed. Horace studied them all carefully. Nobody was smiling. But he knew by now that that meant nothing with the Nihon-Jan. He sensed there was a joke he was missing but he couldn't think of a way to find out what it might be. Best maintain his dignity, he thought.

'Well, I should think so,' he told them, and rode on.

Shortly after crossing the river, Mikeru led them to a cleared patch of ground on the side of the trail, set at the edge of a sheer cliff that dropped away into the valley below. This was the lookout Shukin had wanted to reach. He, Shigeru and Horace dismounted and moved closer to the edge. Horace drew in his breath. The cliff edge was abrupt, as if it had been cut by a knife. The mountain dropped away several thousand metres to a valley. They could see the mountains they had been climbing and, beyond them, the low-lying flatlands.

Horace, who never enjoyed the sensation of being in high places, kept his distance from the cliff edge. Shukin and Shigeru had no such qualms. They stood less than a metre from the awful drop, peering down into the valleys, shading their eyes against the bright morning sun. Then Shukin pointed.

'There,' he said briefly.

Shigeru followed the direction of his pointing finger and grunted. Horace, standing several metres away from the edge, tried to crane his neck and see what they were looking at but his view was obstructed. Shukin noticed and called to him.

'Come closer, Or'ss-san. It's quite safe.'

Shigeru smiled at his cousin. 'Shouldn't that be *Kurokuma*?'

Shukin smiled in return. 'Of course. Come closer, *Kurokuma*. It's quite safe.'

Horace shuffled closer to the edge, instinctively keeping his weight leaning back away from the drop. Bitter experience in the past had taught him that, even though he hated being in high places, he was paradoxically drawn towards the edge when he stood on one, as if he found the drop irresistible.

'Quite safe, my foot,' he muttered to himself. 'And what is this *Kurokuma* you all keep calling me?'

'It's a term of great respect,' Shigeru told him.

'Great respect,' Shukin echoed.

Horace looked from one to the other. There was no sign on either face that they were joking.

'Very well,' he said, continuing to shuffle forward. Then, looking in the direction Shukin indicated, he forgot all about his hatred of heights and terms of great respect.

Across the vast valley, toiling up the trail that clung to a mountainside opposite them, he could make out a long column of men. The sun glinted haphazardly from their equipment as they moved and the light caught on helmets, spear points and swords.

'Arisaka,' Shukin said. He looked from the column of tiny figures to the crest of the mountain they were climbing, then across the next series of ridges. 'He's closer than I'd hoped.'

'Are you sure?' Horace asked. 'It could be Reito, and the survivors of the royal army.' But Shigeru shook his head.

'There are too many of them,' he said. 'And besides, Reito-san should be closer to us.'

'How far away are they, do you think?' Horace asked. Even though he had been riding through this countryside, he had no idea how fast a large party could cover ground — and he had no real idea what lay between Arisaka's army and themselves.

'Maybe four days behind us,' Shigeru estimated, but Shukin shook his head.

'Closer to three,' he said. 'We're going to have to move faster if we want to reach Ran-Koshi before they catch us.'

'That's if we can find Ran-Koshi,' Horace said. 'So far nobody seems to know where it is.'

Shukin met his gaze levelly. 'We'll find it,' he said firmly. 'We have to find it or we have no chance at all.'

'Ayagi-san was confident that there would be people in Riverbank Village who would know about it. Some of the older folk in particular, he said.'

'Well, we're not getting any closer to it standing here talking,' Horace said and Shukin grinned appreciatively.

'Well said, *Kurokuma*.'

Horace tilted his head and regarded the Senshi leader. 'I think I prefer that to Or'ss-san,' he said. 'I'm not absolutely certain, mind you.'

'It's a term of great respect,' Shukin told him.

'Great respect,' Shigeru confirmed.

Horace's gaze switched back and forth between them. 'That's what makes me uncertain about it.'

Shigeru grinned and slapped him on the shoulder. 'Let's get back to the horses. As you say, we're not getting any closer to Riverside Village while we stand here talking.'

They reached the village in another two hours. As they rode in, a familiar figure strode out from one of the cabins to greet them. Horace recognised Reito, the Senshi who had brought them the news of Arisaka's rebellion. He glanced around the village and became aware that there were other Senshi there, the survivors from Shigeru's army in Ito. Many of them were injured, with bloodstained bandages on their wounds. Some were moving around the village, often limping heavily. But too many of them were lying still on rough stretchers and litters. He heard Shukin heave a deep sigh.

'We're going to be moving a lot more slowly from now on,' the Senshi leader said.

Fifteen

There was a lone horseman riding along the northern bank of the Assaranyan Channel, keeping pace with the ship, parallel to their course. The man wore white, flowing robes and a white turban on his head, with a wide tail of material that protected his neck from the sun. It was similar in purpose to the *kheffiyeh* that Selethen wore, Will guessed.

'Now where do you suppose he came from?' Gundar asked, squinting to gaze more closely at the newcomer.

'There's probably a *wadi* just behind that crest,' Selethen told him. Gundar looked at him, uncomprehending, and he explained, 'A shallow gully.'

Earlier, they had been able to see for some distance across the desert on either side of the channel. At this point, though, the bank rose a little, so that it was several metres higher than the water level. Now, they could see no further than the elevated banks.

'Oh . . . yeah. I see.' Gundar paused. 'What do you think he's up to?'

'I should imagine nothing that's good for us,' Selethen told him. 'Hello. He's got friends.'

Three more riders had appeared, seeming to rise out of the ground at the top of the bank. They joined with the first rider in a loose formation. None of them seemed to show any interest in the ship that continued to glide along the channel, sixty or seventy metres away from them. Selethen had been right about the quicksand, Alyss thought. The riders stayed well back from the crumbling, darker-shaded ground at the edge of the channel.

Halt studied them and could make out the short cavalry bows slung across their backs. Selethen's people used such bows. They were effective at close range but lost power after fifty or sixty metres. Still, there was no harm in being prepared.

'Will,' he said quietly, 'fetch our bows, would you?'

Will gave him a quick glance, then nodded. Their bows were stored in the low, enclosed sleeping quarters in the stern of the ship. He hurried away to get them.

'Expecting trouble, Halt?' Evanlyn asked.

The Ranger shrugged. 'It'd be silly not to,' he said. 'Unless you can suggest a reason why those four riders just happen to be riding along beside us.'

'Seven,' Evanlyn told him.

Halt looked again to see that their number had indeed grown. He also saw that Evanlyn's sling had appeared in her hand and was swinging slowly back and forth in a pendulum motion. There was obviously a missile loaded into the pouch at its centre. He smiled grimly at her.

'Bit far for that stone chucker of yours,' he said and Evanlyn shrugged.

'You never know. Besides,' she pointed past the bow, 'the channel seems to be narrowing.'

They all looked forward then and they could see that she was right. Sandbanks had formed on the northern side of the channel, cutting the width down considerably.

Halt rubbed his beard as he studied them. 'Hmmm. Not sure that they'll be able to come any closer, even with that. Those banks look pretty soft to me.'

Will returned and handed Halt his bow and a quiver of arrows. He had his own quiver slung over his shoulder and both his bow and Halt's were already strung. Halt nodded his thanks and flexed the bowstring experimentally.

'Maybe we should edge over to the south bank anyway?' Selethen suggested. That side, they could see, was significantly clear of sandbars. The bank itself seemed to be cut straight and clean, rising almost vertically from the water to a height of five or six metres.

'It's very inviting,' Halt said. 'Perhaps too much so.'

'You're right, Ranger,' Gundar told him. His sailor's eyes, used to looking for signs of submerged obstacles, had detected several suspicious eddies on the surface on the southern side of the channel. 'I'd say there are obstructions just below the surface on that side, waiting for us to get tangled up on them.'

'Sandbars, you mean?' Selethen asked.

Gundar shook his head. 'More likely spikes and logs and heavy cables set to stop us and hold us fast.'

'So the lads beyond the ridge on that side can come visit us at their leisure,' Halt put in. He had been studying the south bank, suspicious of the fact that the riders on the north bank had revealed themselves, and that the southern part of the channel seemed to offer safety. A few seconds previously, he had caught a flash of light, as if the sun had briefly reflected off a sword or helmet. He was willing to bet there were several score of warriors concealed on the south bank, waiting for the moment when the ship became entangled in the underwater barriers that Gundar had detected.

He told the others what he had seen and they all looked carefully at the south bank. After a few seconds, Will caught sight of a small movement as well.

'There's someone there, all right,' he said.

'And there are quite a few of them,' Selethen added. 'There's just the faintest haze of dust in the air where they've been moving into position. Not enough wind to disperse it.'

'I guess they expected our attention to be focused on the riders,' Alyss said.

Even as she said it, the seven horsemen on the north bank spurred their horses to move a little ahead of the ship. Then they reined in and unslung their bows, fitting arrows to their bowstrings.

Halt glanced warningly at Gundar but the skirl had seen the movement.

'Shields on the bulwarks!' he called and the relief rowing crew clambered down into the rowing well and set eight of the big Skandian shields in brackets on the bulwark to cover the rowers. In many years of raiding and fighting, the Skandians had been shot at before and knew how to protect themselves.

'I doubt they have the range to reach us,' Halt said. 'But it never hurts to play it safe.'

They heard the familiar clatter and hiss of the arrows leaving the bows and arcing through the air towards the ship. As Halt had predicted, the range was too great for the short bows. Six of the arrows fell harmlessly into the water. The seventh struck the hull a metre above the waterline but, devoid of energy, it dropped away with a dull splash.

'Out of range,' Will said. 'You were right.'

'I'm not sure if they really meant to hit us or just divert our attention,' Halt replied. 'But either way, I think we might show them it's a bad idea to ride along there.'

He nocked an arrow to his own bowstring. Will did the same. The riders released another volley, which again fell short of *Wolfwill*.

'Take the one at the back with the purple turban, Will. I'll take the one beside him,' Halt said quietly. Will nodded.

'Now,' said Halt and they brought their bows up, drew and released in almost one movement.

The two arrows, one black and one grey, shot away, climbing into the hot air, then arcing down.

The riders Halt had singled out were in the act of shooting again when the two long, heavy arrows hissed down and struck them. Halt's target yelled in pain, dropping his bow and clutching at the arrow that had suddenly slammed into his upper arm. The man in the purple turban made no sound. He toppled sideways out of his saddle and hit the brown sand with a dull thud.

There were yells of confusion as their five companions scattered in panic. The message was all too clear. Their own volleys had fallen short of the target, while the two return shots had hit targets at the rear of their group, farthest from the ship. Which meant all of them were within easy range. Suddenly, they felt very, very exposed. They wheeled their horses away from the bank and rode over the crest to safety, the riderless horse following them.

Only the man in the purple turban remained, lying unmoving on the sand.

A few seconds later, the men on the south bank seemed to realise that their ambush had been detected. They appeared above the crest of the bank, waving weapons and yelling insults and curses at the ship as it glided arrogantly by. There were over two score of them, raggedly dressed and armed with an assortment of swords, spears and daggers, with several short bows among them. The bowmen shot a few ragged volleys but they were all well short of the ship. Will looked at Halt, then glanced down at the bow in his hands, but the bearded Ranger shook his head.

'Leave them,' Halt said. 'They can't hurt us and now they know it's safer to leave us alone.' He turned to Gundar. 'All the same, it might not be a good idea to anchor anywhere midstream for a rest.'

The sun was setting astern of them, a giant ball turned blood red by the tiny particles of sand that hung in the desert air, when they slipped quietly out of the Assaranyan Channel into the Blood Sea — a narrow gulf that led eventually to the wide spaces of the Eastern Ocean.

'I guess that's where the name comes from,' Will said, jerking a thumb at the water's surface behind them.

The intense glow of the sunset was reflected in the surface of the water, turning it to the same spectacular red colour, shimmering and shifting on the waves as they trapped and reflected the last light of the day so that the water itself looked like a sea of blood.

A gentle sea breeze sprang up from the south once they were several hundred metres offshore. It was warm, but nonetheless welcome after the stultifying heat that had engulfed them as they rowed through the channel.

'Make sail,' Gundar ordered. In the absence of roaring wind and waves, he could give his commands in a much calmer voice than his normal bellow. The sail handlers hurried to unfurl the port sail and hoist the slender boom that supported it to the masthead. As the wind caught the canvas and it bellied out, he gave more quick orders.

'Sheet home. In oars.'

The long oars rose, dripping, from the water. There were a few seconds of clattering and banging as the rowers drew them inboard and stowed them along the line of the ship. At the same time, the sailing crew hauled in on the sheets controlling the triangular sail. Initially bellying out loosely in the wind, it now hardened into a smooth, efficient curve and the passengers felt the harnessed thrust of the wind take effect. *Wolfwill* heeled a little to port, then Gundar leaned his weight on the tiller, heading the ship at right angles to the wind.

'Loosen off,' he called. He could sense that the sail, sheeted too tightly, was causing the ship to heel further than was necessary and this was costing them speed. *Wolfwill* steadied, came a little more upright, then swooped over a long, slow swell like a gull.

Gundar looked around at his passengers and couldn't help grinning at them.

'I never get tired of that!' he said and they smiled in return. The ship's motion was exhilarating, particularly after the hours of heat and tension as they passed through the Assaranyan Channel.

'So what can we expect from the Blood Sea, Gundar?' Will asked the big, burly Skandian.

Gundar braced the tiller with his hip and spread the Genovesan sailing notes on the small chart table beside him. He consulted the carefully lettered script for a few minutes, then looked up at Will.

'At this time of year, we should have steady winds,' he said. 'Although in a month or two there'd be a good chance of being becalmed.'

Sailors, Will noted, always wanted you to know the worst news, even when things were looking good.

'And,' Gundar continued, 'the notes say to avoid other ships as much as possible. Apparently the sea here is crawling with pirates.'

'Pirates?' Halt asked.

Gundar nodded, jerking a thumb at the notes. 'That's what it says here. Pirates.'

Halt raised both his eyebrows for once.

'Pirates,' he said. 'Oh, goody.'

Sixteen

'Yes. I know the way to Ran-Koshi,' the timber worker told them. Shukin and Shigeru exchanged a quick glance. They had begun to fear that the fabled fortress of Ran-Koshi was just that — a fable. Now, it seemed, they might have found a guide.

'You've been there?' Shukin asked. It was one thing to say you knew where a place was, another entirely if you'd actually been there.

'It's where we get our supplies of the fragrant timber,' the villager said.

Shigeru frowned, wondering what trees he meant.

Seeing the expression, Shukin said quietly, 'Camphor wood.'

Toru, the villager, nodded. 'Yes. I've heard it called that.' He saw the relieved expressions on the faces of the two Senshi and added a warning. 'It's a difficult place to get to. You'll have to go on foot from here. Horses will never manage the mountain trails.'

'Then we'll walk,' Shigeru said with a smile. 'I may be the Emperor, but I'm not a fragile little flower. I've done my share of travelling hard.'

'You may have. But what about those?' Toru said, sweeping his hand around the cleared communal space at the centre of Riverside Village. The three men were seated on low stools on the polished wood verandah of the village headman's house. The headman, Jito, had summoned Toru to speak to the Emperor when he learned that the Senshi party were seeking the ancient fortress of Ran-Koshi.

Now, at Toru's gesture, Shukin and Shigeru looked at the rows of injured men gathered around the square. At least a third of the Senshi who had escaped Arisaka's army were wounded — some of them seriously. Many would have to travel on litters or stretchers, and even the ones who could walk could only travel slowly because of their wounds.

'Our village headman would offer to look after them here if you asked him,' Toru said. 'But you would be causing great hardship to the villagers if you did so.'

Shukin made an apologetic gesture, touching his hand to the money purse at his belt.

'Naturally, we would pay,' he said but Toru shook his head.

'Winter is nearly here. The villagers have stockpiled barely enough food to last them through the cold months. They can't eat money and there wouldn't be enough food in the local markets for them and these extra people.'

It had been a different matter at the previous village, Shukin thought gloomily. There, the villagers only had to provide for a dozen people for one night. He knew Toru was right. They couldn't ask a small village to care for and feed thirty wounded men for several months. And in any case, he was reluctant to leave the Senshi behind. Many of them would recover and that would provide Shigeru with a nucleus of trained warriors. Not an army, perhaps, but a start towards one. They couldn't afford to abandon such a potential force.

'The wounded will come with us,' Shigeru said, interrupting them. His tone showed that there would be no discussion. 'We'll just have to manage. And we'll have to move quickly.'

Toru shrugged. 'Easily said. Not so easily done.'

He was respectful to the Emperor but not in awe of him. The Kikori were practical people and he saw no reason to agree with Shigeru when he knew he was wrong. That would not be doing the Emperor and his men any favours.

'Nevertheless, we will do it,' Shigeru said. 'Perhaps some of the stronger men of the village would act as stretcher bearers for us. Again, we would pay.'

Toru considered this. The season for wood gathering was over. Some of the younger men might be willing to supplement their income. Hard cash like that could be set aside for the warmer months, when the markets would have more items for sale.

'That's possible,' he agreed. Ever the bargainer, he was about to add that the men would be entitled to charge extra for the hardship of leaving their homes and families and trekking through the mountains in the oncoming winter weather when raised voices from the edge of the forest distracted them all.

They turned to look and saw a group of people emerging from the trees. Roughly twenty of them, and Kikori, by their dress, Shukin thought. Then he frowned. The thickset man leading the group, an axe held casually in his hand, looked familiar.

'Strangers,' Toru said. 'What brings them here, I wonder?'

He looked pointedly at the two cousins. His thought process was obvious. One way or another, they had brought the strangers to Riverside Village. Then Shukin recognised the leader of the newcomers and it seemed that Toru was right.

'It's Eiko,' he said, rising from his low stool.

Shukin and Shigeru stepped down off the verandah and walked towards Eiko and his companions. Toru followed them as other members of the village gathered around the newcomers. The Kikori weren't a particularly gregarious lot. Individual villages tolerated their neighbours but tended to keep to themselves. Each group had their own secret sources of timber and they guarded the locations of these resources from outsiders. The villagers greeted the strangers politely, but not effusively.

The headman stepped forward.

'I am Jito, headman of Riverside Village. What brings you here, stranger — and how can we help you?' His tone left no doubt that his offer of help was a formality only.

Eiko bowed politely — a quick lowering of the head that was all protocol demanded for a village headman.

'Greetings, Jito-san. My name is Eiko.' Then, looking past Jito, he saw the Emperor and Shukin, easily distinguished from the villagers in their Senshi robes. This time, he bowed more deeply. 'Greetings, Lord Shigeru.'

Jito looked sharply at the Emperor as he heard Eiko's words. He was not entirely happy to have even more strangers descend upon his people. The wounded Senshi had put a heavy strain on Riverside Village's resources. At a time when they should be making final preparations for the coming winter, the villagers were distracted by having to care for the wounded warriors.

'Good morning, Eiko. Is there some kind of problem?' The Emperor's keen eyes had noticed that some of the newcomers were injured. Half a dozen were bandaged and three others were being assisted by friends.

'You know these people, my lord?' Jito asked suspiciously.

Shigeru nodded. 'They offered us their hospitality last night. I'm afraid that may have cost them dearly.' The last statement was really a question to Eiko, but even before the villager answered, Shigeru thought he knew the answer.

Eiko nodded. 'That's true, Lord Shigeru,' he said. 'But no fault of yours. Arisaka's men reached our village a few hours after you were gone.'

Shigeru heard a quick intake of breath from his cousin.

'But we saw Arisaka's army! They were two or three days behind us!' Shukin said.

'His main force, yes. This was a scouting party who had come on ahead. A dozen warriors, well mounted and travelling light.' Eiko's lip curled in contempt. 'So light that they didn't bother bringing their own supplies. They simply took whatever they wanted from our people.'

There was a murmur from the Riverside Villagers who were listening to this exchange. It was a mixture of anger and fear in equal amounts. In the past, they had all experienced the depredations of marauding Senshi parties. Eiko acknowledged their reaction with a meaningful nod.

'You're right to worry about it,' he said. 'They're checking all the villages in the region. They'll be here before too long.'

That statement evoked a storm of exclamations from the villagers. Some were of a mind to abandon the village and hide in the forest. Others wanted to stay and protect their belongings. Jito held up his hand to still the babble of excited voices..

'Be quiet!' he shouted and the voices died away to an embarrassed silence. 'We need to plan calmly, not run around like headless chickens.' He looked back to Eiko. 'Some of your men are injured. I take it these Senshi didn't simply stop at stealing supplies?'

Eiko shook his head bitterly. 'No. They searched the village for anything of value — as they usually do. And —'

'And they found the coins we gave your headman,' Shigeru finished for him, his face grim.

'Yes, lord. They saw the royal crest on those coins and wanted to know how we had come by them.'

Horace had been a silent spectator to all of this. After days of hard riding, he had indulged in the practice of all experienced warriors to catch up on sleep whenever the opportunity arose. Hearing the voices from the village square, he had emerged, rubbing his eyes and pulling on a shirt as he came. He had been in time to hear Eiko's account of events and he remembered the coins Shukin had given to the Ayagi, the headman. They were gold, which would have been enough to raise suspicions in such a poor village. But to compound the problem, they had been clearly marked with the Emperor's symbol of three cherries. They could only have come from one source.

'Ayagi-san refused to tell them where he had got the coins,' Eiko continued. 'They killed him. Then they ran amok through the village, burning cabins, killing women and the old people.' He indicated his companions. 'Some of us managed to escape into the forest in the confusion.'

Shigeru shook his head bitterly. 'He should have told them,' he said. 'They would have known anyway.'

'Perhaps, Lord Shigeru. But Ayagi was a proud man. And he was loyal to you.'

'So I'm responsible for his death,' Shigeru said in a tired, defeated voice.

Eiko and Jito exchanged quick glances. The individual Kikori villages might treat each other with suspicion. But they were true to the ancient ways and they were united in their loyalty to the Emperor — both the concept and the man himself.

Jito said firmly, 'You were not the cause, Lord Shigeru. The blame lies with the oath-breaker, Arisaka. These actions have set him against the Kikori.'

'If anyone was to blame, it was me,' Eiko said. The pain was all too evident in his voice. 'We watched like cowards from the forest as they killed our people and destroyed our village. We did nothing!'

Shukin shook his head. 'You couldn't do anything against trained Senshi,' he said. 'And losing your own lives wouldn't have helped your people.'

Horace had been edging forward through the crowd. Now, he decided, it was time for him to take part.

'Nor would it have helped your Emperor,' he said, and all eyes swung to him. 'He needs men to help him fight Arisaka, not to throw away their lives to no purpose.'

He saw Eiko's shoulders straighten and sensed the new resolve in the stocky timber worker. A murmur of assent ran through the people of both villages. Years of resentment at their high-handed treatment by the Senshi were suddenly focused into an opportunity for defiance — an opportunity centred on the person of their Emperor.

'Well said, *Kurokuma*!' Shukin called to him, smiling. He turned to the assembled Kikori. He too could see the new sense of purpose infusing them. The tall *gaijin* had an excellent sense of timing, he thought, and an excellent choice of words to fire the spirits of these people.

'We do need you. The Kikori will be the loyal heart of the Emperor's new army. We will train you. We will teach you to fight!'

A roar of enthusiasm and defiance greeted these words. Many felt that arrogant, overbearing Senshi such as Arisaka had enjoyed their own way far too long in Nihon-Ja. Even without the cold-blooded destruction of the neighbouring village, Arisaka's act of treason towards the Emperor was enough to harden their hearts against him. But there were still some who favoured caution. As the cries of defiance died down, one older woman voiced their thoughts.

'But what if Arisaka's men come here? We're not ready to fight them yet.'

Horace saw the doubt begin to spread among the Kikori. They didn't believe in their own ability to face armed Senshi warriors. But they were forgetting one important fact. He stepped forward into the clear space around the Emperor, Eiko and Jito.

'You said there were a dozen in the scouting party?' he asked.

Eiko nodded. 'A dozen. Maybe a few more.'

Horace smiled at the answer. He looked around the assembled group of Senshi loyal to the Emperor — a dozen in his immediate bodyguard and at least another twenty-five uninjured survivors from the battle at Ito.

'It seems to me,' he said, 'that for once we have Arisaka's men seriously outnumbered.'

Seventeen

Evanlyn and Alyss were practising their fencing skills on the foredeck, under the somewhat bemused eye of Selethen.

Evanlyn's exploits in Skandia and Arrida in recent years had been widely reported throughout Araluen — she was, after all, the crown princess and enjoyed a certain amount of celebrity. As a result, many Araluan women and girls had been influenced to take a greater interest in weapon skills. Alyss was one of these, but her motivation went beyond following what was currently seen to be fashionable. She had been more than a little frustrated by her inability to defend herself effectively when she was captured by the traitor knight Keren at Castle Macindaw. She had determined that she would never let that happen again. This new emphasis on martial skills was evidenced by the fact that her dagger, part of the Courier uniform, had changed from a narrow, needle-pointed ceremonial design to a more practical — and more lethal — heavy-bladed fighting knife.

In addition, she had taken to practising the javelin and to wearing a lightweight sabre while on assignments. It was a style of sword rapidly gaining popularity with girls her age. Evanlyn had a similar weapon and, when they discovered the fact, it was only logical that they should practise together.

Logical, perhaps. But not wise.

One of the ship's crew had carved wooden practice weapons for them and the two girls began a daily training routine. Selethen had offered his services as an instructor and referee after watching the first few sessions and both girls had accepted the offer.

'Very well,' he said now, 'fighting positions, please, ladies . . .'

'That's debatable,' Halt said in an undertone to Will as they stood watching. A number of the off-duty crew had gathered to watch as well. There was a certain enjoyment to be had in watching two extremely attractive girls trying to split each other's skulls open with wooden swords.

'The "fighting" part or the "ladies" part?' Will replied with a grin.

Halt looked at him and shook his head. 'Definitely the "ladies",' he said. 'There's no debate about the "fighting".'

Will shrugged. He knew that there was an edginess to the girls' relationship and that it had something to do with him. Why that should be so was beyond him.

'Weapon a little higher, Evanlyn,' Selethen said. 'You tend to drop your guard too low.'

He waited as she adjusted the position of her sword, then glanced at Alyss to see if she was ready. The blonde girl had an edge over the princess in skill, he had noticed. Probably because she had a more focused approach to her swordsmanship. When she practised, a small furrow formed between her brows, evidence of the concentration and sense of purpose she was putting into her moves. Evanlyn, on the other hand, was a little slapdash in her approach. She had taken lessons in the sabre for some time, but never with any particular dedication to the weapon. She was faster than Alyss, but Alyss, tall and athletic, had a longer reach and stride, and Evanlyn tended to let herself get off balance too often.

'Begin,' Selethen said, with a sense of resignation in his voice. He had a fair idea what was about to happen.

Evanlyn lunged forward to attack, as he knew she would. She was too impulsive, he thought, too inclined to want to get things started, without any preliminary sparring.

Alyss knew it too. She had waited calmly for Evanlyn's rapid attack. She swayed to one side as Evanlyn lunged, deflecting the thrusting wooden blade past her body. Evanlyn staggered slightly, losing her balance, then Alyss cut back with a quick wrist movement, laying her own blade across Evanlyn's knuckles with a crack that made the spectators wince. Money changed hands among the watching Skandians.

'Ow! Ow! Damn it!' Evanlyn yelled. Her sword clattered to the deck and she nursed her bruised hand, glaring at Alyss. Then she turned angrily to Selethen. 'She did that on purpose!'

But before Selethen could reply, Alyss chimed in with equal vehemence, colour flaring into her cheeks. 'Well, of course I did it on purpose! That's why we're practising, isn't it? To do things on purpose? Or are we trying to practise accidents and flukes?'

'Please, ladies,' Selethen began. He was unmarried and so had little experience with women. He was beginning to wonder if he ever wanted any.

'But it's true, Selethen!' Alyss protested. 'She always leaves herself open to that reply.'

'Which you always manage to make,' Evanlyn said angrily, taking her sword from the grinning Skandian who had retrieved it for her. 'Thank you,' she said briefly.

The sea wolf leaned a little closer to her.

'Kick her in the shins next time, Princess,' he said in a whisper. 'I've got money on you.'

Alyss failed to notice the exchange. She was still appealing to Selethen as the referee of the bout. 'I mean, she's got to learn, hasn't she? If this was a real fight, she wouldn't get a do-over. She wouldn't have a *hand*.'

'On the other hand,' Selethen said, instantly regretting the words as he heard the Skandians snigger at the unintended pun, 'if you simply do that *every* time, we will never progress past this point, will we?'

Alyss seemed to consider the point. Then, reluctantly, she agreed. 'Very well, Selethen. If you say so.' She turned to Evanlyn. 'All right, Princess, your hand's off limits from now on.'

Will shook his head despairingly. 'Oh, Alyss, Alyss, Alyss,' he said under his breath, just loud enough for Halt to hear him.

Wisely, the bearded Ranger said nothing.

'Don't do me any favours,' Evanlyn said, through

gritted teeth. She flexed her hand on the sword's hilt, trying to ease the pain in her bruised knuckles.

Selethen looked doubtfully at the two girls. Both had high colour in their cheeks now.

'Perhaps we should call it a day?' he suggested.

'You can,' Evanlyn said, her eyes fixed on Alyss. 'I don't feel like it.'

Alyss smiled at her, a smile completely devoid of good humour. 'Well, neither do I,' she replied sweetly.

There was a long pause, then Selethen accepted the inevitable with an eloquent shrug of the shoulders.

'All right then — ladies.' He glanced at Halt and rolled his eyes at the word. Halt nodded gravely. 'Positions . . .'

Selethen noted that Evanlyn's guard position was correct this time. Perhaps she will learn from all this and not go rushing into the fight, he thought. And perhaps the Great Blue Whale that the Skandians believe to cause the rising and falling tide will leap from the ocean, sprout wings and fly in a circle around the ship.

'Begin,' he said in a resigned tone.

And there went Evanlyn, like an arrow from a bow, springing across the deck and swinging a series of rapid overhead cuts — backhand, forehand and backhand again. The strokes were clumsy but her speed made up for the fact. Alyss, expecting another long thrust, was caught by surprise and forced to give ground, backing away and parrying the blows desperately with her own blade, so that a series of clacks and cracks rang out across the deck.

There was a low murmur of encouragement from the Skandians who had backed Evanlyn to win. It should be noted that they had only done so because their shipmates had offered generous odds of three to one — hard to resist in a two-person contest.

But then Evanlyn's impulsiveness got the better of her. At the point where she should have seen that Alyss had recovered her own rhythm and weathered the attack successfully, she persisted with one stroke too many. Unable to sustain the lightning speed of her first half-dozen blows, she had slowed noticeably and Alyss, now back in control, flicked her final stroke to the side, then threw in another wristy back-hander.

This time, however, her blade cracked painfully off Evanlyn's elbow.

'Ooooow!' Evanlyn screeched. 'You great gangly cow!'

The sword dropped to the deck once more. Her arm and hand were numb and tingling. Alyss's riposte, whether intentionally or not, had caught her on the nerve at the point of the elbow.

'Alyss!' Selethen said angrily. 'We agreed —'

'We agreed that her hand was off limits,' Alyss said, all injured innocence. 'I hit her elbow, not her hand. If we're going to . . . Ooooowwwwoooooooh!'

The sudden howl of agony was wrung from her as she felt a searing pain in her right leg. Evanlyn, cradling her numb right arm with her left, had stepped in and swung her boot hard into Alyss's shin, tearing her tights and scoring a long, shallow wound on the edge of the bone. Alyss, her face wrinkled in pain, hobbled sideways to the bulwark and rested against it. She glared at Evanlyn, then glanced down and realised she still had her own sword in her hand, while Evanlyn was unarmed. She started forward.

'ENOUGH!' Halt bellowed.

All eyes turned to him in surprise. Even the Skandians looked impressed at the volume he'd mustered. Halt looked angrily at the two girls, both nursing their injuries, each furious with the other.

'Will you two stop squabbling and squalling like a pair of spoilt, self-centred brats?' Halt continued. 'I am sick and tired of it. Both of you should know better.'

Alyss's eyes dropped from his and she stood, shame-faced, before him. Evanlyn, however, was still angry — and ready to assert her own dignity.

'Is that so, Halt? May I remind you that this particular "spoilt, self-centred brat" is your royal princess?'

Halt spun round on her. His eyes were glittering with fury and Evanlyn, in spite of herself, took a pace back. She had never seen Halt so angry.

'Royal princess?' he said with contempt. *'Royal princess?* May I suggest, *royal princess*, that you tell that to someone who gives a flying fig about it? If you weren't nearly full-grown, I'd put you over my knee and tan your backside for you!'

Evanlyn was scandalised by the idea. 'If you laid hands on me, my father would have you flogged!'

Halt snorted derisively. 'If your father were here, he'd hold my cloak while I did it!'

Evanlyn opened her mouth to reply, then paused. Truth be told, knowing her father, she thought Halt was probably correct.

'Now for god's sake, will you two start behaving like a princess and a Courier?' Halt told them. 'If you don't, I'll have to think about sending Will home.'

'Me?' Will said, his voice breaking into a high-pitched

squeak of indignation. 'What's it got to do with me?'

'It's all your fault!' Halt shouted irrationally.

And as he said it, the two girls realised he was right. Jealousy over Will was making them behave like little children. Alyss was the first to respond. She thought that was only fair, as she'd been the one most at fault. She dropped the sword, took a step towards Evanlyn and held out her hand in peace.

'I'm sorry, Evanlyn. I behaved atrociously,' she said miserably. Her sincerity was obvious and Evanlyn, who was quick to anger, was equally quick to forgive and to see her own faults. She took the hand.

'My apologies too, Alyss. I shouldn't have kicked you. Is your shin all right?'

Alyss looked down to where a trickle of blood was running down her shin. 'Not really,' she said, with a lopsided grin. 'But I guess I deserved it.'

'No guessing about it,' Halt said. 'You definitely deserved it.' But he regarded the girls keenly and nodded in satisfaction. He was all too aware of the tension that existed between them and he'd known this day would come, sooner or later. Better to have it sooner and be done with it, he thought. When he spoke, his voice had lost the harsh edge of his previous statements.

'Perhaps we should forego further fencing lessons for a while,' he said and the girls nodded.

Selethen gave a deep sigh. 'I'm for that.'

There was an awkward pause. Finally, it was Gundar who broke it.

'I don't know if anyone's interested,' he said tentatively, 'but there appears to be a pirate ship heading our way.'

Eighteen

The party of Senshi riders emerged from the forest in a ragged formation and drew rein in the small communal area of Riverside Village.

Nothing stirred in the village. The forest birds, which had grown silent with the noisy passage of the strangers, gradually began to sing again in the trees around the little circle of cabins. The small river that ran on the far side of the village, and gave the place its name, gurgled and chuckled over the rocks in its shallows. The noise seemed abnormally loud in the silence.

The lead rider twitched his reins impatiently, glaring round at the silent, seemingly empty huts.

'Kikori!' he shouted. 'Show yourselves! We want food and drink and we want them now!'

The forest seemed to swallow his voice. There was no reply, only the birds and the river.

'There's no one here, *Chui*,' said one of the riders, using the leader's rank of lieutenant. The officer glared at the man who had spoken. He was tired. He was saddle sore. And he was becoming increasingly angry with these damned Kikori, who either refused to answer his questions or fled into the forest at the first sign of him and his men. Time these insolent peasants were taught a good lesson, he thought.

He dismounted stiffly, taking a few paces to stretch his tired muscles. Riding in this mountainous terrain, with its constant switching of slopes and angles, was an exhausting business.

'Dismount,' he told his men and they followed his example. He jerked a thumb at the man who had spoken.

'You. Go and search those cabins.' He indicated three of the larger cabins, grouped together and facing onto the common ground. 'You go with him,' he ordered a second warrior.

The two men, hands on the hilts of their long swords, strode with a stiff-legged swagger. They mounted the steps of the closest pair of cabins. The first man kicked open the door, shattering the doorpost so that the door hung crookedly from one leather hinge, and strode inside, his muddy boots marking and scratching the carefully polished wooden floor. It was the ultimate act of arrogance among the Nihon-Jan to enter a home without removing shoes. Those outside heard his boots ringing on the floor as he moved through the cabin. After a short while, he appeared at the doorway.

'Empty!' he called.

The other man had been searching the next cabin and now he too reappeared.

'Same here, *Chui*!' he said. 'They've all gone, it seems.'

The lieutenant mouthed a quiet curse at the absent villagers. Now he and his men would have to forage for food in the village, and prepare it themselves. That wasn't work for Senshi, he thought. It was work for the peasants who were born to serve them. He reflected angrily that the villagers would probably have hidden their stores before they fled. More time wasted. More inconvenience.

'All right!' he said curtly. 'Burn those cabins!'

The cabins, judging by their prominent position, probably belonged to elders of the village. Well, they'd learn not to make a Senshi warrior stand waiting when he required their service, he thought. There was a light breeze blowing and the odds were that if he burned the three cabins he'd indicated, the flames would spread to the rest of the buildings, destroying the village completely. Too bad, he thought harshly. Next time, they mightn't run away if they knew this could happen.

The men had taken a lantern from the verandah of the largest cabin and they were now busy with flint and steel to light it. Once they had a source of flame, they'd fashion rough torches and use them to set the timber and thatch cabins alight. The lieutenant rubbed his back with his clenched fists, stretching away the stiffness. He'd enjoy seeing the cabins burn, he thought. It always gave him a certain feeling of satisfaction to see a building flare up, then eventually collapse in upon itself in a pile of smoking ash.

The men had two bundles of straw and kindling gathered now and they set the lantern's small flame to them, letting them flare up. They looked questioningly at their leader and he made an imperious gesture with the back of his hand.

'Get on with it!'

As they turned towards the largest cabin, a voice called from behind them.

'Lord! Please! Don't burn my house! I'm begging you!'

A ragged figure, in a plain Kikori robe, came running from the trees that circled the village.

Two Senshi moved to intercept him but the officer curtly told them to let the man through. He stopped a few metres from the officer and dropped to his knees, head bowed.

'Please, lord. Don't destroy our village,' he said in a servile tone.

The officer's hand dropped to the hilt of his sword and he took a pace closer to the kneeling figure. 'Who are you?'

'I am Jito, lord. I am headman of this village.'

'How dare you keep me and my men waiting!' the officer raged at him and Jito's head sank lower. 'Where are the villagers?'

'Lord, they ran away. They were frightened.'

'And you didn't stop them?'

'I tried, lord. But they wouldn't listen to me.'

'Liar!' The word was shouted and the kneeling man flinched at the violence behind it. 'You are a liar! You ordered them to go! And you told them to hide any food in the village from me.'

'No, lord! I . . .'

'Liar!' The word was shouted even louder this time. The officer was working himself up into a frenzy of hate. His men exchanged glances. They had seen this happen before and they knew what fate lay in store for the kneeling village headman.

'No, lord! Please . . .'

'You are lying to me! And you have insulted me and my

men! Where is your hospitality? Where is the respect due to members of the Senshi class? You filthy Kikori should be on your knees, begging us to eat your food and drink your rice wine. We honour you by coming to your village and you shame yourselves and insult us by running away into the forest like thieves!'

'No, lord! Please. We will be glad to —'

'Shut your lying mouth!' the lieutenant screamed. 'I'll show you how we deal with thieves. And then I'll burn your village to the ground!'

There was a ringing hiss of steel against lacquered wood as he drew his long sword from its scabbard, taking a two-handed grip.

'Kneel straight and bow your head, thief!' he shouted.

Finally, the headman seemed to accept that pleading would do no good. He had been sitting back on his haunches but now he knelt upright and bowed his grey head forward, resigned to the lieutenant's sword.

The lieutenant raised the long weapon above his head, preparing to sweep down. He emitted a grunt of animal pleasure as he paused at the top of the stroke. Then things happened very quickly.

The kneeling headman suddenly came up onto his right knee. There was another ringing hiss and his hand emerged from under the ragged Kikori cloak with a gleaming Senshi short sword. Using the purchase of his still-grounded left foot, he thrust forward, burying the blade in the lieutenant's midsection.

The lieutenant looked in startled horror at his attacker. Now, as the ragged cloak was cast aside, he saw that this was no elderly, whining villager. It was a fit, strong Senshi warrior, his black hair powdered with ash to make it look grey. On the breast of his fine leather vest was emblazoned a triple cherry symbol.

The sword fell from the lieutenant's hand and he doubled over, dead before he hit the ground. Quickly, Shukin switched the short sword to his left hand, stooped and retrieved the lieutenant's longer weapon.

The men of the raiding party had been stunned for a few seconds but now they drew swords and prepared to avenge their leader's death. They weren't completely sure how it had happened. One moment the villager had been cowed into submission. The next, their officer was staggering and falling before him. Whatever had happened, the treacherous villager would die for it.

But even as they moved, other figures appeared from the trees behind them, running to flank them and cut them off from Shukin.

The two men who had been sent to fire the cabins were close to him and he turned to face them. He blocked the first man's cut easily, flicking the sword to one side and, in the same motion, cutting back so that his own blade bit into the man's neck. As the man fell, Shukin blocked the second man's cut with the short sword in his left hand, then spun to his right, his long sword reaching back over his right shoulder as part of the movement and taking the enemy Senshi high in the chest.

He stepped clear as the man fell, a few seconds after his comrade.

Now the remaining raiders had no time to avenge their fallen leader. They found themselves surrounded by thirty armed Senshi warriors, all wearing the Emperor's crest.

For a few brief minutes, the clearing rang with the clash of swords and the cries of the injured. Arisaka's men fought fiercely, but they never had a chance. Horace, assigned to guard the Emperor in one of the second row of cabins, watched the fight curiously. Each of the enemy was surrounded by two or sometimes three of Shigeru's men. Yet they never attacked all at once, choosing instead to engage the raiders in a series of single combats. He remarked on this to the Emperor and Shigeru simply nodded.

'This is the way it is done,' he said. 'It's not honourable to fight three at a time against one man. We win or lose as individuals.'

Horace shook his head. 'Where I come from, once a fight starts, it's all in and devil take the hindmost,' he said. He saw that Shigeru didn't understand the expression but he made no attempt to explain.

Gradually, the sounds of fighting died away as the last of Arisaka's men were cut down. But they hadn't gone easily. Four of Shigeru's warriors also lay silent on the bloodstained soil of the common ground and another two were nursing wounds.

Shigeru and Horace left the cabin where they had been concealed and moved out to join Shukin. Gradually, the villagers began to reappear, drifting back in from their hiding places in the forest. They regarded the fallen Senshi with something like awe.

Jito looked at Shigeru and inclined his head slightly. 'This was good work, Lord Shigeru.'

Eiko too had a look of satisfaction on his face. These were the men who had killed his friends and neighbours and destroyed his village, while he was forced to stand by and watch. It was good, he thought, to see the shoe was on the other foot.

But Shigeru was looking troubled. He indicated the bloodstained forms on the ground.

'Arisaka will hear of this. He'll hold you responsible and he'll declare war on the Kikori people,' he said.

Jito threw a disparaging glance at the dead raiders. His shoulders straightened and his head came up proudly.

'Let him! Lead us to Ran-Koshi and teach us to fight, Lord Shigeru. The Kikori are declaring war on Arisaka.'

There was a growled mutter of agreement from the people of both villages as they heard his words. They gathered around Shigeru, touching him, bowing to him, pledging their loyalty.

Shukin and Horace exchanged grim smiles.

'We have men,' Shukin said.

Horace nodded. 'Now we just have to turn them into warriors.'

Nineteen

The pirate ship was a long, low galley, narrow waisted and mounting twelve oars a side. She had a small mast and a square sail but for the moment the sail was furled. As she approached the wolfship, the two banks of oars rose and fell in perfect unison.

'Can we outrun her, Gundar?' Halt asked.

As ever, Gundar glanced at the sky, the sail and the other ship, then sniffed the air experimentally before answering.

'As long as this wind holds, no problem,' he said. He called an order to the sail trimmers and they hauled on the sheets, bringing the sail to a harder curve. At the same time, he nudged the tiller slightly so that the bow of the ship swung a few degrees to port. Instantly, Will felt a tremor run through the deck as the ship leaned, then accelerated.

Halt was rubbing his beard thoughtfully, still watching the pirate galley behind them. He estimated that there were forty or fifty men in her crew and he could see her captain leaning forward to yell encouragement to his rowers as he realised that they were losing ground to this strange ship with its triangular sail.

'And if the wind drops?' Halt asked.

Gundar shrugged. He, too, studied the pirate craft.

'Twelve oars a side to our eight,' he mused aloud. 'Under oars, she's probably faster than us.'

Halt turned that information over in his mind, then added, 'And she's not likely to be the only one of her kind we sight.'

Gundar nodded. 'The sailing notes say these waters are infested with pirates.'

The Ranger studied the pirate galley again. Under a renewed effort from her rowing crew, she had made up a little distance on *Wolfwill*. But now, after that initial surge of enthusiasm, they were beginning to drop back again. *Wolfwill*'s oars were shipped and at least half her crew were relaxing on the rowing benches, out of sight. Chances were that the pirates thought she was a trader, manned by only a dozen or so men.

'Can you let her catch up to us without them realising you're doing it?' he asked.

Gundar, for once, answered immediately. 'Easily,' he said, grinning evilly. 'I take it you want to give them a little surprise?'

'Something like that.' Halt glanced at the men on the rowing benches. 'Get your weapons ready, but stay out of sight,' he called. He was answered by at least a dozen wolfish grins from the Skandians. Sea wolves loved a fight, Halt thought.

Gundar, meanwhile, eased the bow a little back to starboard, and called more orders to the sail trimmers. The sail came even tauter, and the ship heeled a little further. It looked impressive, but the reality was that she came off her best point of sailing and lost speed in the manoeuvre. The pirates began to gain on them once more. There were a dozen of them gathered in the prow of the galley, yelling threats and waving weapons at their quarry.

'They're a raggle-tail bunch,' Will remarked. 'Do you want me to start the ball rolling?'

He had an arrow nocked to the bowstring and the galley was in easy range now. But Halt shook his head.

'Not yet.' He glanced to where Evanlyn and Alyss were standing by the rail. Evanlyn had her sling ready, slowly swinging it back and forth. Alyss, he saw, had changed her practice sabre for the real thing. She had it belted around her waist.

'You two move back here,' he said, indicating a position in the stern of the ship. Reluctantly, they obeyed. They might have argued with him earlier, but both of them knew that when the ship was about to go into a fight, Halt's orders were to be obeyed without hesitation.

'You can knock a few over with that sling as we get closer,' Halt told Evanlyn. Then he glanced at Alyss. 'You watch her back in case any of them get on board.'

Alyss nodded. 'Is that likely?' she asked, with a faint grin. She'd seen the fighting qualities of Skandians — particularly this crew — in the past.

'I doubt it.' Then, addressing Gundar and his crew, Halt laid out his plan. 'We'll turn up into them as they get closer and take them bow on bow. Grapple them, then board them over the bows and disable their ship.'

'What about their crew?' Nils called from the rowing benches.

'If they get in the way, disable them too,' he said shortly. 'Get rid of their mast, knock holes in the hull, then get back on board.'

'You want us to sink her?' Gundar asked and Halt shook his head.

'No. I want her badly damaged but capable of making it back to port. I want the word to go out that the strange ship with the red falcon ensign,' he gestured to Evanlyn's ensign, flying from the mast top, 'is manned by dangerous, hairy maniacs with axes and is to be avoided at all costs.'

'That sounds like us,' Gundar said cheerfully. And a rumbling growl sounded in the throats of the crew. 'Jens,' he said now to one of the sail handlers, 'you take eight men up to the bows. Have grapnels ready and lead the boarding party when we've got her secured.'

'I'm going too, skirl!' It was Nils Ropehander, from his position on the front port-side rowing bench. Gundar nodded.

'First four rows from either side follow Jens aboard her,' he said. 'But stay out of sight for now!'

'Show yourselves only when I give the word,' Halt called. 'We want the sight of your lovely faces to be a big surprise for these lads.'

Again, a growl of assent from the crew. They lived for this sort of encounter, Will realised. Several of them were already chuckling at the thought of the panic that would fill the pirates' hearts when they realised that the helpless-looking, apparently unarmed sailing ship was literally a wolf in sheep's clothing. A sea wolf in sheep's clothing, in fact.

'Evanlyn, let's see what you can do,' Halt said quietly. The princess needed no further urging. She already had an egg-shaped lead shot loaded into the pouch of her sling. Glancing around to make sure she was unimpeded, she whirled the sling up, let it circle twice, then released and sent the shot whizzing on its way.

They could follow the flight of the shot for a few seconds, then lost it against the mass of the galley. But a second later, one of the shouting, gesticulating pirates in the bow suddenly toppled over, folding up like an empty garment. His companions stepped away in shock, silenced for a moment, then redoubled their threats and insults, urging their rowers to go faster and catch this insolent intruder. They were a ragged group, as Will had mentioned, wearing tattered white and coloured robes and dirty turbans. They were generally thin and dark skinned. As they grew closer, Will could see that their weapons were a mixture of curved swords, dirks and knives. There seemed to be no uniformity among them and Will guessed that they were more accustomed to slaughtering helpless crews than fighting trained warriors.

Halt nodded approvingly at Evanlyn's successful shot.

'Interesting. Just two spins,' he said. 'In Arrida you spun the sling round and round a lot more before releasing.'

'I've been practising,' she said. 'Spinning it too much warns your enemy and leaves you exposed to return shots. The ideal is to get maximum velocity in one spin, but I'm not up to that yet.' She reached into a leather pouch slung over her shoulder and took out another of the specially shaped lead projectiles. The days of using river pebbles were long past.

'Shall I do another?'

Halt regarded the oncoming pirates, his eyes slitted against the glare of the sun from the sea.

'No. I think we've stirred up that hornets' nest enough. Once we've grappled them, you can let fly at that group around the tiller as much as you like.' He turned away to Gundar. 'Any time you're ready, skirl.'

Gundar judged distance and the angles and the set of his sail.

'Coming about!' he bellowed and leaned on the tiller. The ship swung neatly, the wind going out of the sail as she turned, leaving the canvas flapping wildly.

'Down sail!' he roared and the boom and sail thundered down to land on the deck. Hastily, two of the sailing crew gathered the flapping canvas in out of the way.

On board the pirate galley there was a sudden silence as their quarry unexpectedly swung round to face them.

'Show yourselves, sea wolves!' Halt yelled and sixteen big, heavily armed men appeared from the rowing benches to supplement those already in the bow of the ship.

The pirates, expecting to attack a dozen or so lightly armed sailors, suddenly found themselves facing at least thirty yelling, hairy denizens, all armed with double-headed battleaxes.

At the same moment, two grapnels sailed out from the bow of the ship and thudded into the woodwork of the pirate galley. The captain, aft at the tiller, started to scream orders to his men to cut the ropes that were now drawing his ship closer to the foreigners' craft. He gesticulated to the rowers to back water and pull them away from this unexpected danger.

Will heard a quick whizzing sound as Evanlyn whirled and cast again. The pirate skipper abruptly reared up, clutching his forehead, then crashed over backwards onto the deck.

There was a grinding crunch as the two ships drew together and the yelling, battle-mad Skandians poured over their own bow and onto the deck of the galley. Most of the pirates gathered in the bow took one look at the huge men and their huge axes and ran for the stern. Some of them took a shorter escape route and dived over the rail into the sea. The few who remained to fight had little time to regret their choice. The boarding party, led now by Nils, who had forced his way past Jens, smashed through them, scattering their limp bodies to either side.

Several of the boarders, directed by Jens, dropped into the rapidly vacated rowing benches and smashed their axes into the hull's planks below the waterline. Seawater gushed in through the massive rents they created. Satisfied with their work, they then busied themselves throwing oars overboard, while their companions hacked at the stays holding the ship's low mast in place. One man swarmed up the mast itself and released the sail, then slid rapidly down again. The sail filled with wind and strained at the mast. Unsupported, the mast withstood the pressure for a few seconds, then there was an ugly crack and it sagged to leeward, taking a tangle of sailcloth and cordage with it.

Gundar glanced at Halt. The Ranger had been assessing the damage to the galley and her crew. Nearly half the pirates were killed or disabled and the ship was already settling at the bow. Time to let the remaining pirates make repairs and take news of this very unwelcome foreign ship back to their lairs on the coastline.

'Bring 'em back,' he said and Gundar bellowed to his men.

'Back on board! Sea wolves! Back to the ship!'

The men began to scramble back to the bow of the galley, clambering from there up to *Wolfwill*, which stood higher than the pirate ship. Their comrades on board helped them over the bulwark. Nils was the last to come. Initially, he was fighting a one-man rearguard action. Then the pirates seemed to realise that there was no future in coming within reach of that whirling battleaxe and they left the deck to him. Annoyed, Nils spread his feet, brandished his axe and yelled a challenge at them.

'Come on, you raggedy-bum backstabbers! Come face a real pirate!'

But there were no takers and he actually began to advance down the deck towards them again.

'Nils! Get back on board, you great idiot!'

Gundar's bellow cut through the fog of anger and battle madness that filled Nils's mind. He stopped, shook his head, then turned and grinned sheepishly.

'Coming, skirl!'

Will had to smile. Nils sounded like a naughty boy answering his mother's call to dinner.

Nils made one last insulting gesture at the pirates, then turned and ran lightly back to the bows. Disdaining help, he sprang from the pirate's bulwark back aboard.

'Cut the grappling ropes!' Gundar called and two axes swung and thudded in quick succession, severing the two ropes. No longer fastened together, the ships began to slowly drift apart. Gundar looked down at the last four ranks of rowers on either side — the men who had remained aboard *Wolfwill* through the brief, one-sided battle.

'Out oars! Give way!' he ordered. As the men reacted instantly, Will realised that the Skandians had done this sort of thing many, many times before. *Wolfwill* slowly gathered sternway under the thrust of the eight oars, and the gap to the pirate ship widened.

'Hoist the sail!' Gundar ordered and the boom and sail ran smoothly up the mast.

'Sheet home! In oars!' he called and the sail handlers hauled in on the sheets and hardened the flapping sail to the wind. *Wolfwill*'s bow swung downwind and as the skirl leaned on his tiller, she began to gather way.

Behind them, the pirate galley was bow down in the water and her men were swarming forward to repair the massive holes smashed in her planks before she went under.

Gundar nodded in satisfaction. His men had performed well. He jerked a thumb at the half-submerged pirate ship.

'I doubt we'll be hearing from them again,' he said.

Selethen was watching the wallowing ship as her crew worked to stop her sinking.

'You know,' he said to Halt, without any trace of a smile, 'it might have been simpler to have the two girls board her with their practice swords.'

They exchanged a long look, then Halt shook his head. 'I needed to leave some of them alive,' he said.

Twenty

With each passing day, their numbers grew. As the Emperor's party clawed and stumbled up the steep, muddy mountain tracks, climbing one ridge, descending the other side, then climbing the next, which always seemed to be steeper and higher than the one before it, more and more Kikori quietly joined their group. They would emerge silently from the trees, having travelled secret and dangerous paths known only to the mountain people, make a simple obeisance to Shigeru, then attach themselves to the column.

The leaders of the column learned, without too much surprise, that the Senshi patrol they had defeated at Riverside Village was not the only advance party sent out by Arisaka. There were more than half a dozen other small groups combing the mountains, brutalising the Kikori, burning their villages and torturing their leaders in an attempt to learn Shigeru's whereabouts.

This barbaric behaviour, intended to cow the Kikori into submission, was actually self-defeating. The Kikori were a profoundly law-abiding people and they placed great value on the concept of legal and rightful succession to the throne — even if they had never seen the Emperor himself. Shigeru was the rightful Emperor and their deeply felt sense of morality told them that he must not be deposed by force. Arisaka's depredations only served to convince them that he was a would-be usurper, whose attempts to gain power bordered on sacrilege and must be resisted. And, as a corollary to that, Shigeru must be supported.

So, as villages were plundered and burned, the Kikori joined Shigeru's party, in dribs and drabs, until there were several hundred of them — men, women and children — toiling up the precipitous tracks over the mountains, helping carry the wounded in their litters and bringing much-needed supplies of food with them. It was hard going, even for the mountain-bred Kikori, and the need to carry the wounded slowed them down. Shukin, Shigeru and Horace were constantly aware that Arisaka's main force was somewhere behind them, closing the gap between them each day.

'If only we knew where he was,' Shukin said. He had called a brief halt at noon and the bearers had gratefully set down the litters and sprawled beside the track. Some took the opportunity to eat a little of the food they carried. Others simply lay back, resting and regaining their strength, trying to let a few minutes' respite ease the ache of strained muscles.

Without anything being said, Horace had become one of the small group leading the trek. Shigeru had recognised his worth as an expert warrior and an experienced campaigner and was grateful to have someone share the burden that his cousin Shukin had assumed. Looking at his two main supporters now, the Emperor smiled ruefully. They were far from the idealised picture of a royal party, he thought. Exhausted, mud stained, grimy and soaking wet, their robes and tunics torn in a dozen places by thorns and sharp branches along the track, laden with rough packs of food and blankets, they looked more like a group of wandering vagabonds than the Emperor and his two principal advisers. Then he glanced at the swords the two men wore — Horace's long and straight in the Araluan style, and Shukin's *katana*, shorter, double hilted and slightly curved. There was no mud there, he knew. Both blades, inside their scabbards, were scrupulously clean and razor-edged — a result of their owners cleaning and sharpening them each evening.

'When do you expect the scouts to come back in?' Horace asked. Two days before, Shukin had asked for volunteers among the Kikori to go back along their trail to look for some sign of Arisaka's position. There had been no lack of numbers willing to take on the task and he had sent four of the fittest younger men back down the mountain.

'It'll depend how long it takes them to find Arisaka,' Shukin said. 'I'm hoping we hear from them later rather than sooner.'

Horace nodded. If the scouts returned this evening, he thought, they would have good cause to worry. Allowing for the fact that the lightly laden Kikori, expert in traversing this country, would travel much faster than Arisaka's men, they would still have to travel double the distance — there and back. If they returned in the next twelve hours, Arisaka couldn't be more than two days behind them.

'How far now to Ran-Koshi?' Shigeru asked.

Shukin shrugged in reply. 'Toru says about five leagues, as the crow flies.'

Horace grimaced. 'We're not crows,' he said and Shigeru smiled tiredly.

'More's the pity.'

Five leagues was over twenty kilometres, Horace estimated. But travelling up and down ridges as they were, and traversing around rearing mountainsides, the distance they covered on the ground could be five or six times as much as that and it would be hard going, all the way.

'We should be there in four days, if all goes well,' Shukin said hopefully. Neither Horace nor Shigeru replied, although Horace couldn't help asking himself the question, why should things start doing that now?

They heard voices raised further back down the column and they all rose and turned to see what was causing the disturbance. Horace saw two young men trotting tiredly up the track, past the rows of resting Kikori, who called questions to them as they came. The two arrivals shook their heads in answer to the questions. Unlike most of the travellers, they were lightly dressed, without heavy robes or cloaks to protect them from the chill air of the mountains. They wore breeches and shirts and stout leather boots, and carried small packs that could have held only the barest minimum of food and water. They were dressed and equipped to travel quickly and Horace felt a cold hand close over his heart as he recognised them as two of the scouts Shukin had sent back.

'This doesn't look good,' he said, noting the serious expressions on the arrivals' faces. Shukin grunted in reply and the three of them moved down the track to meet the scouts.

The young men saw them and redoubled their pace, dropping to one knee and bowing their heads before the Emperor. Gently, Shigeru put them at their ease.

'Please stand, my friends. This muddy track is no place for ceremony.' He looked around and saw several interested bystanders watching them, curious to know what the scouts had discovered. 'Can someone bring food and a hot drink for these men? And warm clothing.'

Several of the bystanders hurried away to do his bidding. The remainder crowded a little closer, eager to hear the report. Shukin glared at them and waved them back.

'Give us room,' he said. 'You'll hear the news soon enough.'

Reluctantly, they backed away, although their eyes remained riveted on the small group. Shukin ushered the two scouts to the spot where he had recently been resting.

'Sit down and rest first,' he said. They sank gratefully to the wet ground, unslinging their packs. One of them began to speak but Shukin held up a hand to stop him.

'Eat and drink first,' he said, as food and hot tea were placed before them. The people who had brought the food stood by, wanting to linger and hear what the scouts had to report. But Shukin's quick glance and a jerk of his head moved them away. Horace realised that his order for the men to eat first was more than simple kindness. He didn't want anyone to overhear what they had to say.

The scouts noisily slurped down their bowls of rich pork broth and noodles. As they ate, Horace saw the strain and weariness fading from their faces.

Shukin waited till they had eaten most of the noodles.

'You found Arisaka?' he said quietly.

Both men nodded. One, his mouth momentarily full of hot broth, looked to his companion to answer.

'His army is barely a day's travel from here,' the scout said and Horace heard Shukin's quick intake of breath. Shigeru, as ever, seemed unmoved by the news, simply accepting it for what it was.

'A day!' Shukin repeated, in a troubled voice. He ran his hands through his hair. Horace recognised the distress in his action. Burdened with the task of keeping his Emperor safe, Shukin could see his enemies drawing ever closer. 'How can they be moving so quickly?'

The first scout had gained his voice now. 'Arisaka is driving them cruelly, my lord,' he said. 'He is determined to take Lord Shigeru.'

'His men won't thank him for it,' Horace said thoughtfully but Shukin made a dismissive gesture.

'His men will accept it. They're used to his lack of regard for their wellbeing.' He looked up at the scouts. 'Where are your two companions?'

'They stayed behind to watch Arisaka,' he was told. 'When he gets within half a day's march, they'll come on to warn us.'

'At the rate he's catching up, that should be some time late tomorrow,' Shukin said thoughtfully. He unrolled the map of the mountains that he and Toru had drawn up and pondered it. Arisaka was a day away from their present position. If they moved out now and kept moving, they would extend the time it would take him to catch them, but even so, he was making ground on them too quickly.

He looked up and nodded his gratitude to the scouts.

'Thank you both. You've done well. Now go and get warm clothing and a little rest. We'll be moving out shortly.'

They bowed and turned to go, but he called them back.

'Ask Toru to come here, would you?' he said. They nodded and trotted away. Horace and Shigeru said nothing as Shukin studied the rough chart, tapping his fingers on his chin as he did so. A few minutes later, Toru arrived.

'You sent for me, Lord Shukin?'

'Yes. Yes. Never mind that,' Shukin said, waving away Toru's formal bow. 'Sit down here.'

The Kikori guide sank to his knees, feet folded under him. Horace shook his head. He could only hold that position for a few minutes, then his knees and thighs would begin burning. The locals, he knew, could sit comfortably for hours in that pose.

'Arisaka is a day away from this point,' Shukin told Toru. The guide showed no sign of emotion at the news. 'At the current rate he's catching us, we've probably got a day and a half. Maybe two days if we push the column as hard as we can.'

He paused to let Toru absorb this information.

'How long do you think it will take us to reach Ran-Koshi?'

The Kikori raised his eyes to meet Shukin's. 'At our current speed, at least four days.'

Shukin's shoulders sank. He had expected the answer but had been hoping against hope that Toru might have better news.

'Then we have to find some way to delay him,' Shukin said, after a moment's thought.

Toru's face brightened and he reached for the map, turning it towards him and studying it. Then he jabbed a forefinger at a spot.

'Here, lord,' he said. 'This ravine is impassable — except for a simple footbridge. If we destroy it, Arisaka will have to take a long detour . . . along this ridge . . . down another, then across this narrow valley. And then he'll have to regain all that lost ground.' His hand swept in a long curve across the map. 'It will take him at least two weeks.'

Shukin nodded in satisfaction. 'Excellent. We'll destroy the bridge. When will we reach it?'

Toru's face fell as he saw the fault in his suggestion. 'Lord, the bridge is two days away. Arisaka will catch us before we reach it.'

There was a long silence, then Shukin took the map and deliberately rolled it and replaced it in the leather tube that protected it from the elements.

'Then we'll have to buy a little more time along the way,' he said.

Twenty-one

The western coast of Nihon-Ja lay before them as the ship rocked gently on a long, glassy swell.

The flat land at the coast quickly gave way to a succession of heavily timbered hills. Behind them, ranges of steep mountains rose high into the air, their peaks already covered in snow and intermittently concealed by cloud driven on the wind.

It was rough-looking country, Will thought, as he leaned on the bulwark beside Halt, studying this new land. After weeks at sea, breathing the freshness of the salt air, he was conscious of a new smell borne to him on the wind: charcoal or woodsmoke, he realised. They must be relatively close to a town or large village, although at the moment none was visible.

'There,' said Halt, reading his thoughts and pointing to a long cape that thrust out into the sea to the north of them. Will peered at it but could see no sign of buildings or people. Then he realised what Halt had been pointing at as he made out signs of smoke haze in the air. Judging by the extent of the smoke, he thought, there must be a sizeable town beyond the cape.

'Is that Iwanai?' he asked Gundar. The skirl went through his usual routine of air sniffing, sail checking and spitting over the side.

'We've come a little south,' he said. He sounded disgruntled and Will smiled to himself. He'd seen enough of Skandian skirls to know they prided themselves on making perfect landfalls – even in places they'd never actually been before. After weeks at sea, using only the stars, instinct, his northseeker needle and a cross staff, Gundar had brought them to within a few kilometres of their destination.

'You've done well, Gundar,' Halt said quietly.

The skirl looked at him and shrugged. 'Could have been better.' He checked the wind tell-tale and leaned on the tiller to bring the bow around to the north-west, setting a course to weather the long cape before them. *Wolfwill* heeled to port, then began to swoop over the swell.

'What do we do when we reach Iwanai?' Will asked Halt. For so long now, the seaside town in the middle of Nihon-Ja had been their goal. Now they were nearly there, it was time to consider their next course of action.

'According to the message George sent, the man who guided him down from the mountains will be in the town,' Halt said. 'We need to make contact with him. He's loyal to the Emperor and should be able to take us to him.'

'As easy as that?' Will said. 'We just stroll ashore in a strange town in a foreign country and ask, "Has anyone seen George's friend, please?"'

Evanlyn was consulting the message she had received from George so many weeks ago.

'His name is Atsu,' she told them. 'And they should be able to put us in touch with him at a *ryokan* called the Shokaku.'

'What's a . . . *ryokan*? And what's a *shokaku*?' Will asked and she smiled helplessly.

'I haven't the faintest idea,' she said. She glanced at Alyss for help. The blonde girl had taken a copy of the message when they left Toscana and had been studying it in the past few days, referring to the book of Nihon-Jan words and phrases that Lady Pauline had sent to her.

'A *ryokan* is an inn,' she told them. 'And *shokaku* is a crane of some kind.'

'For lifting things?' Will asked.

'For flying. A large bird type of crane,' she corrected him. 'In fact, as near as I can work it out, *shokaku* means "a flying crane".'

'Seems like a logical thing for a crane to do,' Halt mused. 'I suppose you wouldn't expect it to mean "a hiking crane" or "a waddling crane".' He paused, then studied Alyss carefully for a few seconds. 'Are you sure you'll be able to make yourself understood here?'

Alyss hesitated. 'Pretty sure. It's one thing practising a language with another foreigner, another to hear it spoken by the natives. But I'm fairly sure I'll manage. One thing, though,' she added. 'I think when we go ashore looking for this Atsu person we should keep the numbers down.'

The trace of a smile touched Halt's mouth. 'You're right,' he said. 'After all, we are an exotic bunch, aren't we?

I suspect the sight of Selethen, Gundar and Nils walking the streets would draw a lot of attention. We'd be better to keep as low a profile as possible.'

'So it'll just be the four of us?' Evanlyn said and Halt shook his head.

'Three. Alyss because she speaks the language. Will because I want someone to watch my back.'

'But . . .' Evanlyn began, her cheeks reddening. His unspoken words were all too obvious. There was no useful role she could play in the search for George's former guide. Yet she hated the idea of being left out. Evanlyn had a keen sense of curiosity and always liked to be at the centre of things.

Halt raised an eyebrow at her now. 'But?' he repeated.

'Well, it's not really fair, is it?' Evanlyn protested. 'After all, this is my expedition.' The words sounded weak as she said them.

'Fair has nothing to do with it,' Halt replied. 'But you're right, it is your expedition . . .'

Before he could continue, Evanlyn seized on his words, thinking he might be showing signs of relenting.

'That's right! If it weren't for me, none of us would be here.'

'Actually, I think credit for getting us here goes to Gundar,' Will interposed, and she glared at him.

Halt stepped in quickly to nip any further discord in the bud. 'As I say, it is your expedition — and I'm sure you'd want to see it carried out in the most efficient way possible. Correct?'

'Well . . . if you put it that way . . . of course,' Evanlyn was forced to concede.

'And that means a small party going ashore initially,' Halt said, his tone indicating that this was the end of the discussion. Then his voice softened a little. 'Bear with me on this, Evanlyn. I know you're anxious about Horace.'

Will was a little puzzled by Halt's words. 'No more anxious than the rest of us, surely?' he said.

Halt turned away and raised his eyebrows as his gaze met Selethen's. Sometimes, he thought, his former apprentice could be remarkably slow on the uptake. He saw the Arridi's slow nod of understanding.

'I think we all agree, Halt,' Selethen said. 'We should keep a low profile until we know the situation here. And you Rangers are very good at that.' He smiled at Evanlyn. 'I'm sure the rest of us will have the chance to play a role in due course, Princess.'

Evanlyn gave in. She was disappointed, but she could see that Halt's decision made sense. A large party of foreigners arriving and asking questions would draw attention. And that could lead to the locals being reluctant to give out any information at all. If there had in fact been a rebellion against the Emperor, the situation could be extremely touchy in Iwanai.

'You're right, Halt,' she said and he nodded acknowledgement of her backing down.

'Nice to hear someone else saying that for a change,' Will said cheerfully. 'Seems I've said those words an awful lot in my time.'

Halt turned a bleak gaze on him. 'And you've always been correct.'

Will shrugged and grinned at Evanlyn. She was reconciled now to the plan and she smiled back at him. The most important thing, she realised, was to find out where Horace had gone. It didn't really matter who found that out, as long as they did.

Nihon-Jan sailors leaned on the railings of the ships to either side of them as *Wolfwill* nosed carefully into a berth in Iwanai harbour. More than one of them cast suspicious glances over the length of the wolfship. Her lines told them that she wasn't a trading vessel — the hull was too narrow to allow for any large amount of storage below decks. She was a fighting ship, they sensed. A raider. And as such, she would be treated with reserve. Several captains, watching her slide in towards the mole, took note of the wolf figurehead at her prow. Appropriate, they thought, and resolved to keep a close watch on her all the time she was in port.

'In oars!' Gundar yelled. Water cascaded down over the rowers as they raised their oars to the vertical, then lowered them and stowed them. The ship was coming into the mole at an angle, her bow pointing at the middle of the gap left between two other ships. Gundar, intent on his task, eased the tiller to the right and the bow swung to port.

'Stern line!' he called and the sailor beside him sent the mooring line curling high into the air to land on the mole. Instantly, three shore men seized it and began hauling on it. The ship's stern swung into the pier and they took a turn around a wooden bollard, checking her way as they heaved on it, allowing the rope to run increasingly slowly.

'Bow line away!' Gundar called. The second rope sailed in a high parabola, and was hauled in in its turn. The ship had lost all forward way now and was sliding sideways through the water towards the pier. Four of the starboard-side rowers tossed wicker fenders over the bulwark, letting them hang down to protect the ship's planking from the rough stone of the mole.

The fenders creaked a protest as *Wolfwill* made contact with the land, the sound gradually diminishing to a few low squeaks as she stopped moving. Two of the ship's crew sprang ashore and supervised the fastening of the mooring lines. Gundar never trusted local shore idlers to carry out that task. He let go a deep breath and turned to his expectant passengers.

'Well,' he said, 'here we are.'

Twenty-two

Shukin found a suitable spot for his plan midway through the following morning.

They had descended a deep valley between two massive ridges, and a fast-running river ran through the lowest point. The trail they were following led to a shallow ford, wide enough for only two men to cross at a time. On the upstream side of the ford, the river tumbled down a steep, rocky cliff. Downstream was a deep, wide pool. Either side, the banks were sheer and steep. Shukin paused as he surveyed the site, waiting for the last of the Kikori to cross. They waded through the water with difficulty — the shallow water of the ford made the river run even more quickly.

'A few men could hold this for hours,' he said. 'Arisaka's men can only come at us two at a time.'

Horace surveyed the spot quickly. 'Those high banks upstream and downstream will stop them coming ashore there. You're right. This is the only point where they can cross. The only danger is if there's another ford somewhere downstream, where they could get across and flank your position.'

'Even if there is, the trees are too thick for them to move downstream quickly. No, this is where they'll have to cross.'

Shigeru was nodding. 'Besides, it's not in Arisaka's nature to look for an alternative crossing,' he said. 'He'll want to try to bull his way across the river here. He's not renowned for subtlety and he has little regard for the lives of his men.'

'That's what I was thinking,' Shukin said.

'We could reinforce this side with stakes driven into the sand on either side of the ford,' Horace said. 'That'd make sure they have to cross on a narrow front.'

'Good idea,' Shukin said. He glanced around, saw Eiko watching them and passed on instructions for some of the Kikori to cut and sharpen stakes from the trees and hammer them into the ground, set at an angle and jutting out over the river's surface. Immediately, a dozen men set about the task.

'Helps to have skilled timber workers with you,' Horace said with a small grin.

'So, cousin,' Shigeru said, choosing his words carefully, 'your plan is to leave a small party of men here to hold the ford and delay Arisaka's army as long as possible?'

But Shukin was shaking his head before Shigeru finished speaking — as the Emperor had suspected he would be.

'I'm not leaving a party of men here,' he said. 'I'm staying with them. I can't ask them to do this unless I'm willing to share the danger with them.'

'Shukin, I need you with me,' Shigeru said quietly. But Shukin's face had a determined set to it and Horace could see that his mind was made up.

'My task is to make sure you're safe,' he said. 'The best way I can do that is to delay Arisaka's men and give you a chance to reach the fortress at Ran-Koshi. You'll be safe there once the snows come.'

'And in spring?' Shigeru asked. 'Do you think I won't need you then?'

'By that time, a lot of things may have happened. Believe me, Shigeru, I've thought about this and this is the best way I can serve you. Besides, once we've delayed them long enough, we can slip away into the trees and rejoin you later.'

The fact that he used Shigeru's name and neither a formal or informal title was proof of the depth of his conviction. And the pretence that he and his men could escape through the trees fooled nobody.

Shigeru continued to regard him sadly. 'At least half a dozen other warriors would be willing to command this rearguard,' he said. 'I understand that your personal sense of honour might lead you to do it. But there's more than your honour at stake.'

'That's true. And I'm not doing this from any misguided sense of honour. But what do you imagine will happen here?'

Shigeru shrugged. 'Arisaka's men will try to cross. You and your men will repel them. They'll try again. Eventually, they will make it across. You can't hold them back forever.'

'That's right,' Shukin said. 'And unfortunately, the advantage this position gives us is also a disadvantage.

They can only attack us two at a time but, by the same token, only two of us can face them at any one time. So it's important that the men defending the ford are our best warriors. Do you know anyone in our group who could best me with a sword?'

Shigeru went to answer, hesitated, then dropped his eyes as he realised that Shukin wasn't boasting. He was speaking the simple truth.

'No,' he said. 'You're the best we have.'

'Exactly. And so I have the best chance of holding off Arisaka's men for the longest period.'

'Eventually, of course, Arisaka will realise this. He'll send his best warriors to face you and, if necessary, he'll come at you himself,' Shigeru said.

Shukin allowed himself a grim smile. 'And that might solve the entire problem.'

Shigeru said nothing. They both knew that, as fine a warrior as Shukin might be, Arisaka was one of the best swordsmen in Nihon-Ja. In a one-on-one battle, the odds were vastly in his favour.

'I'll stay with you,' Horace said suddenly, breaking the silence. But both his friends shook their heads.

'I can't ask that,' Shigeru said. 'It's bad enough that my cousin is ready to do this. I can't ask an outsider to sacrifice himself as well.'

'And besides, *Kurokuma*, I'm depending on you to advise Lord Shigeru in my absence,' Shukin told him. 'He needs an experienced soldier standing beside him. I can see now why you were sent to us. I can command this rearguard with a much clearer mind if I know the Emperor will have your experience and knowledge to call on. You can serve him in my place. That will be worth more to me than having another sword to help me.'

Horace drew breath to argue but Shigeru laid a hand on his forearm.

'Shukin is right, Or'ss-san,' he said, foregoing the use of the Horace's joking nickname. 'I'll need all the help I can get.'

After a few seconds, Horace capitulated. He nodded sadly, eyes cast down to the ground.

'Very well.' He looked up and met Shukin's gaze. 'You can depend on me,' he said simply and the Senshi leader nodded.

'I know that, Or'ss-san.'

Horace looked around for some way to break the awkward silence that fell over them.

'Keep some of those sharpened stakes and have your unengaged warriors use them as pikes,' he said. 'You can stop some of Arisaka's men before they reach the bank.'

Shukin nodded, recognising a good idea.

'You see?' he said, smiling. 'This is why I want you to stay with Shigeru.'

'Just don't let your ideas of honour get in the way. Stop Arisaka any way you can. All right?'

'You have my word. Now give me your hand, Or'ss-san. It's been a pleasure knowing you.' All pretence that Shukin and his men might escape from the ambush site was now abandoned. Horace gripped his hand and Shukin embraced him around the shoulders with his left arm.

'There's a gift for you in my pack,' Shukin told him. 'It's wrapped in yellow oilcloth. Something for you to remember me by.'

'I don't need any gift to remember you. Take care, Shukin.'

As he said the words and stepped back, Horace realised how ridiculous they were. But Shukin merely smiled. Then he embraced Shigeru. The two men moved a few paces away from Horace and he turned away to give them a moment of privacy. They spoke softly in their own language. Shukin dropped to one knee, his head bowed, and Shigeru placed his right hand on his cousin's head in benediction.

Then the private moment was over. Shukin rose to his feet and briskly called the names of half a dozen of the Senshi. They stepped forward as he called them.

'We're staying here to swat these annoying mosquitoes who are following us,' he told them and they all smiled, then made stiff little bows towards Shigeru. No calling for volunteers, Horace noted. These men were all volunteers anyway.

'Now, cousin, you had best get on the move. You need to be at that bridge before Arisaka finds another way across the river.' Shukin had returned to the pretence that they would stop Arisaka permanently at this spot.

Shigeru nodded and turned away. Horace, after a moment's hesitation, followed him and they began the long, difficult slog up the next ridge.

Behind them, Horace could hear Shukin issuing instructions to his small party, pairing them off in teams of two.

The ridge they were climbing was one of the highest and steepest so far. The track was cut into its side in a series of switchbacks, so that they continually reversed direction and passed above the spot where Shukin waited to meet their pursuers — each time a little higher. Occasionally, in places where the trees cleared, they could see the small figures by the ford quite clearly. Shukin had despatched one of his men to the far side of the ford, sending him several hundred metres back up the track to give warning of the approach of Arisaka's men. The others sat on the grass beside the ford, resting. Their weapons were kept close to hand, however. Once, Shukin looked up as they passed a clear spot and waved to them.

Reito, as the senior surviving adviser of Shigeru's bodyguard, had taken command of the column and kept pushing the pace as they wound slowly upwards, zigzagging back and forth along the face of the ridge. They were two-thirds of the way up, and had just reached another switchback in the trail, when one of the Kikori let out a warning cry, pointing across the valley to the ridge opposite.

Horace stopped, leaning heavily on the staff he had cut to help him keep his footing on the steep, muddy trail. The rain misted down, preventing the track from ever drying out. It came and went in waves, alternatively shrouding them in mist, then passing so that they could see clearly across the valley. One such shower had just gone over and now the air was clear again. He looked across the valley as the Kikori pointed and saw movement on the mountain-side opposite.

Tiny figures were making their way down the track.

'Arisaka,' he said quietly. This was no advance party. There were several hundred warriors and they were moving at a brisk pace. Halfway along the column he could see banners waving in the brisk mountain wind. That would be the command party, he thought. Arisaka himself was probably there. He squinted, straining to see if he could make out the enemy leader, but it was impossible to pick out an individual from the group. Even if he could have done so, the distance was too great to make out any detail.

The Kikori had come to a halt, watching the pursuing army nervously. In a straight line across the valley, they were less than a kilometre away — although the distance they would have to travel to catch up was many times that. But it was unnerving to see them so close.

He caught Reito's eye and gestured to the opposite ridge.

'They're moving fast,' he said. 'Faster than we are.'

Reito nodded. 'They don't have wounded to carry with them,' he said. 'Lord Shukin will slow them down,' he added confidently.

'Maybe,' Horace said. He wondered how much time Shukin would be able to buy them. 'But let's keep moving anyway.'

Reito turned away and shouted an order. The column began to move again, slipping and sliding in the mud. Those at the rear had the hardest time, as the surface of the track was churned by hundreds of feet before them. Eyes were turned towards the far ridge as they continued upwards. But then the trees blocked it from sight. Horace wasn't sure which he preferred. Seeing how close the enemy were might be an unnerving experience, but not seeing them, yet knowing they were there, seemed worse somehow.

Reito called a ten-minute rest stop and ordered a change of stretcher bearers. Those who had been carrying the wounded set their burdens down gratefully and fresh bearers came to take over the load. The rest period seemed to pass in an instant and Reito had them on the move again. He moved up and down the column, sometimes chivvying the weary travellers to greater efforts, sometimes joking and encouraging them as the situation seemed to demand. Horace thought wearily that Reito, with all his back and forth movement along the column, was covering twice as much ground as the rest of them.

They were close to the top of the ridge when Shigeru pointed to a rocky outcrop, where a gap in the trees afforded a clear sight of the valley. As the group of Kikori and Senshi toiled upwards, he and Horace clambered onto the rocks and looked down.

The ford was below them. On the far side, Arisaka's men were massed. A small group of warriors was struggling across the river, waist deep in the swift water, to attack the defenders. It was obviously not the first attack. Several bodies were slumped over the hedge of sharpened stakes that had been driven into the ground of the river bank. More were visible, drifting slowly downstream in the deeper water below the ford. The river itself was streaked with red ribbons of blood.

Horace looked carefully but he could see only four defenders on the near side of the bank. He heaved a sigh of relief as he made out Shukin's blue-lacquered leather armour. The Senshi leader was positioned now to meet the next attack. One of his men stood beside him, sword drawn. The others crouched behind them, each armed with a long, sharpened stake. As the attackers came within range, they thrust forward at the leading men. One of the attackers was knocked off balance and fell, to be swept away into the deep water beside the ford. Another swept his sword at the probing stake and shattered it. Instantly, the defender withdrew, leaving Shukin and his companion room to fight at close quarters.

Swords flashed in the dim shadows of the valley. The sound of steel ringing on steel carried faintly to them, but it was delayed by the distance and out of time with the actions of the men below, making Horace feel strangely disoriented.

Five of the enemy fell in the first rapid exchanges, Shukin accounting for three of them, and the other attackers drew back to the middle of the stream to regroup. But now Horace could see that Shukin's companion had sunk to his knees as well. One of the others tossed aside his stake, drew his sword and stepped up beside Shukin. The injured man crawled back to the bank. He managed to creep a few metres away from the ford, then lay still.

Shigeru touched his hand to Horace's arm.

'Look,' he said, pointing.

On the far side of the ford, a figure was striding purposefully into the water. He was flanked by at least ten warriors and he wore brilliant, vermilion-coloured armour.

'Arisaka?' Horace asked, although he already thought he knew the answer.

Shigeru nodded gravely. 'Apparently he thinks Shukin has delayed them long enough.'

Horace looked at his friend. Shigeru's face, normally so enigmatic and composed, was drawn with worry.

'Does Shukin have any chance against Arisaka?' he asked.

Slowly, the Emperor shook his head. 'No.'

The latest attack was taking shape now. The ten men with Arisaka crowded forward, slashing and stabbing, in a compact mass. Shukin and his companion met them, cutting at them so that men reeled away in pain or fell and lay still in the river. But sheer weight of numbers was pushing the defenders back. The attackers had managed to gain a foothold on the bank now, inside the hedge of sharpened stakes. Most of them were concentrating their efforts on Shukin's assistant. Shukin launched himself in a flank attack on the knot of fighting men, and two fell in quick succession. But he had to turn aside to do it and that left him vulnerable. Suddenly, the vermilion-armoured figure charged forward, shoving some of his own men aside, and Shukin found himself flanked. He turned to face Arisaka, parried the general's blade and cut backwards with his own. Arisaka recoiled.

'He cut him!' Horace called excitedly. His hand gripped Shigeru's shoulder. But the Emperor shook his head.

'Not badly,' he said and Horace saw he was right. Arisaka was advancing again and Shukin was forced back by the wheeling circle of light formed by Arisaka's blade.

'Be careful, Shukin! Remember he will . . . Aaaah!'

The cry of despair was torn from Shigeru as Arisaka launched a sudden, confusing attack. He struck two blindingly fast blows at Shukin, from the left and the right, swinging in a high downward stroke each time and wheeling in a full circle to give his sword extra force and momentum. As Shukin parried desperately, Arisaka pirouetted for a third strike, and Shukin's blade went up defensively again. But this time, the anticipated blow never came. Instead, as he was halfway through his turn, Arisaka reversed his grip on the sword and delivered a lightning-fast backward thrust. Caught by surprise, Shigeru's cousin staggered to one side, his sword falling from his hand. He doubled over in agony and fell to one knee.

Almost contemptuously, Arisaka took a pace forward and struck again.

Shukin fell face down on the sandy riverbank. He didn't move. Belatedly, delayed by the distance, Shigeru and Horace heard the concerted yell of triumph that came from Arisaka's men.

They had been kneeling to watch the battle and now Horace put his hand under the Emperor's arm and raised him to his feet.

'We'd better get moving,' he said. 'We have to use the time he's bought us.'

Twenty-three

They had been moored alongside the pier for several hours before the Iwanai authorities showed any interest in them. Halt was eager to go ashore and begin the search for Atsu, but he knew this would be a mistake.

'Never a good idea to go ashore before you've paid your mooring fees,' Gundar had told him. It was normal practice in any port to wait for permission to land — which was usually granted after a hefty payment had been handed over. If he ignored that practice, he'd only draw attention to his actions and might even be banned from further visits ashore.

In the midafternoon, a party of four Senshi warriors swaggered down the quay, sending the dockside workers and fishermen scattering hurriedly out of their way. They boarded *Wolfwill* without invitation and their leader conversed briefly in the common tongue with Gundar. The five passengers watched proceedings from the cramped confines of the sleeping quarters in the stern.

The leader of the warriors seemed uninterested, even contemptuous, when the skirl told him the ship had travelled from Skandia, and that the country lay many leagues to the west. It was obvious that, in the Nihon-Jan warrior's eyes, a foreigner was a foreigner, no matter where he came from, and all foreigners were beneath the interest of a member of the Senshi class.

After some minutes, the Senshi came to the real purpose of his visit. He and Gundar bargained over a payment of harbour fees. When they eventually agreed on a figure, Gundar's scowl told the Senshi that he was unhappy with the amount but knew he could do little about it. That seemed to put the warrior in good spirits for the first time. With a sarcastic smile, he accepted the gold coins Gundar weighed out. Then he and his cohorts swaggered off in their stiff-legged strut, looking back at the ship and laughing at some comment the leader made.

Once they were safely away, Halt and the others emerged from the cabin.

'I take it he drove a hard bargain?' Will said, mindful of the scowling expression on Gundar's face as he handed over the money. To his surprise, the skirl emitted a booming laugh.

'That one? He couldn't drive a bargain with reins and a whip!' he said, smiling broadly. 'He was so busy being insulting about *gaijins* . . .' He paused and looked at Alyss. 'What is a *gaijin*, anyway?'

'It's a foreigner,' she said.

Gundar frowned thoughtfully. 'Then why would he call me that? After all, *he's* the foreigner, isn't he?'

The vaguest hint of a smile touched the corners of Halt's mouth. No matter where he was, Gundar would never see himself as the interloper.

'So, about the harbour fees?' he prompted, and the smile reappeared on Gundar's broad face.

'Barely half what I was willing to pay! That lad hasn't been in the job too long, I'd say.' He chuckled to himself, remembering the discussion with the arrogant but inept Senshi official. 'Incidentally, he kept saying he was collecting the cash for the honour of Lord Arisaka. He's the bantam rooster who's giving the Emperor grief, isn't he?'

'I do like the way you put it,' Selethen interjected quietly. The strutting, stiff-legged warriors' manner did bring a rooster to mind. But Halt was nodding in answer to Gundar's question.

'Yes. And that may explain why the fee was so small. Chances are, that particular official has only had the job since Arisaka seized power.'

Evanlyn frowned thoughtfully. 'If Arisaka's men are in power here, that might make it difficult to make contact with Atsu.'

Halt nodded. 'You're right. It might take a little longer than we expected.' He looked at Alyss. 'Perhaps we should take a couple of rooms in this *ryokan* of yours, the one with the waddling crane.'

'That's the flying crane, Halt,' she told him. 'But you could be right. That way, we'll give Atsu a chance to come to us unobtrusively. He might not want to be seen boarding a foreign ship.'

Halt turned to Gundar. 'We'll go ashore tonight after

dark,' he said. 'No sense in letting more people than necessary get a good look at us. Will you be giving your men a run ashore?'

Gundar nodded. 'They've earned it. But I'll make sure they stay out of trouble.'

'I'd appreciate that. We may have to stay at the inn for more than one night, so try to keep your men confined to the dock area. Don't let them wander further afield.'

'Most of what they'll want will be in the dock area,' Gundar said. 'If it foams and goes in a tankard, that's what they're looking for.'

Halt turned apologetically to Selethen and Evanlyn. 'I'm afraid I'm going to ask you to remain aboard and stay out of sight as much as possible,' he said. Both of them nodded immediately, understanding his reasoning.

'You're right, Halt,' Selethen agreed. 'Too many exotic *gaijins* wandering around will draw comment, and that might frighten our man off.'

Evanlyn smiled at the *Wakir*. 'Do you include me as an exotic *gaijin*?' she asked and he nodded gravely.

'Perhaps the most exotic of all, my lady,' he said.

Halt was pleased to see that Evanlyn had accepted his decision that she should not go ashore. That reminded him of something else that had been on his mind.

'Alyss, do you think you might do something to make yourself a little *less* exotic?' he asked. 'I was thinking about your hair, in particular.'

She nodded agreement. 'I've been thinking the same thing. I'll get busy on it right away.'

As she turned away, Evanlyn surprised her by asking, 'Can you use any help with that?'

Alyss turned back and smiled at the princess. 'I'd appreciate that,' she said. 'A girl always likes a second opinion when she tries a new style.'

The two girls disappeared into the stern cabin once more. Will watched them go, then asked Halt, 'Anything you'd like me to do? Grow a beard? Learn to walk like a rooster?'

'If you could stop asking facetious questions, that'd be a start,' Halt told him. 'But it's probably a little late in life for you to do that.'

Halt and Will were waiting by the gangplank for Alyss to emerge from the cabin. The two Rangers looked relatively anonymous in their mottled cloaks, and with their cowls drawn up to conceal their faces. Their massive longbows couldn't be concealed, of course, and Halt had wondered if they should leave them aboard. But then he reasoned that they were going into unknown territory and he wasn't willing to do that without his principal weapon.

The hatch to the rear cabin slid open and Alyss emerged onto the deck.

She wore a long, dark cloak, also with a cowl pulled up and masking her face. She was tall — there wasn't a lot Alyss could do to conceal that fact. But she walked stooped over, and that helped a little. When she came abreast of them and flicked back the cowl, Will muttered in astonishment.

Her long hair was gone, cut short to frame her face. And where it had been a gleaming blonde in colour, now it was black — jet black. Alyss's familiar face smiled out at him from this decidedly unfamiliar frame. And yet, there was something different about her face as well. He peered more closely in the uncertain light of the gangway lantern and realised that she had applied some kind of stain to her skin to darken her complexion, changing it from its normal fair colouring to a light olive brown.

'Good grief!' he said. It was disconcerting in the extreme. She was Alyss. But then again, she wasn't. It was like a stranger with Alyss's eyes and Alyss's familiar smile.

'Not perhaps the most flattering reaction,' she said, and he added to the list, Alyss's familiar voice.

'Well done, Alyss,' Halt said approvingly. 'You've worked wonders.'

'Evanlyn did most of it,' Alyss said, indicating the princess as she emerged on deck. 'I couldn't have cut the hair by myself and it was her idea to stain my skin a darker shade.'

'Good grief,' Will said once more. Alyss frowned at him. Alyss's familiar frown, he thought.

'*Must* you keep saying that?' she said.

'But . . . how did you do it?' Will asked, and Alyss shrugged.

'I'm a Courier,' she said. 'We never know when we might have to go undercover, so part of our standard travelling equipment is a disguise kit. Skin dye, hair colouring and so on. We cut the hair short because I only had a small bottle of dark hair colour.'

'Well, you won't be mistaken for a local,' Halt said. 'But you'll excite far less comment than you would as your usual, blonde self.'

Selethen had been eyeing the results of the girls' work for some minutes.

'Personally, since I'm used to ladies with darker skins, I find this new look quite glamorous indeed,' he said.

Alyss smiled at him and dropped a small curtsey in his direction. She saw Will draw breath for another comment and said, without looking at him, 'If you say "good grief" again, I'll kick you.'

Since that had been what he was going to say, he said nothing.

The three of them slipped down the gangplank and headed down the quay. As they reached the street that ran parallel to the harbour, they hesitated.

'Right or left?' Halt asked.

'Or straight ahead?' Will put in. There was a broad road ahead of them, flanked by the lights of what might be shops, taverns and bars. It was difficult to tell as the signs were all in incomprehensible Nihon-Jan characters. The road itself was erratic, zigzagging haphazardly, and they could see numerous smaller roads and side alleys branching off from it. Of the three choices, straight ahead seemed the most likely, Halt thought. He took an uncertain pace towards in that direction, then hesitated.

'Why will men *never* ask directions?' Alyss said. She had noticed a small group of locals perched on the harbour wall, fishing rods protruding out over the dark water. She strode towards them now and, as they became aware of her approach, she stopped and bowed politely. One of the fishermen scrambled down from the wall and bowed in return. Alyss spoke quietly to him for a second or two. There was a certain amount of pointing and arm waving, obviously indicating a sequence of direction changes. Then the man held up three fingers to make sure she understood fully. She bowed again and turned back to where Halt and Will were waiting.

'What did he say?' Will asked.

She smiled at him. 'He said my Nihon-Jan was excellent. Then he sort of spoiled that by adding "for a *gaijin*". Still, a compliment's a compliment, I suppose.'

'Was your excellent Nihon-Jan good enough to understand his directions to the *rillokan*?' Will asked sarcastically.

'That's *ryokan*, and yes, it was. Straight along that main road to the third lantern. Then left, then fourth right. There'll be a graphic of a crane outside the inn — a flying one,' she added, forestalling any comment from Halt. The Ranger simply shrugged.

'So I was right. It is this way,' he said as they set off.

The buildings were set close together, built from timber and with thatched roofs. Doors and windows were covered with sliding screens whose translucent panes showed the warm yellow of lanterns shining inside. Halt stepped a little closer to one and studied the small panels in the door.

'It's paper,' he said. 'Heavy paper. Probably waxed or oiled to make it rain proof. But it lets light through and preserves privacy at the same time. Ingenious.'

'Not so ingenious if a burglar wants to get in,' Will said. The doors and windows looked decidedly flimsy, he thought.

'Perhaps the locals are all law abiding,' Alyss commented.

They reached the third street lantern, which hung from a pole and swung from side to side in the gusty wind, and turned left into a side street. The buildings on either side seemed to close in on them in the narrow confines of the street. The main street, broad and windswept as it was, had been virtually deserted. But here more people hurried along, the women shuffling quickly in their long, narrow robes, men striding with a more open stride. Passers-by peered at them. Their clothes marked them as strangers, even if their faces and features were hidden by the deep cowls they all wore.

They heard babbles of conversation and sudden gusts of laughter from many of the buildings they passed. Occasionally, doors slid open and figures emerged, calling farewells back to their friends inside. As they emerged onto the street, they usually stopped to watch the three foreign figures passing by, hurrying through the shadows. But their interest was cursory. In a seaport like this, the locals were used to seeing foreigners.

'It seems we're being noticed,' Will said softly. Halt glanced sidelong at him.

'Not as much as if we came blundering down here in full daylight,' he said. 'And at least so far, we're only being seen by the townsfolk, not Arisaka's soldiers.'

'Maybe they don't come down these side alleys at night. How are we doing, Alyss?'

Alyss's face, in the shadow of her cowl, was contorted in a frown of concentration. The side street was even more erratic than the main street had been, twisting and turning and opening onto alleys and side entrances to the buildings. It was difficult to keep track of what was actually a street and what was simply a blind alley.

'Shut up. I'm counting,' she said. Then she pointed to a narrow opening on the right. 'That looks like it.'

They plunged into the alley. There were more people on the street now and they had to jostle their way through the slow-moving crowd as people stopped to read what appeared to be menu boards outside eating houses.

'*S'mimasen,*' Alyss said repeatedly as they brushed against passers-by.

'What does that mean?' Will asked, as they reached a stretch of street bare of any other pedestrians. He was impressed by Alyss's grasp of the local language.

'It means "pardon me",' Alyss replied, then a shadow of doubt crossed her face. 'At least, I hope it does. Maybe I'm saying "you have the manners of a fat, rancid sow". I'm told a lot of the meaning is in the pronunciation.'

'Still, that could be a useful phrase to know,' Halt said. But he'd noticed people's reactions to Alyss's apologies. They'd simply nodded acknowledgement and gone on their way. He was pretty sure she had the correct word. He, too, was impressed with the way she was coping. Pauline would be proud of her, he thought, and made a mental note to tell his wife about Alyss's language skills.

'There it is,' the girl said suddenly, pointing to a two-storey building on the opposite side of the street. It was more substantial than its neighbours. Its walls were constructed of solid logs, with the space between them filled in with clay or mud. There were several of the waxed-paper windows along the front of the building and four more on the upper floor, facing the street. The door was made of solid wood planks.

Beside the door, projecting over the street, was a signboard bearing a painting of a bird in flight. There were several Nihon-Jan ideograms written vertically down the signboard.

'That looks like a crane, sure enough,' Will said, 'and it's flying.'

Halt studied the board. 'Could be a pelican,' he said critically. 'But let's give it the benefit of the doubt.'

Leading the way, he pushed open the door, to be confronted by a wave of warmth. He paused for a second, studying the room beyond, then led the way inside.

Twenty-four

Wet, muddy and exhausted, the Emperor's party finally reached the narrow footbridge.

Horace paused as he looked at it. It was a flimsy structure. There was a narrow, planked footpath, wide enough for only one person to pass at a time. Four heavy rope cables supported it: two on either side of the foot planks and another two, set a metre higher and further apart, that acted as hand rails. Short lengths of lighter rope were tied in a zigzag pattern from the lower cables to the higher, forming a flimsy side barrier to prevent travellers falling through. With the handrail cables set wider apart than the footpath, the bridge formed a truncated, inverted triangle. When he looked at the yawning drop below, and noticed that the bridge was swaying and vibrating gently in the wind, Horace decided it was not a structure that filled him with overwhelming confidence.

Horace didn't like heights. But he gathered himself, took a deep breath, and stepped out onto the narrow planks, grasping the side ropes firmly as he did so.

The minute his foot touched it, the bridge seemed to come alive, swaying and dipping as it described a giant circle in the air. Far below him, he heard the river rushing and tumbling over the rocks. Hastily, he stepped back onto solid land, realising that he'd be a handicap to the others. The Kikori, used to this sort of terrain, would move more quickly across the bridge than he could. They would be held up if he went first.

'I'll cross last,' he said and motioned for the nearest Senshi to lead the way.

The warrior stepped onto the bridge. He paused while he absorbed the rhythm of its movement, then strode confidently across. Reito and several other Senshi followed, reaching the far side quickly. Then Shigeru crossed, followed by the first two of the Kikori stretcher bearers. They stepped carefully onto the bridge, moving more slowly, with both men having to adapt to the bridge's plunging, swooping motion. Eiko, who had watched their progress, called a suggestion to the next pair of stretcher bearers. They stopped and set their stretcher down. One of them slung the wounded man over his shoulder and set off across the bridge. Horace could see that he moved faster this way. The second man followed his companion, with the folded stretcher balanced over his shoulder.

That set the pattern for moving the wounded across the gorge. When they were safely over, the remaining Kikori followed. Since they were unhampered, they didn't have to wait for one person to cross before the next followed. Soon a steadily moving line was formed as they stepped lightly across the bridge. Once the Kikori were across, the Senshi warriors began to follow. They didn't manage the task with as much composure as the Kikori, but by moving carefully, they found three or four could negotiate the bridge at one time and the group waiting to cross quickly dwindled.

Horace waited anxiously. He had now watched three hundred people cross the bridge, so any doubts as to its strength were dispelled. Now he spent the remaining minutes in a fever of impatience, watching back down the path for the first sign of Arisaka's men.

'*Kurokuma!* It's time!'

The last of Shigeru's Senshi plucked at his sleeve, indicating the bridge behind them. Horace nodded.

'Go,' he said. 'I'll be right behind you.'

He waited until the other man was halfway across the bridge and then stepped onto the planks once more. He settled himself, adjusting to the swooping and swaying motion, then shuffled across, moving his feet carefully, placing them as close to the centre of the footplanks as he could. Still the motion was disturbing and he struggled not to look down. A memory suddenly shot into his mind — of Will at Morgarath's huge bridge in Celtica, running light-footed across the narrow beams where the footpath was yet to be laid.

'Wish you were here, Will,' he said quietly, then shuffled onwards.

He was two-thirds of the way across when he heard the cry of alarm from the far side. Stopping, he twisted his upper body to look back over his shoulder. He could see men running along the track at the rim of the gorge. In another five minutes, they'd reach the bridge. He hadn't expected them to catch up so soon and the thought struck him that Arisaka must have sent yet another advance party forward at top speed, unburdened by anything but their weapons.

'Don't stop, Or'ss-san!' It was Reito, shouting to him from the far side of the gorge. 'Keep moving!'

Galvanised into action, he plunged forward, careless now that his motion might set the bridge moving and swinging. He gripped the rope side rails fiercely, almost running to clear the bridge. He could see half a dozen Kikori standing where the handlines and cables that supported the bridge were anchored, axes ready. Behind him, he heard more shouting as Arisaka's men grew closer.

'Get a rope ready!' he yelled. 'A long rope!'

He lurched onto solid ground and turned to see the first of Arisaka's men stepping carefully onto the bridge. They hesitated at the wild movement. Unlike the Kikori, they weren't born and bred in this mountain territory. But they began to advance, slowly.

The Kikori's axes thudded against the cables supporting the bridge. But the thick rope was braided together and heavily tarred, and the tar had hardened to an almost rock-like consistency over the years. It was going to be a close thing whether Arisaka's men would make it across before the axemen could sever all four cables.

Horace saw one of the Kikori standing by with a length of rope and beckoned him forward.

'Round my waist! Quickly!'

The man realised what he wanted and stepped forward, fastening a loop of the rope around Horace's waist, knotting it securely behind him.

'Now pay it out as I go!' Horace said. He shrugged his shield around, ran his arm through the support straps, and drew his sword. Then he took a deep breath and stepped out onto the bridge again. The Kikori who had tied the rope now paid it out slowly, keeping a little slack between them so that Horace's movement wasn't impeded. He called for help and three of his companions ran to assist him.

This time, Horace moved with a purpose in mind. Any nervousness he might have felt was overborne by the necessity to hold back the advancing Senshi coming to meet him. Horace knew the real danger on such an unsteady platform would come if he let himself tense up. He had to relax and ride the motion of the bridge. He was a superbly co-ordinated athlete and now he hit upon the way to relax the tension in his muscles.

'Think you're on horseback,' he told himself, and instantly, he found he could attune himself to the swirling, plunging movement of the bridge. He advanced five metres and waited. The first of the Senshi stopped a few metres short of him, looking uncertainly at the tall figure who rode the bridge, balanced lightly on the balls of his feet. The Senshi had no such sense of ease. He was tense and nervous, out of his comfort zone. But he came on, swinging a clumsy overhead stroke at Horace.

Horace took the blow with his shield slanted, deflecting it rather than blocking it. As a consequence, his attacker felt no resistance to his blow and stumbled forward, off balance. As he tried to recover, Horace made a quick, darting lunge and took him in the left thigh, through the gap in his armour there.

With a hoarse cry of pain, the warrior dropped his sword as his left leg collapsed under him, sending him lurching into the thin web of side ropes. Horrified as he realised he was about to plunge through and fall to his death, he scrabbled for a handhold. The man behind him was impeded by the awkwardly sprawled, struggling body. As he attempted to step past, Horace advanced suddenly, shuffling quickly forward. The Senshi swung an awkward cut at him but once again the shield stopped the blow. The blade bit into the rim and stuck there for a second. As the Senshi jerked it free, Horace's return side cut hit him in the side.

The Nihon-Jan swords were sharper and harder than Horace's blade. But his sword was longer and heavier and it crumpled the lacquered leather body armour the Senshi wore, crushing the ribs behind it. The man gasped in pain, lurched against the side rail and lost his balance, toppling over to fall into the massive gorge below them.

The next man hesitated as both he and Horace felt a violent tremor run through the bridge and the left side rail sagged downwards. They faced each other, each waiting for the other to make a move. But Horace knew time was on his side now.

On the brink of the gorge, Shigeru spoke quickly to the men holding Horace's lifeline.

'Take a turn round that tree stump there!' he ordered them. 'When *Kurokuma* falls, slow him down before the rope runs out!'

They grasped his meaning instantly and ran the rope around the stump — which was thick as a man's waist. The axemen were working faster and faster now and the bridge trembled with each blow. Shigeru saw the enemy soldier closest to the far side turn and begin to run back, yelling a warning. His companions followed but they were too late.

The bridge suddenly fell clear, spilling Horace and the four remaining Senshi into the drop.

'Let the rope out!' Shigeru ordered. He knew if the rope simply snapped tight, Horace would swing against the cliff face with brutal force. But as the rope came tight, the Kikori let it run, using the loop belayed around the stump to slow it and allowing Horace to drop clear into the gorge, below the overhang where the bridge had been set.

Horace felt the bridge go, felt himself drop into space and his stomach rise into his throat. He waited for the sudden snap of the rope jamming tight, then realised what was happening. The rope was tight but yielding. There was no sudden stop so he let himself go limp and tried to turn to face the cliff face, so he could break the impact with his arms and legs.

The overhang, and the belayed rope, saved him. If the cliff had been sheer, he would have swung into it like a pendulum, at the bottom of its arc, moving too fast to prevent himself being injured. But as he began to swing inwards, he was also still moving vertically, and his momentum was being gradually reduced. He hit the rock wall twenty metres down, with enough force to crack a rib or two and jolt the breath out of his body. He cursed as the impact shocked the sword from his hand and it spun away into the giddy drop below. Then he felt the rope tightening under his armpits as the Kikori began to draw him upwards.

As he drew closer to the rim of the gorge, he could see Shigeru's anxious face among those peering down at him. He used his legs to fend himself off from the overhang as he reached it and was eventually hauled over the edge, sprawling on the muddy ground. He must look like a landed fish, he thought.

Shigeru seized his arm, then instantly released him as Horace's injured ribs flared with pain and he cried out.

'Are you all right, Or'ss-san?' Shigeru asked.

Horace felt his sore ribs under the mail shirt and grimaced.

'No. I've cracked my ribs. And I lost my sword, damn it,' he said.

Twenty-five

In contrast to the noisy taverns and restaurants they had passed so far, the interior of the *ryokan* was an oasis of calm and quiet.

Halt, Will and Alyss found themselves in a large entry room, walls and floor finished in polished timber. The sweet smell of beeswax hung in the air, evidence of constant polishing. It was overlaid by a mixture of incense and scented woodsmoke, the latter from a fireplace set against one side wall, where a log fire sent a warm glow through the room. This subdued lighting was augmented by several hanging lanterns, each consisting of a candle burning inside a paper globe. Opposite the fireplace, and set in symmetry to it, a small raised pond sent reflections of light ribboning across the walls.

The decor of the room was sparse but elegant. A large table faced them, with two beautifully lacquered boxes, one at either end, and a heavy journal in the centre. Writing implements were arranged neatly beside the journal.

Behind it was a framed wall painting — not a picture, but a large Nihon-Jan ideogram. To the left, a timber staircase ascended to the next level, and a wooden railed gallery ran round four sides of the open space above them. Halt, glancing round, assumed that access to the guest rooms led off from this gallery.

There was a single step in front of them, so that the main area of the room was slightly higher than the entry. Will went to step onto the raised area and approach the table, but Alyss had noticed several pairs of sandals ranged along the lower part of the floor. She recalled an item from George's background notes on Nihon-Jan customs and stopped him with a hand on his arm.

'Just a moment, Will,' she said. 'Your boots.'

'What about them?' he asked but Halt had noticed the discarded sandals, and a shelf of soft slippers set to one side.

'Take them off,' he said.

'It's a Nihon-Jan custom,' Alyss explained. 'They don't wear boots inside.'

Halt was already stripping off his boots and placing them against the shelf. He looked appreciatively at the polished wood floor, the colour of dark honey in the fire and lantern light.

'With floors like these, I'm not surprised,' he said.

Will and Alyss followed suit. They stepped up onto the raised platform and selected slippers. They all seemed to be the same size, but they were a simple slipover style, with a matting sole and a soft felt band that stretched over the instep of the foot to hold them in place.

'Just as well Horace isn't here,' Will said. The young

warrior's big feet would have overhung the compact slippers. The others smiled at the thought. Then, as if he had been waiting for them to don the slippers, a man emerged from a curtained doorway behind the long table. He stopped and bowed. The three of them approached the table and bowed in return. It seemed a lot of bowing went on in this country, Will thought.

'How may I serve you?' the man said. His voice was soft and slightly sibilant. Alyss glanced at Halt. The man had spoken in the common tongue and she assumed that Halt would conduct the conversation with him. He nodded briefly to her.

'We would like rooms,' he said. 'For two nights, possibly three.'

'Of course. That will not be a problem. You are from the foreign ship that entered the harbour today?'

Halt nodded and the man opened the large book on the table. He picked up what Will had assumed to be a pen but now saw was a fine brush. He dipped it in an inkwell made from polished blackwood and made two neat entries in the book — which was obviously the register of rooms available.

'Did you want to dine?' he asked. 'There is a dining room downstairs, or we can serve your meal in one of the rooms.'

'I think in the room upstairs,' Halt said. He indicated Will. 'My assistant and I will take one room and the lady will have the other. You can serve the meal in our room.'

The man bowed slightly. 'As you wish. Is there anything else or shall I show you to your rooms now?'

Halt exchanged a quick glance with Alyss. He wondered if the man already suspected the reason behind their visit. After all, this was where George had spent several nights before he left Iwanai. He came to a decision and leaned forward, lowering his voice a little.

'We were told that we might find a friend here,' he began. 'A man by the name of Atsu. He came —'

He was interrupted by the sound of the door slamming back on its hinges behind them. They all turned as two Senshi strode into the inn, their boots ringing loud on the wooden floor. Contemptuously, they ignored the slippers and stepped, hard-shod, onto the raised inner platform. One, obviously the leader, was a pace ahead of the other. The innkeeper's eyes flickered briefly with annoyance but he quickly recovered and bowed to the newcomers, his hands tucked inside his sleeves.

'Bow,' Halt muttered to his companions. He'd felt a momentary surge of apprehension, wondering whether the innkeeper might inform the Senshi that they were inquiring about Atsu. But it was obvious that the man was no friend to Arisaka's soldiers.

The Senshi made a derisive noise in his throat as they bowed deeply to him. He disdained to return the compliment, then turned and fired off a stream of rapid Nihon-Jan at the innkeeper. Will heard the word 'gaijin' used several times. He glanced at Alyss and saw she was frowning slightly as she tried to keep pace with the conversation. The innkeeper replied courteously, withdrawing a hand from the sleeve of his robe to indicate his guests with a graceful gesture.

The Senshi turned to them. Singling out Halt as the leader, he stepped closer to him — too close for politeness — and stood, feet apart and hands on hips, studying him. Will noted the symbol on the breast of his robe — a red owl.

They had learned that this was the mark of Arisaka's clan — although Will felt they could also be identified by their overbearing, arrogant manner.

Halt, who could appear deceptively obsequious if the occasion demanded it, dropped his eyes from the direct, challenging gaze of the Senshi. The man grunted again, seeing the simple action as an act of weakness.

'*Gaijin!*' he said abruptly, jabbing a forefinger at each of them in quick succession. 'From the *gaijin* ship?'

Halt inclined his head. 'That is correct, lord,' he said. He was sure the Senshi was anything but a lord but it would do no harm to call him that.

'Uncover your face in front of a Senshi!' the man ordered. He reached forward and slapped the cowl of Halt's cloak back from his face with the back of his hand. Will drew a sharp breath, sure that Halt would react explosively to the insult. But the bearded Ranger merely bowed his head again. The hand had made no contact with his face, merely catching the brim of the cowl and knocking it back. The Senshi nodded to himself in satisfaction, then turned to Alyss and Will.

'You and you! The same!'

They pushed back their cowls. Alyss bowed as she did so and Will followed suit, glad that his lowered head would mask the anger that he knew was showing in his eyes.

When he had recovered his equanimity, he straightened again.

'Why are you here?' The Senshi had turned his attention back to Halt.

'We are here to trade in precious stones,' Halt replied. It was the answer Gundar had given earlier in the day to the harbour official. Trading in precious stones explained the lack of large cargo space on board the ship, and went some way towards explaining her speedy lines. A ship with a cargo of jewels would need to be fast, after all. But the Senshi reacted angrily to his answer, stepping even closer to shout in his face.

'No! No! No! Why are you *here*?' He stamped his foot, scuffing a mark into the soft polish, and pointed at the floor. 'Why in this *ryokan*?'

The innkeeper intervened with an explanation in Nihon-Jan. His voice was low and respectful and he kept his gaze lowered, avoiding eye contact with the angry Senshi. The warrior listened to the explanation, then turned his gaze on the three Araluans and made a comment to his comrade. They both laughed and then, with a contemptuous gesture, the Senshi indicated that he had no further interest in the foreigners. The two men turned and stumped out of the *ryokan*, slamming the door shut behind them.

'And what was that all about?' Will asked.

He had addressed the question to Alyss but it was the innkeeper who answered. 'I told them you had come for the baths. The *ryokan* is built over a hot spring. The Senshi check on the movements of all foreigners in the town — they enjoy showing how important they are. Someone must have seen you arriving here and reported it. There are informers everywhere these days,' he added sadly.

'That could make travelling north a little difficult,' Halt said thoughtfully, and the innkeeper nodded agreement.

'It won't be easy.'

'Actually, after so long at sea, a hot bath sounds like a good idea,' Halt said. On the journey, with fresh water at a premium, they had been forced to use seawater for bathing.

'And what was Mister Smileyface's closing sally?' Will asked. 'It seemed to put them both in such a good mood.'

'He said, judging by the way we smell, we need a bath,' Alyss replied. Will raised an eyebrow at the insult but Halt uttered a short laugh.

'If it wasn't so true, I might be insulted,' he said. He turned to the innkeeper.

'Perhaps we might use the baths first, then eat?' he suggested.

The innkeeper nodded. 'I'll show you the way,' he said. 'And while you're relaxing, I'll send a messenger to see if Atsu is still in Iwanai. He comes and goes.'

Before she left the others to go to the women's bath area, Alyss gave them careful instructions. The hot baths themselves were not for washing. They were for soaking and relaxing. Accordingly, they washed and rinsed off in an annex, scooping hot water from tubs and pouring it over themselves, and then plunged into the near-scalding water of the bath. At first, it was agony, but Will gradually became accustomed to the heat and felt it soothing the aches and pains of several weeks standing braced on a heaving, uncertain deck and sleeping on hard planks. Reluctantly, he finally emerged, dried himself and wrapped himself in a soft robe the *ryokan* provided.

Alyss was waiting for them when he and Halt returned to their room.

In the centre of the room, a low table, barely thirty

centimetres from the floor, had been placed in position. It was laden with bowls and plates and small, candle-fired food warmers.

Will looked around hopefully for a chair but, in keeping with the minimalist decor of the *ryokan*, there were none available. Alyss sat, resting on her heels, her legs folded under her at the table.

Halt groaned softly. 'I was afraid of this,' he said. 'I suppose we have to sleep on the floor too.'

He'd noticed earlier that there were no beds in the room. When he'd enquired, the innkeeper had shown them thick mattresses stored behind one of the sliding screens that masked a closet.

Will grinned at him as he helped himself to a skewer of grilled chicken, covered in a delicious, salty, dark sauce.

'You've been sleeping on the ground for years when we camp,' he said. 'When did you become so fussy?'

'When we camp,' Halt replied, 'we are out in the open. I accept that I have to sleep on the ground when I am in a forest or a meadow. But this is a room and this a floor. When I am indoors, I prefer to sleep in a bed.' He removed the lid from a polished wood bowl and eyed the steaming broth inside. Looking round, he could see no sign of a spoon, so he drank directly from the bowl. 'This is actually very good,' he said.

Alyss was helping herself to another dish — a broth of noodles heavily laced with shredded pork. She looked puzzled at the two wooden sticks that seemed to be the only implements, then held the bowl close to her mouth and shovelled some of the noodles and pork in with the sticks, slurping in a highly unladylike fashion.

'You know, I rather hope Atsu doesn't show up in too much of a hurry. I could take a few more days of this,' she said.

Halt shifted position for the third time in thirty seconds, easing the strain in his thighs by sitting sidelong on one buttock.

'Tell that to my poor old aching knees,' he said.

Twenty-six

In spite of Halt's earlier grumbling, the beds — essentially no more than thick mattresses spread out on the floor — were quite comfortable.

After they had doused the small lantern that lit their room, Will lay on his back, listening to Halt's deep, regular breathing. As his eyes became accustomed to the darkness, he could discern a pale crack of light that showed at the edge of the sliding door leading to the gallery outside, although the innkeeper had dimmed the gallery lanterns some hours previously.

The sliding, paper-paned window panel was open and a chill breeze entered the room. Will pulled the down-filled bedcover higher around his ears. The innkeeper had offered them a small charcoal brazier to warm the room but they had declined. Both Rangers preferred fresh air.

Not for the first time, he found himself marvelling at the amazing turns his life had taken in recent years. He knew that some people he had grown up with had never strayed more than a kilometre or two from Castle Redmont and others had never gone outside the boundaries of Redmont Fief. Even his wardmate Jenny, who was now a famous chef, had barely gone further afield.

Yet here he was, on the far side of the world, having travelled through an amazing channel in the desert, cut by unknown, ancient hands, on an ingenious ship designed to sail against the wind. Before this, he had crossed the heaving, tossing Stormwhite Sea and seen the barren crags of Skorghijl, then travelled on to the snow-covered mountains of Skandia, where he had faced the fierce riders from the Eastern Steppes.

More recently, he had crossed the burning deserts of Arrida and made firm friends among the nomads of the Bedullin tribe. He had faced the wild Scotti tribesmen in the north. Then, with Halt and Horace, he had travelled the length of Clonmel, one of the six kingdoms of Hibernia.

Sometimes, when he thought about how much he had seen and done in his young life, his head swam. And at those times, he thought about his childhood ambition of becoming a knight. How circumscribed his life would have been in contrast to this amazing existence! He knew that most of the knights who had trained in the Redmont Battleschool with Horace had never left Araluen's frontiers.

He wondered if Halt, who had seen all these things and more, ever felt the same sense of wonder and excitement about his life. Without thinking, he spoke.

'Halt? Are you awake?'

'No.' The ill humour in the one-word reply was unmistakable.

'Oh. Sorry.'

'Shut up.'

He pondered whether to apologise again, decided this would go against the instruction to shut up so remained silent. He glanced at the open window. The light of a half moon was beginning to creep through it. The same moon would be shining now on Horace, somewhere in the mountains, he guessed. Then he yawned hugely and, shortly after, in spite of his sense of wonder, he fell asleep.

He'd barely been asleep a few minutes when Halt's voice woke him.

'Will? Are you asleep?'

His eyes shot open, instantly alert. Then he realised there had been no sense of alarm or warning in Halt's words and his tensed muscles relaxed.

'I was,' he said, a little indignantly. 'I'm not now.'

'Good,' Halt replied, a trifle smugly. 'Serves you right.'

And the bearded Ranger rolled onto his other side, gathered the bedclothes under his chin and dozed off.

A sound.

Slight, barely audible. But outside the normal pattern of night sounds that Will's subconscious had studied, filed away and learned to ignore. His eyes were open again and he listened carefully. The moon no longer shone through the open window. He must have been asleep for some hours, he thought.

Halt's breathing remained deep and even but Will knew that his teacher would be wide awake too. Rangers trained to maintain their breathing pattern even when awakened unexpectedly, so that a prospective attacker would have no warning that his quarry was awake and ready for him.

Another sound. The light, creaking noise of wood moving, ever so slightly, against wood. It was the sound of a careful tread on the stairs, he realised. So the intruder, if it was an intruder and not one of the *ryokan* staff, was not in their room. Moving slowly and with infinite care to make no noise, he raised himself on one elbow and laid the bedcover back. Across the room, he saw the dim shadow of Halt doing the same thing. Halt raised a warning hand, signalling him not to make any further movement. Lying low to the floor like this, it would be difficult to rise without making any noise. The general construction of the *ryokan*'s interior was exceedingly light — with interjoining panels of wood and oiled paper and more panels of woven reed matting covering the wooden floors. Movable panels like that would almost certainly have free play in them and would make noise — just as the stairs were doing. They heard another two slight squeaks from the stairway as if in confirmation. Will glanced down to make sure his saxe knife and throwing knife were next to the mattress, in easy reach.

Now that they knew there was no intruder in the room, there was no need to continue the pretence of deep breathing. They both breathed lightly, almost inaudibly, their ears tensed for any sound coming from outside.

Will was grateful that their room was closer to the stairwell than Alyss's. An attacker would have to pass their room to get to Alyss. A soft scuff of fabric against the wall, then another slight squeak, told them that whoever it was had reached the gallery and was moving slowly along it.

They followed the slight sounds that marked his progress until the pale crack of light at the door panel was obscured and they knew he was outside their door. The sounds of movement ceased and Will felt a sense of relief. Whoever it was, Alyss was not the target.

He strained his ears, his head cocked slightly sideways towards the door. There was a gentle scratching sound — fingernails on the oiled paper surface, he guessed. Hardly the act of someone whose intention was to take them by surprise.

Halt mimicked the sound, rustling his fingernails on the reed floor mat. There was silence for a few seconds, with no movement perceptible outside the door. Then a low voice, barely audible, hardly more than a whisper, came to them.

'I am Atsu.'

They exchanged a quick glance. Halt nodded to the wall beside the door. Will rose, making as little noise as possible, and moved, barefooted, to stand beside the opening, his saxe knife in his hand. Halt remained seated on the mattress.

'Come in, Atsu,' Halt said softly.

The door scraped open. A figure was framed in the opening. He looked left and right, saw Will beside the doorway and spread his hands to show he was unarmed. Will gestured for Atsu to go forward, into the room, and he complied, sliding the door shut behind him. He moved to where Halt sat sideways on the mattress, his legs crossed, and dropped to his knees, facing him. He bowed.

'Greetings, friends,' he said.

Will moved from the doorway now and stood to one side, so he could observe the man as he spoke to Halt.

He was slightly built, shorter than Will or Halt, but wiry. He was almost bald, with just a fringe of hair around the sides and back of his head. He appeared to be unarmed, but he could well have a knife concealed under the long cross-over robe that was standard attire for most Nihon-Jan.

'Do you always move around so late at night?' Halt asked him.

Atsu nodded. 'Since Lord Arisaka's men have imposed themselves upon us, it is safer for me to avoid them.'

'You helped another *gaijin* recently,' Halt said. It was a statement, but it was also a question. If this was not Atsu, chances are he wouldn't know the name of the *gaijin* he had brought down from the mountains. Atsu understood the challenge.

'You are talking about George-san,' he said. 'Friend to Or'ss-san.'

Halt frowned momentarily, not recognising the name.

'Who?' he said suspiciously. This time, Atsu enunciated the name carefully.

'Or'ss-san,' he said. 'The tall *gaijin* warrior.'

Will suddenly deciphered the name. He knew that the word 'san' was a Nihon-Jan term of respect, added as a suffix to a person's name. If he ignored that, he was left with 'Or'ss' — and that was a little more recognisable.

'Horace,' he said quickly and Atsu turned his head towards him and bobbed it quickly in affirmation.

'Yes. Or'ss-san,' he said. 'He saved the Emperor's life.'

'Did he now?' Halt said thoughtfully. 'I imagine that didn't make him Arisaka's favourite foreigner.'

'No indeed. Arisaka was enraged when he heard.

Or'ss-san killed two of his Senshi.' Atsu allowed a note of satisfaction to creep into his voice as he added the last comment.

'That sounds like Horace, all right,' Will said.

'And our friend here doesn't sound too heartbroken at the thought of Arisaka's men leaving us for a better place,' Halt said wryly.

'Which makes it more likely that he is, in fact, a friend,' Will agreed.

Halt paused a moment, thinking. Will would seem to be right, he thought. But a few more questions might be in order.

'What else can you tell us about George?' he said.

Atsu considered the question, sifting his thoughts to ensure that his answers advanced his credibility in the eyes of these two *gaijin*.

'He is no warrior. He is a talker.'

Will smothered a small laugh. 'That sounds like George.'

Atsu looked at him again. 'But he saved Or'ss-san's life in the mountains,' he added and Will raised his eyebrows in surprise.

'*George* saved Horace's life?' he said, incredulous.

'We were ambushed in the mountains. One of the ambushers shot an arrow at Or'ss-san. George-san saw it and pushed Or'ss-san to one side. The arrow struck George-san in the arm.'

Halt and Will exchanged another glance.

'Alyss did say George mentioned a wound in his message,' Will said. 'Although this bit about saving Horace is news to me.'

'Speaking of Alyss,' Halt said, 'perhaps you should fetch her. She should hear what Atsu has to say.'

His tone of voice said that he was now convinced that this really *was* Atsu and that he could probably be trusted. Will turned towards the door but, as he did so, there was a light tap on the door frame and the sliding panel opened, revealing Alyss in the Nihon-Jan robe she had been wearing earlier.

'Do you two always bellow at the top of your voices in the middle of the night?' she said. Then, catching sight of the third figure in the room, her voice lost its joking tone. 'I take it this is Atsu?'

It was a logical assumption, Will thought. No one else was likely to be in their room at this time of night.

'Indeed it is. Atsu, this is the Lady Alyss.'

The small Nihon-Jan swivelled round on his knees and bowed from his kneeling position to Alyss.

'Hr'ady Ariss-san,' he said. Alyss, diplomat though she was, raised an eyebrow at the unusual pronunciation of her name. Wait till she hears what he makes of Horace, Will thought, seeing the expression.

'Delighted to meet you,' Alyss said, her features under control again. She closed the door and crossed the room to sit on the end of Halt's mattress, her legs tucked up to one side.

'Can Atsu tell us what has become of Horace?' she asked Halt.

'I was about to ask him that,' the Ranger replied. But Atsu needed no further urging.

'Or'ss-san has offered to serve Lord Shigeru, the Emperor of Nihon-Jan, against the usurper, Arisaka. They have gathered some of Lord Shigeru's men and are retreating into the mountains, heading for the ancient fortress of Ran-Koshi.'

'So the Emperor has an army with him?' Halt asked.

Atsu shook his head. 'No army. Just the survivors of his men from the garrison in Ito. Barely fifty men. There are also the Kikori, but they're no army.'

'The Kikori?' Alyss asked. She wasn't familiar with the word. Atsu turned to her.

'Timber workers and wood cutters,' he said. 'They live in the mountains and they are loyal to the Emperor. Arisaka made the mistake of raiding and burning their villages in his search for the Emperor. As a result, he has alienated the Kikori and many of them have joined the Emperor.'

'But they're not soldiers?' Will asked and Atsu shook his head.

'Sadly, no. But they know the mountains like the back of their hands. If they are hiding the Emperor, Arisaka will never find him.'

'What's this fortress you mentioned?'

'Ran-Koshi. It's a legendary fortress, with high walls that are many metres thick. Even with a small force, the Emperor can hold it against Arisaka's army for months.'

The three Araluans exchanged glances. Will and Alyss left it for Halt to voice the question they all wanted answered.

'So how do we get to Ran-Koshi? Can you guide us?'

Their hearts sank as Atsu shook his head sadly.

'It's said to be somewhere in the north-western mountains. Only the Kikori would know its location for sure

— it's been so long since anybody's seen it that many people say it's a legend only.'

'Is that what you believe?' Alyss asked.

'No. I'm sure it's real. But even if I knew exactly where it is in the mountains, it would take weeks, even months, to get there. You'll be crossing mountainous country, one high ridge after another. It's incredibly slow going and, of course, you'd be caught by winter before you were halfway there. And you'll be moving through territory controlled by Arisaka's men.'

Halt rubbed his chin thoughtfully. 'Do you have a map?' he asked. 'Can you show us the approximate area?'

Atsu nodded quickly. He reached into his robe and withdrew a roll of vellum. He spread it out and they could see it was a chart of the north island of Nihon-Ja.

'Ran-Koshi is said to be in this area,' he said, his finger circling a small area in the top left-hand corner of the island. It's wild, difficult country. As you can see, it's in the heart of the highest mountains and it backs onto this enormous lake. To get there, you'd have to traverse all of this . . .'

His forefinger traced a route up through the centre of the island. The markings on the map indicated that the route would take them through mountain country — steep and heavily forested. He looked up, apologetically.

'As I said, it would take weeks to make that trip. And I simply don't have the time to guide you. There is a resistance movement growing against Arisaka and I'm one of the organisers. I sympathise with your desire to find Or'ss-san, but I have my own tasks.'

Halt stared at the map thoughtfully for a few seconds.

Then he pointed to a spot a little to the west of the area Atsu had indicated.

'If we were here, could you put us in touch with people who might help us find the Emperor? These Kikori you mentioned.'

Atsu nodded. 'Of course. But as I say, it would take weeks to reach that spot — we might not even make it if the snows come. And I can't spare that time. I'm sorry.'

Halt nodded, understanding his predicament. He'd been considering the problem of travelling through this hostile countryside controlled by Arisaka's forces ever since the encounter with the two Senshi. Now he thought he saw an answer.

'Can you spare four or five days?' he asked.

Twenty-seven

They were near the end of their journey. Horace trudged wearily up the rough trail that wound along the floor of a narrow valley. On either side, steep, unscaleable cliffs rose high above them. The further they went, the narrower the valley became, until it was barely twenty metres wide. A few snowflakes fluttered down but they were yet to see the first really heavy snowfalls of winter.

Reito finally called for a rest stop and the long column of Senshi and Kikori slumped gratefully to the ground, easing packs off their shoulders, lowering stretchers to the ground. It was late afternoon and they had been travelling since before dawn. They had travelled long and hard every day for the past week, with Reito hoping to maintain the lead they had gained over Arisaka's force. Horace found a large boulder and leaned against it. His ribs were still aching from the impact with the cliff face. Shigeru's physician had bound them for him but there was little else he could do. Time would be the real healer. But now the muscles protecting the cracked ribs were stiff and sore and the actions of sitting and then rising again would have stretched them, causing sharp pain to flare again.

'How much further?' he asked Toru. The Kikori who had been guiding them considered his answer before replying. Horace could tell by his expression that he didn't know, and he was glad the Kikori made no attempt to pretend otherwise.

'This is the valley. I'm sure of that. How much further we have to go . . . I'm not sure.'

Horace caught Reito's eye. 'Why don't we go ahead and reconnoitre?' he suggested and the Senshi, after glancing once at Shigeru, reclining against the base of a large rock, nodded. Since Shukin's death, Reito had taken his responsibility for the Emperor's safety very seriously. It was a charge that weighed heavily upon him. Shukin, a long-time close friend and relative of the Emperor, had found it easier to handle the responsibility. He had grown used to the task over a period of years. But it was all new to Reito and he tended to be oversolicitous. Now, however, considering the situation, he decided that Shigeru would be safe enough in his absence.

'Good idea,' Reito said. He hitched his swords up and turned to face the valley before them. Toru, without being asked, rose to his feet as well and the three of them set out, walking carefully over the tumbled rocks and stones that littered the valley.

They rounded a left-hand bend. The narrow valley snaked its way among the towering mountains, rarely continuing in one direction for more than forty metres.

Ahead of them they could see the blank wall of rock that marked another twist, this time to the right. They trudged on, their boots crunching on the rocks and sand beneath them.

No one spoke. There was nothing to say. The fortress of Ran-Koshi was somewhere ahead of them. Talking about it wouldn't bring it one centimetre closer.

They rounded the bend and, suddenly, there it was.

'Is that it?' Horace said, the disbelief evident in his voice.

Reito said nothing. He shook his head slowly as he studied the 'fortress'.

Ahead of them, the valley floor straightened and ran up a steep incline. A hundred metres away, a ramshackle wooden palisade, barely four metres high, had been thrown across the narrowest part of the valley, where the steep rock walls closed in to leave a gap barely thirty metres across. Beyond the palisade, the ground continued to rise and the valley widened out once more. They could see several ruined huts, their timbers grey and brittle with age, their thatched roofs long rotted away.

Reito's face darkened with anger. He turned to Toru.

'This is Ran-Koshi?' he said bitterly. 'This is the mighty fortress that will protect us from Arisaka's army?'

For weeks now they had sought this goal, thinking of it as their final sanctuary, as a place where they could rest and regather their strength, where they could train the Kikori to fight, protected by the fortress's massive walls of stone.

Now here they were, with no more than a derelict line of logs and planks to shelter behind. On the left-hand side, the western side, the palisade was actually half-collapsed,

Horace saw. A determined effort by an attacking force would bring it crashing down and open a five-metre gap in the defences, meagre as they were.

Toru was unmoved.

'This is Ran-Koshi,' he said. He hadn't been present at the discussion weeks ago, when Shigeru and Shukin had described the massive, fabled fortress. He had simply been asked if he could lead the way to Ran-Koshi and he had complied. He had known that Ran-Koshi was this simple palisade across a valley — many of the Kikori knew — and he had assumed that so did Shigeru and his followers. There had been no reason for him to think otherwise. He faced the angry Senshi nobleman calmly.

Reito made a frustrated, infuriated gesture with both hands. He felt suddenly helpless. Worse, he felt that he had betrayed the trust that Shukin and Shigeru had placed in him. They had struggled through the mountains for weeks, carrying their wounded, fighting their way up treacherous, muddy tracks where a false step could lead to disaster. Shukin and his men had given their lives to buy them time. And they had done it, they had endured it, for . . . this. For a moment, he was within an ace of drawing his long sword and running the Kikori guide through. But he mastered the impulse. He looked at Horace, his face stricken.

'What can I tell the Emperor?'

But Horace, after his initial surprise, was nodding slowly as he studied the terrain around them.

'Tell him we've found Ran-Koshi,' he said simply. Reito went to make a bitter reply but Horace stilled him with a raised hand, then gestured at the sheer mountains that enclosed them on all sides.

'These are the mighty stone walls of the fortress,' he said. 'It's the valley itself. This is the fortress. No army could scale these walls, or break them down. The palisade is merely the gateway.'

'But it's derelict! It's falling down on itself!' Reito burst out in despair.

Horace placed a calming hand on his shoulder. He knew the reaction was caused by the sense of duty and obligation Reito felt to the Emperor.

'It's old, but the structure is sound enough apart from the western end — and it can be rebuilt,' he said. 'We simply need to replace some of the larger logs in the main wall — and after all, we have two hundred skilled wood workers with us.' He glanced at Toru. 'I'd say your people could put this to rights in three or four days, couldn't they?'

'Yes, *Kurokuma*,' he said. He was glad that the *gaijin* warrior had seen the bigger picture. 'And we can rebuild the cabins so that we have warm, dry quarters for the winter.'

Slowly, the sense of anguish was draining from Reito as he looked at their surroundings with new eyes. *Kurokuma* was right, he thought. No army could scale or breach these massive walls. And the palisade was a mere thirty metres wide — it could be easily held by the two or three hundred defenders they had at their disposal.

Another thought struck Reito. 'Once the snows come, this pass will be metres deep in snow. An enemy couldn't even approach the palisade in any numbers,' he said. He turned to Toru and bowed deeply. 'My apologies, Toru-san. I spoke without thinking.'

Toru returned the bow and shifted his feet uncertainly. He was unaccustomed to having Senshi warriors apologise to him, or bow to him. He mumbled a reply.

'There is no call for you to apologise, Lord Reito,' he said.

But Reito corrected him. 'Reito-san,' he said firmly, and the Kikori's eyes widened in surprise. The Senshi was eschewing the honorific of 'Lord' for the more egalitarian 'Reito-san'. Horace watched the interplay between the two men. By now he was familiar with the etiquette of forms of address and he realised the giant gulf Reito had just bridged. That boded well for the coming months, he thought. It would be better to have the Kikori as willing partners, rather than inferior subjects. He clapped both men on the shoulders, drawing them together.

'Let's go and tell Shigeru we've found his fortress,' he said.

They made their way back down the valley to where the column waited for them. Horace was conscious of a new spring in his step. After weeks of climbing and staggering onwards, they had reached their objective. Now they could rest and recuperate.

Shigeru saw them coming, saw the positive body language among the three of them and rose expectantly to his feet.

'You've found it?' he said.

Horace deferred to Reito. The Senshi felt the responsibility of leadership deeply and Horace thought it only fair for him to deliver the good news.

'Yes, lord,' he said. 'It's barely a few hundred metres away.' He gestured up the valley behind him. 'But Lord

Shigeru, I should tell you. It's not . . .' He hesitated, not sure how to proceed.

Horace, seeing him falter, filled in smoothly for him. 'It's not exactly what we expected,' he said. 'It's a natural fortress rather than a man-made one. But it will suit our needs just as well.'

For the first time in many days, Shigeru smiled. Horace saw his shoulders lift, as if a giant weight had been taken from them.

'The entrance needs repairing,' Horace continued. 'But the Kikori will handle that easily. And we can build huts and a proper shelter for the wounded.' He was all too conscious of the fact that the wounded men, who had travelled without complaint, had been constantly exposed to the bitter cold, sleet and snow while they had been travelling. Several had succumbed to their wounds already. Now, with the prospect of warm, dry quarters, the others would have a greater chance of survival.

Word had quickly travelled down the column that Ran-Koshi was within reach. Without any orders being given, the Kikori and Senshi had risen to their feet and were forming up in their marching order once more.

'Thank you, Reito,' Shigeru said, 'for bringing us safely through the mountains to this point. Now perhaps we should inspect my winter palace?'

They climbed through the ruined western end of the palisade, picking their way carefully over the splintered timber. As they emerged on the far side, Horace stopped in surprise.

The valley widened out here, the ground still rising gradually. But there was a considerable open space behind the timber wall. And the area was dotted with huts and cabins.

'Somebody's been here recently,' Horace said. Then, as they moved further up the valley and he could see the condition of the buildings more clearly, he revised his estimate. 'Maybe not recently,' he said to Reito. 'But certainly a lot more recently than a thousand years ago.'

The timber of the buildings, like the palisade itself, was grey and dried out with age. The roofs were made of split shingles and in most cases, the support beams had collapsed, leaving only sections of the roofs still in place.

The newcomers stared around in wonder, puzzling over who the most recent inhabitants might have been. Then one of the Kikori emerged from a cabin that he had been inspecting and shouted excitedly.

'*Kurokuma!* Here!'

Horace moved quickly to join him. The cabin was larger than most of the others. There were no window spaces. The walls were blank and solid, with just a door at the end.

'Looks more like a warehouse than a cabin,' he said softly. And as he stepped gingerly inside, glancing up to make sure that the roof wasn't about to come crashing down on him, he saw that he was right.

The interior was littered with old, decaying wooden boxes and rotted scraps of woven fabric that might have been the remnants of food sacks. They were scattered in all directions. Obviously, animals had been at work here over the years, rummaging through the contents of the building in search of anything edible. But what caught his interest was a rack running down the centre of the room.

'Weapons, *Kurokuma*!' said the Kikori who had called him. 'Look!'

The rack held old weapons. Spears, pikes and simple swords — not the carefully crafted weapons used by the Senshi, but heavier, straight-bladed weapons. The leather bindings and wooden shafts were rotten with age and looked as if they would crumble at a touch. And the metal heads were pitted with rust and age. Unusable, Horace saw at a glance. They hadn't been good quality when they were new. He guessed they were iron, not tempered steel. They would be more dangerous now for the user than an enemy.

'Can we use them?' the Kikori asked, but Horace shook his head. He touched the blade of one of the swords and rust came away in red flakes.

'Too old. Too rusty,' he said. He turned to Reito, who had followed him into the cabin. 'Any idea who might have built all this?' he asked, sweeping a hand round the interior of the ancient warehouse. Reito stepped forward and examined one of the swords, noting the poor quality.

'At a guess, I'd say bandits or brigands,' he said. 'This would have made an ideal hideout for them while they preyed on the Kikori villages and travellers through the valleys below.'

'Well, they're long gone now,' Horace said, wiping traces of rust from his fingernails.

'I think we'll build our own cabins,' he added. 'I'd prefer to sleep at night without worrying that the roof is going to fall on me.'

They set up camp in the wider area behind the palisade. For the moment, they would shelter in tents, but Horace directed the senior Kikori as to where cabins and a hospital shelter should be located. With such a large number of skilled workmen at his disposal, he also gave instructions for the renovation and reinforcement of the palisade to begin, with priority to be given to the collapsing left-hand side.

He was glad to take this load off Reito's shoulders, leaving him free to look after Shigeru's wellbeing. Reito was a Senshi but he was a courtier, not a general, and Horace was better qualified to see to the defence of Ran-Koshi. He strode about the valley with a new energy in his step, followed by a group of a dozen Kikori elders – the leaders from the villages that had joined their party. He was pleased with the way they quickly accepted his right to give orders. Even more gratifying was the fact that they were willing to co-operate with each other. Any inter-village rivalries that might have existed before were snuffed out by the current situation.

One of them pointed out that there was little in the way of heavy timber in the valley itself. Work parties would have to travel back the way they had come to fell timber outside the valley and drag it up to the fortress.

Horace nodded acknowledgement of the fact.

'Then tomorrow we will rest,' he said. 'After that, work starts.'

The assembled Kikori nodded agreement. A full day's rest would make the work go faster, they all knew.

'Get your work parties detailed,' he told them. The senior Kikori all gave perfunctory bows and he returned them with a quick bob of his own head. Interesting how quickly it became a natural action, he thought. Then, as they drifted off to their respective groups, he looked around for Eiko and Mikeru. The two were never far away and over the past weeks he had become accustomed to detailing them to specific tasks.

'Eiko, can you organise scouts to go back the way we've come and keep watch for Arisaka's approach?'

'I'll go myself, *Kurokuma*,' the heavily built lumberjack said but Horace shook his head.

'No. I may need you here. Send men you can trust.'

'Will I go with them, *Kurokuma*?' It was Mikeru, the youth who had guided them from the first Kikori village and, as a result, had escaped the brutal attack of one of Arisaka's patrols. He was keen and intelligent and energetic, always ready for something to break the monotony of the long, hard march. He was the ideal person for the task Horace had in mind.

'No. I have something else I need you to do. Get three or four of your friends and explore this valley. Find the secret path out to the flatland below.'

Mikeru and Eiko both frowned, puzzled by his words.

'Secret path, *Kurokuma*? Is there a secret path?' Mikeru looked around the rock walls that enclosed them. They seemed impenetrable. Horace smiled grimly.

'This was a fortress. But it's also a trap. A dead end. No military commander would put his men in a fortress like this unless there was a secret way out. Trust me. It'll be there all right. It'll be narrow and it'll be difficult but it'll be there. You just have to find it.'

Twenty-eight

Wolfwill glided into the narrow cove under oars. There was no breath of wind and the surface of the water was calm and glassy, marred only by the sixteen rippling circles left by each stroke of the oars and the arrow-straight wake the ship left behind her.

Four days previously, they had left Iwanai and sailed up the west coast of Nihon-Ja. A brisk southerly wind was blowing and Gundar had raised both starboard and port sails, and sheeted them home out to either side. They stood at right angles to the hull. In this position — Gundar called it goose-winging — they formed a giant M shape. With the wind astern, he could use twice the normal sail area.

The sea had been calm and with this extra thrust behind her, *Wolfwill* had flown up the coastline. As Halt had seen when he studied the chart, three days' easy sailing had saved them weeks, compared to the alternative — slogging over hundreds of kilometres of mountain ranges.

And they had avoided the attention of Arisaka's patrols. Now they had reached the northern part of the island and somewhere, not far inland, lay the fortress of Ran-Koshi.

'That's far enough, I think, Gundar,' he said quietly. Gundar called an order, also in a muted tone, and the oars ceased their constant motion. It seemed right to keep their voices down. Everything here was so still, so peaceful.

At least, for the moment. Time would tell what lay beneath the trees on the thickly forested shore of the cove. Behind the first few tree-covered hills, the mountains began to rise again, now covered to halfway down their height in snow.

Wolfwill drifted, seeming to rest on her own inverted image, while her crew and passengers studied the shoreline, looking for signs of movement.

'Have you been here before, Atsu?' Selethen asked and the guide shook his head.

'Not to this province, lord,' he said. 'So I don't know the local Kikori. But that shouldn't be a problem. The Kikori are loyal to Emperor Shigeru. I will simply have to make contact with the local tribes.'

'Just so long as you don't bump into Arisaka's men instead,' Halt said dryly.

'We don't know that Arisaka's men have penetrated this far north-west,' the guide said.

Halt shrugged. 'We don't know they haven't, either. Better to assume the worst. That way, you're not disappointed when it occurs.' Halt turned to Gundar. 'I thought you could camp on that island we passed, rather than in here on the mainland.'

The skirl nodded. 'My thought too. We could be here for weeks, even months, while the winter passes. We'll be safer on the island.'

It had been decided that Gundar and his men were not going to accompany them into the mountains. A captain was always reluctant to leave his ship for even a short time, and they could be at Ran-Koshi for months. Instead, the Skandians would take Atsu back to Iwanai, then return to this point and spend the winter in a camp, beaching their ship and hauling her high above the tide mark to protect her from winter gales. They planned to build huts in the shelter of the trees. Skandians often wintered like this while they were travelling. Gundar had re-provisioned the ship while they were in Iwanai so they had plenty of food on board. Plus they could come to the mainland to hunt and fetch water if there were none on the island. The island was a lucky break. Four hundred metres offshore, it would provide security and early warning of any possible attack.

'Put us ashore in the skiff,' Halt continued. 'Then get out to the island. We'll camp on the beach tonight while Atsu tries to contact the locals.'

Forty minutes later, the shore party watched as the wolfship's oars went forward on one side and back on the other, pivoting the neat craft in her own length. Then both banks of oars began to pull together and the ship gathered speed, heading out to sea. On the stern, Gundar waved farewell.

As *Wolfwill* rounded the point and disappeared from sight, Will felt strangely alone. But there was no time for introspection. There was work to be done.

'Right,' said Halt. 'Let's get a camp set up. Atsu, do you want to wait till morning? Or will you try to make contact with the locals tonight?'

Atsu looked at the low sun. There was probably an hour of daylight left.

'It might be better if I go right away,' he said. 'It's highly likely we've been seen, so the sooner I can make contact and explain our intentions, the better.'

Halt nodded agreement and while the others set about erecting their small tents and gathering stones for a fireplace, Atsu slipped into the forest. Will watched him go, then turned back to the task of tightening the guy rope on his tent. Selethen, beside him, was unfamiliar with the Araluan tent design and was puzzling slightly over the arrangement of ropes and canvas. Will quickly moved to help him get them sorted out.

'Thanks,' said the *Wakir*. He added, with a faint smile, 'I usually have a servant to do this for me, you know.'

'Happy to be of assistance,' Will told him. 'So long as you break out some of your supply of coffee.'

'Good idea,' the Arridi replied and began rummaging in his pack. His coffee beans were superior to the ones Will and Halt carried. They had more flavour and were far more aromatic. During the trip, they had all rationed their supplies carefully — coffee seemed to be unknown in Nihon-Ja. But now Will thought it was time to enjoy a good cup.

Evanlyn and Alyss had found a freshwater stream a little inland from the beach and had taken the water skins and canteens to fill them with fresh, cold water. While they waited for the girls to return, Will and Selethen set about making a fire. Halt, sitting with his back to a log and studying the map, glanced up as they did so. Will hesitated.

'Are we all right to have a fire, Halt?' he asked.

The older Ranger thought for a moment. 'Why not?' he said. 'As Atsu pointed out, the locals probably know we're here anyway.' He glanced towards the trees, where the two girls were visible, filling the canteens.

'Are you expecting trouble?' Will asked, aware that Halt had been keeping a watchful eye over the girls as they worked.

Again, Halt hesitated before replying. 'I'm always edgy when I'm in a country I don't know,' he said. 'I find it's the best way to be.'

'It's certainly kept you alive so far,' Selethen said, with a hint of a smile.

Halt nodded. 'Yes. So far so good. Plus, I've been thinking . . . Atsu seems confident that all the Kikori villages will be supporting the Emperor. But there's no iron-clad guarantee that some of them haven't gone over to Arisaka.'

'Do you think that's likely?' Will asked and Halt turned his gaze on his young protégé.

'No. But it is possible. We're going a lot on Atsu's word for things and we have no way of knowing how good his judgement is.'

Evanlyn and Alyss returned as they were discussing this. The girls were burdened with filled canteens and two large waterskins and they carried the load between them. Evanlyn glanced around the camp site approvingly.

'What a cheery little home away from home,' she said brightly.

Alyss, who had noticed the sombre expressions on the faces of Selethen and the two Rangers, added, 'And what serious faces you're all wearing. Is something wrong, Halt?'

Halt smiled at her. 'Now that we have water for the coffee, no,' he replied. 'Everything is just as it should be.'

They made coffee, then Will set about preparing an evening meal. The market in Iwanai had supplied them with several chickens and he set about jointing them and preparing the meat in a marinade of oil, honey and the dark salty sauce that was a staple in Nihon-Ja.

Atsu had taught him how to prepare rice, which he had never cooked before, and he set a covered pot steaming in the coals of the fire while he prepared a green salad, using small onions and green leaves that resembled spinach. As ever, he had his cooking kit with him, with his own personal staples that went to create a light, tangy salad dressing.

'Nice to know a man who cooks,' said Alyss, sitting comfortably by the fire, her back against a log and her knees drawn up.

'I've heard you can whip up a pretty good meal too, Halt,' Evanlyn said, gently teasing him.

Halt took another sip of the coffee they had prepared. His eyes smiled at her over the rim of his mug.

'It's part of a Ranger's training,' he said. 'There's no law that says we have to exist on hard tack and cold water when we're in the field. A good meal does a lot to restore the spirits. Some years back, Crowley had Master Chubb prepare a set of recipes and instructions for us. All Ranger apprentices do a three-month course in their third year.'

'So what are you planning to whip up for us?' Selethen asked. He was smiling but he thought such a course was an excellent idea. As Halt said, good, simple food could go a long way towards making a camp more comfortable.

Halt drained the last of his coffee. He looked at the dregs in his mug wistfully. For a moment he was tempted to make a fresh pot. But they couldn't afford to squander their limited supplies.

'I won't be cooking,' he replied. 'Will enjoys doing it and I wouldn't want to spoil his fun.'

Will looked up from where he was threading the marinated chicken meat onto thin skewers of green wood.

'Besides, Halt has been known to burn water when he boiled it,' he said and they all laughed. He was about to add to the tale of Halt's failed cooking attempts when he stopped, his eyes fixed on the shadows at the edge of the trees fringing the beach. He laid down the skewer he'd just prepared and rose to his feet, his hand going to the hilt of his saxe knife.

'We've got company.'

There were figures emerging from the trees. Roughly dressed in fur and sheepskin and all of them carrying weapons — spears and axes, mainly.

The others rose to their feet as well. Halt had his longbow in his hand and he quickly retrieved his quiver from where it lay on the ground beside him, slinging it over his shoulder. In a continuation of the same fluid movement, he took an arrow from the quiver and laid it on the string. Selethen laid a cautioning hand on his forearm.

'There are too many of them, Halt. This might be a time for talking.'

Selethen was right, the Ranger saw. There were at least twenty men coming towards them.

'Where the hell is Atsu when we need him?' Will said bitterly. He was scanning the trees for some sign of their guide, but with no success. His own bow was close to hand but Selethen was right. There were too many armed men to make resistance worthwhile.

The newcomers formed a half circle around the little group by the camp fire. Their eyes were hard and suspicious. Halt laid down his bow and spread his hands in a gesture of peace. Following his lead, Selethen took his hand away from the hilt of his curved sabre.

One of the men spoke. But Halt couldn't recognise the words.

'Did you get that, Alyss?' he asked. The blonde girl glanced quickly at him, not totally sure of herself.

'It's Nihon-Jan,' she said. 'But it's a pretty strong regional accent. Makes it hard to pick up. I think he's asking who we are.'

'Logical question,' Will said.

The speaker looked at him and spat out a few words. The tone was obvious, even if the meaning wasn't. He was angry.

'Best if Alyss does the talking, Will,' Halt cautioned in a low voice. The Nihon-Jan speaker swung his gaze back to him but as Halt was obviously the leader of this group, he didn't seem to be annoyed that he was talking.

'Ask if he's seen Atsu,' he said and Alyss spoke, choosing her words. The others heard the word 'Atsu' among them. The Nihon-Jan replied dismissively. Obviously he had no idea who Atsu might be. He repeated his original question, more pointedly this time.

'He's still asking who we are,' Alyss said. There was

no need to translate the negative reply to her question about Atsu.

'Tell him we're travellers,' Halt said carefully. 'Our ship was damaged and the crew left us here.'

Alyss gathered her thoughts to frame the necessary sentences. The Nihon-Jan spokesman greeted her words with a grunt. Then he fired another question.

'He wants to know where we're going,' Alyss said. She looked at Halt. 'Should I say anything about Shi—' She stopped herself saying the Emperor's name, realising that the Nihon-Jan would probably recognise it. Instead, she changed her question at the last moment. 'About . . . the Emperor?'

'No,' Halt said quickly. 'We don't know whose side these people are on. Just tell him we're looking for the Kikori.'

It was a tricky situation. The odds were good that these men were opposed to Arisaka. But it was no certainty. If Alyss told them they were looking for Shigeru, they could find themselves made prisoners by the usurper.

Alyss began to translate the statement. But the man had heard the word 'Kikori'. He pounded his own chest repeatedly and shouted at them. The word 'Kikori' was repeated several times.

'I assume you understood that,' Alyss said. 'These are Kikori.'

'The question is, whose side are they on?' Evanlyn asked. But Alyss had no answer for that.

Then the man turned to his followers and made a swift gesture. The Kikori moved in on the camp site, surrounding the five foreigners and making imperious gestures.

The meaning was obvious. They were to come along. Will noticed that the Kikori made no attempt to relieve them of their weapons, and they gestured for the Araluans and Selethen to pick up their rucksacks and other gear. Will made a tentative move towards one of the tents but the Kikori closest to him made a negative gesture and shouted at him. He seemed to repeat the same word over again: *Dammé! Dammé!*

Will shrugged.

'I guess the tent stays,' he said.

Twenty-nine

Horace was studying the collapsed western side of the palisade with the foreman of the work gang assigned to repair it. This section of the work had lagged behind the rest of the repairs. The greater part of the palisade was in good condition now, the walkways had been reinforced and in some places replaced entirely, and the wall timbers refurbished where necessary with new, strong logs.

But the collapsed section had problems beyond the simple ravages of time.

The foreman pointed to a deep channel cut in the ground beneath the ruined palisade.

'This area becomes a water course when the snow melts, *Kurokuma*,' he said. 'The runoff water has gradually undermined the foundations of the wall at this point and washed them away. We'll have to set new foundations.'

Horace scratched his chin. 'And hope it doesn't rain. No point in repairing it if it's all going to be swept away again,' he said thoughtfully. But the foreman shook his head.

'It's too cold for rain. It'll snow. But there'll be no water running through here until spring, when the snows melt. Even then, it would take a few seasons for enough damage to be done. This didn't happen in one or two years.'

Horace studied the man for a moment. He looked confident and he certainly seemed to know his craft.

'Very well. Let's get on with it. I won't be happy until I know the entire palisade is up to strength.'

'We should be able to fix it in a few days. Now the other repairs are almost finished, I can assign extra work gangs to this part.'

'Very well,' said Horace. He gestured for the man to go ahead and turned away, heading back up the slope to the small settlement of cabins that had already been created by the hard-working Kikori.

A small group of the younger men had been excused from labouring work and the commander of Shigeru's personal guard had begun their instruction in the art of Senshi sword technique. He was demonstrating the basic movements to them now, calling a tempo for each cut, block or thrust. Horace stopped to watch, fascinated by the different style. It seemed far more ornate and ritualistic than the drills he was used to. More — he searched for a word and then found it — flamboyant, with its spins and sweeps. But beneath the foreign technique he could discern a similarity of purpose.

Now Moka, the guard commander, ceased his demonstration and called for the Kikori to repeat the sequence. They were armed with swords taken from the raiding party wiped out at Riverside Village.

Moka watched, stony faced, as the young Kikori tried to

emulate his movements. They were sadly unco-ordinated and clumsy in their execution. Reito was standing nearby, watching as well. He saw Horace and moved to join him.

'They're not too good, are they?' Horace said.

Reito shrugged. 'Senshi begin learning this when they're ten years old,' he said. 'It's asking a lot for timber workers to learn it in a few weeks.'

'I wonder if they'll learn in a few months,' Horace said gloomily. 'They'll be facing warriors who *have* been training since they were ten.'

Reito nodded. He thought the same thing. 'But what's the alternative?'

Horace shook his head. 'I wish I knew.' Even if the palisade and the massive cliffs either side kept them safe for the winter, he found he was dreading the confrontation with Arisaka's Senshi army in the spring.

'Sometimes I think we're just postponing the inevitable,' he said. Before Reito could reply, they heard Horace's name being shouted. They turned and looked down the valley, to where they could see the excited figure of Mikeru and two of his young companions. Several of the Kikori stopped their sword drill to turn and look as well. As they did, their instructor shouted angrily at them to get back to work. Sheepishly, they resumed their practice.

'Let's see what Mikeru wants,' Horace said.

'He looks excited,' Reito observed. 'Maybe it's good news.'

'That'd make a change,' Horace said as they walked down the sloping valley floor to meet the young man. Mikeru saw them coming and stopped running. He paused, hunched over with his hands on his knees, while he got his breath back.

'We've found it, *Kurokuma*,' he said, still slightly breathless. For a moment, Horace wasn't sure what he was talking about. His head was still filled with thoughts of the repairs to the palisade and the seemingly hopeless task of turning timber workers into skilled swordsmen in the space of a few months. Then he remembered the task he had set for Mikeru a few days prior.

'The secret exit?' he said. The boy nodded, beaming triumphantly at him.

'You were right, *Kurokuma*! It was there all the time! It's narrow and it's difficult and it twists and turns. But it's there!'

'Let's take a look at it,' Horace said and Mikeru nodded eagerly. He bounded away at a half-run, then stopped after a few metres, looking back to see if Horace and Reito were following. He reminded Horace of an eager puppy, waiting restlessly for its master to catch up.

'Slow down, Mikeru,' he said with a smile. 'It's been there hundreds of years. It's not going anywhere now.'

As the boy had said, the well-hidden path was narrow and difficult. It was a steep gully that ran down through the mountain, carving its way through the rock. In some places, Horace thought, it appeared to have been dug out by hand. Seemingly, the original occupants of Ran-Koshi had found a series of narrow gullies running down the mountain and connected them to form an almost indiscernible path leading down through the rock walls.

They slithered and slid down one steep patch, sending a shower of small pebbles cascading before them, rattling off the rock walls either side.

'Not too easy to come up this way,' Reito remarked.

Horace glanced at him. 'That's how you'd want it. Most people would look at this and not recognise it as a back way into the fortress. And even if an attacker knew about it, I've seen half a dozen spots where ten men could hold off an army.'

'Plenty of places to build deadfalls and traps as well,' Reito said. 'You could only come up here in single file.'

'Same going down,' Horace said casually. 'You'd need a lot of time if you wanted to get a force down here.'

'Down? Why would you want to go down? I mean, it's as well to know this route is here. We'll certainly need to fortify it and set up defensive positions to stop Arisaka using it and catching us by surprise. But why would you want to take a force down?'

He knew Horace couldn't be thinking of this as an escape route for the entire party. There were over four hundred Kikori with them now, many of them women and children. It would take weeks to get everyone down this steep path to the mountain plateau below. And even if you could get everyone down, they would be seen almost as soon as they tried to escape across the open ground at the bottom.

Horace shrugged and didn't answer. It was just a vague idea stirring in his mind. Everything he had done so far had been purely defensive. Rebuild the palisade. Find this track, which instinct had told him must be here, and set up defences. But it was in Horace's nature to attack, to take the fight to the enemy, to surprise them. This track could make that possible. Although how he was going to mount an attack against professional warriors with only hastily trained timber workers, he had no idea. Not for the first time, he recognised the fact that he wasn't a planner or an innovator. He knew how to organise defences. He could study a position, assess its potential weaknesses and move to strengthen and reinforce them. But when it came to devising an unexpected or unorthodox method of attack, he simply didn't know where to begin.

'I need Halt or Will for that,' he muttered to himself.

Reito looked at him curiously. 'What was that, *Kurokuma*?'

Horace shook his head. 'Nothing important, Reito-san. Let's follow this goat track down to the bottom.' He set out after Mikeru. As usual, the young man had forged ahead of them, leaping like a mountain goat from one rock to another.

At the bottom, the narrow track let out onto level ground. The entrance was well concealed. After a few metres, the gully made a sharp turn to the right. To a casual glance, it appeared to be a blind rock wall ending in a shallow indent in the face of the mountain. Shrubs and trees had grown over the entrance as well and larger rocks were piled across it. Horace was willing to bet that hadn't happened by chance. The main entrance to the valley that led up to Ran-Koshi was around a bluff, about three hundred metres away and hidden from sight.

Horace studied the ground.

'Say you brought a hundred men down. Single file. No packs. Just weapons. It would take the best part of a day.

You could keep them concealed here while they formed up. Maybe do that in the dark so there was less chance of being seen.'

Once again he didn't realise he had spoken his thoughts aloud. He was a little surprised when Reito answered him.

'You could do it,' he agreed. 'But who are these hundred men you're talking about? We have barely forty Senshi fit and ready to fight now and Arisaka will have ten times that many.'

Horace nodded wearily. 'I know. I know,' he said. 'I just can't help thinking. If we had a decent fighting force, we might be able to give Arisaka a nasty jolt.'

'And if we had wings, we might be able to fly safely over the top of his army,' Reito replied.

Horace shrugged. 'Yes. I know. If, if and if. Well. We've seen the back door. Let's get back up to the valley.'

Climbing back up took even longer. It was near dusk when Reito and Horace emerged from the tumble of rocks. Their clothes were torn in several places and Horace was bleeding from a long scrape on his right hand, where he had unsuccessfully tried to stop himself sliding back down a steep pile of gravel and shale.

'You were right,' Horace told his companion. 'It would be impossible to climb up there *and* fight a determined defender at the same time.'

'Let's just make sure we've got defenders in place,' Reito said.

Horace nodded. Another detail to take care of tomorrow, he thought.

As they stumbled down the last of the slope leading to the gully, voices began calling out to them. Horace narrowed his eyes against the gathering dark. There seemed to be a large group of people assembled by the open-sided hut that had been constructed as a communal eating house. He led the way towards them but one of the Kikori detached himself from the group and ran to meet them.

'*Kurokuma!* Come quickly. We've caught five spies!'

Thirty

The assembled group of Kikori and Senshi parted before them as Horace and Reito pushed their way through. The young warrior saw the captives, surrounded by an escort of armed Kikori, and his heart lifted with indescribable joy. For the moment, the five newcomers were facing away from him and hadn't noticed his arrival.

'*Kurokuma!*' called the escort leader, shoving through the small crowd to greet Horace. 'A patrol caught them on the lowlands, near the coast. They won't say why they're here. We think they're spies. They're foreigners,' he added, as an afterthought.

'So they are,' Horace replied. 'Perhaps we should have them flogged. That might loosen their tongues.'

At the sound of his voice, the prisoners turned and saw him. There was a moment of non-recognition, due to the fact that he was wearing Nihon-Jan clothing — trousers and a thigh-length Kikori robe over his shirt, held in place by a sash. A fur cap, low down on his head and with side flaps to protect his ears from the cold, completed the outfit.

Then Evanlyn let out a rising shriek of delight.

'Horace!' Before the startled Kikori could stop her, she bounded to him and threw her arms around his neck, hugging him so fiercely that he found it difficult to breathe properly. Two of the men who had been guarding the group moved to drag her away but Horace stopped them with a hand gesture. He was quite enjoying having Evanlyn hug him.

'It's fine,' he said. 'They're friends of mine.' A little reluctantly, he disengaged from Evanlyn's hug, although he was pleased that she remained close by him, her arm possessively around his waist. He grinned at Halt, Will and Alyss as they, too, recognised their old friend in the guise of a shabbily dressed, unkempt Nihon-Jan lumberjack.

'I have no idea how you all got here,' he said. 'But thank god you did!'

The Kikori, still puzzled but now realising the foreigners posed no threat, stood aside as the three Araluans surged forward to greet Horace, slapping his back — in the case of Will and Halt — and hugging him again in the case of Alyss. Evanlyn didn't relinquish her hold around Horace's waist and, when she deemed the hug had gone on long enough, she moved him subtly away from the Courier's embrace.

For a few garbled moments, they all spoke at once, in a mad babble of unanswered questions and declarations of relief. Then Horace noticed an unfamiliar figure, hanging back from the others. He looked more closely.

'Selethen?' he said, surprise in his voice. 'Where did you spring from?'

The tall Arridi stepped forward then and, in the manner of his people, embraced Horace, then made the graceful hand gesture to mouth, brow and mouth.

'Horace,' he said, a broad smile on his face. 'How good to see you alive and well. We've all been worried about you.'

'But . . .' Horace looked from one familiar face to another. 'How did you come to . . .?'

Before he could finish the question, Will interrupted, thinking to clarify matters but only making them more puzzling – as so often happens.

'We were all in Toscana for the treaty signing,' he began, then corrected himself. 'Well, Evanlyn wasn't. She came later. But, when she did, she told us you were missing, so we all boarded Gundar's ship – you should see it. It's a new design that can sail into the wind. But anyway, that's not important. And just before we left, Selethen decided to join us – what with you being an old comrade in arms and all – and . . .'

He got no further. Halt, seeing the confusion growing on Horace's face, held up a hand to stop his babbling former apprentice.

'Whoa! Whoa! Let's take it one fact at a time, shall we? Horace, is there anywhere we can talk? Perhaps we should sit down quietly and catch up with what's been going on.'

'Good idea, Halt,' said Horace, relief evident in his tone.

Will stopped, a little embarrassed as he realised that he had been running off at the mouth.

'Anyway, we're here,' he said. Then the embarrassment

faded and he couldn't stop a broad grin breaking out on his face at the sight of his best friend. Horace responded in kind. He instinctively understood that Will's outburst was the result of intense relief that he, Horace, was safe and well.

Horace introduced his friends to Reito, who bowed in the Nihon-Jan fashion as he greeted each of them. The Araluans bowed but Horace, accustomed now to the action, saw that they were a little stiff and uncertain in their reply. Selethen was the only one who managed a graceful response, combining the bow with the standard Arridi hand gesture. The assembled Nihon-Jan stood by, interested spectators to all this. Once Reito had greeted his friends, Horace introduced them *en masse* to the watching Nihon-Jan. The Kikori and Senshi all bowed. Again, the newcomers responded.

'Lot of bowing goes on in this country,' Will said, out of the corner of his mouth.

'Get used to it,' Horace told him cheerfully. The sense of relief that he felt at the sight of his old friends was almost overwhelming. He had been beginning to feel out of his depth.

The assembled Nihon-Jan, seeing that the newcomers posed no danger, began to drift away.

'We'll go to my cabin to talk,' Horace said. 'Reito-san, would you ask the Emperor if he would see us in half an hour? I'd like to present my friends.'

'Of course, *Kurokuma*,' Reito replied. He bowed briefly and turned to hurry away. Horace responded automatically with a swift bow of his own.

Will, watching, mimicked the action uncertainly, not

sure if he was supposed to join in or not. 'Does everyone bow to everyone here?' he asked.

'Pretty much,' Horace told him.

The one-room cabin that the Kikori had built for Horace was roomy and comfortable. His bedroll was folded away in a corner. A low table had been built and was placed in the middle of the timber floor, while a small charcoal-burning grate created a cheerful circle of warmth. The group of friends sat around the table and exchanged details of events over the past few months.

'I don't know what's happened to Atsu,' Halt said as they came to the end of their tale. 'He's probably going frantic down there at the camp.'

'I'll send someone to let him know you made it here. He won't find any of the local Kikori,' Horace said. 'They're all here with us. The ones who ran into you were a patrol we sent out to watch for Arisaka's men,' Horace said. 'But tell me, why didn't you just say you were looking for me — or Shigeru?'

He addressed the question to Alyss, as she was the Nihon-Jan speaker in the group. She shrugged.

'We weren't totally sure who we were dealing with,' she explained. 'We didn't want to mention the Emperor in case they were allied to Arisaka. I guess they felt the same way about us. They seemed to think we were spies. They probably distrusted us because we're foreign.'

Horace nodded thoughtfully. 'I guess so.' He was still a little overwhelmed by the sight of Alyss with short, dark hair.

'And they never mentioned you,' Will put in. 'All we

could get out of them was that they were taking us to *"Kurokuma"*. We didn't know if that was a place or a person. What does it mean, by the way?'

'I'm told it's a term of great respect,' Horace said, unwilling to admit that he didn't know.

'Tell us more about the Emperor,' Halt said. 'You're obviously impressed with him.'

'I am,' Horace agreed. 'He's a good man. Kind and honest and incredibly courageous. He's trying to better the lot of the common people here and give them a bigger say in things.'

'Which is, of course, why Arisaka hates him,' Halt said.

'Exactly. Shigeru has the courage not to back down from Arisaka, but unfortunately, he isn't a military leader. He was trained as a Senshi, of course. All members of his class are. But he doesn't have the wider military skills — no idea of tactics or strategy.'

'That was Shukin's role, I take it?' Evanlyn said.

A sad look came over Horace's face. 'Yes. He took care of that side of things. I think his death has shaken the Emperor very badly. He needs help.'

'Which you've been providing,' Selethen said quietly. Horace shrugged.

'I couldn't just leave him to fend for himself. His other advisers are courtiers, not war leaders. And any experienced warriors are too junior to plan a major campaign.' His face brightened. 'Which is why I was so glad to see you lot.'

'Perhaps we should go and meet this Emperor of yours,' Halt said.

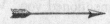

Shigeru greeted them courteously, welcoming them to his country and asking for details of their journey. He apologised for the situation they now found themselves in.

'Arisaka has thrown my country into disarray,' he said sadly. 'I'm afraid I can't welcome you with the honours you deserve.'

Halt smiled at the Emperor. 'We don't deserve too much in the way of honours, your excellency.'

'Any friends of *Kurokuma*,' Shigeru said, indicating Horace with an inclination of his head, 'deserve great honour in this country. Your young friend has served me well, Halto-san.'

On the way to the Emperor's cabin, set at the head of the valley, Horace had quickly explained some of the vagaries of Nihon-Jan pronunciation.

'They seem to find it difficult to finish a word with a hard consonant, like "T",' he said. 'Usually they'll add a vowel after it. So if you don't mind, Halt, I will introduce you as "Halto". Will can be "Wirru".' He paused to explain further. '"L" is not a sound they're totally comfortable with, either.'

'I suppose that'll make me "Arris"?' Alyss said and Horace nodded.

'What about Selethen and me?' Evanlyn asked.

Horace considered it for a moment. 'The L's in your name will probably be a little slurred,' he said. 'And they'll pronounce all three syllables in your names with equal emphasis. You won't be E-*van*-lyn or Sel-*eth*-en, as we say them. They don't stress any one syllable more than the other. They'll say all three in a sort of staccato rhythm.'

He had proved to be correct. Shigeru listened attentively as Horace introduced his friends, using the adapted names he had given them, and then repeated them carefully. Of course, the polite term 'san' was added to each name as well.

After the formalities were taken care of, Shigeru sent for tea and they all sipped gratefully at the hot drink. There was a sharp edge in the weather — the heavy snows would soon be starting.

Horace regarded his cup. Green tea was all right, he thought. But it wasn't his favourite beverage.

'I don't suppose you brought any coffee with you?' he asked the two Rangers.

'We've got some,' Will replied and as Horace's eyes brightened, he continued, 'But it's all at our camp site on the coast.'

'Oh. Just when you got my hopes up. I'll send men to bring your gear up here,' Horace said.

Shigeru had been following the exchange with a smile. Horace's relief was obvious now that his friends were here — particularly the older, bearded man. Shigeru knew that Horace had taken on a lot after Shukin's death and he had worried it might be too much of a burden for such a young man. Now, he could share that burden, the Emperor thought. And he instinctively felt confidence in the abilities of this Halto-san to find a way to oppose Arisaka. Horace had told him a great deal about the enigmatic Ranger over the past weeks.

'*Kurokuma* has been missing his coffee,' Shigeru said.

'Your highness?' It was the younger of the two Rangers, obviously with a question, and Shigeru nodded for him to continue. 'What is this name you've given him? *Kurokuma?*'

'It's a title of great respect,' the Emperor replied gravely.

'Yes. So Horace told us. But what does it mean?'

'I think,' Alyss began uncertainly, 'it has something to do with a bear? A black bear?'

Shigeru inclined his head towards her. 'You have an excellent understanding of our language, Arris-san,' he told her.

She flushed a little and bowed in response to the compliment.

Horace, who had been trying to find out the meaning of *Kurokuma* for some time now, was pleased to hear the translation.

'Black bear,' he repeated. 'It's undoubtedly because I'm so terrible in battle.'

'I'd guess so,' Will put in. 'I've seen you in battle and you're definitely terrible.'

'Perhaps,' said Halt quickly, heading off any further exchange between them, 'we might take a tour of the defences. We've taken up too much of his excellency's time.'

'Please, Halto-san, call me Shigeru. I don't feel like an excellency in these mountains.' His gaze travelled round the others. 'All of you, please, call me Shigeru-san. It will save a lot of bowing and scraping.'

His smile embraced them and they all murmured acknowledgement. Then, as they began to rise to their feet, he held up a hand.

'Princess Ev-an-in,' he said, 'perhaps you and Arris-san

can stay and talk further. I would like to learn more about your father and his Kingdom of Araluen.'

'Or course, your exc—' Evanlyn began, then stopped herself at his admonishing finger. 'I mean, of course, Shigeru-san.'

Thirty-one

First order of business was to inspect the progress of repairs to the palisade.

Halt was silent for several minutes as he studied the weakened western section. The Kikori work gang assigned there were busy digging foundations for new vertical beams. They were well organised and the work was proceeding smoothly. The Kikori, after generations of cutting and hauling the immense mountain trees, were used to working together, with minimum confusion. Everyone was assigned a task and carried it out efficiently. Will watched one group as they went about raising a massive baulk of timber over one of the foundation holes. They worked smoothly and efficiently, reacting instantly to instructions shouted by their foreman.

'They're well disciplined,' Will commented.

Horace nodded. 'Yes. They co-operate well. I'd say it's because they need to work as a team when they fell really large trees and then move them down the mountains.

Each man has to be able to depend on the men next to him.'

'Horace,' Halt interrupted, 'just stop them for a moment, will you? Stop them from what they're doing.'

Horace looked at him in surprise, then called to the foreman and told him to let the men stand down. He turned back to Halt.

'Is something wrong, Halt?' he asked and the Ranger shook his head.

'No. No. We just might have an opportunity here.' His eyes narrowed as he studied the damaged section. Then he seemed to come to a decision. 'How many men does Arisaka have? And how long before they get here?'

'Five or six hundred warriors, as near as our scouts can figure,' Horace told him. 'The bulk of his army is about three weeks away. We forced them into a long detour when we cut the footbridge down. But if he runs true to form, he'll send a party on ahead at double time to try to get in here before the snows block the valley.'

Halt nodded. It was what he had expected. 'So we might expect a party of maybe a hundred men sometime in the next ten days?'

'That's right. It could be sooner, but I doubt it. Even travelling light and with no real baggage, it's difficult country.'

'And if we could give them a bloody nose, it would be helpful,' Halt said.

Again, Horace agreed. 'Any reduction to Arisaka's numbers would be helpful.'

'All right. Here's what we'll do. Stop the repairs on that section. Patch it up but do it badly. Use the old rotten timbers that were there. Make it an obvious weak point.'

Horace nodded thoughtfully. 'You're planning to concentrate their attack in one area?' He wasn't sure if it was a good idea, but he'd never known Halt to have a bad one.

'A little more than that. Inside the weakened section, build a second wall — make it U-shaped and a little lower than the palisade so they can't see it. We'll let them create a breach. When they charge through, they'll find they've got walls on three sides — strong ones this time. We'll have them concentrated in one area and we can really do some damage to them. We'll have logs and rocks on the palisade walkway so that once they're inside, we can drop them into the breach and trap them. At least, we'll make it hard for them to retreat.'

Selethen was nodding, his eyes roving the palisade and the steep stone wall beside it.

'We could also pile up rocks and logs on that rock face,' he added. 'It'll be easy enough to build a retaining wall to hold them in place. Then, once the enemy are inside, we collapse the retaining wall and bring an avalanche down on them.'

Halt glanced quickly at the Arridi. 'Nice,' he said.

For the first time in several weeks Horace could smile at the thought of the impending conflict. There would be little hand-to-hand combat involved. The Kikori would have the advantage of fighting from the top of the palisade. Rocks, spears and logs would be effective weapons. They could destroy any small attacking force before they ever got to close quarters.

'I'm so glad you lot turned up,' he said.

'At the very least, we'll cut Arisaka's numbers down,'

Halt said. 'The trick will only work once, but it'll slow him down and by then the snows might be here.'

Horace beckoned the foreman over and they explained the new plan to him. His eyes lit up as he grasped the idea and he nodded eagerly, smiling at Halt and Selethen as the authors of the stratagem. There was no need to give him detailed plans for the new section of wall. He would be more than capable of planning that. They left him to reorganise the workers and moved on to watch the small group of Senshi who were practising their swordcraft. As Horace had been, the three new arrivals were impressed with the speed and precision of the Nihon-Jan warriors' technique.

'They're good,' Selethen said. 'Very good.'

Horace looked at him. 'Man for man, I'd say they're better than our Araluan knights,' he said. It pained him to admit it, but the fact was unavoidable. 'Our best warriors would be pretty much equal to their best, but it's the next level down where they hold the advantage. The rank and file Senshi are more skilled than the average graduate from an Araluan Battleschool.'

Halt agreed with him. 'It makes sense,' he said. 'You told us they start practising when they're ten years old. Our Battleschools don't accept pupils until they're fifteen.'

Selethen stroked his beard. 'I agree,' he said. 'As individuals, they're impressive.'

The words fanned a spark of vague memory in Will's mind. He frowned as he tried to place it, but for the moment it escaped him. He looked away, distracted, to the workers down the valley, who were climbing over the palisade, placing new timbers in position and now working on the logs that would form the new inner wall section. He noted how well they worked in harmony with each other. There seemed to be no wasted effort and no confusion in their actions. He shook his head, a little annoyed, as he tried to retrieve the tantalising thought that was stirring in his memory. What had Selethen just said? *As individuals, they're impressive.* That related somehow to the sight of the disciplined teams of Kikori at work.

'It'll come to me,' he told himself, and hurried to catch up with the others.

Once again, Moka was working with his small group of Kikori, trying to turn them into swordsmen. There was some improvement, Horace thought. The Kikori were fit and well co-ordinated. But the gap between these new trainees and the Senshi they had just been watching was all too evident.

'How many fit Senshi do you have, ready to fight?' Halt asked.

'Maybe forty. Enough to hold the palisade against one attack. But after that . . .' Moka gestured doubtfully. He knew Arisaka would not be daunted by early casualties. Once he had overwhelming numbers in place, he would keep throwing his men at the wooden wall.

'And Arisaka has . . . how many? Five hundred?'

'Something like that.' Horace's tone was dejected. No matter what tactics they could devise to delay Arisaka, sooner or later, they would have to face his large, expertly trained warriors.

'And you've got two hundred Kikori who'll fight?' Selethen asked and, as Horace nodded, he added, 'What about weapons?'

'Axes,' Horace said. 'Some knives. And most of them

- 271 -

have spears. We did find a stockpile of old weapons further up the valley when we first got here. The place has been used as a fortress more than once over the years. But they were old and mostly rusty. I wouldn't trust the temper of the blades, they're hardly usable.'

Halt looked at the sky. There were grey clouds scudding low above them, their bellies swollen with moisture.

'Let's hope it snows soon,' he said.

'So, how are things between you and Will?' Horace asked. Alyss turned to him and a slow smile lit up her face.

'Lovely,' she said. 'Just lovely.'

It was two days since the Araluans and Selethen had arrived at Ran-Koshi. In that time, the work that Halt and Selethen suggested had advanced well. As Horace had remarked earlier, the Kikori were a useful group to have with you if you needed to build in timber. The young warrior had felt a sense of relief at being able to hand over these details to older, more experienced heads.

'I'm not a planner,' he had said to himself. 'I'm a doer.'

Today, Halt and the Arridi *Wakir* were supervising the placement of the retaining wall Selethen had suggested. Evanlyn was cloistered in another long discussion with Shigeru. The Emperor was interested in learning about the social structure in Araluen. It was a far less oppressive hierarchy than the one that had existed in Nihon-Ja for centuries and he thought he might be able to use it as a model for his new society.

Horace and Alyss, finding themselves with no pressing duties, had taken the opportunity to have a few hours off together. The two were old friends. They had grown up together as orphans in the Ward at Castle Redmont and they were at ease in each other's company. They had taken their midday meal to a rock outcrop above the valley, where they could relax and look down upon all the work going on. The sounds of hammering and sawing, and the cries of the Senshi drill masters, mingled together and drifted to them.

'You know,' Horace said, 'when we were riding home from Macindaw that time, I thought I was going to have to take you two and knock your heads together. It was so obvious that there was something going on and neither of you would admit it.' He smiled at the memory. He was delighted with the relationship that had developed between Alyss, whom he thought of as a sister, and Will, his best friend.

'Yes,' Alyss said, 'each of us was afraid to say anything in case the other person didn't feel the same way.'

Horace laughed quietly at the memory. 'Trouble is, you two think too much. I said that at the time. I believe if you feel that way about someone, you should just come out and say it.'

'Is that right?' Alyss said and Horace nodded, doing his best to look wise and knowledgeable.

'Always the best plan,' he said definitely.

'So, how're things between you and the princess?' Alyss asked abruptly and was delighted to see that Horace's face went a shade of pink as he hesitated to answer.

'Well . . . ah . . . what do you mean, me and the princess?' he managed to blurt out after a few seconds. But the hesitation told Alyss all she needed to know.

'Oho!' she said. 'I thought as much. Why, she could barely keep her hands off you when we first arrived! She was all over you like a coat of paint.'

'She was not!' Horace insisted.

'Oh, come on! I'm not blind. She went rushing to you, threw her arms around you and hugged you.'

'So did you,' Horace pointed out but she waved that aside.

'I didn't re-crack any of your ribs,' she said. 'Besides, do you think it's completely normal for the Crown Princess to set off across the world on a quest to find one knight who's gone missing?'

He dropped his gaze and she saw a shy grin forming on his face.

'Well, maybe, since you put it that way . . .'

Alyss hooted with delight. 'So there is something between you! I knew it! I told Will but he wouldn't believe it.'

'Well, let's not make too much noise about it, all right?' Horace said. 'It mightn't come to anything. It's just that, before I left Araluen, we had been . . . seeing quite a bit of each other.'

'I guess that's why Duncan sent you away,' she teased and was instantly sorry when she saw the doubt cloud his face.

'Do you think so? That did occur to me. After all, she's the princess and I'm a nobody . . .'

She took his arm and shook it, annoyed with herself for putting this doubt in his mind.

'Horace! You are definitely not a nobody! How could you say that? Duncan would be happy to have you paying court to his daughter!'

'But I was an orphan. I've got no noble background . . .' he began but she cut him off.

'Duncan doesn't care about that! He's no snob. And you are a hero, don't you realise? You're the foremost young knight in the Kingdom. He'd be delighted to have you as a son-in-law.'

Now panic flared in Horace's eyes at her words. 'Whoa! Not so fast! His son-in-law? Who said anything about being his son-in-law?'

'It was just a passing thought,' Alyss said. 'Figure of speech. Nothing more than that.' Horace relaxed a little but she smiled inwardly. If Horace seriously had no thoughts in that direction, he would have simply laughed off the idea. I knew it, she thought. I wonder if he knows it too?

Looking for a way to change the subject, Horace cast around and his gaze lit on Will. The young Ranger was lower down the valley, sitting on the ground, deep in conversation with a group of the older Kikori.

'What's he up to?' he asked.

There was a lot of gesticulating and sketching on the ground with sticks. Hands would wave, voices would babble, adjustments would be made to whatever was drawn and then the group would reach agreement, nodding and laughing, slapping each other on the shoulders as they reached a common point of view.

Alyss was still smiling to herself over what she considered to be Horace's slip. 'Don't know. He's been quiet for the past two days. Wanders off a lot by himself. Something seems to be wrong. I've asked him but he shies away from the subject.'

But Horace had seen this sort of behaviour from his friend several times before and he knew what was happening.

'There's nothing wrong,' he said. 'He's planning something.'

Thirty-two

In the small cabin she shared with Alyss, Evanlyn was hunched over a map drawn on a sheet of linen paper, chewing distractedly on one of the fine brushes that the Nihon-Jan used as pens. It was late. The single lantern on the table left dark shadows in the corners of the room, and was really inadequate to allow her to read the finer details of the map. She had contemplated lighting another lantern but Alyss was curled up on her mattress against one wall and Evanlyn didn't want to disturb her.

The two girls had spent more time in each other's company since arriving at Ran-Koshi. They were the only two females in their group, and now that they were surrounded by an even wider group of warriors and timber workers they tended to be thrown together. There were women in the Kikori settlement, of course, but they treated the two foreigners with awed respect, and the language differences, along with the heavy regional accent of the Kikori, made it difficult to become close to them.

It couldn't be said that Alyss and Evanlyn had become good friends. But they were both making an effort to get along with each other — aside from the occasional moment of friction. Had they been close friends, Evanlyn probably would have lit another lantern. But, because they tended to tiptoe round each other, she didn't want to give Alyss any cause for complaint.

She rubbed her eyes and leaned closer to the map. She wished she had a normal-height table and a comfortable chair. These low Nihon-Jan tables and benches were hard on the knees and the back. She heard a rustle of bedclothes as Alyss turned over.

'What are you doing?' the tall girl said. Her voice was thick with sleep.

'Sorry,' Evanlyn said instantly. 'I didn't mean to wake you.'

'You didn't wake me,' Alyss replied. 'The light did.' Then, realising that Evanlyn might take this as a sign that she was annoyed, she added quickly, 'That was a joke.'

'Oh . . . well, sorry, anyway,' Evanlyn told her. 'Go back to sleep.'

But Alyss was sitting up. She shivered in the chill mountain night and hastily draped a Kikori sheepskin coat around her shoulders. Then, disdaining to rise, she moved on all fours across the room to sit beside Evanlyn.

'Light another lantern,' she said. 'We'll go blind trying to read that in the dark.'

Evanlyn hesitated, but Alyss gestured impatiently for her to do as she suggested.

'You might as well,' she said. 'I'll never get back to sleep wondering what you're doing.'

Evanlyn nodded and lit a second lantern, pulling it close to the first so that the light was doubled. Alyss moved a little closer and studied the map with her.

'Where did this come from?' she asked. She could see it was a chart of Ran-Koshi and the country to the north.

'Shigeru and I drew it up, with advice from Toru and some of the other Kikori. Of course, the general lie of the land here was no secret. The only unknown factor was the exact location of Ran-Koshi.' She tapped a finger on the section of the map that showed the valley and its steep surrounding walls.

Alyss nodded thoughtfully, then she pointed to a broad, featureless expanse directly to the north of the valley.

'What's this?' She read the name lettered on it. 'Mizu-Umi Bakudai?'

'It's a huge lake. And round here, on the far side, is the province where the Hasanu live.'

'I've heard people mention them several times. Who are the Hasanu?'

There was a teapot on the table and Evanlyn reached for it to pour herself a cup of green tea. 'Like some? It's still quite hot.'

Alyss shook her head. 'I'm fine.'

'The Hasanu are a wild mountain tribe that live in this remote area on the other side of the lake. Some people think they're monsters. There are apparently a lot of legends about weird mountain creatures, trolls and demons and such. But Shigeru thinks that's superstition. He believes the Hasanu are human. They're simple folk. They're said to be much taller than the average Nihon-Jan and covered in long, reddish body hair.'

'How attractive,' Alyss commented.

Evanlyn allowed herself a brief smile. 'Yes. But they are apparently amazingly loyal to their lord, a Senshi noble called Nimatsu, and he's loyal to Shigeru. And they're quite formidable warriors,' she added meaningfully.

'Hmmm. So if Shigeru could recruit them, he might have a reasonable force to engage Arisaka,' Alyss said. Like all of the Araluans, she was aware of the shortcomings of the Kikori as warriors. 'Are there many of them?'

'Thousands,' Evanlyn told her. 'That's the beauty of it. There are plenty of clans loyal to Shigeru who would oppose Arisaka, but they're all small in numbers and they're not organised. Arisaka's supported by his own clan, the Shimonseki, and one other, the Umaki clan. Numerically, they're the two largest clans in the country, so he has a strong, co-ordinated power base.

'But if we could call on the Hasanu for help, we'd have Arisaka badly outnumbered. Which might encourage the other clans to stand up for Shigeru. Only problem is . . .'

She paused and Alyss finished for her. 'The Hasanu are on the far side of this huge lake.'

'That's right. And the path around the lake goes through mountains even wilder than the ones here. Shigeru says it would take at least two months to get there and another two back.'

'By which time, things will probably be all over here,' Alyss said and Evanlyn nodded, wordlessly.

The two of them studied the map in silence for a few minutes. Then Alyss said slowly, 'Why not take a leaf out of Halt's book? Go across the lake, not around it.'

She was referring to Halt's tactic of sailing north along

the coast from Iwanai, and cutting out weeks of hard travel over the mountains. But now Evanlyn pointed out the obvious fault in her plan.

'We could do that if we had a ship,' she said, but Alyss shook her head, her excitement mounting as the idea grew.

'We don't need a ship. We need a kayak.'

'A what?' Evanlyn asked. The word was unfamiliar to her.

Alyss took the brush from her and began sketching quickly on the margin of the map, laying out a rough design of a long, narrow boat.

'A kayak. It's a small, light boat — with a timber frame and an oiled linen or canvas covering. The Skandians use them for fishing. I've actually got one back at Redmont. I use it on the river and lakes there. It's great exercise,' she added.

Evanlyn studied the rough drawing critically.

'Could you build one?' she asked.

'No,' Alyss told her and Evanlyn's spirits sank, only to rise again when Alyss continued, 'But I'll bet the Kikori could, if I showed them the rough idea.' She pulled the map around so she could see it more clearly and traced a path across the lake with her forefinger. 'We could do it in easy stages,' she said. 'There are plenty of islands where we could camp at night.'

'We?' Evanlyn asked and Alyss looked up to meet her gaze.

'Well, of course "we". They're going to need every available man they have here once Arisaka's army arrives. There's not really a lot we can achieve here.' She saw Evanlyn was about to protest and went on quickly, 'Oh,

I'm sure you could knock a few of them over with that sling of yours. But if we did this, we'd be doing something much more valuable! Come on,' she said, after a brief pause, 'in the back of your mind, you always intended to do this, didn't you?'

'I suppose so,' Evanlyn said.

'Then let's do it together! I'll come with you. You might need an interpreter and I can handle a kayak. Plus we won't need an escort if we do it this way. We'll be perfectly safe on the lake and that means we won't leave Halt and the others short-handed.'

Evanlyn thought for a few seconds, then squared her shoulders, reaching a decision.

'Why not?' Then she thought further. 'I wonder what Halt will say when we put it to him?'

Alyss shrugged. 'Well, it's such a logical idea, he can hardly say no, can he?'

'No!' said Halt. 'No, no, no — and, just in case you missed it the first time, no.'

'Why not?' Evanlyn said, her voice rising in pitch to indicate her anger. 'It's a perfectly logical solution.'

Halt regarded her as if she'd lost her senses. 'Can you imagine what your father would say to me if he heard I'd let you go haring off on this half-baked expedition?'

Evanlyn shrugged. 'Well, for a start it's not half-baked. We've planned it pretty well.' In fact, she and Alyss had sat up for most of the rest of the previous night noting down details and equipment they would need for the trip.

'And secondly,' she continued, 'if we don't do it, my father will never hear about it anyway because we'll all be dead.'

'Don't be ridiculous!' Halt snorted.

'Halt, you've got to face facts,' Alyss put in. 'Evanlyn is right. If we don't get help Arisaka will overrun this place in the summer. Oh, we'll hold out for a while, of course. But sooner or later, his men will break through. This is our only chance.'

'I expected more sense from you, Alyss,' he said coldly. 'I know Evanlyn tends to go off on wild ideas, but I'm surprised at you. What do you think Pauline would say about this?'

Colour flared in Alyss's cheeks as he spoke. Then she replied, measuring her words carefully so that anger would not get the best of her.

'What would you say to Pauline if it was *her* idea?' she replied.

Halt hesitated. They all knew he would never dare to tell Pauline she was reckless or hare-brained.

Seeing his hesitation, Alyss continued quickly. 'Tell me, Halt, aside from the simple fact that you'd be worried about us, what's the flaw in this plan?'

He opened his mouth to reply, then paused again. Truth be told, there was no flaw, other than the fact that he hated to see the girls place themselves in danger. He looked at them for a few seconds and realised that that fact was not a sufficiently good reason to reject the plan. Both girls had been in dangerous situations before. Both would be in dangerous situations again. Neither of them were shrinking violets. And Evanlyn was right. If she and Alyss went, they wouldn't be taking any fighting men away from the valley. They'd need help scaling the sheer cliffs that led down to the lake. But once that was done, the Kikori who helped them could return.

'I just . . . I . . . I don't like it,' he said.

Evanlyn stepped closer to him and placed her hand over his. 'We don't ask you to like it,' she said. 'I don't like the idea that we'll be leaving you and Will and Horace to fight Arisaka with a bunch of half-trained lumberjacks as an army. These are hard times and we have to make tough decisions.'

He let go a deep sigh. The girls were right and he knew it.

'All right,' he said. The two faces before him were suddenly wreathed in excited smiles and he added heavily, 'But God help me when Will and Horace find out about it.'

Whatever answer the girls might have made was cut off by the sound of shouting outside Halt's cabin. Then the door flew open and young Mikeru burst in, too excited to exhibit the normally impeccable manners of the Nihon-Jan.

'Halto-san! Come quickly! Arisaka's men are here!'

Thirty-three

Mikeru's excited warning was a little premature. Arisaka's army were not actually charging up the valley, as he implied. But the first elements had been sighted, just a day away.

As Horace had surmised, Arisaka had repeated his earlier tactic and sent a fast-travelling advance party ahead of his main force. The Kikori scouts had counted a hundred armed Senshi, carrying minimal baggage and moving towards the valley at a steady jog.

'How did they know we're here?' Horace asked.

Halt shrugged. 'They may not know your exact location. They're probably just tracking you. After all, a party as large as this one would leave plenty of signs for a halfway decent tracker.'

'So what is our best move now, Halto-san?' Shigeru asked. They were gathered in his cabin to discuss this latest eventuality. Shigeru, observing how Horace deferred to the bearded Ranger, and knowing Reito's limitations as a combat commander, had questioned Horace at length about Halt's background and experience. Horace had left him in no doubt that they were lucky to have such an experienced tactician at their disposal and Shigeru had appointed the Ranger in command of the defence of Ran-Koshi.

'The palisade is repaired,' Halt said. 'And the trap at the western end is just about complete. Another half day should see that done. I suggest we sit tight behind the palisade, wait for them to attack and then bring down our avalanche on top of them.'

'Will they attack?' Shigeru asked. 'Perhaps they will wait for Arisaka's main force to catch up.'

Halt shook his head. 'I doubt it,' he said. 'It makes no sense to come racing across country after us only to sit down and wait when they eventually catch up. Arisaka knows that the snow is coming.' They all glanced at the open doorway. It was snowing outside. With each day, the flakes became bigger and heavier and the snowfalls longer. Already the cover on the ground was eight to ten centimetres deep. 'He'll want his men to hit us before the real storms come. After all, he knows you only have thirty or forty warriors with you.'

'There are around two hundred Kikori men as well,' Will said but Halt made a dismissive gesture.

'From everything the Emperor and Reito-san have told us, Arisaka won't be expecting them to fight. That could give us a big advantage.'

'If they *will* fight,' Horace said gloomily. He worried that when the time came, the Kikori might be affected by centuries of tradition and history. They had rarely rebelled against the Senshi in the past and when they did, the results had been catastrophic. He felt the chances were high that they would, at the last minute, be overwhelmed by their sense of assumed inferiority. Assisting the Emperor to escape and standing up against the highly trained Senshi warriors of Arisaka's army were two entirely different matters.

'They'll fight,' Will said firmly and Halt turned a questioning eye on him.

'You seem sure of that. What have you and Selethen been up to? You've been spending a lot of time with the Kikori.'

Will and the Arridi leader exchanged a quick glance. Then Will shook his head.

'Early days yet,' he said. 'Just an idea we're working on. We'll tell you when the time is right.'

'In any event,' Halt said, dismissing the matter for the time being and returning to the point Horace had raised, 'the Kikori will be fighting from behind a defensive position, not facing the Senshi in open combat. That'll make a difference. All they'll have to do is keep shoving them back down off the wall.'

'As easy as that?' Horace said, grinning in spite of his earlier misgivings. But he thought Halt had a point: fighting from behind a defensive position was less daunting than facing an enemy on an open battlefield. With any luck, not many of Arisaka's warriors would get close enough for individual combat.

'When do you think they'll attack, Halt?' Selethen asked.

'Our scouts say they should be here late tomorrow.

I would assume they'll size up the situation, rest for the night, then hit us first thing the following morning.'

Selethen nodded agreement with the estimate, but Shigeru was a little surprised at the speed things were moving.

'So soon?' he said. 'Won't they have . . . preparations to make?' he asked vaguely.

'They don't have any heavy weapons or siege equipment with them,' Halt said. 'After all, they had no real idea that we would find us in a ready-made fortress like this one. My guess is they'll spend the night getting a few scaling ladders ready then try and rush us. After all, they have nothing to gain by waiting.'

The sky was overcast and heavy with clouds. In the east, through a gap between mountain peaks, the sun could be made out as a red, watery ball rising into the sky. A cold wind blew up the valley, bringing snowflakes with it.

Above the soft keening of the wind, Halt could hear the rapid tread of feet, crunching on the rocky ground before them.

'Here they come,' he muttered, as Arisaka's advance party, moving in three uneven columns, rounded the last bend before the palisade. He turned to Will.

'Don't waste arrows on the ones at the foot of the wall. Rocks and spears will do for them. Save your shots for any who make it to the top. They're the ones we need to stop, before they get a real foothold.'

Will nodded. They were pacing the timber walkway on the inner side of the palisade. Shigeru's few Senshi warriors were in defensive positions. Beside them and behind them, the Kikori crouched, out of sight. Some had their heavy axes ready, but most were armed with spears or long poles they had cut to use as pikes. The tips were carved into points which had been hardened in fires the night before. Every five metres, piles of large, jagged rocks stood ready for use against the attackers.

'Stay down, Kikori,' Halt said quietly, as he passed the crouching timber workers. They grinned nervously up at him and he added, 'We'll soon be giving Arisaka a very unwelcome surprise.'

They reached the decrepit western end of the palisade. Here ten Senshi and the same number of Kikori were stationed on the planked walkway behind the badly patched, dilapidated wall.

'They'll concentrate here once they realise,' Halt called. 'Be ready to get off the wall as soon as you feel it's going.'

The mixed group of defenders nodded, their faces serious, their thoughts focused on the coming fight. Halt surveyed the new inner wall with satisfaction. It was lower, but much sturdier than the old palisade – altogether a much more defensible position. He glanced up to the piled rocks, earth and timber balanced precariously above on the rock wall. The Kikori had contrived to cover the rocks with branches and bushes, even leaving one small sapling springing out from the mound so that it appeared more natural. Looking carefully, he could just make out the ropes trailing away from the deadfall.

'Get ready!' It was Horace's voice. He was at the mid-point of the palisade. He had his shield on his left arm. The unfamiliar shape of a Nihon-Jan *katana* was in his right hand. Behind them, they heard and felt feet on the ladder that led up to the walkway from below. They both turned to see Shigeru, in lacquered leather armour, stepping onto the walkway, closely followed by Reito.

'Your highness, I'd really prefer it if you'd stay back from the fighting,' Halt told him. He knew Shigeru was no expert with the sword. Capable, perhaps, but expert? Never.

'Your preference is noted, Halto-san,' said Shigeru, making no move to retire back down the ladder. Halt met his gaze for a few seconds, then shrugged.

'Well, I tried,' he said.

At a shouted order, the attacking force suddenly broke into a run. They had no particular formation. They spread out in a rough line as far as the narrow valley walls would allow. The line was three or four men deep. Halt made out five rudimentary scaling ladders — each one nothing more than a single thick sapling trunk, notched to accept crosspieces, which were then bound in place to act as rungs. At least another ten men were carrying ropes and grapnels. The plan was obviously to assault the wall at fifteen or sixteen different points at once to overextend the thirty-odd Senshi who could be seen defending the palisade.

The attackers had no idea that a hundred Kikori were crouched below the wooden ramparts. The first three ladders crashed against the wall almost simultaneously at three different points and Shigeru's men moved to bar the way to the men climbing them. Halt waited until each ladder had several men on it.

'Kikori! Now!' he yelled.

The waiting timber workers rose to their feet with a wordless roar of defiance. Rocks showered over the ramparts, hurled down into the mass of Senshi at the bases of the ladders. The first attacker to reach the top of a ladder cut at a Kikori, who ducked the whistling blade just in time. Moka thrust with his sword and the man screamed and plummeted off the ladder.

Elsewhere, Horace blocked another attacker's sword with his shield. Before he could retaliate, however, a wild-eyed Kikori spearman shoved him aside and buried his spear in the Senshi's shoulder. With a screech of pain, the man fell back onto his comrades, massed below.

A third ladder was sent toppling as four Kikori pikemen thrust their long poles against it, shoving it sideways until it crashed over. The Senshi closest to the top managed to spring onto the rampart. It was only a momentary respite. He barely regained his balance before a Kikori axe sheared through his armour. He toppled forward, crumpled over the rampart. Another defender shoved a spear handle under his shoulders and levered him back, sending him crashing back to the side he came from.

Grapnels were rattling against the walls now as Arisaka's men tried to clamber up hand over hand. Halt heard Reito and Moka, the two senior members of the Emperor's Senshi, shouting instructions to the defenders, and he knew the gist of their words. *Let them get at least halfway up before you cut the ropes!* They had determined this strategy the night before. A man falling from three or four metres stood a good chance of being injured — particularly if his comrades below were brandishing weapons.

At the midpoint of the wall, Halt saw one of Shigeru's bodyguard engaged in swordplay with an attacker who had made it over the wall. The still forms of two Kikori were at the attacker's feet. As Halt watched, an arrow slammed into the defender's chest and sent him staggering back off the rampart.

Before the attacking warrior could take advantage of his momentary respite, Selethen's tall form moved gracefully to the attack. His curved sabre cut into the gap between the Senshi's helmet and the neck piece of his armour.

Satisfied that the threat had been taken care of, Halt glanced around and saw another defender, a Kikori axeman this time, fall to the planks with an arrow in his chest. The Ranger searched the valley below the wall. Five Senshi, armed with the long, asymmetrical recurve bows favoured by the Nihon-Jan, had stopped some thirty metres behind their comrades and were picking off the defenders.

'Will!' he shouted. His apprentice had moved away to cut through a grapnel rope with his saxe knife. Now he looked, saw Halt's outstretched arm pointing to the group of archers and slipped the bow off his shoulder.

'You from the left. Me from the right!' shouted Halt and Will nodded. Once before, they had made the mistake of shooting at the same enemy in a battle. Now both long-bows sang their dreadful song and the Senshi at either end of the line of archers staggered back, staring in horror at the arrows that had punched through their leather armour as if it weren't there. Before their comrades registered the fact that they were down, the Rangers dropped the next two within a heartbeat of each other. The fifth man searched in vain for the source of these deadly return shots. He had an arrow nocked, ready to draw and shoot as soon as he saw his opponent. He never managed it. Will's third arrow slammed into him. He dropped his bow, clutching at the terrible shaft, then fell and lay still.

Now a captain among the attackers, realising that the first blind, formless rush had failed, was taking stock of the situation. He saw the patched and sagging western section of the palisade and realised this was an opportunity. He gestured for two men to pick up a fallen ladder and follow him. Along the way, he gathered three more, equipped with grapnels and ropes. The hastily assembled assault party ran along the base of the wall, dodging rocks that showered down from above, to the weakened section. As they went, the captain rallied more men until at least thirty Senshi were following him. He gestured at the single-trunk ladder, then at the rotting beams of the wall.

'Use it as a battering ram! Smash through the wall!' he yelled. Half a dozen more men, suddenly seeing what he was about, joined the two Senshi wielding the log. They charged at the wall and, with one of them counting tempo, slammed it again and again into the brittle timbers of the palisade. Two of the old logs shattered and split, a third sagged away at the next strike of the ram. More rocks hailed down on them, but the defenders' aim was not as accurate as before. Panic, the captain thought. He screamed at the men with grapnels, pointing to the top of the palisade.

'Don't try to climb it! Pull it down!' he ordered. The grapnels whirred around, then sailed upwards, each one trailing a tail of rope behind it. One clattered back but two bit into the wood and held fast. Instantly, eight or nine men tailed onto the ropes and heaved and strained backwards. A three-metre section of the wooden parapet gave way and came crashing down in a cloud of dust and splinters. The men heaving on the rope staggered and fell but recovered quickly and cast again. The grapnel that had missed with the first cast was now solidly buried in the timber at the top of the wall. As the attackers further down the wall saw what was happening, more of them streamed to join the assault on the western section. The tree-trunk battering ram smashed into the wall again, tearing a rent between two of the upright timbers. More men joined in the assault, swinging the ram with even greater force.

Rocks and spears showered down on them now but the attackers were mad with battle rage and they knew that the section of wall was almost breached. They could see the defenders deserting the ruined wall, running in panic to escape before it came crashing down. Yelling their battle cries, they surged forward triumphantly as, under the combined force of the ram and four grapnel ropes, the wall finally gave way and a four-metre breach appeared. They clambered up over the shattered timbers, swarming through the gap.

The first men through stopped, bewildered, faced by a new, lower wall that enclosed them on three sides. But the press of their companions behind them forced them forward into the enclosed space. More and more of them poured in before they realised they were in a trap. Horrified, they saw a line of heads appear over the top of the new palisade — at least fifty of them. Then a storm of hurled rocks and spears broke over them — and this time, the defenders seemed to have regained their former accuracy.

'Go forward! Keep going forward!' The captain who had begun the assault was still alive. He brandished his sword now to lead the Senshi to a new attack. There was no way they could get back through the crowded, crammed breach. Their only hope was to scale this new, lower wall in front of them.

As they started forward, he heard a strange cracking, grinding noise from above. Looking up, he saw what appeared to be a section of the mountain wall suddenly tearing loose. A vast pile of rocks, earth and timber tumbled end over end down the wall, bouncing, smashing, crushing anything and everything in its path.

A log smashed the sword from his hand and a jagged rock slammed into him, driving him to his knees. As earth and rock thundered around him, he toppled sideways, knowing the assault had failed — then everything went dark.

The stunned attackers, with almost of a third of their number killed or injured in the trap devised by Halt and Selethen, slowly began to withdraw from the palisade, leaving their fallen comrades behind them. They straggled back down the valley in small groups, to face the wrath of their commander. General Todoki, leader of the advance party and one of Arisaka's most ardent supporters, watched in disbelief as his defeated men shambled out of the valley, bruised, bleeding and disheartened. He screamed at them, his rage making him lose all control and all sense of dignity. For the most part, they ignored him. He hadn't been there with them and they'd left over thirty comrades behind them, without any chance of decent burial.

That night, winter took care of that for them. The snow began in earnest, and by morning, there was nearly two metres piled up in the valley. The pure white carpet obliterated all sign of the previous day's carnage.

Thirty-four

'**H**ow do you propose to get this thing down the cliffs to the lake?' Halt nudged the kayak dubiously with one toe. The narrow craft was nearly four metres long, with a light wooden framework covered by oiled linen, stretched to drumskin-tautness. He'd seen kayaks before. As Alyss had said, she had one herself at Castle Redmont, and this one looked similar, so far as he could remember. The Kikori had done an excellent job constructing it, under Alyss's watchful eye.

'Eiko solved that problem for us,' Evanlyn replied. 'The Kikori will lower it down by rope, doing it a stage at a time.'

They were standing in a half circle around the newly completed boat. Evanlyn and Alyss wore an air of excitement and proprietorial pride. Will and Horace looked extremely doubtful about the whole project. Halt, who had known about it for some time, was more or less resigned to it. But he wasn't enthusiastic.

'That's going to take a bit of handling,' he said. But Alyss put up a hand to stop him saying any more and knelt beside the kayak.

'Aha, that's the beauty of this design. Watch,' she said. She worked two wooden retaining pins out of their sockets and removed one of the four bulkhead sections that created the cross-section profile of the kayak. The ribs that ran the length of the boat collapsed inwards slightly, and the oilskin covering lost some of its tension. She repeated the action with the other three formers and within minutes, the kayak was nothing more than a bundle of light ribs, frames and oilskin. She rapidly gathered them together, then used the oilskin to wrap the ribs into a tight bundle. She stood back from the result — a narrow bundle of long, light wooden stakes.

'There!' she announced. 'We simply collapse it so that it's a much more manageable bundle. Tie a rope round one end and we lower it down the cliffs, hanging vertically.'

Will stepped forward and eyed the narrow bundle critically. When it was assembled, it had looked like a boat. But now the frailty of the design was far more evident. It was nothing more than sticks and cloth.

'Will it float?' he asked doubtfully and Alyss smiled at him. She knew the reason behind his lack of enthusiasm and she couldn't help being a little pleased by it. By the same token, she wasn't going to allow it to go too far. Will might worry about her, and she knew he loved her. But that didn't mean he owned her or could dictate what she might or might not do.

'Of course it will float,' she told him. 'And if it doesn't, we'll just have to come back up the cliffs.'

'Well . . . I don't like it,' Will said.

Horace echoed the sentiment. 'Neither do I.'

'Your dislike for the project will be duly noted,' Evanlyn told them coolly.

'And ignored,' Alyss added. The two girls exchanged a quick smile.

Will opened his mouth to speak further but Selethen stepped in to prevent any unfortunate statements.

'Personally, I think it's a good plan,' he said smoothly. 'What's more, I'll sleep soundly through the winter knowing that there is the prospect of a relieving force arriving in the spring.'

In Arrida, the women of the desert tribes lived in a hostile environment and took their share of dangerous tasks. They often ranged far into the desert, hunting for food and fighting off the predators that attacked their herd animals. He knew these two girls and was confident they had the ability and the courage to carry out the mission they had taken on. And his comment about feeling a sense of comfort at the prospect of a relieving force was the truth. Selethen, like the others, knew that they could not simply occupy this defensive position indefinitely once the snows melted. Arisaka would eventually be victorious, by dint of his overwhelming numbers.

'Yeah . . . well . . . maybe,' Horace said. He was a little surprised that Selethen was supporting the girls. Will looked at Halt.

'What do you think about this, Halt? Are you really going to let them go?'

At the words 'let them' both girls bristled with indignation. But Halt held up a hand and they held their peace for the moment.

'I can't say I'm happy about it,' he began and Will nodded knowingly, glad to see that his mentor was in agreement with him and Horace. But Halt's next words wiped out any sense of satisfaction he might be feeling.

'But I wasn't happy in Arrida when you went off searching for Tug,' he said. His gaze moved around to include Horace. 'Nor when I heard you two had assaulted Castle Macindaw with just thirty men.'

'Thirty-three,' mumbled Horace. He was beginning to see where Halt was heading.

The Ranger gave him a withering look. 'Oh, pardon me . . . Thirty-three men. That makes a lot of difference. Look, we live in a dangerous world, and both Evanlyn and Alyss have decided they want to do more than sit by and watch while we menfolk take care of them.

'They don't want to be spectators. They're courageous and imaginative and adventurous. That's why you like them. They fit into the world you've chosen for yourselves. If you'd wanted a pair of silly, primping maidens who are good for nothing but gossip and needlepoint, there are plenty of those around. But I doubt they'd interest you.'

He paused, watching to see if his words had sunk in. Slowly, Will and Horace began to nod agreement with what he'd said. Halt himself had come to terms with all these points many years ago, when he had fallen in love with Lady Pauline. He'd had to accept that she would fulfil the duties of a Courier — which would inevitably take her into harm's way. And he had to trust in her ability to look after herself — as she had learned to trust in his.

'Now, what Selethen says is true. We *are* going to need help in the spring. We can't simply sit behind the palisade and hope to hold Arisaka off forever. And the only available source of that help lies across the lake, with the Hasanu. Is that right, Lord Shigeru?'

The Emperor nodded. He had been following the discussion with great interest. The evenings he'd spent talking with Evanlyn had shown her to be a young lady of remarkable courage and determination. And she was highly intelligent and articulate — qualities that would be necessary if she were going to carry his request for help to Lord Nimatsu.

'Lord Nimatsu has the only viable force that can help us defeat Arisaka,' he said.

'Then it makes sense for Evanlyn and Alyss to enlist his aid,' Halt finished, eyeing the two young men.

'I know all that,' Horace replied. 'But I can't help feeling —'

He got no further. Alyss interrupted him.

'Stop *feeling*, Horace, and start thinking! Let's face it, when it comes to straight-out battle, you have an advantage over us. Right or wrong, you men are physically stronger than we are. That's a fact of nature, and physical strength plays a big role in close combat. I could work on my skills with the sabre till I was blue in the face. But even if I were as fast and as skilled as you, Horace, you would still be stronger than me. That's the way of things. And I know Evanlyn might knock one or two, or even a dozen, of the enemy over with her sling. But once they came to close quarters, she'd be in trouble.'

'This is our chance to do something constructive in this war!' Evanlyn said, taking up the theme. 'Our chance to contribute! And if we do it, we don't weaken your forces. That's the beauty of Alyss's kayak. If we travelled overland we'd need some of the Kikori to come with us as guides and bodyguard. But on the lake, who can touch us?'

There was a long silence while Horace and Will digested all of this. In their hearts, they knew that Halt and the girls were right. The plan was logical and well thought out — even down to the detail that Evanlyn had just pointed out. Travelling across the lake, they wouldn't need the services of any of the Kikori. It was just that . . .

'I'll worry about you,' Will said, looking into Alyss's eyes. She smiled at him and took his hand in hers.

'Well, of course you will. I'd hope you would. Just as I'll worry about you, trapped here with hundreds of Arisaka's men baying for your blood. Just as I worried about you when you were in Hibernia. Or in Arrida. Or on any of your other missions. Of course I worry about you. But I never tried to stop you going, did I?'

'No,' Will agreed reluctantly. 'But . . .'

Alyss held up one finger in warning. 'Don't dare say "this is different",' she said and he closed his mouth hurriedly. Selethen gave vent to a deep chuckle and they all turned to look at him.

'A good tactician always knows when to retreat from an untenable position, Will,' he said. The young Ranger grinned reluctantly.

Evanlyn turned to Horace. 'What about you, Horace? Will you worry about me?' she said, a smile lurking behind her lips.

Horace went red in the face and shuffled his feet. He didn't meet her gaze.

'Ah . . . well . . . yes. Of course. And Alyss too, of course. Both of you. I'll worry about both of you.'

Evanlyn turned to the others and shrugged. 'I guess that's all a girl can expect from a strong, silent type like him.'

'I'm glad that's settled,' Halt said. 'Now, down to details. When do you plan to leave?'

'We thought tomorrow,' Evanlyn said and Alyss nodded assent.

'Tomorrow!' Will and Horace chorused in surprise. All eyes turned to them.

'I mean, isn't that rushing it a little? Why go so soon?' Will added uncertainly.

Alyss shrugged. 'Why wait? The weather will only get worse. And the sooner we go, the sooner we'll be back.'

'That's true, I suppose. But . . . tomorrow?' So far, they'd been discussing the *concept* of the girls' leaving. But now there was a reality and an immediacy to the whole thing.

Halt dropped a hand on his shoulder. 'Best get used to it, Will. If you're involved with a Courier.' He paused and then included Evanlyn. 'Or a madcap princess . . .' He favoured her with a faint smile so she wouldn't take offence. 'This is not going to be the last time you see them off on some hare-brained scheme.'

For a moment, he studied the two girls. He had to admit to a certain proprietorial feeling about them. Alyss was his wife's protégée and he'd watched her grow into a resourceful and courageous young woman. Will's account of her strength of purpose and her coolness under pressure during the siege of Castle Macindaw had confirmed his favourable opinion of her. As for Evanlyn, he'd watched her in action, battling the Temujai riders in Skandia and the Tualaghi bandits in the desert. There was no question of her courage or her ability. They would make a good team, he thought. And if they could overcome the residual jealousy that still existed between them, they would be formidable. Perhaps this trip would help them do that.

'I'll compose a letter for you to take to Lord Nimatsu,' Shigeru said to Evanlyn. 'And tonight, I'll ask my servants to prepare a suitable farewell meal for you both.'

'Sounds good,' Evanlyn said cheerfully. 'What will we be having?'

Shigeru smiled at her. 'The same hard rations we have every night,' he said. 'But tonight, the table setting will be exquisite.'

Halt looked around the group, satisfied that the matter had been settled and that Horace and Will realised the need for the girls to contribute to the campaign, and the value in their doing so. But there was something else that had been on his mind for some time now. He caught Selethen's gaze. The Arridi saw the challenge in the Ranger's eye and smiled, knowing what was coming.

'Tomorrow it is then,' Halt said. 'But before Alyss and Evanlyn leave, I think we'd all like to see what Selethen and Will have been up to these past weeks.'

Thirty-five

'It's a little early to be showing you this,' Will said, as he led the curious party uphill towards a secluded corner of the valley. 'So far, we only have equipment for ten men. The others have to take it in turn to train and practise.'

'Practise what?' Evanlyn asked but Halt signalled her to wait.

They stopped at a point where a grove of trees screened a smaller gully. Will and Selethen ushered them forward and they came to a flat section of land, forty metres by twenty.

Horace pointed to a line of fascines — bundles of light branches tied together, each about the size of a man — standing at the far end of the gully.

'What are they?'

Will grinned at him. 'They're the enemy.' He looked at Selethen. 'Do you want to take over?'

The Arridi warrior shrugged deferentially. 'It was your idea. I'm just an assistant.'

Will nodded, gathered his thoughts for a second, then proceeded.

'I got the inklings of this idea when we first arrived here and I saw the Kikori at work. Their group discipline was excellent.'

Shigeru nodded. 'It has to be. Timber cutting is a dangerous business.'

'Exactly,' Will said. 'Then Horace, I think, said that the Senshi, with their years of training, excelled at individual combat. How one on one, they were generally superior to our Araluan warriors.' He glanced a question at Horace, who also nodded.

Halt settled back, leaning comfortably against a rock, smiling at his former pupil. He thought he could see where this was heading, but he wasn't sure how Will planned to achieve it.

'Now all of this rang a bell in my memory. I'd heard this sort of thing before. It drove me mad for a few days, then I remembered where it had been.' He paused and Halt's smile widened as the others unconsciously leaned forward, waiting for him to continue. His young pupil couldn't resist the opportunity for a little drama.

'I recalled General Sapristi saying much the same things.'

'General who?' Horace asked, totally puzzled.

'He was a general in Toscana who arranged a demonstration of their fighting methods for us,' Will explained. 'The Toscan legions have developed a system of fighting as a team. It's simple, so there's no need for them to learn or practise complex swordplay. They just have to jab and stab and shove. The secret is, they all work together.' He paused. His throat was a little dry with all this talking and he gestured for Selethen to take up the story.

'As the general told us, individually his legionnaires would be no match for expert warriors. Their strength lies in their teamwork, and their equipment.' Selethen paused, then turned and called out an order.

'Kikori! Show yourselves!'

He and Will had sent a messenger ahead to let the trainees know they were coming. Now, on his command, a file of ten Kikori trotted out from behind a pile of boulders halfway up the valley.

But they were equipped as no Kikori had ever been equipped before. Shigeru stared at them, fascinated.

Each man carried a long rectangular shield. It was slightly curved and made of wood, reinforced at the top and sides with strips of iron. In the centre, a plate-sized iron boss protruded. The men also wore hard leather breastplates and leather helmets. These too were trimmed with iron strips, for extra protection. As they ran, moving at a steady jog, they held long wooden javelins sloped over their shoulders.

Horace moved forward to look more closely. 'They're pretty primitive,' he said. The javelins were roughly trimmed wooden stocks, about a metre and a half long, each with an iron rod bound to it, protruding some fifty centimetres past the wooden stock. The iron rod ended in a barbed point.

'They don't need to be anything more than that,' Will told him. 'Selethen, will you conduct the drill, please?' He turned to the others. 'Let's move down a little, to the side. You'll be able to see better.'

He led the way to a small rock outcrop halfway down the gully. Selethen kept the ten Kikori in a line, waiting expectantly. When his companions were settled, Will called to Selethen.

'Enemy sighted!'

'Battle formation!' Selethen barked the command. Instantly, every second man in the line took two paces backwards. Then both lines closed up, so that where there had been ten men in one line, there were now two ranks of five. The movement was accomplished in seconds.

'Forward!' Selethen commanded. The two ranks stepped off together, pacing steadily forward, with the Kikori on the right end of the second rank calling time.

'Impressive,' said Horace softly.

Will glanced quickly at him. 'As I said, their sense of discipline is excellent. They pick up these drills quickly.' Then he looked away and shouted to Selethen again.

'Enemy archers!'

'Halt!' cried Selethen. The steadily advancing Kikori crashed to a stop.

Halt remembered Will's phrase at the display in Toscana: *A cloud of dust and a line of statues*. General Sapristi would have been impressed, he thought.

'*Kamé!*' Selethen ordered.

The Emperor leaned back and looked at Will, a little confused. 'Tortoise?'

But Will gestured towards the ten trainees. The front rank had raised their shields to head height, while the second rank held theirs higher, parallel to the ground, the edges overlapping the tops of the front rank's shields.

The ten men were now protected from the front and above by an uninterrupted carapace.

'Ah . . . yes. Tortoise. I see,' Shigeru said thoughtfully.

'*Kamé* down!' Selethen ordered and the shields came back to their original position. 'Front rank, *yari*!'

Now the front rank took a large pace forward. The men turned side on, reversed their grips on the rough javelins and, as one, leaned their weight onto their right feet, the long weapons going back over their right shoulders, pointing up at a thirty-degree angle.

'Throw!'

They released as one, each man putting the strength and power of his entire body behind the cast. The weapons sailed high, then arced down as the weight of the iron tips took effect. Three of the fascines were struck and knocked to the ground, while the other two javelins bounded and slithered harmlessly past them. Already, Selethen was ordering the second rank forward. They moved through the first rank and repeated the sequence of movements. Another five javelins soared across the short distance. Another fascine was hit.

'Imagine that, but with fifty javelins each time instead of one,' Will said.

Horace nodded thoughtfully. A barrage of fifty of those rough-looking weapons could be devastating to an opposing force. His military mind had seen the value of the soft iron tips — understanding how a warrior, even lightly wounded, would be impeded by the dragging weight of the javelin.

'But now they are unarmed,' Shigeru said. He had been looking carefully, but could see no sign of the long *katana* that were the principal weapon of the Senshi. No sooner had he said the words than he heard the scraping rattle of blades being drawn. He saw now that each of the Kikori was armed with a short weapon.

'*Issho ni!*' Selethen called. The two ranks began to advance, shields locked together.

'*Issho ni!*' The shout was echoed from ten throats, then repeated as they moved steadily forward.

Will looked at the Emperor. 'We're using Nihon-Jan for the more important commands,' he explained. 'Less chance of misunderstanding that way.'

'Appropriate,' Shigeru answered.

Evanlyn cocked her head to one side curiously. 'What does "*issho ni*" mean?'

'Together,' Alyss told her.

'It's their battle cry,' Will said. 'It reminds them of how they fight — as a team.' He cupped his hands and called to Selethen. 'Bring them towards us!'

The Arridi waved acknowledgement and called an order. The left-hand marker on each rank began to march in place while his comrades wheeled to the left in a steady, co-ordinated movement.

Horace whistled softly. 'They might have been born to do this.'

Now the two ranks were facing the spectators and Selethen called another sequence of orders. The wheeling movement stopped and the formation, still intact, began to advance again. Shigeru and the others could see the value of the large shields. The men themselves were virtually invisible, only the tops of their helmets showing above the wall of shields.

There was nothing for a swordsman to engage, the Emperor realised. But darting out from narrow gaps between the shields, he could see the short weapons the Kikori carried, flickering like so many snakes' tongues.

'How can they see?' he asked.

Will smiled. 'Not very well. Their commander controls the direction of the advance. But they stab at anything that comes into sight through the gaps in the shields. Arms, legs, bodies. It's just stab and move forward, stab and move forward. We don't teach them any of the sort of sweeping, scything strokes that the Senshi use. They don't need to learn any complex techniques. Just stab quickly and withdraw the weapon immediately. If a Senshi warrior attacks one of them, he's confronted by a huge shield. And if he presses the attack, the man next to his opponent will probably stab him as he does so.'

'Where did their swords come from?' Halt asked.

'Some of them are the short swords carried by the Senshi killed at Riverside Village or at the palisade. The rest are cut-down spears, with the shafts reinforced with iron strips.'

'But a good *katana* will shear easily through iron like that,' Shigeru protested.

Will conceded the point. 'Admittedly. That's why each man will carry two reserve swords. But they're not using their short swords to parry or block the Senshi's *katana*. That's what the shields are for. And if a *katana* cuts into the iron and wood of a shield, its owner could find himself in trouble.'

'I don't understand.' The Emperor frowned.

But Horace had seen the truth of what Will said. In fact, he'd used the same idea as a tactic in times past.

'If the *katana* cuts into the shield, it will be jammed for a few seconds while its owner gets it free. And in that time, he'll have two or three Kikori stabbing at him. He stands to lose either his sword or his life.'

'Yes.' The Emperor fingered his chin thoughtfully. He had to admit that this display was a little unnerving. He was raised in the Senshi tradition and, egalitarian as he might be, it was unsettling to see that two foreigners had so quickly devised a way to counteract Senshi techniques.

Will held up his hand now and Selethen called the troop to a halt. Another command and, as one, they grounded their shields and bowed to their Emperor. Shigeru rose from where he had been seated on the rock and bowed deeply in return. His qualms of a few minutes ago were gone. These were his people, just as much as the Senshi were, he realised. They were willing to fight for him, and to learn new ways of doing so. They deserved his respect and loyalty.

Will slid down from the rock and walked among the Kikori troops, slapping them on the shoulder and offering words of congratulation to them as he went. Then he and Selethen dismissed them and rejoined the others.

'We've got three months,' he said to Halt. 'We plan to train and equip two hundred men in these techniques.'

Halt nodded. 'With two centuries of trained men, you could give Arisaka a very nasty surprise indeed. Well done, Will. And you too, Selethen.'

The Arridi bowed and made his traditional greeting gesture. 'As I said, it was Will's idea,' he replied. 'But like you, I think it will be very effective.'

Horace dropped an arm over Will's shoulder and shook his head. His slightly built friend never ceased to amaze him.

'You seem to have a habit of creating armies out of nowhere,' he said. 'Pity there aren't a hundred Araluan slaves here you could train as archers.' He was referring to the potent force of archers Will had formed to fight the Temujai army. 'One thing,' he added with a slight frown. 'You're going to need a lot of iron for helmets and shields and stabbing swords. Where are you going to find it?'

'We have it already.' Will grinned. 'The Kikori metal workers are busy melting down the cache of old weapons you discovered. We don't need finely tempered steel and they should do the job nicely.'

'I wonder,' said Horace, 'if I'll ever ask a question you can't answer.'

Will considered the idea for a second or two, then shook his head.

'I shouldn't think so.'

Thirty-six

Evanlyn spun slowly on the end of the rope as the team of Kikori above her gradually paid out line, allowing her to descend.

She was hanging in space, several metres clear of the cliff face. But a few metres below her, a large outcrop of rock bulged out, barring the way. As she turned back to face the cliff once more, the waiting Kikori let out a few more metres of rope until her feet touched the rock. Bracing her feet against it, she walked herself backwards down the cliff, using her legs and feet to keep her clear as the men above continued to lower her. Then she was past the outcrop and slowly spinning in space again as she descended.

'You're nearly here,' Alyss called from below. Evanlyn looked over her shoulder and could see the Courier waiting at the foot of the cliff, barely fifteen metres below her. She looked back up to where the rope now slid over the rock outcrop. Too much of that and the rope would fray and eventually break, she thought. But the rock was smooth and there wasn't far to go. She felt her feet touch solid ground, and Alyss's hand on her elbow to steady her. The rope went slack and she let out a huge sigh of relief. She hadn't realised she'd been holding her breath. Her legs were a little unsteady, a reaction to the fact that she had been dangling in space over an enormous drop, like a spider on a strand of web. Alyss hurried to help free her from the harness of rope that the Kikori had created to hold her safely while they lowered her down the cliff face.

'I'm glad that's over,' Evanlyn said.

Alyss nodded in heartfelt agreement. 'If there's one thing that terrifies me, it's heights.'

Evanlyn looked at her in surprise. 'But you volunteered to go first.'

'Only because I thought if I watched you go, I'd never have the nerve to follow. I spent most of the time with my eyes shut tight.'

They cast loose the last of the rope that had been tied around Evanlyn, and Alyss tugged hard on it four times — a prearranged signal to tell the Kikori above that Evanlyn was safely at the bottom of the cliff. The rope suddenly began a rapid ascent while the two girls took stock of their situation.

The cliffs were over two hundred and fifty metres high and they had made the descent in three stages, with the Kikori climbers choosing suitable staging points along the way. At each point, a climber had waited with Alyss and Evanlyn while the rest of the team descended, then the girls were lowered down the next stage. The kayak, tied in a narrow bundle, lay on the rocks beside them. One of the Kikori had made the final stage of the descent with it, guiding it past the obstruction of the rock outcrop and untying it at the bottom. He had then climbed swiftly back up, aided by his companions hauling in on the rope, to report that all was well.

A few metres away, the waters of Mizu-Umi Bakudai lapped gently against the shore. Evanlyn was relieved to see that the water was calm. The day had been sufficiently hair-raising, she thought, without the added complication of rough water for her initiation into the art of kayaking.

'I guess we'd better start getting the boat assembled,' she said. But before Alyss could reply, a small shower of pebbles rattled off the rock outcrop above them. They both covered their heads against any stray pebbles that might come down, then looked up as a pair of boots appeared over the edge of the rock. The Kikori who had made the descent called for his companions to stop lowering. He braced himself out from the rock and slipped a pad of sheepskin between the rope and the rock face. Obviously, he shared Evanlyn's earlier thought about the rope fraying. Then he signalled and the lowering recommenced. He dropped quickly to the rocks beside them, then looked up, grinning.

'You came down faster than we did, Eiko,' Evanlyn said.

He shrugged. 'Do this many times,' he told them.

The girls noticed that he had disdained to use the harness arrangement that had been devised for them. He had simply tied a loop at the end of the rope and placed one foot in it as the others lowered him. Alyss shuddered at the thought.

Eiko had their travel packs over his shoulder and he unslung them and set them on the ground beside the bundle of timber and oilskin. He gestured to it.

'You need help?'

Alyss shook her head. 'We should get used to assembling it ourselves.'

He nodded and stood back, watching as they quickly unrolled the bundle, arranged the frames and ribs, then fastened and braced the timbers so that the skeleton of the boat took shape.

As they began to stretch the oilskin cover over the frame, straining against the lacing to bring it tight, he made a clicking noise with his tongue and stopped them.

'Better this way!' he said. Removing the retaining pins, he slid one of the main frames sideways, relaxing the tension so that the ribs of the boat collapsed slightly.

'Tie now,' he said, accompanying the word with gestures. 'Then tighten ribs again.'

The girls quickly grasped the idea. They stretched the oilskin tight over the partially collapsed boat, lacing it firmly in place, then straightened the frame, levering it into its original position, so that any remaining slack in the skin of the boat was now tensioned out.

'Good thinking,' Alyss said appreciatively. 'That makes it much easier.'

'Yes. I was afraid I was going to break a fingernail,' Evanlyn added.

Alyss looked up at her sharply, about to make a disparaging remark, when she realised the princess was joking. Feeling a little foolish, she bent her head to the task of fastening the last of the laces. When the last knot was tied, they stepped back and surveyed their handiwork.

'Excellent,' said Alyss.

Evanlyn nodded. 'You'd almost swear it was a boat.'

This time, Alyss didn't react. She had a feeling that Evanlyn's jokes were intended to conceal her nervousness about venturing across the lake in this seemingly frail craft. Alyss could understand that. But she also knew that the kayak was far more robust and seaworthy than it looked.

The two double-ended paddles had been tied in the original bundle and she picked them up and carried them the few metres to the water's edge. When she returned, she saw that Eiko had been busy, blowing up the two pigskin air-bladders that served as buoyancy chambers in case the boat was swamped in heavy weather. They pushed them into the bow and stern of the kayak, wedging them in place between the stringers, then stowed their travel packs into the space between the two seats, fastening an oilskin cover over them to keep them dry.

'Right,' said Alyss. 'Grab an end and let's go.'

The girls stooped to pick up the boat but Eiko waved them back. He lifted it easily onto his hip, balancing it there, and smiled at them.

'Eiko,' Evanlyn said, 'we told you. We have to —'

'Yes, yes!' he said, waving his free hand disdainfully. 'You have to do yourselves. You can do tomorrow and tomorrow and tomorrow. I do today.'

Alyss and Evanlyn exchanged a look. Then Alyss shrugged.

'Why not?' she said. 'After all, we can do it tomorrow and tomorrow and tomorrow.' She bowed and swept one hand towards the edge of the lake. 'Eiko, my friend, after you.'

Grinning, the Kikori strode towards the lake, the two girls following. He set the kayak down in the shallow water at the lake's edge, leaving it half in and half out of the water. The two girls looked out over the wide expanse of water. From the clifftop, they had been able to see the far shore, a long, long way away. From water level, there was no sign of it. They might have been at the edge of an ocean.

'It's certainly a big lake,' Evanlyn said quietly. She looked up at Eiko. 'Eiko, what does "Mizu-Umi Bakudai" mean?'

The stockily built timber worker frowned uncertainly. 'It means "Mizu-Umi Bakudai",' he said. Evanlyn made an impatient gesture.

'Yes. Yes. Obviously. But what do those words mean?'

Alyss coughed and Evanlyn turned to her. The Courier was repressing a smile. 'They mean "Big Lake",' she said.

Eiko nodded cheerfully and Evanlyn felt her cheeks colouring. 'Oh, of course. Logical, I suppose.'

'The Nihon-Jan have a penchant for literal place names, I've noticed,' Alyss told her. Then, briskly, she dusted her hands off and stooped to the kayak, shoving it fully into the shallow water. 'Let's check the boat for leaks.'

The water was only a few centimetres deep at the shore but the bank shelved steeply so that, after two or three metres, it was half a metre deep. From there, it rapidly became deeper and the sand and stone bottom, easily visible close in, became lost from sight. Alyss waded in, reacting to the shock of the icy water.

'Ow! That's cold! Make sure you don't tip us over, Evanlyn.'

'Make sure yourself,' Evanlyn replied crisply. But secretly, she knew that if anyone were going to tip the boat, it would be her. She went to step into the water to help, but Alyss waved her back.

'Eiko can help me. He's heavier.' She turned to the Kikori and gestured to the boat. 'Push it down as far as you can, please, Eiko.'

He nodded his understanding and waded in beside her. Reaching down, he braced his hands against the gunwale ribs and leaned his weight onto the boat. The hull sank deeper into the water under his weight and Alyss leaned in, searching up and down its length for any sign of water coming in. But the tight oilskin created an excellent water-tight barrier and there was no sign of a leak.

'That's great,' Alyss said, straightening. She beckoned to Evanlyn. 'Okay, grab your paddle and come and get aboard. Take the front seat. That way I can keep an eye on you.'

Eiko moved quickly towards Evanlyn, gesturing to indicate that he would lift her into the boat, but Alyss stopped him.

'No, Eiko. Better if she gets used to doing it without help. Getting in can be a little tricky,' she explained to Evanlyn. The other girl nodded and, paddle in hand, waded into the water. She, too, caught her breath at the icy touch of the lake.

'I can see why you don't want to tip over in this.' Moving awkwardly, she raised one dripping wet foot and went to step over the kayak, planning to straddle it. But Alyss stopped her.

'Not that way. Turn your back to it and get your behind in first. Sit in sideways with your backside on the seat. That gets the greater part of your body weight inside the boat, with only your legs to follow.'

Carefully, Evanlyn lowered herself backwards onto the

wooden seat. The boat tipped and she tensed nervously. But Alyss held it steady.

'I've got it. Loosen up. Now lift your feet and swing them into the boat. Put them on the ribs or the footrest in front of your seat, not the oilskin,' she added. 'Don't ever put weight on that.'

Evanlyn looked up at her. 'Any other blindingly obvious advice you've got for me?' she asked sarcastically and Alyss shrugged.

'Never hurts to be sure,' she said. She waited as Evanlyn swung her legs and feet into the boat, settling herself in place. Then Alyss released her hold on the stern and moved to the side of the kayak. Eiko stepped forward to hold the boat steady as she had been doing but she waved him away.

'I'm fine,' she said. She handed her paddle to Evanlyn, who was waiting, a little anxiously. 'Evanlyn, the boat is going to rock when I get in. Boats do that. It's perfectly normal. Don't try to counteract it. It'll recover itself. Just keep your weight central and keep your body loose, okay?'

Evanlyn, tense as a fiddle string, nodded acknowledgement.

Moving quickly and smoothly, Alyss settled her weight into the rear seat and swung her legs inboard. The boat rocked under her weight – violently, it seemed to Evanlyn, who couldn't help emitting a small squawk of alarm. Then it steadied and she realised they were floating, drifting clear of the bank and the spot where Eiko stood, knee deep in the water. He grinned encouragingly at them and waved. The tiny wavelets made a constant *pok-pok* sound against the tight skin of the kayak and, for the second time that day, Evanlyn let go a breath she hadn't realised she was holding.

'Okay, hand me that paddle,' she heard Alyss say and she turned awkwardly to hand the paddle back to her companion. As she did so, the boat lurched and she instantly tensed up once more, turning quickly back to face the bow.

'Relax,' Alyss told her. 'Just go with it – the way you would on a horse. If you suddenly go rigid, you'll find it harder to keep balanced and relaxed. Now let's try with that paddle again. And see if you can avoid dropping it overboard.'

This time, Evanlyn slid the paddle behind her without turning. She heard a slight grunt of pain as the blade caught Alyss in the ribs.

'Thank you for that,' the Courier said.

'Sorry,' Evanlyn replied. She hated the feeling of being out of control.

'Now, let's get this boat moving,' Alyss told her. 'Left side first. Paddle smoothly and slowly. Don't try to do too much. Above all, try not to throw water all over me. On my count.'

Evanlyn raised the unfamiliar paddle, waiting for Alyss to call time.

'All right . . . left side first. One . . . and two . . . One . . . and two . . . that's good. Keep it going. Nice . . . and smooth. One and . . . Ow, damn it! If you splash me again I'll throw you overboard. Now be *careful*!'

Which, Evanlyn thought, was no way to speak to the Crown Princess of Araluen.

Thirty-seven

'They're moving well,' Horace said as the fifty Kikori trainees, in two extended ranks, advanced at a steady jog across the drill field.

Selethen shouted a command and the men at the left-hand end of each rank stopped in place, still jogging in time, and turned ninety degrees to their left. The two lines went with them, those on the outer end of the arc having to move faster than the ones closer to the pivoting point. For a few seconds, the ranks wavered and curved, losing their straight-edge precision. Then the outer third of each line came back into position and the ranks were properly formed again. As soon as they were, another command from Selethen set the fifty men jogging forward once more, now moving at ninety degrees to their original path. The entire evolution took less than thirty seconds.

Will hadn't answered. He had been watching the manoeuvre carefully, looking for any signs of sloppiness or lack of precision. There had been none that he could see. Now he looked up at his friend and grinned in reply.

'Yes. Their co-ordination is first-rate.'

'I see you've got more weapons for them now,' Horace remarked. The entire front rank was now equipped with the big, rectangular shields and crude javelins. Each man in the fifty wore several of the short stabbing weapons at his side.

'They've all got stabbing swords now. Most of them have made their own by cutting down their spears. And the wood and metal workers are delivering new shields and javelins all the time. Soon we'll have enough to equip a full *hyaku*.'

'*Hyaku?*' Horace asked.

'It's Nihon-Jan for "one hundred". That's the standard Toscan fighting formation — one hundred men in a group. They call it a century — three ranks of thirty-three men each plus a commander.'

'And how many of these *hyakus* do you plan on having?'

'I figure two. It'd be nice to have more but we just don't have the men. And Halt says a small force, properly trained and disciplined, can be very effective.'

'That makes sense,' Horace said.

The troop halted now and those in the front rank passed their javelins back to the men behind them. 'We share what we have,' Will explained to Horace. 'Since so much of the training depends on moving and turning as one unit, it doesn't matter if not everyone is armed yet.'

As the troops waited, twenty of their fellow trainees ran onto the drill field, and placed dummy warrior figures in a line facing them, about fifty metres away. Once that was done, they hurried from the field, and Selethen gave the order for his troops to advance once more.

'*Kamé!*' Selethen shouted. Instantly, the front rank raised their shields above head height, while the second rank mimed holding shields horizontally to form a roof. Thus protected, they continued their steady advance, boots tramping in unison on the packed ground. After a few seconds, Selethen called another order and their shields, real and imaginary, returned to the normal marching position. The dummy enemy soldiers were now a mere forty metres away.

Another order from Selethen saw the front rank continue to march while the second rank halted and drew back their javelins. As one, on command, they hurled the weapons over their marching comrades, sending them arcing up and over to come smashing down into the line of fascines forty metres away. Then they marched in double-time to regain their position behind the front rank. Half of the fascines had been struck by javelins. Some were spilled over on their sides, while others leaned drunkenly, supported by the heavy javelin shafts that now sagged to the ground.

Selethen upped the tempo and the entire fifty moved forward at a steady jog, stabbing blades flickering menacingly in the narrow gaps between the shields. As the front rank reached the 'enemy' line, the second rank instantly closed up tight behind them, shoving and adding their weight to the impetus of the leading rank.

Finally, Selethen called a halt to the drill and the trainees relaxed, grounding their shields. The rear rank moved to collect the javelins.

'Selethen's doing a good job,' Horace said, as the tall Arridi moved among the men, making comments to them, encouraging some, praising others, offering words of advice and correction where needed. 'Will he command both *hyakus*?'

'No,' Will replied. 'They need to work independently. That's something I wanted to talk to you about. Will you take command of one of them?'

'Me?' Horace said, a little surprised. 'I assumed you'd want to command one of them. After all, it's your idea.' But Will was shaking his head.

'We need two good battlefield commanders,' he said. 'You're better at that than I am. Halt and I can stand off and keep an overall view of things. We'll keep Shigeru's Senshi back as a reserve and send them in wherever they're needed.'

Horace couldn't help a grin forming. 'Ah, you Rangers,' he said. 'You love to be the puppetmasters, don't you?'

Will hesitated, about to deny the joking accusation. Then he spread his hands in defeat.

'Well, yes. Actually, we do. But also, we're better suited to long-distance fighting. You're the close combat expert.'

Horace had to admit that the potentially devastating effect of Will's and Halt's archery would be a valuable resource to have in reserve.

'I'd be honoured to command one of the *hyakus*,' he said. 'I've been feeling pretty useless lately, sitting around in my cabin doing nothing.' He paused as a thought struck him. 'I'll have to learn all the commands and drills.'

'That won't take you long. We've kept it all pretty simple — no insult intended. It's something Halt always says: *Do a few simple things really well, instead of a lot of complicated manoeuvres that can go wrong in the heat of battle. You'll pick it all up in a day or so. And with you and Selethen both working the men, we'll get them trained in half the time.'*

Horace nodded. The thought of having something constructive to do was a satisfying one. After the tension and danger of the flight through the mountains, the past few weeks of inactivity while his injured ribs healed had left him feeling stale and empty. Now, he felt a sense of purpose once more. He slapped the hilt of his sword and frowned as he encountered the unfamiliar shape of the *katana* that he now wore.

'I'll have to do something about this sword,' he said. 'After years of training with an Araluan cavalry sword, this Nihon-Jan *katana* just doesn't feel right.'

The opportunity to do so came sooner than he expected. After spending several more hours with Will and Selethen, taking notes of the drills and commands that he would need to learn, Horace returned to his cabin that afternoon. One of Shigeru's retinue brought him food and hot tea and as he sat down to enjoy the meal, the man bowed.

'*Kurokuma*, his excellency requests that once you have eaten you should visit his cabin.'

Horace went to rise immediately but the man waved him back down.

'No! No! His excellency said you should enjoy your meal first. He will welcome you whenever it is convenient to you.'

Smiling, Horace acknowledged the message and sat down again. With most rulers, he knew, the words 'whenever it is convenient for you' meant 'right now, and five minutes ago if you can make it'. With Shigeru, he had come to learn, they meant exactly what they said. The Emperor set no store in having his people drop everything to attend him on a whim. It was one of the reasons why his immediate followers loved him as much as they did.

Even so, an Emperor was an Emperor and Horace didn't waste any undue time finishing his meal. Once he had eaten and washed, he donned his warm outer robe, tied the sash around it and pushed the *katana* in its scabbard through the sash. His boots were sitting ready on the sheltered step outside the cabin and he donned them and set out through the falling snow. How different it all was to Araluen, he thought. And yet, in so many ways, it was the same. This little encampment in the mountains reflected many of the values he had learned in his home kingdom. Friendship and comradeship, loyalty to a thoughtful and considerate ruler. And, he reflected sadly, the ever-present problem of those who would usurp that ruler and seize power for themselves.

His boots crunched in the dry snow as he made his way to Shigeru's cabin. It was somewhat grander than the others the Kikori had built. Shigeru had protested at this, saying he needed nothing more than his companions had. But the Kikori were scandalised by such a suggestion. He was their Emperor and this was their opportunity to show him how much they revered and respected him. Consequently, Shigeru's cabin had a covered porch and two interior rooms — one large room where he could meet with his advisers and a smaller room where he could retire in privacy.

One of the Senshi stood guard on the porch. He smiled and bowed in greeting as he saw Horace approaching through the curtain of falling snow.

'*Kurokuma!* Good afternoon. His excellency is expecting you.'

Pausing only to respond to the man's greeting and to take off his snow-encrusted boots, Horace stooped and entered through the low doorway. Shigeru was seated, cross-legged, on a reed mat on the floor. A small, but brightly glowing, charcoal brazier proved a welcome source of warmth in the room. The Emperor had a fine brush pen in his hand and a frame holding a stretched piece of rice paper across his knee. He was writing the same Nihon-Jan ideogram on the paper, over and over again, striving each time for a better rendition of the loops and careful swirls. He looked up and smiled.

'Ah, *Kurokuma*, please sit with me.' He gestured towards a low stool.

Horace bowed, then sat. He knew it was normally a breach of etiquette to sit in a higher position than the Emperor. But Shigeru was aware that Araluans did not spend years sitting with their legs tucked up under them and, as a consequence, their knees tended to burn in protest after some minutes in that position. It was another example of the man's consideration for his subordinates, Horace thought.

'Would you like tea, *Kurokuma*?'

Horace, of course, had just had tea. But he knew there was a rhythm and etiquette to Nihon-Jan society. To refuse would jar that rhythm.

'Thank you, your excellency,' he said, bowing from his sitting position. He felt a little silly, sitting on his low stool with his knees drawn up in front of him — rather like a giant in a children's playroom. Shigeru, by contrast, looked dignified and balanced, sitting back on his heels.

A servant emerged from the inner room and served them both tea. Horace sipped his gratefully. Even the short walk from his cabin to Shigeru's had exposed him to the shivering cold in the valley and he felt the heat of the tea flood through his body.

'You wished to see me, your excellency?' He had a vague notion that George would have disapproved of such a blunt opening. Probably, he should have commented on the Emperor's calligraphy, admiring it while Shigeru modestly pointed out its mistakes and shortcomings. But he was intrigued to learn the reason for the summons. Since the battle at the palisade, a certain lack of activity had overcome them. There was no urgent need each day for Shigeru to consult with his advisers and the Emperor had withdrawn into himself a little. Horace knew that Shukin's death weighed heavily on the Emperor and it was highly likely that Shigeru, sensitive and kindly as he was, also felt a deep responsibility for the fate of those who had rallied to his aid — the Kikori, his own Senshi and the group of foreigners who had arrived and offered their service. It would be little wonder if the Emperor had retreated out of a sense of depression.

These thoughts all went through Horace's mind. But the Emperor showed no sign of doubt or uncertainty. His expression was calm and his demeanour was serene. He smiled now at the young man sitting before him, hands on his knees.

'You have been busy, *Kurokuma*?' he asked.

Horace shrugged. 'Not really, excellency. There has been little to do. But that will change. I have been asked to take command of one of the *hyaku*.'

'Ah, yes. The troops your friend Wirru-san is training,' Shigeru said. 'Tell me, do you think the Kikori will stand a chance against Arisaka's Senshi?'

Horace hesitated. He recalled his thoughts at the drill field — how the Kikori appeared as an inexorable force, advancing across the cleared ground behind the deadly shower of javelins.

'I think they *could*, your excellency,' he said. 'So long as they believe in themselves and keep their nerve. But all of Will's training and special tactics will come to nothing if the Kikori don't believe they can win.'

'Do they believe this?'

Horace shook his head. 'Perhaps not now. But they will. We'll make them believe it. It's up to us to build that spirit in them.'

'I thought you might say that. And it occurs to me that if you are fighting beside them, leading them in fact, you will need a sword.' Shigeru gestured to the hilt of the *katana* where it protruded from Horace's sash. 'How do you find your *katana*?'

'It's a fine weapon,' Horace said, careful not to offend. 'But it feels unfamiliar to me. It's not what I've been trained with.'

'Hmmm. I thought this might be so. A warrior needs the weapon he knows and trusts. In that case . . .' Shigeru turned towards the smaller side room, where his servant had retired after serving tea.

'Tabai! Bring the sword!'

The servant entered again, carrying a long bundle wrapped in oilcloth. He went to present it to the Emperor, but Shigeru clicked his tongue and pointed to Horace. Tabai proffered the parcel to the young knight, who took it curiously. He glanced up at Shigeru.

'I found it yesterday among Shukin's baggage,' the Emperor said. 'I couldn't bring myself to go through his things any sooner and frankly, I had forgotten about this.' He gestured for Horace to unwrap the parcel.

Horace cast the oilskin cover aside, coming forward onto one knee to inspect the parcel more closely. Inside was a sword. *His* sword, in a finely oiled leather scabbard. The plain steel crosspiece, the brass pommel and the leather binding of the hilt were all familiar.

'But . . . this is my sword!' he said, in amazement. The sword had plunged into a deep ravine, with a rushing torrent at its bottom. He couldn't conceive how it could have been recovered.

'Look more closely,' Shigeru told him. When he did, Horace noted that the leather binding on the hilt was fresh and new, unstained with the perspiration of a score of encounters and hundreds of practice drills. He went to draw it from its scabbard, then remembered that this was a gross breach of protocol in the Emperor's presence. But Shigeru gestured for him to go ahead.

The blade zzzz*inged* clear of the scabbard and Horace held it aloft, a little confused. The balance was perfect — just as he remembered. It could have been his old sword. But now he could see the blade itself, slightly blued, showed a repeating pattern of half circles beaten into the steel that appeared as a series of wavy lines. It caught the dim light and gleamed as his old sword had never done.

'It was Shukin's gift to you,' Shigeru explained, and Horace remembered Shukin telling him to look for a parcel when he had left them to defend the ford. 'He "borrowed" your sword one night in the summer lodge and had his own swordsmith copy it exactly.'

'But . . .' Horace began, wondering why Shukin had gone to such trouble.

Shigeru, sensing what the question was going to be, held up a hand to forestall it.

'There is one difference. This blade is Nihon-Jan steel — much harder than your old sword and able to take a much sharper edge. Now if you fight against the Senshi, you will do so on even terms.'

Thirty-eight

Their first night had been uneventful, save for Evanlyn's groans as she lay in their small tent, trying unsuccessfully to ease the waves of pain that swept through her shoulder and thigh muscles. She and Alyss had paddled for several hours across the placid waters of the lake, eventually landing on a small island. A quick scouting trip showed them that the island was uninhabited — it was barely more than a rock thrusting up out of the water, dotted with shrubs. They had made camp on a tiny sandy beach and settled in for the night.

'There are muscles here I never knew I had,' Evanlyn told Alyss the following morning. 'And every one of them is burning like fire.'

Evanlyn was fit and in excellent physical condition. The active life she led saw to that. But the action of paddling, hour after hour, had her using muscles that she never normally put under strain.

Alyss, more used to the motion, was stiff herself. But

she knew it was worse for Evanlyn. Still, she reasoned, there was nothing to gain by allowing the princess to wallow in misery. Evanlyn's constant low moaning through the night had kept Alyss awake, and this morning she was a little snappy about it.

'You'll get used to it,' she said.

Evanlyn looked at her sharply, saw she'd get no sympathy from that quarter and set her mouth in a grim line, determined to show no further sign of discomfort.

The water was boiling on the fire and she took the kettle out of the coals and poured it into a small metal teapot, over the leaves of green tea they'd brought with them.

'Wish we had coffee,' she said. In her travels with the Rangers, she'd grown to like the beverage nearly as much as they did. She passed a cup to Alyss, who was studying her map of the lake, planning the next stage.

'Me too,' Alyss replied absentmindedly. She sipped at the tea, enjoying its warmth, and spread the map on the sand between them. It was a simple chart. There was, after all, little to show on a map of the lake, aside from the islands that dotted its surface at irregular intervals.

'Today will be a long day,' she said. 'The closest island to us is way over here.' She tapped the map, indicating a land mass marked in the expanse of water.

Evanlyn looked at it, compared the distance to it to the distance they had already travelled, and whistled softly under her breath.

'That's quite a way,' she said.

'There's nothing closer,' Alyss told her. 'We're just going to have to do it. And I'd prefer to make it before dark. At least the wind hasn't got up.' She knew from experience how difficult it could be paddling into a headwind. 'I figure we're going to be paddling for five, maybe six hours.'

Evanlyn groaned softly. 'Oh my aching arms and shoulders.'

'You'll be okay once we get going,' Alyss told her. 'The kinks will ease out when you're working the muscles and you get warmed up.'

Evanlyn began to gather up their breakfast utensils. She felt a little encouraged by Alyss's comment. 'Well, that's something, at least.'

'Of course,' Alyss added, a trifle maliciously, 'once you cool down tonight, and they stiffen up again, they're going to hurt like merry hell.'

Evanlyn paused in the act of strapping her travel pack shut. 'Well, thank you for those kind words of encouragement,' she said. 'It's nice to know I have that to look forward to.'

They packed their supplies into the kayak and pushed it clear of the beach. Once again, Evanlyn climbed in first, still a little clumsily, while Alyss held the boat steady. Then Alyss boarded as well. This time, when the boat rocked suddenly under her weight, Evanlyn didn't tense up. The previous day had seen her grow accustomed to the fact that their little craft moved on the water. It rocked and plunged from time to time. But she'd learned that such movements didn't presage sudden disaster. Once she managed to relax, she found that she could counteract the kayak's motion with a loose-muscled response, balancing her weight without panic or tension.

Her paddling still left a little to be desired and from time to time she miscued a stroke, sending a shower of near-freezing water splashing back over her companion. The first few times this happened, Alyss had responded, with icy politeness, 'Thank you for that, your majesty.'

After that, her comments were less audible, consisting of indecipherable mutterings.

Each time, Evanlyn gritted her teeth and resolved not to make the same mistake again. Inevitably, she did and had to endure more of the almost, but not quite, inaudible comments from the rear seat — comments that she knew were unladylike and uncomplimentary in the extreme.

But there was nothing she could do about it, as she realised that she was in the wrong each time she unwittingly threw a faceful of water at Alyss.

They paused every thirty minutes or so to rest. When the sun passed the midday mark, Alyss announced that they could take a break to eat and drink. They sat drifting on the lake, lulled by the now familiar *pok-pok-pok* of the wavelets against their hull. There was little wind and no current, so they tended to stay pretty much in one position. When they had rested, but before Evanlyn's muscles had time to cool and stiffen, Alyss called a start again. She had a Northseeker needle with her and she turned the kayak to face west of north-west, then began to paddle once more. As the little boat moved off, Evanlyn glanced back over her shoulder to get the timing of the stroke and joined in. The kayak surged forward under the increased thrust, then yawed as Evanlyn missed a stroke and threw more spray onto Alyss.

'Thank you so much,' Alyss said.

Evanlyn said nothing. She had apologised so many times that the words now seemed meaningless. Besides,

Alyss should know by now that she wasn't doing it on purpose. Grimly, she concentrated on her paddling, digging the blade deep into the water, and finishing the stroke before she raised it again. This time, a good forty minutes passed before Alyss caught another bladeful of water in the face.

'Thank you so much,' she said mechanically.

Evanlyn wished her companion would come up with something new to say, or revert to her bad-tempered muttering.

In the midafternoon, the wind rose, blowing sharply across their course from the south-west. Alyss had to consult the Northseeker more frequently to keep them on course. The wind also raised a spiteful little cross-swell and larger waves than they had previously encountered began to slap against the left-hand side and bow of the kayak. Spray sloshed over the gunwales and into the boat.

At first, it was no more than an inconvenience and a discomfort as the icy cold water swirled around their feet. But as more and more water slopped in, the little boat became heavier.

'I'll keep paddling. You bale her out for a while,' Alyss ordered. They both leaned to the side as Evanlyn stowed her paddle down the inside of the little boat, then took the baling bucket that Alyss passed forward to her.

'Mind the skin of the boat,' Alyss warned her, as she scooped water out of the bottom of the kayak and tossed it overboard. Unthinkingly, she threw the first bucketful over the left, or windward, side. A good proportion of it was caught by the wind and flung back over the two of them.

'Thank you for that,' Alyss said.

'Sorry,' Evanlyn said. Next time, she threw the water to the right.

It was a wet and cold and exhausting afternoon. Evanlyn's arm muscles, shoulders and elbows were aching from the alternate actions of paddling and baling. Alyss stayed doggedly to her task of paddling throughout and, in spite of the acid comments when Evanlyn accidentally soaked her, Evanlyn felt a growing admiration for the tall girl's strength and endurance. Alyss never flagged, keeping the narrow craft driving forward through the waves.

'At least,' she said at one point, her words coming between grunts of exertion, 'this wind is giving me something to steer by. So long as I keep it on our left front quarter, we're heading more or less for the island.'

'Unless it shifts,' Evanlyn said, sending another bucketful overboard.

There was a long silence. Finally, Alyss spoke again. 'Hadn't thought of that. Better check.'

The kayak gradually slowed and sagged off downwind as Alyss stopped paddling and produced her Northseeker. It took a few minutes for the needle to settle, then she grunted in satisfaction.

'No. It's held steady. Let's go.'

Evanlyn had used the brief stop to clear most of the water out of the boat. She took up her paddle again and joined Alyss in driving the boat forward, quickly regaining the distance they had lost as they drifted. Her shoulders were on fire. No more groaning, she told herself grimly, and she bit the side of her mouth to prevent herself from making a sound. Head down, she reached forward with the paddle, placed it in the water and dragged the boat forward. Then she lifted it out, feathering the blade as she did so, and reached forward on the other side. With each stroke, her shoulder muscles and the muscles on the underside of her upper arms sent shafts of pain stabbing through her. But she was determined not to stop before Alyss did. No more groaning. Just keep going. The unspoken words formed a rhythm in her mind and she worked to it, hearing the two phrases like a strange mantra.

At least I'm not cold, she thought. Although her feet and hands were frozen, she could feel perspiration on her body. She paddled on, determined not to stop before Alyss did. The light was fading now as the winter sun sank low to the horizon. Her viewpoint was confined to the sharp prow of the kayak ahead of her and the pewter-coloured water around her.

No more groaning. Just keep going. Over and over again. Stretch, thrust, pull, lift. Stretch, thrust, pull, lift. She hated the lake. Hated the icy water. Hated the paddle. Hated the kayak. Hated everything about this journey. And above all, she hated Alyss.

'We've made it,' Alyss said. 'We're there.'

Evanlyn could have kissed her. She looked up and there was the island, fifty metres away. It was larger than the one they had camped on the previous night and there were trees here, where there had been nothing but low shrubs on the other island.

They dragged the boat up onto a shingle beach, then fell exhausted to the ground, both groaning in agony as they lay there. Alyss gave them a few minutes of rest before she roused Evanlyn, shaking her shoulder.

'Come on,' she said. 'We have to set up camp before we stiffen up.'

As Evanlyn rose wearily to her feet, she decided that she had been too quick to forgive Alyss. She hated her again. But she also knew the tall girl was right. Staggering with weariness, they built a fire and pitched their tent close to it. Then they changed out of their sweat-dampened inner clothing and fell on their bedrolls, pulling their blankets around them, too tired to eat.

The long, mournful howl penetrated through the fog of exhaustion that had wrapped around Evanlyn, bringing her awake.

Had it been close by, or far away? She had no way of telling. She'd been asleep when the cry came. Maybe, she thought, she had dreamed it.

Then it came again and she knew it was real. And it was close. It sounded as if it were only a few metres away from the back of the tent.

'Alyss?' she said uncertainly. Nobody could have slept through that noise, she thought.

'What is it?'

'That's what I want to know. It sounded like a wolf. Are there wolves on these islands?'

'Well, it certainly didn't sound like a kitty cat, did it?' Alyss threw off her blankets and crouched in the low headroom of the tent, fumbling with the gear stowed beside her bed. Outside, the fire they had built up before going to sleep was almost dead. A few yellow flames flickered and cast weird shadows on the tent walls.

Evanlyn heard the quick hiss of a blade being drawn and saw Alyss with her sabre in her hand. 'Where are you going?'

'Out to see what all the noise is,' Alyss told her. Hastily, Evanlyn tossed off her blankets and scrabbled around in the dim light for her own sword. She pulled on her boots, leaving them unlaced, and followed Alyss as she crept on hands and knees out of the tent.

'Oh dear,' Alyss said as she emerged.

Evanlyn joined her a few seconds later and she pointed to the half circle of grey shapes ranged around the camp site, at the edge of the pool of light thrown by the fire.

'Wolves,' Evanlyn said. 'Are they likely to attack?'

Alyss shrugged. 'I don't know. But my guess is they didn't just come here to pass the time of day. At least the fire seems to be keeping them back.'

There was only a handful of firewood left — a few branches that they had left to rekindle the fire in the morning. Evanlyn threw two of them onto the small pile of coals and flame. For a moment, nothing happened. Then the intense heat of the coals asserted itself and the two new branches caught and flared up.

The semicircle of silent watchers edged back a few paces. Alyss glanced around. The wolves were on the inland side of the camp. The way to the kayak, and the lake beyond, was clear.

'Back into the tent,' she said. 'Grab your pack. We're making for the kayak.'

'The kayak? What are . . .?'

Alyss cut her off. 'You can wait here until the fire dies down and see what the wolves have in mind if you like,' she said. 'I'm launching the kayak and sitting offshore till morning.'

'Can wolves swim?' Evanlyn asked doubtfully, although Alyss's idea seemed logical.

Alyss shrugged. 'Not as fast as I can paddle when I'm terrified,' she said. 'And if any do come after us, we can brain them with the paddles. Now let's get moving, unless you've got a better idea.'

They backed towards the tent. As they did so, the wolves edged in closer, still staying on the rim of the pool of firelight. Inside, they hastily shoved clothes and gear back into their packs. Then, still carrying their bare swords, they emerged once more. A rumbling growl went round the half-circle of grey watchers. The firelight was down to a few low flames now.

'Don't turn your back on them,' Alyss said. Carefully, they backed away from the camp site towards the kayak. As they went, two of the wolves rose and started to pad slowly after them. Alyss raised her sword and hissed a challenge at them. The steel caught the red light of the fire and reflected it around the camp. The wolves stopped. The girls moved off again and the wolves kept pace with them.

Evanlyn took a light grip on Alyss's jacket. Looking over her shoulder, she steered the other girl towards the kayak.

'You watch them. I'll watch the boat,' she said.

Alyss grunted in reply. She had feared that the wolves might try a flanking movement, circling round to put themselves between the two girls and the boat. But the animals had no idea what the long, narrow shape was. As far as they could see, they had these strange creatures trapped against the water.

They stopped and Alyss could see the kayak in her peripheral vision.

'Get it in the water,' she said. 'And get aboard.'

Evanlyn heaved and got the boat moving, sliding across the small pebbles and into the water. She moved it offshore a few metres, waiting as Alyss backed after her, her sword still presented to the following wolves. Evanlyn sheathed her own sword — she didn't want to risk its sharp edge cutting the oilskin covering of the boat — and sat clumsily into the boat. It rocked wildly for a few seconds but she rode the motion and waited till it steadied. She stowed her sword and took up her paddle.

'Get in,' she said and Alyss splashed hastily through the shallows to the boat. The two wolves who had been shadowing them bounded to the water's edge, then stopped, uncertainly. Alyss was swinging her legs into the boat as Evanlyn was already stroking backwards away from the beach.

One of the wolves threw back his head and howled in frustration.

'I guess that means they don't swim,' Alyss said.

'It also means we don't go back ashore,' Evanlyn replied. But Alyss shook her head.

'They'll be gone by daylight,' she said. 'We'll have to go back anyway to get our camping gear. At least they won't bother that — although they'll probably eat our food supplies.'

'Great,' said Evanlyn.

They paddled until they were about a hundred metres

offshore, then rested to take stock of their situation. The wind had died down after sunset. It was now a gentle breeze — although that was enough to set them drifting away from the island. Evanlyn remembered something she had seen long ago, when she and Will had been captives aboard Erak's ship, *Wolfwind*. She tied a length of light rope to the baler and tossed it over the bow, where it filled with water and streamed behind them.

'It's called a sea anchor,' she explained. 'It'll stop us drifting too far.'

Alyss was impressed. 'And you said you were pig-ignorant when it came to boats.'

'I don't remember saying that,' Evanlyn replied with a frown.

Alyss shrugged. 'Oh? Well, it must have been me.'

When dawn came, they paddled back to the beach, having dozed fitfully in turns through the dark hours of the morning. They gathered up their camping gear, spare clothes and blankets from where the wolves had tossed them as they had looked through their belongings for anything edible. There was a sack of rice split open and spilled on the sand and they carefully gathered it up again. There was no sign of the wolves.

But the girls knew they were still there, still watching.

Thirty-nine

Halt and Will made their way carefully along the narrow ledge. It was wise to take care. The rock was wet and glistening, with patches of ice in places. Fifty metres below them was the floor of the narrow, twisting valley that led to Ran-Koshi.

Mikeru moved ahead of them, unmindful of the sheer drop to his right. He strode casually, sometimes breaking into a trot, occasionally taking a short cut by jumping from one rock outcrop to the next, and all the while looking back and urging them to catch up.

'He's like a damned mountain goat,' Halt muttered and Will grinned.

'He grew up in this country.' Even though he had an excellent head for heights, Will couldn't match Mikeru's easy, almost casual approach to moving along this precarious path.

'Just as well he did,' Halt replied. 'And just as well he's got a restless nature.'

Since his success in finding the secret gully that led down from Ran-Koshi, Mikeru had spent his days exploring the cliffs and mountains around the valley-fortress, searching for new secrets, new hidden paths. The evening before, he had approached Will and Halt as they sat discussing the progress of the Kikoris' training. He was beaming with pleasure and pride at his new discovery.

'Halto-san. Wirru-san. I have found a lookout place. We can see Arisaka's men from there.'

This roused their interest. Since they had beaten the Senshi back after the first attack, they had been unable to gain any further information about Arisaka's movements. Halt had been on the verge of sending a small party down through the narrow secret entrance to see what the rebel lord was up to. He hadn't done so to date, because sending a group down carried the risk that they would reveal the existence of this secret way in and out.

This, however, promised to be an easier way of seeing what Arisaka was up to. But the light was fading and it was too late to inspect Mikeru's find that day. They agreed to leave it overnight.

Accordingly, the following morning, as soon as they had breakfasted, the young Kikori was waiting impatiently to lead them. He hurried to the eastern wall of the canyon, gesturing upwards.

'Track is up there. We climb up little bit, little bit.'

They had told Horace and he had decided to accompany them. But he looked up in alarm at the sheer rock face. He could just make out the ledge some twenty metres above them, now that Mikeru pointed it out.

'Little bit, little bit, my eye,' he said. 'That's a big bit, big bit.' He began to back away from the cliff but Mikeru took his arm and grinned encouragingly at him.

'Easy climb, *Kurokuma*. You do it easily.'

'The hell I do,' Horace said, as he gently disengaged Mikeru's grip. 'That's what we have Rangers for. They climb up sheer rock walls and crawl along narrow, slippery ledges. I'm a trained warrior and I'm too far valuable to risk in such shenanigans.'

'We're not valuable?' Will said, feigning insult.

Horace looked at him. 'We've got two of you. We can always afford to lose one,' he said firmly.

Mikeru was still puzzling over Horace's last remark. He frowned. '*Kurokuma*, these shenanigans . . . what are they?'

'Shenanigans are what Rangers do. They usually involve doing things that risk breaking your neck or your leg.'

Mikeru nodded, filing the word away. 'I will remember this word,' he said. 'Shenanigans. It is a good word.'

'If we've finished the language lesson for the day,' Halt said dryly, 'can we get a move on?'

Horace made a mock bow and waved a hand in the direction of the cliff face. 'Please. Be my guest.'

The ledge hugged the cliff face, and gradually rose higher and higher as they moved along it. Will estimated that they must be close to the mouth of the valley, but any sight of Arisaka's men was hidden behind a large rock outcrop that blocked the ledge. Mikeru, seeing them hesitate, scampered to it.

'Easy!' he said. 'Like this!'

He flattened himself against the rock, reaching out and around with his right hand, all the while keeping a firm grip with his left. He searched for a few seconds, then obviously found a new handhold on the other side. Without warning, he stepped off the ledge, leaving his left foot hanging in space while his right foot found support somewhere on the reverse side of the outcrop.

Then he set his left foot in a tiny vertical crack in the rock and swung himself around to the far side, out of sight. His voice came back to them, cheerful as ever.

'Easy! Plenty of room round here! Come now!'

Halt and Will exchanged glances. Then Will repeated Horace's bow.

'Age before beauty,' he said to Halt.

The older Ranger's eyebrow rose slightly. 'Pearl before swine,' he replied, and stepped towards the outcrop, repeating Mikeru's actions. After a few seconds groping, he swung out and disappeared round the bluff after the young Kikori. Will moved to the outcrop. He glanced down, then ignored the drop below. He knew that if the others could manage this, he could. He'd been an excellent climber all his life. He reached his right hand around, groping at the sheer rock face on the other side. A hand gently seized his and guided it to a firm handhold in the rock. He stepped off the ledge, hanging by his two hands, stretching his right leg around. Almost immediately, he encountered a horizontal ledge some five centimetres wide that gave his foot firm purchase. He moved his left foot to the vertical crack, then was free to reach with his right hand, then his left, swinging his body round the outcrop as the others had done. He found them waiting for him on a wide section of the ledge they had been following, a roomy platform in the rock. Judging by the drill marks visible in the hard surface, the platform had been constructed to serve as a lookout.

And there, below him, was the Senshi encampment.

He frowned. 'There can't be more than a hundred and fifty of them.'

But Halt pointed further to the south. 'The main body's back there.'

Now that Will looked, he could see a much larger camp set among the shelter of the trees, almost two kilometres away. Between that point and the valley mouth, the ground was a high, bare plateau, unsheltered open ground that was swept by the constant wind.

'Not the most comfortable spot,' Will said, gesturing to the smaller of the two positions.

Halt nodded. 'No point in Arisaka keeping all his men — and himself — exposed down there. He's left a force to plug the mouth of the valley and keep us contained, while the rest of them are sheltered in the trees.'

Will was looking keenly at the small encampment at the valley mouth. Very few of the men there were moving around. Those he could see were bundled up in heavy clothing and furs. He guessed that most of them were huddled inside the meagre shelter of their tents, dispirited, cold, resentful. After a while, all they would care about would be finding warmth and shelter from the persistent wind. That meant their vigilance would be lowered. After all, nobody really expected Shigeru and his tiny force to move out from behind the protection of the palisade — unless it was to attempt an escape. And a few sentries could keep track of any such attempt. As Halt had said, they were the cork in the bottle neck, placed there to prevent the Emperor slipping away.

'They're kind of vulnerable, aren't they?' Will said.

Halt glanced at him. 'To the weather?'

Will chewed his lip thoughtfully. 'Yes. But also to us, if we were to attack them.'

Halt studied the rows of tents below them without speaking. Will was right, he thought. The men in that camp would be preoccupied with the task of keeping warm. Judging by what he'd heard of Arisaka, they probably included the survivors of the attack on the palisade, placed there as a punishment for their failure.

'You'd bring men down through Mikeru's Pass?' he asked.

The young Kikori looked up and grinned at the mention of his name. He liked the fact that the secret path was named after him. He hoped maybe this spot would be called Mikeru's Lookout.

'Yes,' Will replied. 'The gully comes out around the far side of this cliff we're on. They won't be watching in that direction. We could bring the men down by night, let them assemble at the bottom, out of sight, then hit that camp before they know we've arrived.'

Halt's eyes followed the terrain as Will spoke. He nodded. 'Thirty or forty Senshi could make a big impact,' he suggested. 'Particularly with surprise on their side.'

Many of the wounded Senshi in Shigeru's party had recovered sufficiently to be ready to fight. They could easily muster a fighting force that size. But Will shook his head in disagreement.

'I was thinking of maybe a hundred Kikori,' he said.

There was a long silence. Halt wasn't surprised. Even though he'd suggested using the Senshi, he had a sense that this was what Will had in mind. The idea had a lot of merit. But Halt felt he should raise the possible flaws, to make sure his former apprentice wasn't just overeager to try the tactics he'd been teaching the Kikori.

'They're untried in battle,' he said. 'No matter how much you train them, nothing takes the place of actual experience.'

'All the more reason to do it,' Will told him. 'It's a perfect opportunity to give them the experience they need. The enemy will be cold and demoralised, not expecting an attack. And there are only about a hundred and fifty of them. We're not facing Arisaka's main force. We'll hit the enemy hard and fast, then head the Kikori back up the gully while Arisaka's men are still wondering what's happened. If the plan works, we'll give the Kikoris' self-confidence and esprit de corps an enormous boost.'

'And if it doesn't work?' Halt said.

Will met his gaze levelly. 'If it doesn't work now, with all the advantages in our favour, we're going to be in deep trouble when the spring comes and we're facing five times as many Senshi. This way we can give Arisaka a bloody nose, reduce the numbers of his army a little, and show the Kikori that they can face up to and defeat Senshi in battle. And that's possibly the most important part of it all.'

'I think you're right,' Halt said. 'When do you want to do it?'

'As soon as possible,' Will said. 'No point in delaying any longer. A few more days' training won't make any difference to the Kikori.'

Forty

vanlyn glanced over the side of the boat as they glided in towards the shore. The water was clear and pristine and looked to be no more than twenty centimetres deep. But she had learned in the past five days how deceptive this could be. The third day, thinking the water was shallow, she had stepped clear of the boat to find herself floundering wildly in waist-deep water. It was only by an enormous effort that she had avoided falling and immersing herself completely.

Her clothes had dried that night in front of the blazing fire they built. Since the encounter with the wolves, it had become their standard procedure to keep a fire burning all night and take turns keeping watch. It meant they each got less sleep each night, but at least when they did sleep, they did so soundly, each secure in the knowledge that her companion was keeping watch and making sure that the fire was maintained through the dark hours.

Whether because of the fire or not, there had been no

further disturbances since that second night. Of course, Evanlyn thought, it may have simply been the case that there were no wolves on any of the other islands.

Now, she reached down with her paddle, satisfying herself that the water was barely knee deep. She swung her legs over the side and stood up quickly, then guided the prow of the kayak towards the shingle beach. They had learned to beach the little boat unoccupied. On the third night, letting the bow grate into the sand and rock of the shore, they had torn a hole in the oilskin covering.

Alyss had watched Evanlyn sew a patch over the hole with a piece of spare oilcloth, then cover the seam with melted wax to seal it.

'Very neat,' she had said approvingly. Evanlyn smiled and brandished her needle.

'Needlepoint is one of the skills that are deemed fitting for a princess,' she replied. 'I never thought it would come in handy.'

Alyss's eyes were on her now as she tested the water depth, then dismounted from the boat. Alyss was developing a reluctant admiration for the princess's ability to adapt and learn. Alyss had been tough on her while she was learning the techniques of handling a small boat. Some of this was due to the lingering antipathy that Alyss seemed to feel for Evanlyn, but in the main it had been a practical choice.

Alyss knew, from conversations with Will and Lady Pauline, and from her own observations, that Evanlyn, courageous and resourceful as she was, did have a petulant side to her character. Unavoidable, perhaps, in one raised as a princess, in an environment where there were scores of people ready to leap to and do one's slightest bidding, and attend to the smallest wants. But on this trip, there could be no servants and no passengers. Alyss had sensed that if she had shown sympathy for Evanlyn's aching muscles, or laughed off her clumsy attempts at paddling, Evanlyn could be inclined to take advantage of her good nature. Instead, Alyss's repeated, sardonic *thank you for that* at each mistake had acted as a goad to Evanlyn, urging her to do better, to try harder, to show her tall, self-satisfied travelling companion that, princess or not, she could do the job she had been set.

With these thoughts in mind, Alyss nearly left it too late to step out of the boat herself. Knowing this would result in a tart comment, for she knew Evanlyn wanted nothing more than an opportunity to reply in kind, she swung her own legs clear and helped the princess lift the boat as they slid it up the beach, out of the water.

They set it down and both stretched to ease their cramping back muscles. Alyss took a few paces inland, looking around the little beach, and into the thickly growing trees beyond.

'So this is it,' she said.

They had finally reached the far side of the massive lake. This was the province where Lord Nimatsu ruled over the mysterious and fabled Hasanu. There was snow on the ground here but not in the quantities they had seen at Ran-Koshi. The altitude was lower, and the area was sheltered from the weather systems that blew in from the sea and drove snow and rain clouds onto the mountains behind them.

Here, in an area shielded by those same mountains, the wind was more gentle, more temperate. And it sighed softly through the needles of the spruce trees that towered above them.

'There doesn't seem to be anyone around,' Evanlyn murmured.

'Doesn't mean there's no one here, of course.'

'Of course.'

A knot of apprehension had formed in Evanlyn's stomach as she stood on this quiet, seemingly deserted spot. They had quizzed Shigeru and his senior advisers at some length about the Hasanu but, in truth, they had learned little.

Some held the Hasanu to be remnants of an ancient race of semi-human apes who had survived in this remote territory. Other, more frightening, theories held that the Hasanu were tree or forest spirits and the reclusive Lord Nimatsu was a sorcerer who had bent them to his will.

Other 'facts' they had gleaned seemed to contradict each other. Some said that the Hasanu were shy and nervous of contact with strangers, while others maintained they were fierce and merciless killers. Old legends about them certainly lent credence to this last. Numerous tales were told of their ferocity in battle. It was said that they had never been defeated. These tales, of course, were centuries old and nobody could actually admit to having seen a Hasanu, or to knowing someone who had. Although there were those who claimed to know someone who knew someone else who had seen one.

At the end of a long and confusing briefing session, Shigeru had dismissed his advisers and sat quietly with the two girls to give them a more balanced opinion on these strange people.

'Much is said about the Hasanu,' he had told them. 'And much of it is wild exaggeration. Here is what I know, stripped of rumour, conjecture and hysteria.

'They are said to be a tall and powerful race and reports from the past held them to be covered with long, reddish hair all over their bodies. This could be true. They live in a cold climate and their bodies may well have adapted in this way over the years. But the key point I know, and on which all legends and tales about them are agreed, is that they are fearless in battle and that they have an intense loyalty to their lord. At this time, that is Lord Nimatsu.

'These qualities would seem to indicate positive elements to their character, which give the lie to those wild stories about their bloodthirsty behaviour with regard to strangers. Loyal and fearless do not, to me, equate with bloodthirsty and savage.

'Lord Nimatsu has, on many occasions, confirmed his allegiance to me. That, I believe, will be the key to your dealings with the Hasanu. They are loyal to Nimatsu so, by extension, they are loyal to me – or at least, to the concept of an Emperor. When you reach Nimatsu's province, be patient. Wait for the Hasanu to make contact. They will do so – and they will do so at Nimatsu's bidding. When he knows that you are acting in my name, you will be safe.'

Shigeru had removed his signet ring and handed it to Evanlyn.

'Take this with you. When Nimatsu sees it, he will know you come from me. This will ensure your safety. Once you have made contact with him, I rely on your eloquence, Ev-an-in-san, to convince him to help us. I will send a letter with you, of course. But in my experience, it is the spoken word and the integrity of the messenger that holds most sway in these matters.'

Evanlyn had taken the ring, slipping it onto her first finger.

'I wish I could advise you more fully on this matter,' Shigeru said, sighing deeply. 'But the success or failure of your mission will rest on your own abilities and resources.' He had smiled at them both then and added: 'And I cannot think of two more worthy or resourceful messengers.'

'So,' Alyss said, looking round the silent trees. 'How do we find the Hasanu?'

'Don't worry about that. Remember what Shigeru said. The Hasanu will find us.'

They unpacked their gear from the kayak and set about making camp. Alyss pitched their small tent while Evanlyn gathered stones for a fireplace, then a good supply of firewood. She was using her saxe knife — a gift from Halt some years previously — to cut one long piece of deadfall into manageable lengths when she had the sensation of eyes upon her.

Somewhere in the shadows among the trees, someone, or something, was watching her. She was sure of it. She paused for a moment in her work, then resumed, resisting the almost overpowering urge to turn and look into the trees. She glanced sideways, to see if Alyss had sensed anything. Apparently not. The tall girl was tightening the guy ropes on the tent, testing the tension to make sure that the canvas was evenly positioned.

Evanlyn gathered up the wood and walked casually

back to place it by the circle of stones she had arranged as a fireplace.

'We're being watched,' she said softly.

Alyss froze for a second, then tugged the guy rope one last time, dusted her hands in satisfaction and moved to help Evanlyn sort the kindling from the heavier firewood. As they knelt together, she said, 'You saw someone?'

'No. It was more a sensation than anything. But I'm sure someone's there.'

She half expected a sardonic reply from her companion. But Alyss was never one to deny the value of instinct.

'Then we just keep doing what we're doing,' Alyss said. 'Let's brew some tea. And keep acting casually.'

All the same, Evanlyn noticed, she stole a quick glance to where her sword was resting on top of her pack at the entrance to the tent.

Some minutes later, they sat facing each other across the fire, sipping the warming tea. Alyss had positioned herself so that she faced the lake, leaving Evanlyn looking towards the trees behind them. Evanlyn had sensed the presence of the watcher, she reasoned, so there was a better chance of her seeing whoever it might be. Or whatever it might be, she amended.

As she sipped her tea, Evanlyn's eyes darted from side to side above the teacup. Her head never moved. From a few metres away, there was no indication that she was scanning the dark shadows beneath the spruces.

She gave a satisfied sigh and set her cup down.

'Something moved,' she said in a conversational tone.

A fleeting, shadowy movement had caught her eye. It was all she could do not to suddenly stare in the direction from which it had come but she managed it by an enormous effort of will.

'Can you see him now?' Alyss asked, maintaining the same casual tone.

'No. He's gone to ground. Wait. There he goes again. Can't make out any detail. It's just movement in the ferns under the trees. Whatever it is, it's moving closer to the edge of the tree line.'

They waited, nerves tensed. But there was no further sign of movement.

'I think he's gone,' Evanlyn said after several minutes.

Alyss shrugged. 'Or he's not moving, just watching us. Well, we can't sit here all afternoon. Any ideas?'

Evanlyn rose to her feet, avoiding any sudden movement, and crossed to her pack. Rummaging in it, she found what she was looking for — one of the few food items that the wolves had missed when they ransacked the camp several days before. It was a small twist of greased paper, containing a handful of candied fruit pieces — apples and apricots. They were a confectionery much favoured among the Kikori and Evanlyn had developed a taste for them herself. There were about a dozen pieces left. She hoped that would be enough. She strode back to where Alyss was watching her curiously.

'I've got a thought,' she said. 'Our unseen friend might be a bit more willing to show himself if there weren't two of us.'

She saw Alyss begin to object and held up a hand to stop her. 'No! Hear me out. I'm suggesting that you take the kayak and paddle offshore about a hundred metres and wait there. I'll sit over there, closer to the trees, and see if the Hasanu are willing to make contact.' She held up the small package of candied fruit. 'I'll use this to get the conversation going.'

Alyss frowned thoughtfully. 'One thing most people agreed on,' she said, 'is that the Hasanu like sweet things.'

'And these fit the bill. Look, if you leave — although you'll be seen to stay in the general area — and I sit closer to where they are, it's a pretty unmistakable message, isn't it? We want to make contact. There's a good chance that our friend in the trees will be encouraged to come out into the open.'

'There's also a chance that he'll be encouraged to tear you limb from limb,' Alyss said and Evanlyn nodded uncomfortably.

'That's the part of my plan that I'm not totally delighted with. But I think we have to take the chance and force things along. Otherwise, we could be sitting here for days. And let's face it,' she added, 'if they want to tear us limb from limb, your presence here is hardly going to stop them.'

'Well, thank you for that vote of confidence,' Alyss replied. 'One thing,' she added. 'Just consider my position. It's going to be awfully awkward for me to return to Araluen and tell your father I watched a Nihon-Jan monster dismember you. It won't be good for my career.'

Sensing a new note of comradeship behind the banter, Evanlyn managed a faint smile.

'And after all, your career is important to all of us,' she said. 'I'll try to bear it in mind. Now get going.'

Alyss rose, took her sword, a water canteen and some strips of smoked rabbit that Evanlyn had killed with her sling the day before, and made her way to the boat. Evan-lyn followed. They took Evanlyn's paddle out — Alyss wouldn't be needing it — and she waded into the water, lifting the kayak and sliding it with her. As soon as it could float, Alyss slid gracefully into her seat and took a few smooth strokes, setting the little boat gliding across the calm water. She glanced back over her shoulder to Evanlyn, standing by the water's edge.

'Take care,' she called.

Evanlyn waved in reply. 'Of course,' she said easily.

Walking up the shallow beach, she found a fallen log close to the treeline that gave her a comfortable spot to sit and wait. She took a seat, then produced the packet of candied fruit and spread half a dozen pieces on the log beside her.

She took a piece and placed it in her mouth, feeling the juices begin to run as the combination of tartness and sweetness took effect on her taste buds. She gave an exag-gerated sigh of pleasure, smacking her lips several times to indicate how much she was enjoying the treat.

And waited.

It seemed an age, although in reality it was only two or three minutes, but her straining senses caught the slightest sound — a rustle in the ferns behind her and to her left. Senses as taut as a fiddle string, she strained to hear more.

Was that another slight rustle? It sounded a little closer than the first. Or was it the wind? She looked to her right, examining the ferns there closely. They weren't moving. No, there was no wind, she thought.

There it was again! The hairs on the back of her neck stood up and she could feel gooseflesh forming on her forearms. Something was there. Something was behind her, and moving closer to her. Every nerve in her body screamed at her to stand and turn and see what it was. This waiting, knowing something was there — no, *thinking* something was there — was all but intolerable.

But somehow, she stood it. She swallowed the piece of fruit, forcing it down a throat that had suddenly turned dry.

'Mmmm,' she said appreciatively. 'That was good!'

She popped another piece into her mouth, made another exclamation of enjoyment, then, seemingly as an afterthought, she took a piece and placed it half a metre or so away from its companions, then gestured to it.

'This is for you,' she said, then repeated a little louder, 'For you.'

There was definitely something behind her. She knew it now without any doubt. Something large was less than two metres away. She didn't know *how* she knew it was large. She hadn't heard any heavy footfall, nothing more than the slightest rustle of leaves and twigs. But there was a large presence there, as if the very life force of whatever it was had impinged upon her senses.

She realised she was holding her breath. Her heart was hammering inside her rib cage — so loud she was sure that whatever it was behind her could hear it.

She began to sing — one of the gentle country songs that she'd heard Will singing as he accompanied himself on the mandola.

'Oh, Annalie dancing.
A shaft of light fell on her as I saw
Annalie dancing
and haven't I seen Annalie, somewhere before?'

Her voice quavered with tension. She warbled on and off the notes as she tried to sing them truly.

I sound terrified, she thought. Although maybe this . . . whatever it is . . . will just think I'm a lousy singer.

She drew breath for the next verse but it never came. Out of the corner of her eye, she saw movement.

A large hand, with long, claw-like nails and covered in thick red-brown hair, reached from behind her and took the candied apricot from the log.

Forty-one

The men selected for the attack *hyaku* were paraded on the exercise ground in two groups of fifty. Formed up in three extended ranks, the Kikori looked impressive. The weak sunlight shone off the gleaming points of their javelins, and caught the iron bindings and reinforcing strips on their man-high shields and leather helmets. The lines of their formation were ruler-straight as they stood before Will, Horace, Halt and Selethen. Horace and Selethen would command a group of fifty each — or a *goju*, as they had called the formation. Will and Halt would stand back and stay in overall command — although Halt had ceded this responsibility to the younger Ranger.

'They're your men,' he said. 'You trained them and men deserve to be led by the leader they know and trust.'

Will nodded nervously. He knew Halt was right. All the same, he was glad the experienced grey-bearded Ranger would be on hand if needed. He looked to where Horace was watching him, and nodded. The young warrior drew in a breath, then called out an order in a ringing parade ground voice.

'*Hyaku!*'

The men had been standing at parade rest, their feet apart and their javelins, shafts resting on the ground, extended forward at arm's length. At the warning command, their feet stamped together and the javelins came to the vertical position.

'Open order!' Horace called. The front rank took two long paces forward. The rear rank took two back. The three ranks were now separated by a two-metre gap, leaving room for their commanders to move through and inspect them.

This was Horace and Selethen's job. They selected a *goju* each and moved quickly along the lines, checking equipment, making sure each man had his three short stabbing spears in a quiver-like arrangement at his right hip, checking shields for any sign of looseness or fraying in the straps, glancing at javelin heads to see that they were firmly attached and gleaming from a recent sharpening.

'Looks good,' Halt said quietly.

Horace and Selethen were more than halfway through their inspection and so far, neither had stopped to reprimand any of the troops for missing or faulty equipment. Obviously, the turnout was near perfect. Horace did stop once and straighten a soldier's leather helmet, tugging the chin strap a little tighter to secure it more firmly, but that was all.

The Kikori had risen to the challenge splendidly and Will felt a warm sense of pride in them. Not so long ago, they had been simple timber workers. Now they were soldiers, with a soldier's pride in their own ability and in their own unit.

'Troops inspected and ready,' Horace reported.

Will nodded. 'Close them up and stand them at rest, Horace.'

The tall warrior gave the orders and the front and rear ranks closed back in to their original positions. One hundred feet stamped apart and one hundred javelin heads thrust forward as one.

Will stepped forward, moving closer to the ranks so that they would hear him more clearly. He studied the faces under the leather and iron helmets. The men were grim and determined. But there was a look of subdued excitement in many of the eyes looking back at him. No apprehension or fear, he was glad to see.

'*Goju Kuma! Goju Taka!*' he said, and now every eye was on him. They had named the two *goju* for the two leaders. *Goju Kuma* was the Bear fifty, led by Horace, who was now known to everyone as *Kurokuma*. *Goju Taka* reflected the nickname that had been given to Selethen. *Taka* meant hawk, and Will assumed the name derived from Selethen's prominent nose, which had some similarity to the curved beak of a bird of prey.

'Tomorrow is the time to put all your hard work into practice,' he continued. 'Tomorrow is the day when you will strike the Emperor's first blow at the traitor Arisaka!'

There was a growl of anger through the ranks as he said the name of the hated rebel leader.

'Remember your training. Remember what we have practised. If you do this, you will achieve a great victory for your Emperor. But you must remember your training.

Look around you. Look at the men beside you and behind you! Study their faces.'

He paused while one hundred heads turned, while eyes made contact and heads nodded in recognition. When they had settled again, he continued.

'These men are your comrades. These are your brothers. These are the men you fight with. These are the men you trust to stand beside you. These are the men who trust you to stand firm beside them! Be worthy of their trust!'

Again, a deep-throated rumble of agreement ran through the ranks of armed men. Will felt he had said enough. He had no time for lengthy, florid speeches from commanders on the eve of battle. They were usually made to please the commander's sense of self-importance. He had just one more thing he wanted to remind them of.

'Kikori soldiers!' he shouted. 'How do we fight?'

The reply came in a roar from the ranks.

'Issho ni!' they told him. 'Together!'

'How do we fight?' he asked, louder still, and the roar came back louder as well.

'Issho ni!'

'How?' he asked them one more time, and this time the valley echoed to their reply.

'Issho ni!'

On an impulse, he drew his saxe and brandished it high above his head. The two *goju* responded, holding their javelins high, then pounding them back to the frozen ground with a resounding crash of wood and metal.

Behind him, a deep, penetrating voice called a single word.

'*Chocho!*'

The one hundred troops in front of him responded instantly, echoing the cry and turning it into a chant.

'*Chocho! Chocho! Chocho!*'

Puzzled, and a little taken aback, Will turned to see that Shigeru had approached while he had been speaking. The Emperor was dressed in full armour, but no helmet. His two *katana* were thrust through his belt, their long hilts protruding before him like the crossed horns of a dangerous animal. Shigeru continued to lead the chant, dropping his hand on Will's shoulder.

'*Chocho! Chocho! Chocho!*' the men roared and, vaguely, Will realised that this somehow applied to him. Then Shigeru held up his hand for silence and the roaring voices gradually died down. Will disengaged himself and stepped back deferentially, sensing that Shigeru wanted to address his troops.

Horace was grinning hugely as Will joined him.

'What the devil is *Chocho*?' Will whispered.

Horace's grin broadened. 'You are. It's what the men call you,' he said. Then he added, 'It's a term of great respect.'

Behind them, Halt nodded confirmation. 'Great respect,' he agreed. There was the hint of a smile at the corner of his mouth and Will knew he would have to find out the meaning of the word before much longer. But he had no more time to think about it as Shigeru began to speak.

'Kikori, I am honoured to have you as my soldiers. I am proud of your commitment and your courage and your loyalty. You have your Emperor's gratitude.'

There was silence around the parade ground now. These were simple timber cutters, peasants for whom, up until recently, the Emperor had been a distant and much revered concept, way above their reach and their station. Now he lived among them and spoke directly to them in terms of the greatest respect. His words were simple but the sincerity behind them was all too obvious and the Kikori felt their hearts swelling with pride. Such was the charisma of this man that they would die for him. Shigeru seemed to sense this and he continued.

'Soldiers! I know you would die in my service.'

There was an instant roar of assent and he immediately raised his hands and his voice to quell it.

'But I do not want this!' The shouting died away and the faces that watched him were puzzled.

'I want you to *live* in my service!' he shouted and they roared their acclaim once more. When the sound of their voices died down, he continued. '*Chocho* has taught you a new way to fight. He has taught you the code of *Issho ni*! If you are faithful to this code, you will win a great victory.' He paused. 'And I will be there to see it! I am coming with you!'

Now the cheers were deafening. Shigeru moved forward to walk among his men and they broke ranks to surround him, cheering him, bowing to him, reaching out to touch him.

'What?' Will said. 'What is he talking about?' He made to follow the Emperor, to draw him back.

A hand seized his arm from behind him and he turned to see Halt's face. His old mentor was shaking his head.

'He's right, Will. He has to be there.'

'But if we're beaten! If we fail . . . he'll be taken by Arisaka!' Will said helplessly.

Halt nodded. 'That's right. But he's willing to gamble on these men. He believes in them. Don't you?'

'Well, yes, of course. But if he's there . . .'

'If he's there, they'll fight to keep him safe. You know they can beat the Senshi. I know it and Shigeru knows it. The only people who aren't sure are the men themselves. Oh, they're fine here and now. But when the crunch comes, they're going to be facing an enemy they've never felt worthy to face before. Our biggest potential danger tomorrow is that, faced by warriors who they have always believed are their superiors, they'll lose that confidence. And if they do, they'll break. They'll fight bravely. But they'll die bravely — because they will believe they have no right to win.'

'But —' Will began but now Horace interrupted.

'Halt's right, Will,' he said. 'If they know Shigeru is there and that he trusts in them, they'll have greater trust in themselves.'

'He could be killed or taken prisoner,' Will protested.

'No,' Horace said. 'Your men won't let that happen. He knows he has to be there.'

'He's a great man,' Selethen said quietly. 'The sort of man you're proud to serve.'

'They think so,' Halt said, gesturing to where Shigeru's bare head could be seen, moving among the jostling crowd of helmets and javelin points. 'And they'll need that sort of pride if they're going to win.' He paused, watching the scene on the valley floor through slitted eyes.

'And they *are* going to win,' he added. He saw that Will

was still doubtful about the entire idea and clapped him on the back cheerfully. 'Try and have some faith in your men, Will. At least as much as the Emperor does.'

'Isn't there any way I can stop this?' Will asked despairingly, and this time it was Horace's turn to slap his shoulder.

'Of course. Just figure out a way to tell an Emperor that you forbid him to do something he's determined on. That should be easy for someone as devious as you.'

His three friends all grinned at him. Then Halt jerked his head towards the narrow gully that led to the secret pass.

'Let's get going. We've got a battle to win tomorrow.'

Forty-two

Evanlyn's hair stood on end, literally. She controlled an impulse to leap to her feet and spin around, confronting the unknown creature behind her — although logic told her it must be one of the Hasanu. Her song had died away as the hand entered her field of vision. In a quavering, uncertain voice, she began to sing again, very softly.

'*Round and round she went,*
softly stepping circles in the sun . . .'

She was sure she could hear the sound of chewing close behind her. She took another piece of fruit and put it in her mouth. Then, almost as an afterthought, she selected a second piece and placed it away from her, on the log.

'For you,' she said, then continued humming the melody to the song. After a few seconds, the hand appeared again and took the fruit. She finished her piece and smacked her lips again in appreciation.

'Mmmm. Good.'

'Mmmmmmmm.' The sound was echoed behind her,

along with the lip smacking. She took a deep breath and set another piece of fruit to one side.

'For you.'

Again, the hand appeared. This time, it didn't dart in and out as on the two previous occasions. It took the fruit and withdrew more slowly. Then she heard the voice again — husky and a little slurred. Just the one word.

''rigato.'

Arigato, she knew, was the Nihon-Jan word for thank you. She searched her memory desperately for the correct response, but it eluded her. She settled for, 'You're welcome.'

There was one apricot left. She waited until she could hear no more sound of chewing behind her, then set the remaining piece of fruit out to the side. This time, there was a long pause. Then the voice said:

'*Ié, ié!*'

It meant 'No, no!' It was the Nihon-Jan form of polite refusal. The hand appeared, picked up the fruit and put it back close by her side. She smiled to herself. The odds against her being torn limb from limb seemed to be getting better, she thought. Casually, she drew her saxe knife.

Instantly, there was a rustle of alarmed movement behind her. She paid it no heed, other than to repeat the same phrase.

'*Ié, ié!*' It mightn't be the exact phrase needed but she thought it would do, and she made her voice light and reassuring as she said it. The movement stopped. She sensed that the Hasanu had backed off a few metres. Now she used the saxe to divide the remaining apricot in half. She re-sheathed the big knife, took one half of the apricot and set the other to one side. She heard him move in again, this time not bothering to move silently. The hand came into view once more, took the fruit and exited from her field of vision.

'I think it's time we met each other,' she said gently. Making sure she made no sudden movement, she rose from her seat on the log. She paused, fixed a smile on her face and resolved that, whatever she saw, it would stay there.

Then, she slowly turned around.

The figure crouching on the ground behind the log was massive. Long, shaggy red hair hung down to its shoulders, matched by an equally long, equally unkempt beard. The huge body appeared to be covered in long red-brown hair as well. As yet, she could make out no features. She kept the smile fixed on her face. She felt vaguely like a death's head. Then she swept down in a graceful curtsey, her arms extended to the sides, her head bowed.

The Hasanu stood erect. She glanced up, still smiling, and caught her breath. He was at least two and a half metres tall and now she saw that the long red hair that had appeared to cover his body was nothing more than a long cloak, made of fur or shaggy wool, she couldn't tell which. He bowed clumsily to her and she lowered her gaze, then they slowly stood upright together.

Now she could make out more of his features. The face was broad, with prominent cheekbones and a heavy, flat nose. The eyes were narrow but set well apart under heavy brows with luxurious, untrimmed eyebrows. There was a definite light of intelligence and curiosity in the eyes, she saw. Then he smiled. His teeth were large and even. They were somewhat yellowed and stained, but they were normal human teeth, with no fang-like incisors. Evanlyn touched one hand to her own chest.

'Evanlyn,' she said, enunciating the syllables carefully. 'Ev-an-lyn.'

He frowned. The name structure was unfamiliar to him but he attempted it.

'Eh-van-in.'

'Good!' She smiled encouragingly and he smiled back. She swept her arm around and pointed to the distant kayak, where Alyss waited nervously.

'Alyss,' she said. 'My friend. Al-yss.'

He frowned with effort, then repeated, 'Ah-yass.'

'Close enough,' she said in an undertone, then continued, speaking carefully. 'Alyss, Evanlyn, friends.' She accompanied the words with gestures. Pointing to herself and to Alyss, then miming a hugging gesture to indicate friends. The giant frowned again for a few seconds, trying to interpret the meaning. Then she saw understanding dawn as he repeated the hugging gesture.

'Fwends. *Hai!*'

Hai meant 'yes', she knew. Now she pointed to him, then to herself.

'You . . . Evanlyn . . . friends, *hai?*' She repeated the hugging gesture, feeling a sudden sense of alarm that he might attempt it for real. She didn't know if her ribs could withstand a hugging from this two-and-a-half-metre-tall forest giant.

Fortunately, he understood they were talking in symbols. He pointed to himself.

'Kona,' he said.

She assumed an exaggerated questioning expression and pointed to him.

'You . . . Kona?'

He nodded, smiling again. '*Hai!* Kona.' He pointed to her again, then to himself. 'Eh-van-in. Kona.'

'Friends,' she said, firmly, pointing from herself to him. It wasn't a question, it was a statement, and he nodded eagerly.

'*Hai!* Fwends.'

'And thank the lord for that,' she muttered to herself. He cocked his head to one side, wondering what she'd said, but she made a dismissive gesture with her hand.

'Never mind,' she said, making a mental note to avoid flippant remarks in future. Kona might look like a huge, shaggy ape, but he was no fool, she realised. She pointed to the small camp site, then beckoned to him.

'Come,' she said. She reached for his massive hand. Uncertainly at first, he gave it to her, then smiled broadly once more at the contrast in size between her hand and his. She led him down the beach to the water's edge, where she released his hand and waved to Alyss, drifting offshore about a hundred metres. The tall girl waved in return.

'Are you all right?' Alyss's voice carried faintly across the intervening water. Evanlyn couldn't resist a smile.

'No. He tore me limb from limb! Of course I'm all right! Come ashore!'

As Alyss dug the paddle into the water, Evanlyn turned back to Kona. 'Alyss is coming. Alyss, Kona, friends.'

'Ah-yass, Kona, fwends,' he repeated. But his tone indicated that he would reserve judgement. Alyss, after all, hadn't shared any candied apricots with him.

As it turned out, his doubts were soon dispelled by Alyss's natural grace and charm, and her easy manner with strangers. At her invitation, he studied the kayak with interest. The Hasanu did have boats but theirs were clumsy and heavy craft compared to the slender, graceful kayak. He showed particular interest in the shaping of the paddles. His people merely used thick branches to propel their boats. The idea of a shaped, flattened blade had never occurred to them. Kona filed away the design for future reference.

His inspection of the boat completed, he turned his eyes to their other equipment. The tent created some interest. Like the kayak, it was more advanced in design than the simple shelters the Hasanu built for themselves when they were travelling. He studied their packs and his curiosity was aroused when he saw the two sabres lying in their scabbards.

'Katana?' he said, then pointed from the swords to the two girls. The meaning was unmistakable. *Are these yours?*

Alyss nodded. 'Ours.'

He showed some surprise. Apparently it wasn't common for Hasanu women to carry weapons. They built up the fire and Evanlyn boiled water for tea. She and Alyss shared one cup, leaving the second for Kona's use. The tiny receptacle was almost lost in his massive, hair-covered hand. On closer inspection, they had discovered that the Hasanu, assuming Kona was typical, did have a lot of body hair — although nowhere near as much as legend would have them believe.

They waited until Kona had finished his tea, and some smoked rabbit they offered him. He was impressed with the latter, smacking his lips several times. Then they approached the subject of their visit to this province. At Alyss's suggestion, Evanlyn took the lead. After all, she had been the first to win Kona's trust.

'Kona?' she said, to get his attention. When he looked at her expectantly, she gestured among the three of them. 'Alyss, Evanlyn, Kona . . . friends. *Hai?*'

'*Hai!*' he agreed instantly.

She nodded several times, then said, 'Alyss, Evanlyn . . . Nimatsu-san . . .' She paused at that point, seeing his interest kindled by the name, and a look of respect come over his features. Then she repeated: 'Alyss, Evanlyn . . . Nimatsu-san . . . friends. Friends.'

'Pushing it?' Alyss said mildly. After all, they had never met Nimatsu.

'We will be,' Evanlyn said in a confident aside. 'Now shut up. Alyss, Evanlyn, Nimatsu-san. All friends.'

Kona looked a little surprised. He pointed to the two of them. 'Fwends . . . Nimatsu-san?'

'*Hai!*' Evanlyn told him.

'*Hai!*' Alyss said in her turn.

Kona, they were pleased to see, looked impressed.

'You . . . take us . . . to Nimatsu-san?' Evanlyn reinforced her meaning with gestures.

Kona seemed to understand. 'Eh-van-in, Ah-yass . . . Nimatsu-san *ikimas?*'

'*Ikimas* is "go",' Alyss told Evanlyn in an undertone.

Evanlyn felt a small surge of triumph. '*Hai!*' she said. 'Evanlyn, Alyss, Kona . . . *ikimas* Nimatsu-san.'

'Verb should come last,' Alyss muttered. Evanlyn made a dismissive gesture.

'Who cares? He got it.'

Kona considered the request for some time, nodding to himself as he did so. Then he seemed to come to a decision.

'Hai!' he said emphatically. *'Nimatsu-san ikimas.'*

He stood abruptly and loped across the beach in long strides to the treeline. He paused there, looking back at the two girls, who had been taken by surprise by his sudden acquiescence. He held his hand out to them, fingers down, and made a shooing motion at them.

'Ikimashou!' he said.

Evanlyn, halfway to her feet, paused uncertainly. 'What's he doing? He's waving us away. I thought he was taking us?'

But Alyss had seen the gesture several times before, in the Kikori encampment.

'It's how the Nihon-Jan beckon you towards them,' she said. *'Ikimashou* means "let's go".'

'Then what are we waiting for?' Evanlyn said, hurrying to grab up her pack and sword. 'Let's *ikimashou* by all means.'

Alyss was doing the same thing. 'You don't need to say "let's *ikimashou*",' she said. 'The "let's" is already included in the verb.'

'Big deal,' said Evanlyn. She was feeling a little pleased with herself. Alyss was, after all, the linguist. But Evanlyn had been the one to open effective communications with the enormous Hasanu. 'Are you coming, or what?' she threw back over her shoulder as she trudged quickly up the beach in Kona's wake.

Forty-three

Getting the hundred men of the *hyaku* down the narrow pass was an interesting exercise in logistics and teamwork.

Horace had decided it was too risky for the fighting men to negotiate the steep and rocky path burdened by javelins, shields and armour. Accordingly, when the review parade with Shigeru was finished, he marched the men to the beginning of the secret path and had them pile their shields and javelins in stacks of five. Those Kikori who had not been selected to take part in the fighting now acted as bearers, assisted by the ever-present Mikeru and a group of his young friends.

They lashed the javelins together, assigning one man to carry each bundle of five strapped across his back. The shields were similarly lashed together in flat piles and two men took each bundle of five shields, carrying them as if they were stretchers. The remainder spread them- selves along the column to help the weapons bearers down the more difficult places, or to spell them when they became tired. Mikeru and his friends, unhampered and surefooted as mountain goats, scampered ahead, placing burning torches to light the most awkward places on the trail.

Finally, the fighting men themselves, burdened only by their stabbing blades and body armour, wound their way down the narrow defile in a long line.

Half an hour before dawn, Bear *Goju* and Hawk *Goju* were formed up on the level ground at the bottom of the secret path. They were fully armed and equipped and they'd made the trip down without any casualties. By contrast, there were a dozen sprained ankles and other minor injuries among the bearers.

Horace approached the spot where Will, Halt and Shigeru had watched the men emerge from the pass and form quietly into their formations.

'We're ready to move out,' he said.

Will gestured to the huge bluff several hundred metres away, which obscured any sight of the Senshi encampment.

'Let's take a look at the enemy first,' he said. 'Keep an eye on the Emperor,' he added to Horace. He didn't want Shigeru wandering away or showing himself before they had an idea of the enemy's deployment and situation. Then he and Halt ghosted off, staying close to the edge of the bluff as they went. They reached the end of the bluff and disappeared round, moving out of sight.

Horace looked at the Emperor. Shigeru seemed calm, but his right hand was clenching and unclenching on the hilt of his *katana*. Horace smiled encouragingly.

'What do we do now?' Shigeru asked.

'We wait,' Horace replied.

———➤———

Will and Halt slipped round the rocky outcrop, then climbed up a little from the plateau floor for a better view. They'd had lookouts posted at Mikeru's spot the entire night, ready to send warning if the Senshi moved, or were reinforced, or if there were any other change in the situation. No such message had come but Will preferred to trust his own observation in matters like these. That was the way Halt had taught him.

The camp was largely as they had seen it from the lookout point high above. Tents were pitched in haphazard lines, in a large, amorphous mass. A few sentries could be seen, pacing dispiritedly around the outer perimeter. In the time the two Rangers watched, not one seemed to lift his eyes from the frozen ground a few metres in front of his pacing feet. They were preoccupied with remaining hunched down in their cloaks, conserving as much body warmth as possible. The grey light slowly strengthened and Will and Halt could make out more detail.

In the centre of the low, utilitarian tents stood one larger, and rather ornate, pavilion. Two men stood guard outside and banners were planted at the entrance, streaming out in the wind.

'Can you make out the central banner?' Halt asked. There was a heraldic device on the flag in the centre of the group. The others were inscribed with Nihon-Jan characters. Will shaded his eyes and peered more closely.

'An ox, I think,' he said. 'A green ox.'

'Not that it means anything to us,' Halt replied. 'Although Shigeru should know who it is.'

Will glanced at him. 'Is that important?'

'It's always important to know who you're facing,' Halt said quietly. He surveyed the lie of the land between them and the Senshi encampment. For the most part, it was relatively even ground but there was one section covered in tumbled rocks. Beyond the rocks, to the east, the land fell away in a low cliff. Ahead of them, to the south, the plain sloped down towards the tents.

'That's our position,' he said, indicating it to Will. 'That broken ground will give our left flank some protection and the Senshi will be attacking uphill.'

'Not much of a hill,' Will observed.

'We'll take whatever advantage we can get,' Halt told him. 'Now, let's head back and start the ball.'

They made their way back to their waiting companions and held a quick council of war. Will described the broken ground on the left.

'We'll start there,' he said. 'Then we'll advance in line. Put the men in two ranks so we have a longer front. Selethen, put your men on the right of Horace's *goju* and about ten metres behind. That way, when the enemy try to work round his right flank, you can advance and hit them in the rear. Horace, when they do that, remember the plan we made last night.'

'I know. Swing the gate shut with my second rank,' Horace said. 'I have done this before, you know.'

'Sorry,' Will said. 'Later this afternoon, I'll teach your grandmother to suck eggs.'

The two old friends grinned at each other. Shigeru and Selethen both looked a little puzzled.

'Why does his grandmother want to suck eggs?' Shigeru asked.

The Arridi warrior shrugged. 'I have no idea.' He looked at Halt but the Ranger waved away the query.

'Long story,' he said. 'I'll tell you later.'

'Oh, Shigeru,' Will said, remembering a detail. 'The enemy commander has a green ox as his symbol. Does that mean anything to you?'

The Emperor nodded. 'That is General Todoki. He's one of Arisaka's most ardent supporters. His men attacked the palisade. He'll be eager to avenge that defeat.'

'Good,' Halt said. 'That'll mean he's more likely to act without thinking. Always a good thing to fight an enemy who's angry.'

'Let's get moving!' Will said and the five of them shook hands, then moved to their positions. At a word of command, the men of the two *goju*, who had been resting on the ground, conserving their strength, climbed quickly to their feet.

They formed in three files and set out at a steady jog, their equipment and weapons rattling in rhythm to the thud of their feet. They rounded the bluff and the enemy camp came into view.

As the two *gojus* reached their positions, Halt, Will and Shigeru diverted to a small hillock from where they could observe the battle. They were a little behind the Kikori ranks. Moka, Shigeru's senior bodyguard, had wanted to accompany them but Shigeru refused.

'I want the Kikori to see that my trust in them is complete,' he said.

Moka had remained with ten Senshi at the entrance to Mikeru's Pass. If the worst came to the worst, it would be their task to hold the pass against Arisaka's men while the Kikori made their escape up the secret path.

The *gojus* deployed now, forming into two extended ranks, twenty-five men long. Each man in the second rank held two javelins. The front rank were armed with their stabbing blades only. All of them, of course, had their massive shields on their left arms.

Remarkably, there was no reaction from the enemy camp. Not one of the slouching sentries seemed to have noticed that one hundred armed men had suddenly appeared barely one hundred and fifty metres away.

Halt shook his head in disgust. 'I thought this might happen,' he said. He took out a fire arrow he had prepared the night before — a standard shaft with a bunch of oil-soaked rag tied around the head. 'Light me up, Will.'

The younger Ranger worked briefly with flint and steel and in a few seconds set a tongue of flame to the oil-soaked rag. Halt waited until he was sure the flame had taken and was well established. Then he glanced at the enemy camp, raised his bow to almost forty-five degrees, drew and released.

The fire arrow left a thin black trail of smoke behind it as it rose into the overcast morning sky.

They lost sight of it as it plunged down past the apogee of its flight. Then Will saw a bright tongue of flame flare up at Todoki's ornate pavilion. After a second, the entire roof of the pavilion, daubed with oil to make it waterproof, burst into flames and they could hear shouts from the camp as several men ran out of the tent, one falling in his haste.

'I'm afraid you'll have made Todoki-san very angry now, Halto-san,' said Shigeru.

Halt smiled grimly. 'That was the general idea.' He glanced at Will and nodded. The young Ranger filled his lungs and shouted across the intervening space to Horace.

'Horace! Go!'

Horace drew his sword and raised it in the air. Selethen mirrored the action. There was a rattling crunch as the heavy shields were lifted from the rest position on the rocky ground. Then, at a word from Horace, the fifty Kikori bellowed as one.

'Issho ni!'

Selethen's men echoed the cry.

'Issho ni!'

Then all one hundred men began chanting their war cry as a cadence, marching in time to it as they advanced across the plain towards the Senshi camp. Horace and Selethen halted them after twenty paces, but the war cry continued, booming across the plain.

Todoki's men, roused by the sudden fire in their commander's tent, were now fully awake. Their initial alarm at the sudden sound of the Kikori war cry and the tramp of their boots turned to anger as they realised that they were being attacked by mere Kikori — despised peasants who had no right to raise arms against their betters. Arming themselves, Todoki's Senshi began streaming out of the camp in an unco-ordinated mass, hurrying to attack these presumptuous fools. They formed into a ragged line as they ran towards the waiting Kikori. Then Horace gave an order and a shrill whistle sounded among the two waiting *gojus*.

With a crash, the shields in each front rank were presented round to the enemy and the charging Senshi found themselves confronted by a seemingly solid wall of hardwood and iron. Two quick whistle blasts sounded and the wall of shields started to tramp steadily towards them.

This was an insult that could not be borne! The leading Senshi threw themselves against the shield wall, seeking an enemy to engage. But the Kikori were hidden behind the huge shields. Furious, the first Senshi swung their *katana* in sweeping overhead strokes. But the top edges of the shields were reinforced with iron. The swords bit into it but, with the support of the hardwood beneath it, the iron held, stopping the murderous downstrokes. The Senshi who were engaged struggled to free their swords. But now a new danger arose.

The Kikori had not stopped their steady advance and the men in the second rank were lending their weight to the front rank, shoving them forward. The shields smashed into the Senshi, sending them reeling. In some cases, they lost their grip on the hilts of their *katana*, leaving them embedded in the shields.

Now, those engaged closely could see vague glimpses of the enemy through narrow gaps in the shield wall. Several tried to stab through the gaps but as a blade went between two shields, the Kikori holding them suddenly clashed them together, overlapping them like giant shears and twisting the sword from its owner's grasp. Instinctively, the Senshi reached to retrieve their fallen weapons, only to realise their mistake.

Short, razor-sharp iron blades began to stab out of the gaps in the wall, skewering arms, legs, bodies, aiming for gaps in the Senshi armour. One Senshi warrior drew back his sword for a mighty cut at a Kikori on his left, exposed by a momentary gap in the shield wall. But as he did so, he felt a sudden massive pain under his arm as a blade darted out, wielded by a Kikori on his right — unseen until now. His *katana* fell from his hand and his knees gave under him as he heard the battle cry ringing in his ears.

'*Issho ni!*'

It was the last thing that many of the Senshi heard that day. Horace and Selethen, swords drawn and ready, moved between the two ranks, looking for any weakness where they might be needed. But they found none. The Kikori, drilled and trained for weeks, and with their Emperor's eyes upon them, performed like a machine. A machine that stabbed and cut and smashed and shoved at the Senshi in a perfectly co-ordinated programme of destruction.

Some of the Senshi did manage to cause casualties. They attempted high, overhead stabbing lunges that went over the huge shields and, in some cases, they found their marks. But few of them lived to celebrate the fact. The act of reaching high over a shield left them critically exposed to the men either side of the Kikori they were targeting.

For the most part, they found themselves cramped and forced back, without sufficient room to wield their long swords effectively, without opportunity to employ the elaborate, baffling sequences of sword play they had learned and practised since childhood. And all the while, they were buffeted by the shields, while those wicked iron blades flickered in and out like serpents' tongues, stabbing, cutting, wounding and killing.

Todoki's men had never experienced a battle like this before. A Senshi was accustomed to finding an enemy in the battle line, engaging him in single combat and either winning or losing. But there were no individuals facing them — just this impersonal wall of shields that pressed into them like a mobile fortress. Confused, disillusioned, not knowing how to counteract the inexorable force before them, seeing their comrades falling, dead or wounded — the latter soon to be despatched by the second rank of Kikori — they did what any sensible men would do.

They turned and ran.

Forty-four

'I regret to say that I am unable to help you,' Lord Nimatsu told Evanlyn.

They were seated in the audience room of his castle. The castle itself was a vast, sprawling timber building, four stories high, set on top of a prominent hill and surrounded by a deep moat. Each storey was set back from the one below, creating a series of terraces that would provide comfortable recreation areas in good weather, and defensive positions in the event of an attack.

The roof was constructed in blue tiles. It was a shallow pitch, and the corners swept upwards in an exotic style that was foreign to the two girls, although quite common in Nihon-Jan buildings.

The room was spartan in character. They sat on large cushions on the polished wood floor, around a low black-wood table where Nimatsu's servants had served tea and a simple meal. Several tall banners hung from the walls, each inscribed with Nihon-Jan characters. They were simple in form, yet beautiful, Alyss thought.

Their reception at Nimatsu's castle had been a gracious one. He made them welcome, recognising the ring that Shigeru had given to Evanlyn, and offered them his hospitality. The girls had bathed, revelling in the hot water after the long, cold trip across the lake and a further day spent walking to Nimatsu's castle. They found fresh clothes waiting for them when they emerged from the baths — including the wrap-around outer robes favoured by the Nihon-Jan. They dressed and then joined the castle lord for a meal.

Evanlyn had explained the reason for their visit and put Shigeru's request for support to Nimatsu. The Hasanu lord considered her words for a few minutes in silence. He was a tall, slender man who appeared to be about fifty years old. His head was completely shaved and he wore no beard or moustache. His cheekbones were high and prominent, his eyes steady and deep-set. He met his visitors' gaze without any sense of awkwardness or deceit.

But now he had refused Shigeru's request for aid.

The two girls exchanged a glance. Evanlyn, who had done most of the talking so far, looked a little nonplussed by the unexpected refusal. After all, Nimatsu had been at pains over the meal to point out how much he respected the Emperor and how deep his loyalty to the man and the office ran. She gave a small nod to Alyss, asking her to take up the debate while she, Evanlyn, took time to think and plan their next move.

'Lord Nimatsu,' Alyss began and the dark eyes turned to her. She thought she could detect a trace of sadness in them. If this were related to his refusal, perhaps she could use it as a lever to change his mind. She spoke carefully, choosing her words so that there was no hint of disrespect for his position.

'You are a loyal subject of the Emperor,' she said. It was a statement but it was posed so that he must answer it.

He nodded. 'That's correct.'

'And your people are loyal to you — and the Emperor?'

Again, he nodded his agreement, bowing forward from the waist to do so.

'Surely you have no respect for General Arisaka,' she said and he shook his head immediately.

'I consider Arisaka to be a traitor and an oath-breaker,' he said. 'As such, he is an abomination.'

Alyss spread her arms in consternation. 'Then I cannot understand why you would refuse to help Lord Shigeru,' she said. Perhaps, she thought, she could have phrased it in more diplomatic terms. But she felt it was time for plain speaking.

'Forgive me,' Nimatsu said. 'Of course *I* will offer my help to Lord Shigeru. I phrased my statement badly. I am sworn to support him and so I will.'

Frowning, Evanlyn attempted to interrupt. 'Then . . .'

Nimatsu held up a hand to stop her as he continued. 'But I am afraid the Hasanu people will not.'

'They won't follow you? You won't order them to?' Alyss said. He shifted his steady gaze back to her.

'I won't order them because I won't put them in the position of refusing to obey an order from their rightful lord. To do such a thing would cause them enormous shame.'

'But if you order them, they must . . .' Evanlyn stopped. The frustration was all too obvious in her voice and she strove to control it, knowing that to show anger would not advance their cause. As a princess, she was used to issuing orders and to having them obeyed immediately. She couldn't fathom why Nimatsu was reluctant to do the same.

Alyss, more used to the oblique nature of polite diplomatic negotiation, thought she saw a glimmer of hope. Nimatsu's refusal was a reluctant one. He would obviously prefer to help them but, for some reason, he was unable to.

'Lord Nimatsu, can you tell us why you cannot ask the Hasanu people to help their Emperor?' she asked. She chose the word 'cannot' advisedly. It was less confrontational than 'will not' and she felt that there was more to this than a wilful refusal to help. There was something preventing him from doing so.

He looked back at her now and his eyes told her that she had guessed correctly.

'The Hasanu are afraid,' he said simply.

Alyss leaned back in surprise. 'Of Arisaka?'

He shook his head. 'To travel to Ran-Koshi, we would have to first pass through Uto Forest,' he said. 'The Hasanu believe there is a malign spirit loose in the forest.'

'A malign spirit?' Evanlyn asked.

Lord Nimatsu bowed his head briefly in apology to them. The girls sensed that this was a painful subject. He had no wish to hold his simple followers up to the ridicule of outsiders. Then he seemed to come to a decision.

'A demon,' he said. 'They believe that an evil demon roams Uto Forest and they will not set foot inside it.'

'But this is superstition!' Evanlyn said. 'Surely you won't . . .'

Alyss laid a restraining hand on her arm. There was nothing to be gained by forcing an argument with Nimatsu. He noticed the gesture, registered the way Evanlyn forced herself to cut off her vehement protest.

'This is a superstition that has already killed seventeen of my people,' he said simply.

Evanlyn was completely taken aback. The Hasanu might be shy of strangers. But they were huge and powerfully built and their reputation said they were fierce fighters. What could possibly have killed so many of them?

'Do you believe in this demon, lord?' Alyss asked. Again, those calm, steady eyes met hers.

'I believe there is some terrible predator at large in the forest,' he said. 'A demon? No. I don't think so. But that's not important. The Hasanu believe in demons and they believe there is one in the forest. They will not pass through it. And I will not order them to. There is no point giving an order that I know will be refused. That refusal would shame me and the Hasanu equally.'

'Is there nothing we can do?' Evanlyn asked.

He shrugged his shoulders. 'I can't think of anything you could do to persuade them.'

Alyss took a deep breath, then set her shoulders. 'What if we kill the demon?'

Forty-five

General Todoki watched, first in disbelief, then in mounting fury, as his men began streaming back in retreat. Initially, there were only a few, but as they broke and ran, more of their comrades followed them, trying to place as much distance as possible between themselves and the terrible, impersonal wall of shields and darting blades.

Todoki, surrounded by half a dozen of his senior staff, ran to intercept them. He drew his sword as he ran, screaming orders at the retreating Senshi.

'Cowards! Cowards! Turn and face the enemy! They are peasants! Turn and face them!'

The men nearest him stopped their headlong retreat. But they made no move to turn back towards the two *gojus*, which were now silent. His officers moved among the shamefaced warriors, shoving them back around to face the enemy, shouting insults and threats, striking them with their fists or the flat of their swords. One man resolutely stood with his back to the enemy. Todoki stood before him, their faces barely centimetres apart, and screamed at him, his spittle landing on the other man's cheek.

'Coward! Deserter! They are peasants! You are Senshi! Turn and fight!'

The man raised his eyes to meet the general's. There was shame there, Todoki saw, but also confusion and fear.

'Lord,' he said, 'they killed Ito and Yoki beside me.'

'Then go back and avenge your comrades!' Overcome by rage, Todoki slapped the man hard across the face. A trickle of blood ran down from the corner of the warrior's mouth but he made no move to turn back.

'Kill them!' Todoki screamed. 'Kill five of them for each of your dead comrades! Go back and fight, you coward! Teach them they cannot stand against the Senshi!'

Which was all very well in principle. But these men had just seen at first hand that the Kikori, the despised peasant class, could indeed stand against the Senshi — and kill them. Thirty-five of their comrades lay dead on the battlefield to prove it.

'Lord,' said the warrior, 'how can I kill what I can't see?'

Aware that the eyes of the other Senshi were upon them, Todoki felt an overpowering rage building inside him. These men had shamed him by their craven behaviour. Now this insolent coward was daring to bandy words with him! Rebellion like this could be infectious, he realised. Let one man refuse an order and others would follow.

His sword flashed in a blur of reflected light, striking the man in the gap between helmet and breastplate. With a startled, choking cry, the Senshi staggered and fell. Todoki stepped over his body to face the other Senshi, who backed away before him. He gestured with his reddened sword blade towards the silent lines of the Kikori.

'There is the enemy! Attack! Fight them. Kill them!'

The immediate fear of his sword, and the ingrained discipline in which they had been raised, proved stronger than their fear of the Kikori *gojus*. Shoved and harried by Todoki's staff, the men turned back to face the enemy. They did it reluctantly, but they did it.

Will, watching from his vantage point, saw the Nihon-Jan general rallying his troops. He was tempted to try a shot at the general but Todoki was surrounded by dozens of milling figures and hitting him would be a matter of luck. Better not to waste the element of surprise with a stray shot, he thought. The time would come.

He had suspected that something like this might happen, and now was the time to put the second part of his plan into effect — to catch the Senshi with another unexpected tactic.

Now he put his fingers in his mouth and emitted two short, piercing whistles.

Selethen and Horace heard the signal. Horace gave the order for both *gojus*.

'About face. Double time forward!'

The Kikori pivoted in place, then began to jog back to their opening position, their feet hitting the ground in perfect unison.

'Halt!' shouted Horace and the four lines of men crashed to a stop. 'About face!'

Again, that machine-like precision showed itself, with every man moving in perfect unison.

General Todoki watched the movement and shouted encouragement to his reluctant warriors.

'See? They're retreating! They will not stand against you a second time! Attack!'

His men weren't so sure. They had seen the precise, co-ordinated drill of the Kikori as they withdrew. There was no sign of panic or defeat there. The more astute among his warriors realised that the enemy had simply withdrawn to a better defensive position — and they had done it with great efficiency and speed.

Todoki could see the doubt. He looked around wildly and, for the first time, noticed the group of three men on a small rise behind the Kikori lines. He stared for a moment, not believing what he saw. There were three men standing, observing. Two of them were vague and indistinct shapes, somehow confusing the eye as he tried to make them out more clearly. But the third figure, dressed in a Senshi's full armour, was unmistakable. It was the Emperor. He shouted to his officers and they joined him. He pointed his sword at the distant figure.

'It's Shigeru,' he said. 'Get your bows. If we kill him, then attack, the Kikori will break before us.'

The four officers ran back to the tent lines and returned a few minutes later, carrying their massive recurve bows. Senshi noblemen trained in archery as a matter of course. Now Todoki pointed to Shigeru once more and ordered them to shoot.

'What's happening?' Halt said as they saw the small group detach and run back to the camp. It was difficult to make out what they were carrying as they returned but, as they prepared to shoot, the actions were unmistakable. He and Will unslung their own bows.

Will saw the first Senshi officer release and instantly knew where the arrow was aimed. 'They've spotted Shigeru!' He was about to turn and shove Shigeru to the ground but as he did so, his eye caught a flicker of movement and he spun back.

When asked later about what he did next, he could never explain how he managed it. Nor could he ever repeat the feat. He acted totally from instinct, in an unbelievable piece of co-ordination between hand and eye.

As the Senshi arrow flashed downwards, heading directly for Shigeru, Will flicked his bow at it, caught it and deflected it from its course. The arrow head screeched on the hard rocky ground and the arrow skittered away. Even Halt took a second to be impressed.

'My god!' he said. 'How did you do that?'

Then, realising that there was no time for more talking, he shot the Senshi bowman.

Todoki saw the first shot on its way. He was exultant. His four lieutenants were excellent shots. Shigeru had no chance of surviving a hail of arrows from them. Then he heard a thudding impact and the man who had shot the first arrow staggered, then collapsed. A black-shafted arrow had come from nowhere and punched through his leather breastplate.

Even as Todoki bent towards him, two of his other officers cried out and fell. One never moved again, transfixed by a grey arrow. The other clutched feebly at a black shaft in his shoulder, groaning in pain. The fourth archer met Todoki's eyes and the general saw the fear there. Three of his men struck down in seconds, and they had no idea where the arrows had come from. Even as the man opened his mouth to speak, another grey-shafted arrow came slicing down out of the sky. He staggered under the impact, clutching feebly at the shaft, then fell, mortally wounded.

Todoki was momentarily stunned. He looked back to where Shigeru was standing and realised that the two vague shapes either side of him, masked by dull grey and green cloaks, must have done the shooting. He glanced at a fallen bow on the ground beside him and instinctively knew that if he took it up, he would be dead within seconds. He crouched, gesturing to a group of nearby Senshi.

'To me! Stand with me!'

They were reluctant. They had seen the fate of the four senior officers. But years of discipline asserted themselves and the men grouped around their general. Todoki was shorter than the average Nihon-Jan, and the warriors formed an effective screen. But before he could feel any sense of relief, he heard a massive shout from the Kikori lines.

'Okubyomono!'

The word, emanating from nearly one hundred throats, carried clearly across the the ground to them. Then it came, again and again, as a swelling chant, shouted in derision by the Kikori.

'Okubyomono! Okubyomono! Okubyomono!' Cowards! Cowards! Cowards!

The Senshi stirred uncomfortably as the rolling chant

continued. Todoki saw his opportunity. The men might not respond to his threats, but the taunting from these inferior beings must goad them to attack. The enemy had made a mistake, he thought.

'Attack!' he screamed, his voice cracking. 'Attack them! Kill them!'

His men streamed forward, heading for the nearer of the two groups of enemy.

Horace watched them coming, then shouted an order.

'Shields up!'

The massive shields were too heavy to hold up constantly. As they had stopped, the Kikori had rested their weight on the ground beside them. Now they crashed up and round to the front, slamming together to form a solid wall. A few seconds later, Selethen's *goju* did the same.

'Rear ranks! Open order!' Horace bellowed and the rear rank in each *goju* stepped back a pace.

Each man still held two javelins.

'Ready javelins!' shouted Horace.

As the order came, each of the men set one of the heavy projectiles down on the ground beside him, and prepared the other. Fifty right legs stepped back, fifty right arms extended behind, each holding a javelin at the point of balance, the wicked iron tips angled upwards.

Horace waited until the approaching Senshi were barely thirty metres away. They had seen no sign of the second rank's movement. They were concealed behind the shield walls.

'Throw!' shouted Horace and fifty javelins soared up and over, turned their points down, and crashed into the mass of advancing Senshi.

The effect was devastating. Men went down all along the Senshi line as the heavy projectiles crashed into them. Then, as the line stalled and hesitated, horrified by the unexpected, deadly rain of wood and iron, a second volley slammed into them.

Men staggered under the impact. At least thirty of the attackers had been hit and were killed or wounded. But now another command rang out and again the Senshi heard that dreaded war cry:

'*Issho ni! Issho ni!*'

The wall of shields tramped towards them and the deadly stabbing blades began again. Some of the Senshi tried to stab over the shields, knowing that a cutting blow would be useless. But Horace had foreseen that tactic and had one of his own.

'*Kamé!*' he shouted, and the second rank, who had closed up once more after releasing the second volley of javelins, raised their shields to create the tortoise formation, blocking the downward thrusts, enclosing the front rank in a near impenetrable carapace. And now the stabbing and shoving and killing began again as those murderous short blades jabbed out through the shield wall.

Some of the Senshi, realising that they still outnumbered the men of Horace's *goju*, began to flow around the right flank, looking to take them from the rear or the side. As Horace saw that happening, he called another order.

'*Kamé* down! Gate!'

And in a smoothly drilled evolution, the second rank lowered their raised shields and turned to face right, moving smoothly out to form another line at right angles to the front rank, facing the new direction of attack.

It was the manoeuvre Will and Horace had discussed, *shutting the gate*. And viewed from above, that was precisely what it would have looked like.

The Senshi who had tried to flank Horace's men now found themselves facing another solid wall of wood and iron. They crashed against it ineffectually and realised, too late, they had left themselves open to another danger.

Now it was Selethen's turn. His *goju*, in two ranks, swung in a left wheel, then surged forward at a brisk jog to fall on the rear of the Senshi attacking Horace's redeployed second rank.

Caught between hammer and anvil, there was little hope for the Senshi. Confused, bewildered, facing a new enemy and a totally unfamiliar form of fighting, they turned and ran, for the second time that day. They ran past their own camp, heading in panic for the distant encampment where Arisaka's main army were still unaware of what had just happened.

Only now there were pitifully few of them running. The vast majority remained on the battlefield, unmoving.

With one exception. A stocky figure remained, clad in ornate and expensive leather armour — armour that bore the symbol of a green ox.

Maddened with rage and shame, Todoki had emerged from behind the screen of warriors who had surrounded him. Alone now, he advanced on the silent ranks of Kikori. He could see a tall figure among them and he remembered stories of the *gaijin* warrior who had befriended Shigeru. He stood now and screamed abuse and insults at the figure, who slowly stepped forward from the ranks of his *goju*.

Horace's grasp of Nihon-Jan wasn't sufficiently advanced to understand the insults that Todoki's tortured rage was conjuring up but the meaning was obvious.

'That doesn't sound good,' he said quietly to himself as a stream of imprecations was hurled at him.

'Horace!' Will called from his vantage point, but Horace half turned and made a placating gesture in his direction.

'It's all right, Will. I'm tired of this person.'

His sword hissed out of its scabbard and he turned back to face Todoki. With a scream of rage and hate, the enemy general charged towards him.

Todoki had seen the long, straight *gaijin* sword. He knew something about those foreign weapons. They were made from inferior steel and he knew that his own *katana*, forged by one of the finest swordsmiths in Nihon-Ja, would slice through the foreign weapon if he struck hard enough.

Disdaining the grace and balance that went into a normal cutting stroke, he opted for brute strength and put every ounce of his power and weight behind his blow. With a huge cry, he smashed his blade into the foreigner's.

There was a shrieking clang as the two blades met. Todoki's eyes widened in horror as he realised that the *gaijin*'s sword was undamaged. It had withstood his stroke. Off balance from the excessive effort he had put into it, he staggered slightly and his guard dropped.

Horace lunged, stamping his right foot forward then driving with his shoulder and suddenly straightened arm to give maximum impetus to the thrust. He aimed for the gap at the top of Todoki's hardened breastplate, where only a screen of softer leather protected the warrior's throat.

He hit his mark, and the Nihon-Jan forged blade sliced easily through the thin barrier.

Todoki's eyes, startled, still unable to understand what had happened to him this day, stared at Horace for a second from above the half-buried sword blade.

Then they clouded and all sign of life left them as the rebel general sagged to the rocky ground at his feet. Horace freed his sword and turned away, finding himself facing the men of the two *gojus*. The Kikori warriors — for now they truly were warriors — raised their short swords in the air to acclaim him. One voice began the chant, and within seconds, a hundred of them were echoing it.

'Kurokuma! Kurokuma! Kurokuma!'

Horace waved tiredly to acknowledge them. Selethen stepped forward to greet him, smiling broadly. They embraced, then, surrounded by their cheering, chanting Kikori troops, they walked together to where Will, Halt and Shigeru waited.

'I'd still like to know how he got that name,' Will said.

Shigeru turned to him. For once, when he was discussing Horace's nickname, his face bore no trace of amusement.

'However he got it,' he said, 'it truly is a term of great respect.'

Forty-six

Alyss finished lashing the last branch into position and inspected the rough platform she had constructed in the fork of the tree.

'That should do it,' she said. The platform of sturdy branches was approximately two metres by two metres, giving ample room for Alyss and Evanlyn to sit and await the mysterious predator that lurked in Uto Forest.

They were deep in the forest, at a site where four of the Hasanu had been taken by the predator — known to the Hasanu people as *Kyofu*, or the Terror.

Evanlyn, on the ground four metres below, looked around nervously. The sun was setting and it would soon be dark — and the Terror was known to hunt at night. It was one thing to sit in Nimatsu's castle and be critical of the Hasanu's superstitious fears, quite another to stand here in the snow, with the shadows lengthening and the gloomy forest surrounding them. While it had still been full daylight, Evanlyn had gone about the task of collecting branches for the platform without a qualm. But her last foray, which took her further from the site they had selected, had been in the lengthening shadows of early evening and she had found herself glancing fearfully over her shoulder as she worked, her nerves jumping at the slightest of forest sounds.

'Drop me the rope,' she called. 'I'm coming up.'

'Just a moment.' Alyss stood slowly and moved to the centre of the platform. Stepping with extreme care, she tested its strength, making sure the lashed branches were strong enough to bear her weight. Eventually satisfied, she moved to the edge and kicked the coil of knotted rope off the platform, sending it down through the branches to the waiting princess. Evanlyn clambered up the rope hand over hand, moving with slightly undignified haste. Once she was settled high in the fork of the tree, she pulled the rope up and coiled it again, then found a spot to make herself comfortable — although 'comfortable', on this rough platform, was a relative term.

Alyss grinned at her. 'Worried the Terror might climb up after you?'

Evanlyn regarded her coldly and didn't answer. That was exactly what she was worried about.

Darkness stole through the forest and the two girls sat, cold and uncomfortable, on the platform. The only sound they heard was the snuffling and complaining of the young pig they had tied to a nearby tree. The pig was bait, designed to bring the Terror out of hiding. Once that happened, Alyss hoped to kill the Terror, whatever it was, with the two lightweight spears that lay beside her. She had borrowed them from the Hasanu. It had taken her a while to find weapons light enough for her to handle, but eventually she settled on practice weapons, designed for children. She was a competent hand with the javelin and, of course, Evanlyn had her sling and a supply of heavy, egg-shaped lead shot.

'Bit hard on the pig,' Evanlyn said quietly.

'You can change places with it any time you like,' Alyss told her.

'What do you think it is — the Terror, I mean?'

'Some large predator, as Nimatsu suggested. A bear, perhaps. There are bears in this area. And he did say there's evidence that there were snow tigers here many years ago. Maybe it's one of them.'

'It's never been seen or heard. That doesn't sound like any bear I've ever known,' Evanlyn remarked.

Alyss looked at her sidelong. 'Known many bears?'

Evanlyn had to grin.

'Anyway, one thing I'm sure of,' Alyss continued, 'is that it's not a demon from another world. Now be quiet.'

She gestured for Evanlyn to get some rest while she stood guard. Evanlyn lay down on the uneven, knobbly branches and squirmed around to find the most comfortable spot. She closed her eyes but it took a while for sleep to claim her. Her nerves were tensed to a fine pitch as she listened to the soughing of the light breeze through the trees, the soft flutter of a night-flying bird's wing and the dozen or so unidentifiable sounds of nocturnal animals or insects that drifted among the trees.

She seemed to have been dozing for only a few minutes when Alyss's hand on her arm woke her.

'Anything stirring?' she whispered.

Alyss shook her head and replied in the same lowered tone. 'Nothing. The pig was awake about twenty minutes ago but he went back to sleep.'

They both peered down through the branches, across the clearing to where the pig was tethered. The little animal lay sleeping beside the tree.

'Seems peaceful enough now,' Evanlyn said. 'Maybe he was having a pigmare.' She shuffled towards the edge of the platform, picking up the coiled rope. Alyss caught her by the arm. Even though she still spoke in a whisper, Evanlyn could hear the urgency in her tone.

'What d'you think you're up to?'

Evanlyn blushed, although in the dim light Alyss was unaware of the fact.

'Call of nature,' she said. 'I drank too much from my water bottle when we ate. The pickles made me thirsty.' She grinned sheepishly.

Firmly, Alyss took the coiled rope from her grasp and placed it away from the edge of the platform.

'Put up with it,' she said. 'Neither of us is going down that rope before daylight.'

'Alyss, be reasonable. If the Terror was anywhere in the area, that pig would be squealing and snuffling in terror. I'm sure it's perfectly safe. We haven't heard anything in hours.'

'Neither did the seventeen Hasanu that this creature killed. Three of them were taken from the middle of a camp where others were sleeping, remember? Evanlyn, the only place that's safe is this platform. And I'm not even totally sure about that.'

Evanlyn hesitated. Nimatsu had told them some

hair-raising stories about the Terror, that was true. As Alyss pointed out, some of its victims had been taken while surrounded by dozens of sleeping comrades — none of whom ever heard a sound.

'Well . . . all right,' she said, feigning a reluctance she no longer felt. The idea that the Terror might be somewhere close to them, creeping towards the tree where they perched, set the hairs on the back of her neck on end. But she wasn't about to admit that to Alyss. 'You go to sleep. I'll keep watch.'

Alyss eyed her carefully. 'Don't go sneaking off once I'm asleep,' she warned.

Evanlyn shook her head. 'I won't.'

Alyss lay down, pulling her cloak around her shoulders. She seemed to fall asleep much sooner than Evanlyn had managed. Within a few minutes her breathing was deep and regular, punctuated by occasional soft snorts of complaint as she shifted to ease the discomfort of a badly trimmed knot on the branches below her.

Evanlyn sat, bored and cramped, as the moon arced up and over them, eventually descending and leaving the forest black and silent once more. The bird and animal noises had died away. There was only the wind now. Once, just before dawn, it seemed to gust more strongly than before and Evanlyn sat up a little straighter, peering around nervously. But then she realised it had only been a stray gust and she sank back into her bleary-eyed vigil. She yawned mightily. Her eyelids drooped and she jerked upright, realising that her head had dropped to one side and, for a few seconds, she had been asleep. She shook her head to clear it, breathing deeply, then surveyed the dimly lit ground beneath her. The dark form of the pig was still visible in the snow. There was nothing else to be seen.

Shuffling to the edge of the platform, she peered straight down. But she could see nothing there, either.

She yawned again. There was a thin layer of snow on the branches around her. She scooped some up and rubbed the freezing wetness across her face and eyes. For a few minutes, she was refreshed and alert. Then her eyelids and head sagged again. She forced them open, yawned again and wished she hadn't drunk all that water the night before.

She had never in her life been so grateful to see the dawn. The first grey light stole through the trees and she realised that she could make out details now, instead of just seeing vague outlines. Then she began to make out a red glow from the east, faintly visible through the trunks and upper branches.

Then, without her noticing the exact moment when it happened, a steel grey daylight stole over the forest and the clearing above which they sat. Funny, she thought, how daylight made things seem less threatening.

Alyss stirred, then rolled over and sat up, rubbing her eyes.

'Anything happen?' she asked, although she knew that if it had, Evanlyn would have woken her.

'Nothing. We seemed to have picked the most boring stretch of forest possible. There was nothing but the insects and the birds and even they became bored after a while and went to sleep. I think we're going to have to —'

Evanlyn stopped. Alyss's hand was gripping her forearm tightly — so tightly that it was hurting.

'Look,' the Courier said. 'Look at the pig.'

Evanlyn followed her gaze and felt her blood freeze. The snow around the little animal was stained red. Alyss grabbed the climbing rope and moved to the edge of the platform, preparing to let it drop to the forest floor below them. But she stopped, then hurriedly moved away from the edge.

'Look down there,' she said in a barely audible voice. 'Don't stand up!' she cautioned. 'You might fall!'

On hands and knees, Evanlyn moved to the edge of the platform and looked down through the lower branches to the ground below. The snow around the base of their tree was patterned with multiple tracks, where a large animal had circled the trunk repeatedly. Off to one side was an indentation in the snow, where that same animal had lain, waiting for them, watching them.

'You heard nothing?' Alyss asked and Evanlyn, her eyes wide with horror, shook her head.

'Not a thing,' she said, then remembered, 'Once, just before the dawn, I thought the wind seemed to gust a little louder. But that was all.' She indicated the carcass of the pig. 'I never heard that happen! And I swear I was awake all night.'

She trembled with fear as she recalled how she had wanted to climb down from the platform during the night.

'My god!' she said softly. 'I wanted to climb down! It could have been waiting then!'

Alyss nodded. Her stomach was tight with fear as well. They had no way of knowing how long the huge creature — whatever it was — had been lying watching them from the base of the tree.

Eventually, gathering their courage, they climbed down from their perch and studied the tracks in the snow.

'It looks like some kind of giant cat,' Evanlyn said. She couldn't stop glancing back over her shoulder as she studied the paw marks. Alyss had moved to look at the depression where the creature had lain in the snow.

'It must be at least four metres in length,' she mused. 'I wish Will was here. He'd make more sense out of these tracks.'

'I wish he was here too,' Evanlyn said. But she was thinking more about the reassurance that Will's powerful longbow and grey-shafted arrows could provide. Alyss glanced quickly at her, then, as she understood Evanlyn's meaning, the suspicious frown on her face cleared. She rose and moved across to where the pig lay, stiff and cold now. Evanlyn followed her nervously, her hand on the hilt of the sword she wore. Alyss prodded the pig with the haft of one of her spears. It seemed to have been killed by one raking sweep of giant claws across its throat.

'The Terror killed it. But it didn't try to eat it,' she muttered. 'Or take the carcass with it.'

Evanlyn glanced at her fearfully. 'What does that mean?' she asked, although she thought she knew the answer.

'The Terror didn't want the pig raising the alarm. Aside from that, it wasn't interested in the pig. It was stalking us.'

Forty-seven

'Next time,' Halt said, 'we won't get off so lightly.' They had lost only six men in the battle, with another dozen wounded, four badly. In contrast, they had captured over seventy swords, armour breastplates and helmets from the fallen Senshi — and there were many more of Arisaka's men injured as well.

As Shigeru's Senshi and the Kikori warriors were retreating up the narrow pass, Halt had detailed Mikeru and a dozen of his followers to obliterate the tracks leading back to the mouth of the secret entrance. The teenagers did this by dragging large pieces of canvas, sourced from the enemy's abandoned tents, across the snow over a wide area in front of the gully. Mikeru was a very handy person to have around, Halt reflected. He was keen, energetic and he used his initiative. A small group of Senshi from Shigeru's bodyguard remained on watch in the narrow gully, in case the enemy happened to stumble over the entrance.

Now the leadership group were reviewing the battle in Shigeru's cabin. Halt had just voiced the thought that was in most of their minds.

'Arisaka is no fool,' Shigeru agreed. 'He won't rush in blindly, the way Todoki did. He will look for ways to defeat these new tactics devised by *Chocho*.' He nodded at Will, who frowned slightly at the term but knew that now wasn't the time for a language lesson.

'What we have to do is put ourselves in Arisaka's place,' Halt said. 'Try to work out how *we* would counter the tactics used by the two *gojus*.'

'Four,' Will said, and when Halt's eyes swung to him he elaborated. 'We'll have at least two hundred men trained by the time the valley is open again.'

Selethen nodded in confirmation.

'Good,' said Halt. 'But we'll still be outnumbered and this time we won't have the advantage of surprise. Arisaka will know how we're going to fight. So if you were him, what would you do?'

Selethen cleared his throat and the others all looked at him.

'We discussed this in Toscana,' he pointed out. 'Heavy weapons or artillery could break up the *goju*'s formed ranks. Once they lose their integrity, the Senshi can fight in their usual style — one on one.'

'Arisaka has no heavy weapons,' Halt replied. 'And no way of getting any up through the mountains.'

'True,' Selethen admitted. 'Then archers would be the next best thing.' He turned to Shigeru. 'How many archers do you think he could muster?'

The Emperor considered the question for a few seconds.

'Perhaps thirty,' he said. The rank and file Senshi didn't practise archery. It was a skill reserved for the nobility.

'Thirty archers can do a lot of damage,' Will put in.

Horace leaned forward. 'But the *kamé* counters that effectively,' he said, referring to the tortoise formation Will had taught the Kikori.

'Not if they can flank us and then attack from the rear,' Selethen said. 'The second rank will have to turn and face the new attack — and that destroys the *kamé* formation. They can't keep their shields up over their heads if they're facing a flank attack.'

Horace made a dismissive gesture. 'Then we choose a spot where they can't flank us. The valley below the palisade is narrow enough for that. Or we can simply wait behind the palisade itself.'

'We can't do that,' said Halt. 'We'll have to take the fight to Arisaka. He'll have reinforcements coming from the south. With enough men, he could take the palisade. But the problem is . . .' He tailed off, not wishing to voice the thought that was in his mind.

Shigeru looked at him. 'The problem, Halto-san?'

Reluctantly the Ranger answered. 'We can't afford to simply sit behind the palisade and fight a defensive battle indefinitely. If we do that, Arisaka will win. Ideally, he'd like to wipe us out. But if that's taking too much time, he'll simply leave enough men here to keep us bottled up, then march south and claim the throne. He can say you're dead and nobody will be any the wiser,' he told the Emperor.

Shigeru nodded thoughtfully. 'And once he has claimed the throne, it will be twice as hard to unseat him.'

'Exactly. So we need to force him to fight — to make him think it will be worth his while. And if we're to do that, we need to second-guess him, and work out how he'll counter our tactics.'

'In broad terms,' said Will slowly, 'he'll need to smash our shield wall — and outflank us at the same time. Correct?'

The others nodded agreement and he continued.

'We know he has the numbers to outflank us if we fight him on open ground. If he can attack us, but still keep us at a distance, he'll force us to advance. After all, our stabbing blades are only effective at close range. And if we advance from a prepared position to get to close quarters, we expose ourselves to a flanking movement.'

Horace was following his line of reasoning thoughtfully. What his friend said made sense. 'But how can he attack us and keep us at a distance at the same time?' he asked.

'I was thinking of something like the Macedon Phalanx,' Will said.

Shigeru noted the sudden, simultaneous intake of breath from Halt, Horace and Selethen. They all nodded thoughtfully.

'What is the Macedon Phalanx?' he asked.

'The Macedons were warriors who developed a highly effective formation called the Phalanx,' Halt explained to him. 'It consisted of warriors armed with long, heavy lances, up to four metres long. They could smash through the front rank of an army before the enemy could make any reply.'

'And you think Arisaka might know about this phalanx?'

'No,' Halt replied. 'But the idea of using spearmen or pikemen could well occur to him. I'd be surprised if it didn't — it's a logical idea. They could attack our front rank and they'd be safe from our short blades.'

'We'd have to close with them,' Horace said. 'We'd have to advance to fight them or our shield wall would be smashed to pieces.'

'And as soon as we advance, their comrades can out-flank us,' Selethen said.

'We could use our javelins as lances,' Horace suggested. 'We could throw the first volley, then retain the javelins from the second and third rank as stabbing weapons.'

Halt rubbed his chin thoughtfully. 'That might work. The odds are that Arisaka won't have men who could handle anything as long as the Macedon lance. It takes years to develop the strength and skill necessary. My guess is they'll use normal spears, so we'd be fighting spears with spears. But at best, that'll be a stalemate. Eventually, we'll need to get to close quarters. That's where all the advan-tages lie with our men. So we need a way to stop any flanking movement.'

'Fifty or so archers would come in handy,' Will said.

'If we could train them. And if we had fifty bows,' Horace replied.

Will nodded despondently. But as he glanced up at his old mentor, he saw a light in Halt's eyes.

'I might have an idea,' the older Ranger said. 'Will, let's you and I go and find young Mikeru.'

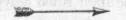

Will, Halt and Mikeru stood on the parade ground where the Kikori *gojus* usually trained. The troops were resting at the moment so they had the ground to themselves.

'Mikeru,' Halt said, 'can you throw a spear?'

The young Kikori nodded enthusiastically. 'Of course, Halto-san. All Kikori learn to use a spear when they are very young.'

'Excellent.' Halt handed the young man a standard Kikori throwing spear and nodded to a pole some forty metres distant, on which he had placed one of the captured armour breastplates. 'Let me see you hit that breastplate.'

Mikeru tested the weight and balance of the spear, then strode forward until the target was thirty metres away. His right arm and body weight went back, his left leg extended and then he hurled the spear in a shallow arc. It smashed into the breastplate, piercing it and knocking it from the pole to clatter on the ground.

Halt noted the co-ordination of the throw, with right arm and shoulder, body and legs all combining to put maximum force behind the spear.

'Very good,' he said. 'Will, would you replace the target please?'

Will moved forward to replace the damaged breastplate on the pole, jerking the spear free as he did so. When he turned back, Halt had led Mikeru back to a point fifty metres from the target. Will rejoined them quickly and Halt took the spear from him, offering it to Mikeru.

'Let's see you do it from here,' he said. But Mikeru shook his head apologetically.

'It's too far. The spear is too heavy for me to throw so far.'

'Thought so,' Halt said. He now opened a rolled piece of canvas he had been carrying and produced a strange weapon, which he handed to Mikeru.

It was a giant dart, over a metre long and made from light bamboo, but with a heavy iron tip at one end. At the other end were three leather fins, laced and glued to the shaft like the fletching on an arrow. Just ahead of these fins, a shallow groove had been carved all the way around the shaft.

'Try it with this,' he said.

But again, Mikeru, after testing the weight of the projectile, shook his head.

'This one is too light, Halto-san. I can't put any force behind it.'

'Exactly,' Halt agreed. Then he produced a leather thong, knotted at one end and with a loop at the other. He wound the knotted end once around the groove at the rear of the shaft, then, holding it firmly in place, crossed the thong over itself, close to the knot, to hold it in place. Then, keeping tension on the thong, he extended it down the shaft to where Will noticed there was a section bound with thin cord, forming a hand grip. He took Mikeru's right hand and slipped the looped end of the thong over it, then placed the boy's hand on the cord-bound grip on the dart, making sure he kept the thong tight as he did so.

Understanding dawned in the Kikori youth's eyes as he held the dart, with the tensioned leather thong extending back over half its length, retained in place by the cord passing over the knot.

'Now try it,' Halt said.

Mikeru grinned at him, sighted on the breastplate, leaned back, then hurled his body and arm into the throw. The leather cord acted as a lever extension for his arm, adding enormous extra thrust to the throw. As the missile hissed away on a murderous, arcing flight, the knotted end of the thong simply came free and fell clear, swinging from Mikeru's wrist.

The dart just missed the breastplate, then thudded point first into the ground some eight metres past it. Mikeru shook his head in wonder.

'This is good,' he said. 'Very good.' He started out to retrieve the dart but Halt stopped him, pointing to the roll of canvas. There were three more darts lying there.

Mikeru was a natural athlete, with excellent hand-eye co-ordination. And he was already an expert spear thrower. It didn't take him long to become accustomed to this new technique. His fourth cast smashed into the leather armour, the heavy iron point tearing a jagged hole.

Halt slapped his back in encouragement.

'Show this to your friends,' he said. 'Make more of them and practise with them till you can all do it. We've got another seven or eight weeks until spring and I want thirty of you trained and ready with these weapons when we face Arisaka again.'

Mikeru nodded enthusiastically. He had been chafing at the fact that so far he had taken no active part in the battle against the usurper. And he knew his friends felt the same way. This would be their chance.

'We'll be ready, Halto-san,' he said, drawing himself up to his full height and bowing formally.

Halt nodded in acknowledgement. Then he and Will turned away, leaving Mikeru to retrieve the darts and continue perfecting his new skill.

'Now let's see what happens if they try to outflank us,' Halt said.

Forty-eight

'**A**re you sure this is a good idea?' Evanlyn asked anxiously.

Alyss glanced up from where she was checking her equipment.

'No. I'm not. But it's *an* idea, and it's the only one we've got. I just hope you're as good as you say you are with that sling of yours.'

'I never said I'm all that good. Other people might have said it, not me,' Evanlyn protested.

Alyss regarded her cynically. 'Maybe. But I never heard you contradict them.'

The discussion was interrupted by a light tap on the door frame of the room they shared.

'Come in,' Alyss called and the screen door slid open to admit Lord Nimatsu. The Nihon-Jan nobleman wore a worried look on his face. He glanced at the bed and saw Alyss's equipment laid out ready.

'Ariss-san,' he said, bowing to her, 'I see you are determined to go ahead with this.'

'I'm afraid I have to, Lord Nimatsu. Your people won't go through that forest unless we show them that we have killed the Terror. And this is the best way I can think of to do that.'

'But couldn't you try with another pig — or a goat, perhaps — as bait?' Nimatsu asked.

Alyss shook her head. 'The Terror has shown it's not interested in animals. It only killed the pig to silence it, so that we'd get no warning that it was there. But once that was done, it didn't touch the carcass. It sat under our tree for hours, waiting to see if we'd come down. It wants people. It's a man-eater. So this time, I'm the pig.' She waited a second and glanced at Evanlyn. 'You could always object to the way I phrased that,' she suggested.

Evanlyn made a disclaiming gesture. 'This is too serious to joke about, Alyss. You're putting yourself in terrible danger. And you're putting a lot of trust in my skill with the sling. Why don't we draw lots to see who's the bait?'

Nimatsu's gaze switched quickly between the two girls during this exchange. He nodded several times.

'You are risking a great deal, Ariss-san. Is Ev-an-in-san as skilled as you say?'

'She's a lot better than I am with the javelin,' Alyss told him. 'So it's logical that I'm the bait and she's the hunter. A friend of ours says she can knock out a gnat's eye with a shot from her sling.'

'I'm not sure I'm that good,' Evanlyn said doubtfully.

Alyss raised an eyebrow. 'Well, this isn't the best time to tell me that.'

Evanlyn let the comment pass. She knew Alyss's sarcasm stemmed from nerves. The tall girl was putting herself into a position of appalling danger. She might try to pass it off lightly, but it was only natural that she should be fearful of what was to come.

'In any event,' Alyss continued, 'once it all starts, I'll be safely tucked up under my shield. You'll be the one out in the open, having to deal with the big kitty cat.'

She indicated the big wooden shield that had been made to her instructions. Almost two metres high, it was rectangular in shape and formed into a shallow curve. It was, in fact, identical to those being used by the Kikori and she planned to use it to protect herself from the *Kyofu*'s attack.

Nimatsu sighed deeply. He admired this tall, courteous girl and he feared that she wouldn't survive the coming night.

'I still say, I don't like this idea,' he said, with a note of finality in his voice. He sensed he would not dissuade her. Alyss grinned at him, but there was little real humour in the grin.

'I'm not mad about it either. But currently, it's the only idea going round.'

Somewhere close to hand, an owl hooted at regular intervals. When she had first heard the sound, Alyss's hair had stood on end. Now she had become accustomed to it and it had become part of the overall tableau of the night, along with the occasional rustle of small, nocturnal animals moving under the trees and the soft breath of the wind through the branches.

She stood with her back to the largest tree she could find, the heavy shield planted in front of her, her arm through the support strap, ready to lift it into position. Only her head showed above the rim of the shield. In a scabbard on her right hip, she wore Evanlyn's saxe knife. The shorter weapon would be more useful and easier to wield than her long sabre — assuming everything went to plan. Her two javelins were rammed point down into the ground beside her. She doubted they'd be any use, but she'd brought them anyway. Her head, face and right arm were wound with tough leather for protection against the Terror's claws. By now she was convinced that it was some form of giant predatory cat. She had heard tales of tigers and their almost supernatural ability to take prey silently and unobserved. She couldn't imagine a bulky, clumsy animal like a bear doing that.

She leaned back against the tree. Her legs were aching. She'd been standing here for several hours and the unrelenting cold was creeping up her legs, stiffening the muscles. She longed to sit down for a few minutes but knew that would place her at a disadvantage if the monster appeared. Standing, she could move instantly, bringing the shield up to face an attack from the front or either side. The tree protected her rear.

She moved her legs, trying to get the blood flowing, easing her weight from one to the other. The momentary ease only made the discomfort worse when she placed her weight on the tired muscles once more. She wondered what time it was. The narrow moon had long departed and the shadows under the trees were deep and inky black. She looked up to the platform they'd built in the tree opposite her position. She could just make it out, and see the dark bulk of Evanlyn's form as she kept watch. At least Evanlyn could sit down, she thought. And that was . . .

Something was wrong.

She sensed it. Something in the forest had changed. Her heart pounded as she tried to pinpoint the difference. Then, she had it.

The owl hadn't hooted. Without realising it, she had been counting in her mind after each hoot. The owl had been making its mournful sound regularly, after she had counted between one hundred and fifty and one hundred and sixty. Yet her automatic, almost subconscious count had just passed one hundred and seventy-three.

There was something here. Something close by. Above the rim of the shield, her eyes darted from one side to another, searching the shadows, trying desperately to gain her first sight of the predator, striving to discover where the attack would come from.

'Alyss! Left! Left!'

Evanlyn's warning cry shrilled through the forest and Alyss swung to her left, lifting the shield as she saw a vague blur of movement coming at her.

Something huge slammed against the shield and sent her flying several metres. She gripped the handles desperately to retain her hold on the shield, her only hope of safety. She crashed onto her back on the ground, skidding in the powdery snow, the breath driven from her body in one explosive grunt. Then something huge and heavy and incredibly strong was on top of her, with only the curved wooden shield between them as she cowered under it, drawing herself up to protect her head and body and feet, clinging desperately to the handles as the monster tried to tear it away to get at its prey. Now she could hear the blood-chilling snarl of the *Kyofu* as it tore at the wood with its claws, and bit at the top rim of the shield with its massive teeth.

As huge cats do, it had drawn up its hind legs to disembowel its prey with one savage downstroke. But the raking claws met not flesh but hard wood, reinforced with iron. They splintered the first and gouged deep grooves in the second.

The beast snarled in frustration and fury as long splinters of hardwood stabbed into the pads of its paws. Somewhere beneath this unyielding surface, it knew, was warm flesh and blood, and it redoubled its efforts to get to it.

Evanlyn saw the sudden blur of movement from the edge of the clearing as the *Kyofu* launched its attack. She just had time to shout her warning before the monster slammed into the shield, sending Alyss flying. So far, Alyss's plan was working. She'd managed to keep the big shield interposed between the predator and herself. Now it was Evanlyn's turn. She kicked the coiled rope over the side of the platform, slid down a few metres, then dropped the remaining distance to the forest floor.

Her sling was already in her hand and as she regained her feet, she was feeding one of the heavy, egg-shaped lead shot into the central pouch. She wanted maximum velocity, so she spun the sling twice, then released, whipping the brutal projectile across the clearing at the predator.

The scene seemed to unfold slowly in her vision. She could see now that the *Kyofu* was a huge cat — much larger than the sand lions Selethen had pointed out to her when they were travelling through Arrida. This was immense, and its coat was white, marked with blurred dark grey stripes.

A snow tiger, she thought. Then her shot hit the animal with a sickening crack, taking it on the left shoulder, smashing and splintering the bone beneath the fur. She moved automatically, reloading the pouch, whirling the sling, releasing again.

Smash! The second shot slammed into the creature's ribs, fracturing them. The tiger howled in agony and fury and swung its head to see where its attacker lay.

Beneath the shield, Alyss heard the violent, thudding impacts as the two shot hit the beast in quick succession. At the first, she felt a lessening of the pressure on her right side, as the creature's left foreleg was smashed at the shoulder, leaving it limp and useless. Then she heard another cracking thud and the *Kyofu* was no longer intent on tearing the shield loose. As it raised its head to search out Evanlyn, the weight on Alyss was suddenly lessened and she could move her right arm. She released her right-hand grip on the shield and, with the strength of desperation, clawed the saxe from its scabbard.

Evanlyn placed her third shot carefully, sending it crashing into the animal's rear left hip. Again, bone crunched and the tiger's left rear leg suddenly went limp, so that its intended leap towards the figure it could now see beneath a tree across the clearing came to nothing. It flopped awkwardly, without thrust on one side.

The agony in its rear leg flared and, mad with pain, it snapped at the injury with its massive fangs.

As it twisted to do this, Evanlyn's fourth lead shot hit its head with shocking force.

And at the same instant, Alyss reached round the edge of the shield and drove the razor-sharp saxe deep into the creature's underbelly, cutting upwards to create a wound almost half a metre long.

The monster roared, a shrill note of baffled terror overriding the heart-chilling savagery of its normal challenge. Crippled, gutted and dying, it collapsed sideways on the snow, now running red with its blood.

Desperately scrabbling with her feet, Alyss forced her way backwards from under the shield, sliding on her back to escape the reach of the horrible creature. Evanlyn ran to her, grabbed her arm and dragged her clear, bringing her to her feet. The two girls clung to each other. Then the *Kyofu* gave one last shuddering screech and lay still.

'It's dead,' Evanlyn said numbly.

Alyss said nothing. Overcome by shock at her ordeal, reacting to the terror of those minutes crouched under the shield, she felt her stomach heave and was violently sick.

Forty-nine

When daylight came, they dragged the monster's dead body back to Nimatsu's castle, hitched behind a pair of horses borrowed from the Hasanu village.

It was, as Evanlyn had guessed when she first saw it, a snow tiger. But it was an immense one, measuring nearly five metres from nose to tail. As the small cavalcade made its way through the main street of the village, the Hasanu came out in awe to watch them pass. There were cries of amazement as they saw the size of the dead cat, its white and grey striped body smeared with blood and dirt. The signs left by Evanlyn's shot were also clearly visible — the left foreleg was smashed and twisted at an oblique angle. The shattered lower jaw was nearly separated from the creature's skull, held in place only by a network of sinew, and the jaw and neck were covered in dried, frozen blood.

Most remarkable was the half-metre-long gash in the beast's belly, with the fur around it saturated in blood as well.

The beast's head bumped over the uneven ground as the two horses drew it slowly through the village. The eyes were half closed, glazed over. But even in death, the animal still earned its title — *Kyofu*. The Terror.

The word flew from mouth to mouth as the Hasanu gaped at the beast that had terrorised the countryside. Then they looked from its enormous corpse to the two girls who had conquered it. Both were drawn and pale, battling shock and the after-effects of fear as much as weariness. Seen beside the limp body, they looked tiny, almost insignificant. Alyss's jacket and breeches were torn and stained from the rough ground she had fallen onto. She had discarded the protective leather from her face and arms. The shield was slung over the left-hand horse's yoke and daylight revealed the extent of the battering it had taken from the *Kyofu*'s claws and teeth. The top edge was splintered and split and there were massive gouges in the curved wood that formed the major part of the shield. The iron reinforcing strips showed bright scars where the creature's massive claws had scored deep into the metal.

As the two slender figures, dwarfed by the *Kyofu* and by the massively built Hasanu people themselves, progressed down the main street of the village, the villagers began to bow, the bending bodies and lowered heads moving in succession, resembling wheat yielding before a sudden breeze that sweeps across a field.

'Should we wave or something?' Evanlyn said out of the corner of her mouth. Trained as she was in protocol, this was a situation that her tutors had never envisaged.

'You can. I'm too tired,' Alyss responded. She looked up to the end of the central street of the village, which ran uphill towards the castle. The tall figure of Lord Nimatsu stood waiting for them. As they came closer, he stooped into the lowest possible bow before them.

Alyss and Evanlyn exchanged a glance, then made vague hand gestures and stiff little bobs of the head in response.

'Ariss-san, Ev-an-in-san,' the nobleman said as he straightened once more, 'you have done my people a great service.'

Evanlyn nodded, looked around and gestured at the huge body on the ground.

'Lord Nimatsu, here is your *Kyofu*. Dead.'

'I can see. I can see,' Nimatsu replied softly. He stepped forward to examine the *Kyofu* more closely, taking in the terrible injuries that these two slightly built foreigners had inflicted on it.

'You are unharmed?' he asked.

Alyss shrugged. 'I'm sore and battered, and my back-side has bruises all over it.'

Evanlyn gave a tired grin. 'And I've had the bejabbers scared out of me. But apart from that, we're fine. You should see the other fellow.' She paused, then added in mock surprise, 'Oh . . . you can.'

'It's a snow tiger,' Nimatsu said softly. He went down on one knee beside the limp body, reaching out to touch the white fur. 'I've never seen one so big. I thought they had been driven out of these parts years ago.'

'Well, this one decided to hang around,' Alyss told him.

Nimatsu looked up from the dead tiger and met the eyes of the two *gaijin* girls. In his life, he had seen many brave deeds in battle. Never before had he seen courage to equal that shown by these two. He turned to the gathered Hasanu, now watching silently.

'Hasanu people!' he said, raising his voice so that it carried down the street, where hundreds of faces were upturned to watch. 'The *Kyofu* is dead!'

It was as if they had been awaiting official confirmation of the fact. There was a giant, wordless roar of triumph from the assembled villagers. Alyss and Evanlyn stood awkwardly, not sure how to respond to the moment. Truth be told, they were both eager to escape from public view and recover from the terrifying night they had spent.

Nimatsu raised his hands and the roar of the crowd slowly died away.

'The *Kyofu* killed seventeen of our friends and neighbours. Now these girls, these young girls from another country, have ended the Terror!' Alyss raised an eyebrow. He didn't use the word *gaijin*, she noticed. Literally, it meant foreigner. But the term had developed slightly pejorative overtones in the way it was sometimes used. Obviously, Lord Nimatsu intended that nobody might infer any kind of slur from his words.

'Hasanu people, give thanks to Ev-an-in-san and Ariss-san!'

Now the roar that rose from their throats was deafening. Alyss glanced at Evanlyn, standing beside her. The princess smiled.

'I think we could wave now,' she said.

They acknowledged the cheers of the villagers, then Lord Nimatsu stepped forward to join them.

'Today, you should rest and recover,' he said. 'I'll send out messengers to gather the Hasanu army. By the end of the week, we should be ready to march to the aid of Emperor Shigeru.'

Alyss lay back in the scalding hot bath, feeling the water ease the bruises and aches of her battle with the *Kyofu*. She could still recall the mind-numbing terror she had felt when the massive beast had stormed out of the night towards her, the mouth-drying fear as she lay curled under the wooden shield, hearing its claws and teeth rip and tear at the wood, feeling it breaking up and knowing that it couldn't withstand the onslaught much longer, then the overwhelming relief as she heard Evanlyn's lead shot begin to pound into the animal's body.

'She's as good as they say,' she muttered to herself.

Reluctantly, she stepped out of the steaming hot water, wrapping herself in a giant, warm robe and groaning slightly as pain twinged in her back muscles. Yet the pain was much less than it had been before the bath, she knew. There was a light tap at the door frame.

'Come in,' she called. The door slid open and Evanlyn entered. She had bathed as well. She wore a wrap-around robe and her short blonde hair was still wet.

'How are you feeling?' Evanlyn asked.

Alyss made her way to a low stool and sat, groaning slightly once more, and indicated for Evanlyn to sit beside her.

'I'll live,' she said, with a wry smile. 'That hot water certainly does wonders. What doesn't parboil me makes me stronger,' she said, misquoting the old proverb. The smile faded and she regarded Evanlyn for a few seconds.

'It occurs to me,' she said, 'that in all the terror and excitement and cheering, I never said thank you.'

'Thank *me*?' said Evanlyn, her tone incredulous. 'I have never witnessed anything to match what you did last night! That was the most courageous act I have ever seen! Where on earth did you get the idea?'

Alyss coloured a little, although, with her face already flushed from the heat of the bath, it was difficult to notice.

'Something Selethen told us when we were in Toscana. He said one of the tribes to the south of Arrida hunts lions that way. They let the lions knock them over, then lie under their shields and stab upwards at them. It struck me that might be the way to deal with the *Kyofu*. Of course,' she said, smiling, 'they don't have the benefit of a friend hurling great chunks of lead at the lion as they do it. You have no idea how relieved I was when you came to the rescue.'

She looked seriously at the smaller girl now. Everyone had made a great fuss about Alyss's willingness to act as bait in the forest. Only Alyss realised that when Evanlyn had come to her aid, she had done so without any protection at all. If her sling shots hadn't been as accurate as they were, she would have been left facing an enraged beast at close quarters, without shield, armour or defensive weapon of any kind.

If Alyss had risked her life to defeat the *Kyofu*, Evanlyn had done no less. She wondered if the princess realised that and she felt a deep regard for the other girl, not just for her skill with the sling, but for her readiness to put herself in danger to save a companion.

If only . . . Alyss resolutely pushed the unworthy

thought aside. But Evanlyn seemed to be thinking along similar lines.

'Alyss,' she said uncertainly, 'one day I'll be queen. And I'm going to want people around me who are courageous and dedicated and imaginative.'

'That's as it should be,' Alyss said.

'Frankly, I'd like quite a few of those people to be women. I think women have a different perspective on things, as your mentor has proven time and time again. I'd like you to be one of my inner circle, Alyss, professionally and personally. I think that we could work very well together.'

Alyss made a half bow from her sitting position and winced as the back muscles stretched again.

'I'll always be happy to serve my queen and my country in any way I can,' she said politely.

Evanlyn spread her hands in exasperation. 'Why do you have to be so formal, Alyss? Why can't I get through to you? I respect you. I admire you. I like you! I want to be your friend! My father has shown that having good friends as advisers is the best way to rule. Halt, Crowley, Baron Arald. They're not just advisers. They've been his friends for years. And friends will tell you when you're wrong. I want that!'

'Have I been unfriendly, your highness? I've always tried to be respectful.' Alyss's face was a mask, but now two spots of colour appeared in Evanlyn's cheeks.

'There always has to be a niggle between us, doesn't there?' she said angrily. *'Thank you for that, your highness. Have I been unfriendly? I've always been respectful.'* She mimicked Alyss's words savagely. 'I'm offering my friendship, but you seem determined to push me away. Why? Let's get it out in the open, once and for all!'

Alyss drew in a deep breath. She hesitated. She was an ambitious girl and she knew she might be jeopardising her future career if she took this any further. But then the dam broke.

'We both know what it is! Keep your hands off Will, all right?' She stood up, dominating the smaller girl with her superior height. But Evanlyn stood her ground and shouted back at her.

'Will? What about Will? What is it with you about me and Will?'

'Because you're in love with him! You're the princess and you think you can have anything you want, and you want Will. Any fool can see that!'

'Then I'm afraid you're the fool, Alyss Mainwaring, because I am not in love with Will. I'm in love with Horace.' Evanlyn had lowered her voice, but her words carried no less weight for the sudden drop in volume.

'Of course you are! Don't deny it. You . . .' Alyss suddenly realised what the princess had said and floundered to a stop. 'You're what?' she said. 'I mean, I know Horace is in love with you. But you . . .'

'I am in love with him. Deeply in love with him. And only him. Why do you think I came halfway round the world to help him? Because he's a good dance partner? Oh, I love Will, Alyss. But I'm not *in love* with him. We went through so much together and he was a wonderful friend and protector for me. Look, years ago, when we came back from Skandia, I thought I was in love with Will. I'll admit I made a play for him then. But he refused me — and he was right. We're friends, good friends. Surely you can deal with that?'

Alyss hesitated. She still wasn't certain. She wasn't sure that she trusted Evanlyn's motives.

'I'm not . . .' she began but Evanlyn erupted in anger once more.

'Oh for god's sake, girl! Tell me, how do you feel about Horace?'

'Horace?' Alyss said in surprise. 'Well, we grew up together. I love him, of course. He's like a big brother.'

'Exactly! Now has that ever seemed to bother me? Or have I coped with it?'

Alyss couldn't help a wry smile. 'Well, when we found him, you nearly broke my arm getting him away from me,' she said and Evanlyn rolled her eyes to heaven. 'But no . . . I suppose it hasn't bothered you. There's no reason why it should. There's nothing like . . . *that* . . . between Horace and me, as I say.'

'Aaaaaaaggggggghhhhh!' Evanlyn let out a frustrated yell. Alyss actually recoiled a pace in surprise. 'That's what I'm trying to tell you! There is *nothing like that* between me and Will, either! Cope with it! For god's sake, cope with it!'

More than a little taken aback, Alyss studied the determined stance of the small figure before her. Alyss was an honest person and she was forced to admit that Evanlyn had an excellent point. Alyss had spent the past few months, and some considerable time before that, acting suspiciously towards her, distrusting her and jealously resenting any time she spent with Will. Yet she realised that Evanlyn, if she chose to, could feel exactly the same way about her relationship with Horace.

But she didn't. She accepted it.

And suddenly Alyss felt very small when she remembered the sarcasm and the taunts and the bruised knuckles that had characterised their relationship. Evanlyn had behaved well, she thought. It was she who had behaved badly, who had been petty and distrustful. This was a noble and courageous girl, she realised. She hadn't hesitated to risk her life when Alyss was in danger. She had acted quickly and resourcefully.

She had offered her friendship and Alyss, as she always had in the past, had rebuffed her.

'I'm sorry,' she said meekly. 'I never thought of it that way.' She felt ashamed and for a few seconds she couldn't meet Evanlyn's eyes. But then she heard the unmistakable smile in the smaller girl's voice.

'Well, thank goodness we got that out of the way. After all, our future husbands are best friends. It'd be damn awkward if we continued to hate each other.'

'I never hated you,' Alyss protested, but she saw Evanlyn's eyebrow raise in a familiar expression.

'Oh really?' the princess said.

Alyss shrugged awkwardly. 'Well . . . maybe a bit. But I'm over that now.' She looked up at Evanlyn and they smiled at each other. There was a new warmth in their smiles and Alyss realised that this was a friendship that would last for her lifetime.

'Are you really going to marry Horace?' she asked, intrigued. Evanlyn nodded.

'I'll be needing a bridesmaid,' she said. 'A tall one. That way, I'll look more petite and feminine.'

Fifty

Halt clapped his hand on the shoulder of the exhausted scout.

'Thanks, my friend,' he said. 'Now go and get some food, then rest. You've served your Emperor well.'

'*Hai*, Halto-san!' the travel-stained young Kikori replied. He had spent a nerve-racking four days avoiding Arisaka's army to bring his report to Ran-Koshi. He bowed to the command group, then again, more deeply, to the Emperor. Then he turned and left. Halt waited until he was gone.

'I think that seals it,' he said. 'We'll have to force Arisaka's hand before his reinforcements get here.'

'Now we know why he's waited,' Horace said thoughtfully. The valley leading to Ran-Koshi had been clear for several days, the last of the snow having melted away. Each day they had expected Arisaka to attack and each day he had failed to do so. Now the reason for his delay was obvious. General Yamada, an unexpected ally, was marching to his aid with a force of three hundred Senshi.

According to the report they had just received, the extra troops could arrive within a matter of days.

Shigeru shook his head sadly. 'I had hoped that Yamada would at least remain neutral. I never thought he would believe the lies that Arisaka has been spreading about me.'

Through the winter, Atsu's network of spies had brought in reports of an extensive disinformation campaign generated by Arisaka and his allies to win over the uncommitted clans. According to these reports, Shigeru had abandoned the throne and fled the country. Arisaka was claiming to have trapped a rebel force that was using Shigeru's name and an impostor who resembled the Emperor, in an attempt to seize the throne.

'The bigger the lie, the easier it is to sell,' Halt said sympathetically. 'People tend to believe that a preposterous story must be true — precisely because it is so unlikely.'

'But surely, once Yamada and his men see Shigeru, they'll know the story's false?' Will said.

Halt shook his head. 'How many of Yamada's men would know you by sight?' he asked the Emperor.

Shigeru pursed his lips. 'Very few. Even Yamada would need to see me at close quarters to recognise me.'

'And by the time he had the chance to do so, you'd be dead. You can be sure Arisaka would see to that,' Halt replied. 'But, if we can break Arisaka's force before Yamada arrives, you'd have the chance to prove you are the Emperor.'

'Arisaka has at least five hundred men,' Will pointed out. 'They'll outnumber us by more than two to one.'

'They'll outnumber us four to one if we wait for Yamada to arrive,' Halt pointed out. 'And this way, we can choose our own battleground.' He turned to where Jito, the former headman of Riverside Village, was standing — a few paces away from the others. Jito was still a little in awe of being so close to the Emperor but he'd earned his place in these councils. Halt had put him in charge of logistics and organising defences. 'Jito, are the hedgehogs ready?'

Jito nodded in confirmation. 'Yes, Halto-san. We have fifty of them. I've had them taken down Mikeru's Pass and they're ready to be assembled and placed in position.'

Those Kikori who weren't training as fighters had been busy during the previous months, constructing defensive measures and equipment. The hedgehogs, portable obstructions designed by Halt that could be assembled quickly on the battlefield, were one example of their work.

'Then deploy them tonight where we decided — between the rocks and the drop-off on our left flank.'

'Yes, Halto-san. It will take four to five hours to assemble them and place them in position.'

'We need them in place by first light. Set your own timetable but make sure they're in place when we need them.'

'Yes, Halto-san.' Jito bowed to the Emperor and turned to leave the tent.

Horace stepped forward to study the map Halt had prepared. 'You plan to engage Arisaka on the same ground where we fought the first battle.'

Halt nodded in confirmation. 'Our right flank will be secured by the bluff. The rocks were good enough on the left flank when we weren't outnumbered, but we'll need more this time. The hedgehogs will extend the protection to this shallow cliff. That way, both flanks are secure.'

Selethen rubbed his chin thoughtfully as he looked at the chart. 'Relatively secure,' he corrected. 'They'll still get through the hedgehogs, given time,' he said and Halt glanced up at him.

'True. So I'll put Mikeru's dart-throwers on the left flank. They can stay hidden among the rocks, then hit the Senshi while they're forcing their way through the defences. The reserve *goju* can take care of any that make it through. And Moka's men can take a hand if they're needed.'

Moka, head of Shigeru's Senshi bodyguard, frowned as the foreigners discussed these dispositions.

'Halto-san,' he asked, 'why don't we simply advance down the valley below the palisade? We could choose a spot where the valley walls protect both our flanks.'

'If we do that,' Halt explained, 'there's no incentive for Arisaka to attack. He'll know we could simply retreat back up the valley to the palisade. If we go out onto the plain here, he'll see we have no real line of retreat.'

'Other than Mikeru's Pass,' Will put in and Halt glanced at him.

'True. But Arisaka doesn't know about that. He'll see this as his chance to defeat us once and for all.'

'If the worst comes to the worst, we'd never make it back up that pass in a hurry. It's too narrow. Our men would be jammed up at the entrance,' Horace said.

'It's a risk,' Halt said. 'But I think we have to roll the dice and take it.'

The Emperor wore a worried expression on his face. He looked at Horace, then back to Halt.

'Halto-san, you're saying that in order to make Arisaka attack us, we have to place ourselves in this dangerous, exposed position?'

Halt met his gaze levelly. 'That's right, your excellency. There are always risks in battle. It's a dangerous business. The trick is to take the right ones.'

'How do you know which are the right ones?' Shigeru asked.

Halt glanced at his two younger companions. They grinned and answered in chorus, 'You wait and see if you win.'

Shigeru nodded. 'I suppose I should have known that.'

Halt smiled grimly at Will and Horace. They knew, as well as he did, that they were taking a huge chance. But the only way to win battles, when you were seriously outnumbered, was to take chances.

'Have your *gojus* ready to move out two hours before dawn,' he ordered. 'We'll jump off from the palisade gate and march down the main valley. It'll be safer and quicker than moving down Mikeru's Pass. And besides, we need to keep that clear for Jito's people.'

After the others had left, Halt stayed behind with Shigeru. The Emperor sat, waiting expectantly. He knew Halt wanted to talk to him and he had a shrewd idea what he wanted to talk about.

'Your highness,' Halt began, 'there is one alternative we haven't discussed . . .'

He paused, searching for the right way to broach the subject. But Shigeru was ahead of him.

'Halto-san, you're going to suggest that I might make my escape from here alone, correct?'

Halt was taken aback that the Emperor had read his thoughts so easily. But he recovered quickly.

'Yes, sir, I am. It needn't be a permanent thing. But I have to admit, the odds are against us here. It might be better if you made your way to the coast. Our ship is waiting at an island only a few days away. They could take you on board and —'

'And turn Arisaka's lie into the truth,' Shigeru said.

Halt shrugged uncomfortably. 'Not exactly. You'd be free to return once things were more settled here. You could even raise some of the southern clans against Arisaka.'

'And the Kikori?' Shigeru asked. 'What would happen to them if I were to abandon them?'

Halt made a dismissive gesture. 'You're using emotive terms here. You're not abandoning them . . .'

Shigeru snorted derisively. 'I'm leaving them on the eve of a battle they're fighting in my name,' he said. 'A battle that even you say is a risky one, with no guarantee of success. Wouldn't that count as abandoning them?'

'But they'd understand. They're fighting for you.' Halt had to keep trying, although he could see he would never convince the Emperor.

'Which is all the more reason for me to stay,' Shigeru told him. Then, after a pause, he continued, 'Tell me, Halto-san, if I were to escape, would you and your friends come with me?'

Halt hesitated. Then he replied, knowing that Shigeru deserved to hear the truth.

'No, your excellency, we wouldn't. We've trained these men to fight. It's up to us to stay here and lead them when they do.'

'Exactly. And I've asked these men to fight in my name. It's up to me to believe in them when they do. So, like you, I have to stay and take my chances.'

There was silence between them for some time. Then, with a barely perceptible lift of his shoulders, Halt capitulated.

'Well, I suppose we'd just better make sure we win,' he said.

Shigeru smiled. 'Which is precisely why I need to be here.'

THE GENERAL
DISPOSITION
OF FORCES
AT THE START
OF THE BATTLE

RAN-KOSHI

The palisade

Mikeru's
Pass

Shark
Goju

Wolf
Goju

Hawk
Goju

Bear
Goju

Hedgehog
fortifications

N

Attacking Senshi

Arisaka's camp

Fifty-one

The four *gojus* slipped through the palisade gate two hours before dawn. With each group of fifty formed up in three files, they set out down the pass.

Discipline was excellent, Halt noted approvingly. Aside from a few muted commands to march, there was no sound other than the jingling of their equipment and the rhythmic tramp of their boots on the rocky ground of the valley below Ran-Koshi. For the time being, at least, the walls of the valley should mask those sounds from the sentries at Arisaka's camp.

When they reached the mouth of the valley, the leading *goju* — the Bears — wheeled left in response to a hand signal from their leader and doubled round the bluff to their appointed position on the flat plain. The Bears, formed now into two ranks, would cover the left of the Emperor's battle line, with the obstructions assembled by Jito's workers protecting their left flank. Selethen's Hawks came behind them, taking position on the right.

The final two *gojus* — the Sharks and the Wolves — took position behind the others, in a slightly staggered formation that covered the gap between the two leading *gojus*.

Moka, with fifty of Shigeru's Senshi warriors, formed a mobile reserve behind the *gojus*, ready to react to any breach.

The battle line formed with a minimum of noise and confusion. Each man knew exactly where he was supposed to be and went to his place without hesitation. They were all in place before the first grey fingers of light started to streak the sky in the east. Will, Horace and Selethen moved among the Kikori, telling them quietly to rest and relax, saving their strength for the coming battle. The men sat in their ranks, laying their heavy shields aside. Some of the women, organised by Jito, moved among them with water, pickled rice and smoked fish.

Other members of Jito's work party were putting the finishing touches to the hedgehogs. Horace strolled over to inspect the devices at closer quarters. You had to hand it to Halt for ingenuity, he thought. First the false wall at the palisade during the first attack, now these.

Each hedgehog was constructed of six sharpened poles, two metres in length. The poles passed through a central rope yoke, with six closely spaced loops to hold them in place. The sharpened poles were thus formed into a shape that resembled three large X's bound together. They were light and easy to assemble. But once in place, they were difficult to push aside, as the wide-spread feet tended to dig into the ground. In addition, each set of four was linked together by stout poles and chains, making them even more difficult to displace. As a final touch, the array of hedgehogs was draped with rope, looped around the arms and trailing loosely between the individual units. The ropes were festooned with sharp iron hooks, Horace knew. They were small, so not easily seen. But they would snag an attacker's clothes or equipment and slow him down while he struggled to free himself.

Beyond the lines of hedgehogs was the drop-off – a small cliff some four metres high, which put an extra barrier in the path of a flanking force from the left.

He heard a slight noise behind him and turned to see that Will had joined him, inspecting the defences.

'All in all, not a bad job,' Horace said.

'I wouldn't care to be one of Arisaka's men tangled up in those hedgehogs,' Will said. 'Have you seen Mikeru and his dartmen practising?'

'I have. They're frighteningly good, aren't they? Another one of Halt's better ideas.'

Will was about to reply when they both heard the sound of distant shouts of alarm, followed by a strident bugle call ringing over the plain. They both looked in the direction of Arisaka's sprawling camp.

'Sounds as if someone's seen us,' Will said. He gripped Horace's hand. 'Good luck, Horace. Take care.'

'Good luck, Will. See you when we've sent Arisaka running.'

'He won't run,' Will answered. 'But if we can settle with him before Yamada's army turns up, we're in with a good chance.'

'And if we can't?' Horace said.

Will met his gaze in silence for a few seconds. 'I don't want to think about that,' he said eventually.

Horace nodded and unconsciously loosened his sword in its scabbard. 'I wonder where the girls are?'

Will's expression, already grim, grew a little more so.

'I'm guessing they didn't make it. If they'd managed to convince Nimatsu and his people to help us, they should have been here a week ago. I'm afraid we're on our own.'

Arisaka's army assembled in their usual loose formation — a large curved front, three or four men deep. They moved steadily across the plain towards the silent, waiting ranks of the four *gojus*. Unlike the Kikori, they didn't march in step, but simply moved in a loose gaggle. The Senshi preferred to fight as individuals and they moved the same way.

There was one change to their normal deployment. Arisaka had been told of the dangers of the Kikori shield wall and he knew he had to break that rigid formation. Will had surmised that he might use something similar to the Macedon Phalanx — a wedge formation armed with long, heavy lances, designed to smash through an enemy's line. His guess was a little off target. Arisaka knew nothing about the Phalanx.

But he knew about battering rams.

At intervals along the line were five young tree trunks, trimmed and sharpened, and borne by six warriors each, the men holding onto rope handles spaced along the logs' six-metre lengths. The sharpened logs, swung underhand at waist height by the long rope handles, would act as battering rams and smash great gaps in the enemy's defences before the Kikori could come to grips with their attackers. No shield bearer could withstand such a shattering impact.

And once the integrity of the shield wall was breached, the Kikori lost their greatest advantage — their ability to fight as a team, with each man supporting and protecting his neighbour.

'So that's what he's got in mind,' Horace muttered to himself. He watched as the Senshi line advanced, overlapping the Kikori line at either end. As the space available closed down, those outer wings would have to fold back in behind Arisaka's front ranks. They'd be poised three and four deep behind the rams.

Will was running across the rear of the two leading *gojus*, shouting to attract Horace's attention.

'Doorway! Doorway!' he called and Horace waved in acknowledgement. They'd practised to defend against a wedge of heavy lances. The rams were essentially the same thing, and they had a tactic they could use against them. Will continued to run to pass on the same message to Selethen.

Horace hurried to join his *goju*. He moved quickly behind the second rank, calling to his men.

'Use the doorway tactic when they get close!' he called and he saw section leaders in the front rank turn briefly and indicate that they understood.

The advancing Senshi were fifty metres away now, almost within effective javelin range.

'Second rank, open order!' Horace yelled and the rear rank responded as one man, stepping back three paces to give themselves throwing room.

'Javelins ready!'

Twenty-five arms went back, the javelins angled upwards.

'Aim for the rams!' Horace ordered. He watched the approaching army, judged they were in range. 'Throw!'

The javelins hissed away on their arcing flight. Several seconds later, he saw sections of the Senshi line collapse in confusion as the heavy missiles struck home. One of the battering rams crashed to the ground as half its bearers were hit and the others were forced to release their grip on the rope handles. The heavy rolling log caused more confusion among the attacking Senshi. But they reformed and came on. There were still two of the battering rams aimed at the Bear *Goju*.

The nearest ram broke from the Senshi front line as its bearers went from a steady tramp to a run. They lunged forward at the Kikori shield wall, their sudden increase in speed catching Horace by surprise. The heavy, sharpened log swung forward on its rope handles, bludgeoning into the front rank. Three of the Kikori went down and the men on the ram moved quickly to consolidate their position. The second rank had closed up again after throwing their javelins. Now they used their reserve weapons to stab over the heads of the front rank, at the ram and its bearers. The ram swung back, then forward to smash into the shields again. More Kikori went down and the waiting Senshi screamed in triumph as they saw the previously impregnable wall disintegrating. The ram went back again.

'Doorway! Doorway!' Horace yelled, his throat dry and his voice breaking.

This time, as the heavy log swung forward, the Kikori facing it stepped back and to the side, opening a gap in front of it. Without any resistance, the battering ram whipped forward through thin air, throwing the men wielding it off balance. The second line of men opened as well and some of the Kikori grabbed the ram and dragged it through their ranks. As the men on the rope handles staggered through the gap left for them, the deadly stabbing blades of the Kikori went to work. The surviving ram wielders found themselves in the clear behind the second rank, bewildered and isolated. As they realised their predicament, ten men from the front rank of the Shark *Goju* moved forward and quickly surrounded them. Within a few seconds, Arisaka's men lay still. But, in the more open style of fighting, they had taken a toll. Five Kikori lay dead beside them.

With a shout of rage, the Senshi line surged forward. But the doorway closed as quickly as it had opened and they found themselves facing that formidable line of shields. They cut and slashed ineffectually, denied the space they needed to wield their swords to best effect. The short swords of the Kikori flickered in and out between the shields, wounding, maiming, killing.

The Senshi backed away, moving out of range of the shorter weapons. Now some of them began a more careful attack, lunging at the small gaps between the shields with their longer *katana*. This time, however, forewarned of the Kikori tactic of jamming shields together, they withdrew their blades almost immediately. It was an effective technique. More Kikori fell, their places taken by men from the second rank.

Horace glanced down the line to see what had happened with the second ram. The men wielding it, having seen what happened to their companions, were more circumspect in their attack. They swung the ram in short, savage jabs at the wall. Shields split, men went down. Then the men on the ram drew their unwieldy weapon back and hurled it into the Kikori front line, immediately drawing swords and following it through the gap they had breached.

For a few minutes, they had the situation they wanted – a disjointed Kikori line, which gave them room to use their long swords. They took a dreadful toll on the defenders. Then the second rank joined in, using their javelins to stab at long range, moving forward as a unit to fill the gaps in the front rank. Horace came charging down the line from his vantage point, his sword swinging and thrusting into the Senshi, his shield deflecting their *katana*. His speed, and the power of his sword strokes, took Arisaka's men by surprise and they began to fall back before his one-man assault. Seeing this, Horace bellowed to his Kikori.

'Advance! Advance! *Issho-ni! Issho-ni!*'

The Bear *Goju*, discipline and formation restored, began to tramp steadily forward, crowding the enemy, buffeting them, shoving and stabbing. But even in retreat, the Senshi's *katana* were taking a toll of the advancing *goju*'s ranks.

On the right flank, Selethen's Hawks were faring a little better. There had been two rams aimed at Selethen's formation and they were some metres behind the rams attacking Horace's section of the line. Selethen was able to order the doorway tactic when the first ram came forward. The Kikori peeled aside, letting the ram blunder through, while Selethen's men stabbed at them with javelins and short swords. Then the line closed again to face the following Senshi.

The second ram never made it to the Hawks' front line. Four of its six bearers were struck down by a salvo of black-shafted arrows. Halt, standing with Shigeru on a raised vantage point thirty metres to the rear, nodded in satisfaction as he saw the result of his shooting. The remaining two bearers, unable to control the heavy log by themselves, allowed it to fall to the ground. It bounced and rolled, knocking over four of the Senshi who were planning to follow it into the enemy's ranks.

Seizing on their confusion, Selethen echoed Horace's order.

'Forward! *Issho-ni!*'

The Kikori, their fighting blood roused, took up the chant as they moved forward like a tide.

'Issho-ni! Issho-ni!'

They slammed into the Senshi and the slaughter began. But, like the Senshi facing Horace's men, these warriors knew better than to allow the Kikori to get too close. They gave ground, all the while stabbing into the gaps and over the tops of the shields. Men died on both sides, although the close quarter fighting suited the Kikori better. Selethen, like Horace, patrolled the line, dashing in where necessary to lend support with his flashing curved blade, using his small hand shield to deflect the thrusts and cuts of the *katana*.

He glanced across at Horace's *goju* and saw that his men were moving ahead of Horace's, opening a dangerous gap. Instantly, he shouted an order.

'Hawks! Halt! Withdraw! Withdraw ten paces!'

Moving as one, the Hawk front line disengaged from the Senshi and moved backwards. As they had trained to do, the second rank seized the shoulders of men in the front rank. They turned to face the direction of the withdrawal, guiding the steps of the front rank so their comrades never had to turn away from the enemy. The *goju* simply moved backwards, formation still intact, any gaps in the shield wall closed by men from the second rank.

Selethen gauged the distance to the Senshi force and glanced back to the Shark *Goju* behind his men. He signalled their commander and the man turned and bellowed a series of orders.

Arisaka's men, their view obscured by the enemy directly in front of them, had no warning of the shower of javelins from the Shark *Goju* as they hurtled down over the heads of the Hawks. Senshi went down all along the line as the heavy weapons struck home. Selethen, seeing that the rams were all out of action, signalled for another volley and watched as great gaps were punched in the Senshi line.

A Senshi commander screamed an order and his men, never knowing when a third volley might arrive, turned and ran clear of the killing ground.

Horace now saw that his men were advancing too far ahead of the Hawk formation. He too called a halt and the two front lines faced each other. The Senshi weren't about to try another frontal assault that would take them within range of those stabbing swords. But now a group of fifty Senshi warriors detached from the main force and began to try to work their way through the wooden obstructions they could see on the enemy's left flank. They shoved and cut their way through the star-shaped hedgehogs, gradually forcing a path through them. Then several of them were pulled up short by the hooks in the tangle of light rope that covered the ground at knee height.

None of them paid any attention to the horn blast that came from the raised ground where Halt stood watching. And very few of them saw the lightly armed group of young men rise from the cover of the rocks on their right.

Mikeru looked to the distant figure in the grey and green cloak. He saw Halt raise his hand slowly, twice, then point to the rear. The young Kikori nodded, understanding, and issued his orders to his thirty dartmen.

'Two darts,' he said. 'Then retreat.' Each man carried eight darts in a leather tube on his back. Halt was obviously aiming to conserve their weapons as far as possible.

'Ready!' Mikeru called. He looked down the line of throwers, saw they were all prepared, and called the executive order.

'Throw!'

The iron-tipped darts, whipped on their way by the taut throwing cords, made a distinctive whistling sound as they flew. Some of the men struggling among the hedgehogs heard it and looked up, curious to know what it was. Then the thirty darts smashed into them and there were screams and cries as they fell, their armour ruptured by the iron tips. Before they could recover, another flight of darts savaged them.

Fifteen of their number were left hanging awkwardly, draped over the hedgehogs. Eleven of the survivors made it through the tangle of obstructions and found themselves facing Moka's fifty warriors, who were eager to strike a blow for their Emperor. There was a brief, uneven battle.

None of the attackers survived. Seeing the result, the remainder of the flanking force withdrew.

Across the field, the same thing was happening. Arisaka's men, thwarted in their attempt to force a way through the shield wall, were drawing back to take stock of the situation. They left a lot of their comrades on the field of battle but they were by no means beaten.

And they had taken their toll of the Kikori. Knowing what to expect, the Senshi hadn't attacked blindly as they had done before. They were more disciplined in their approach and knew when to withdraw.

Now, by mutual consent, the two forces backed off and faced each other, each assessing the damage they had done, the losses they had suffered. Halt looked up as Will approached. He saw that his former apprentice's quiver was half empty. Obviously, Will had accounted for some of Arisaka's men as well.

'How's it looking?' Halt said.

The younger Ranger shook his head. 'It's not great. We've lost over twenty men. And there's another ten wounded.'

Halt whistled slowly. That was a third of the men who had been engaged in the two leading *gojus*. 'Can we stand another attack?'

Will thought about the question before he answered.

'I'd say so. Arisaka lost nearly two hundred men in that attack. We've got two *gojus* intact and ready to fight. They're fresh troops. I'll push them forward to replace the Hawks and the Bears.

'In addition, we've got Mikeru's dartmen. They did a great job. Plus we've got fifty Senshi ourselves.

'I think we can handle whatever Arisaka throws at us —
so long as those reinforcements don't turn up.'

The moment he said the words, he regretted them. The
superstitious thought occurred to him that by mentioning
the possibility, he might make it a reality. Then he
shrugged the thought aside. Things didn't work that way,
he told himself.

Across the field, from Arisaka's army, he heard a sudden
burst of cheering. He looked up.

'What have they got to cheer about?' he asked.

Halt pointed grimly to a file of men, just visible in the
south-west corner of the plain.

'It's Yamada,' he said. 'He's arrived.'

Fifty-two

Stony faced, Will watched the new arrivals approaching from the south-west. They marched in a large, irregular gaggle and the weak midmorning sun glinted off their weapons and armour. At least three hundred of them, he thought.

Halt's voice snapped him out of his grim reverie. 'You'd better get moving if you're going to reorganise your troops,' he said. 'Or do you plan to surrender?'

Will shook himself angrily and ran down from the slightly elevated spot where Halt and Shigeru stood. He sent a detail to recover as many of the javelins as possible, and ordered the Wolves and Sharks forward into the front line, replacing the two badly depleted *gojus* who had borne the brunt of the fighting so far. Horace and Selethen would command the two new *gojus* in the front line. The three friends had a hurried consultation.

'They won't have any rams this time,' Will said, 'so I guess it's business as usual. Use your javelins. Two volleys each, no need to save them for stabbing. And close with them as soon as you can. Our men did well when they got in close — and the Senshi don't like it.'

His two commanders nodded. Horace glanced to where Shigeru stood, in full ceremonial armour.

'Any chance you can convince Shigeru to get away?' he said, lowering his voice.

Will shook his head. 'Halt tried. He'll stand by his men, win or lose.'

'I always thought he would,' Selethen said quietly. All of the foreigners had come to respect the strength of character and the quiet dignity of the Emperor.

'In that case, we'll just have to win,' Horace said. But the very fact that he'd asked the question showed that he didn't believe that was possible now. They all knew their best chance had been to smash Arisaka's force before Yamada's men arrived. That opportunity was gone.

They could hear the irregular tramp of feet and rattle of equipment from Yamada's force as it drew closer. In a few minutes, they'd be fighting for their lives again.

'All right,' said Will, 'I guess this is it. Time we —'

'Chocho! Chocho-san!'

The clear young voice carried to them and they all turned to see Mikeru running towards them. The tube of darts slung across his back slapped up and down as he ran, setting up a rattling counterpoint to the thud of his feet.

'What *is* this *chocho* business?' Will muttered to himself. But his friends overheard the comment.

'It's a term of great respect,' they chorused, and he glared at them.

'Oh, shut up,' he said. But now Mikeru had drawn up with them. He leaned forward, regaining his breath, heaving in deep lungfuls of air, his hands on his thighs.

'Mikeru, we're going to need you back with your men,' Will began. The small but potent force of dartmen was stationed on the far side of the line. But Mikeru was shaking his head as he gathered enough breath to speak.

'*Chocho,*' he managed to gasp, 'there are men coming. Soldiers!'

'We know,' Horace said, jerking a thumb at the approaching Senshi. 'Be a bit hard to miss them.'

But Mikeru waved his hands in a negative gesture. 'Not there!' he said. 'There!' And he pointed to the east.

Three sets of eyes snapped around to follow his pointing finger. To the east of their position, past the end of the left flank and the low cliff, lay another ridge line, two kilometres away. Emerging from behind it, and onto the plain, was a huge body of troops. As the three friends watched, the column kept streaming out from behind the ridge, dust clouds rising to mark their movement.

'It's the girls,' Horace said quietly. 'They made it. And they brought the Hasanu with them.'

'There must be thousands of them,' Selethen said, as the column continued to emerge into sight. And now they could hear the faint sound of a distant chant. Will realised they could hear it because the cheering from Arisaka's army had died away as all eyes turned to the east.

'*Kotei! Kotei! Kotei!*'

'What are they saying?' he asked Mikeru.

The young fighter grinned at him. 'They are saying "Emperor! Emperor! Emperor!"' he told them.

Will let go a huge sigh of relief. He glanced round to where Halt stood and saw his old teacher, his cowl pulled back and his head bared, nod quietly to him.

The Hasanu had deployed fully onto the plain and they began to advance towards Arisaka's Senshi. The chant grew louder and louder as they approached and Arisaka's men turned uncertainly to face the oncoming horde. Even with Yamada's men, they were outnumbered at least three to one and they watched apprehensively as they began to make out details of the Hasanu. Huge figures, over two metres in height, covered in what appeared to be long reddish hair and brandishing spiked clubs, pikes and heavy spears. Unconsciously, the Senshi grouped closer together as they faced this terrifying new threat.

And as they did so, they seemed to forget that behind them were the deadly fangs of the Wolves and the Sharks. Will glanced at the two *goju*, in perfect, disciplined formation. He realised that this was the ideal opportunity to smash Arisaka's army. His small but highly trained force would be the hammer. The huge Hasanu army would be the anvil upon which they broke Arisaka once and for all.

'Mikeru,' he said, 'get your men to advance as far as the hedgehogs. Hit the Senshi from the flank. Let 'em have all your darts, then run for it.'

The young man nodded and sprinted away. Will turned to Horace and Selethen.

'Advance all four *goju* and hit them in the rear,' he said.

The two commanders nodded and ran to their positions. Orders rang out. There was the familiar crashing sound of the massive shields being raised into position, then the Wolves and Sharks stepped out in perfect unison, the depleted *gojus* of Bears and Hawks formed up behind them.

Some of Arisaka's men sensed their approach and turned to face them. The rebel army were trapped. The wings of the massive Hasanu line would encircle them within the next few minutes. And the grim-faced Kikori fighting machine was in their rear. But the Senshi were warriors, and trained in a hard school. They might have no chance, but they would sell their lives dearly. Those at the rear turned to face the steadily advancing Kikori *gojus*. Forty metres out, Horace called for the Kikori to halt, then for the rear ranks to open out, their javelins poised.

'Stop!'

The voice, deep and resonant, rang out over the battlefield.

Will spun round, and saw Shigeru, with Halt beside him, striding towards the Kikori line. After a moment's hesitation, the young Ranger moved to join them. Shigeru was holding a green branch above his head, the Nihon-Jan equivalent of a flag of truce. A hush had fallen over the battlefield as thousands of warriors waited to see what was about to transpire. The green branch was an inviolable symbol and must be respected.

Halt, Will and Shigeru strode across the plain, until they stood between the Kikori *gojus* and the Senshi line. Shigeru stopped, still holding the green branch high above his head.

From the Hasanu force, they saw another group of figures, also bearing a green branch, detach from the main group and begin to move to join them. Will's heart surged with relief as he recognised Alyss, with Evanlyn beside her, trying to match the taller girl's long strides and still retain her dignity. They were walking a pace or two behind a tall, aristocratic-looking Nihon-Jan in warrior's armour. As they drew closer, Will met Alyss's eyes and they smiled at each other.

'Lord Nimatsu,' Shigeru said, 'it's good to see you.'

The tall Nihon-Jan bowed deeply. 'I am at your service, your excellency, as are my people. Give the order.'

Shigeru said nothing for the moment. He turned to the rebel forces, now barely fifty metres away from him.

'Arisaka!' he called. 'We have to talk.'

For a moment, nothing happened. Then a movement rippled through the rebel ranks and the Senshi warriors parted as a group of three men moved through them — Arisaka, his face hidden by the almost demonic-looking red lacquered helmet, and two others. They stopped. On Arisaka's right was one of his lieutenants, a stocky Senshi nobleman, bearing a huge recurve bow. On the left was an older nobleman, also in armour.

Shigeru bowed to this last person. 'Lord Yamada, do you recognise me?'

The older man peered at the figure before him. He wasn't sure. His eyes weren't as good as they used to be and the person was some distance away. But he definitely looked like the Emperor.

'I was told an impostor had taken the Emperor's place,' he said, his voice uncertain.

Suddenly, the bowman on Arisaka's right moved, drawing back an arrow he had already fitted to the string.

'Death to the impostor!' he screamed as he shot. Shigeru stood, unflinching, as the arrow pierced his left upper arm, below the protective armour. Blood began to stream down over his white linen sleeve.

A roar of protest rose around the battleground, from friend and foe alike. The green branch of truce was sacrosanct. To breach it was an abomination in the eyes of the Nihon-Jan. But before anyone else could move, or the bowman could prepare another shot, Will whipped an arrow from his quiver, nocked, drew, sighted and released in one movement.

His arrow punched through the nobleman's armour like a hot knife through butter. The man staggered under the impact, his recurve bow falling from dead hands, then he crumpled to the ground.

The crowd grew suddenly silent, stunned by Will's lightning reply to the treacherous attack. Voices started to murmur again, uncertainly at first. But again, Shigeru stilled the crowd. Quickly, he took a scarf from around his neck and knotted it around the wound in his arm. Then he put his uninjured hand on Will's bow and took it from the young Ranger. His voice rang out once more.

'Enough! Enough bloodshed! Lord Arisaka, let's end this now.'

Arisaka's sword hissed from its scabbard. Once more, a murmur of strong disapproval rippled across the plain, both from his own men and his enemies. To draw a weapon in the presence of the green branch was a gross breach of the Senshi code of behaviour. Even Arisaka's troops could not condone such an action.

'This will only end with your death, Shigeru!' Arisaka screamed.

Yamada turned to him, the anger and shame he felt all too obvious on his face.

'Shigeru?' he repeated. 'Then you've known all along that this is no impostor? You lied to me and my men?'

Arisaka, furious beyond reason, tore the helmet and face piece from his head and hurled them to the ground in rage.

'He's weak, Yamada! Weak and dangerous! He will destroy everything that we hold sacred!' He glared now at Shigeru, his face flushed, his eyes blazing with hate. 'You want to destroy the Senshi class and everything it stands for! I will not allow you! I will stop you!'

'Arisaka.' Shigeru's deep voice was calm and reasonable by contrast. 'I will not destroy the Senshi. I am a Senshi. But for too long, the other people of Nihon-Ja have been repressed and downtrodden. I want to rule for all people. Like the Kikori here, and the Hasanu. The ordinary people have the right to have a say in our country. Tell your men to lay down their weapons now and let's live in peace. Let's live together in peace.'

'No!' Arisaka's voice was a shriek. 'My men will fight you. We will die if necessary! You may defeat us, but this will not be a cheap victory. Thousands will die here today!'

'That's something I cannot allow,' Shigeru said.

Arisaka laughed, a shrill sound that showed how close he was to snapping.

'And how will you stop it?' he demanded.

'I will stand down,' Shigeru said simply.

Arisaka recoiled in surprise, and exclamations of amazement went through the crowd.

'I will abdicate if that is the only way to stop this madness. Appoint another Emperor,' Shigeru continued. 'Lord Yamada, and Lord Nimatsu, I look to you to ensure that a proper choice is made. But I will not stand and watch thousands of Nihon-Jan, my people, lose their lives to preserve my pride. I will stand down.'

'You're bluffing, Shigeru!' Arisaka said. 'You won't give up the throne.'

'I swear that I will, if that will prevent thousands dying here today.' Shigeru let his gaze run round the faces of Arisaka's men as they watched this clash of personalities. 'I swear on my honour, before all of you here.'

Silence greeted his words as those watching realised that he was in earnest. Then Yamada's men began to mutter among themselves. They had come here under a false belief. They realised now that Arisaka had lied to their commander to make them break their oath to the rightful Emperor. If Arisaka ordered them to fight, their commander would refuse. And so would they. Now Arisaka could depend only on his own men.

Matsuda Sato was a low-ranked officer in Arisaka's army. He commanded a small group of twelve men and had led them in the service of his lord for seventeen years. In all that time, he had received scant recognition for his service or his loyalty. He had watched Arisaka brutalise his men, driving them mercilessly and punishing them severely if he believed they had failed him. Arisaka never rewarded good service, only punished that which he deemed to be bad. Sato, knowing no alternative, had always assumed this was the sign of a strong leader. Now he realised he was witnessing real strength — a man who would forsake the highest position in the land to save the lives of his subjects. *This* was leadership, Sato realised. This was a man to follow. Arisaka was exposed as a deceiver and an oathbreaker. Sato slid his *katana*, still in its scabbard, from inside his belt and dropped it to the ground in a sign of peace.

'Shigeru!' he shouted, raising his clenched fist above his head. The men around him looked at him in surprise. Then one of them copied his actions and joined him. Then another. Then two more. Then a dozen.

'Shigeru!'

The cry began to spread throughout Arisaka's men. The rattle of swords hitting the ground became continuous, like some monster hailstorm, and the voices swelled, another dozen, then fifty, then a hundred, then more.

'Shigeru! Shigeru! Shigeru!'

Then the Kikori joined in, letting their shields and javelins fall to the ground and adding their voices to the swelling roar of acclamation. And finally, the deep-throated Hasanu as well, till the mountains around them rang with the name.

'Shigeru! Shigeru! Shigeru!'

Wild-eyed, furious, goaded beyond reason, Arisaka swung his gaze around his followers. The chanting was now deafening and the sight of his own men cheering the Emperor was too much. His sword flashed and the man nearest him fell with a cry.

Matsuda Sato, commander of twelve men, looked up at his former lord, puzzled and wondering why he was seeing him only through a red haze. He felt numb where Arisaka's sword had opened the massive wound in his chest. Then the red changed slowly to black.

A horrified silence spread over the plain as men realised what Arisaka had done. He stepped forward and turned to face his troops, hurling abuse at them as they instinctively stepped back, away from him.

'You have betrayed me!' he screamed. 'You have shamed me! You defile my honour!'

'You have no honour!'

He spun round, the bloodstained *katana* still in his hand. The speaker, whose words had carried clearly to the men around him, was one of the foreigners. A young man, wearing a strange green and grey cloak. Arisaka's eyes narrowed. This was the one who had shot so quickly in reply to his lieutenant's arrow. But now the foreigner's heavy longbow was in Shigeru's hands and he was unarmed.

'You are a traitor and a coward and a man without honour, Arisaka!' the foreigner continued.

Arisaka raised his *katana*, pointing it at the calm young face. 'Who are you, *gaijin*? What do you know about honour?'

'I'm called *Chocho*,' Will said. 'I've seen honour among these Kikori warriors, men I've trained to fight you. They are men who understand loyalty and trust. And I see it now in your own men, now that they recognise the true Emperor of Nihon-Ja. But I see no honour in you, Arisaka. I see a crawling, cowardly, lying traitor! I see a man with no honour at all!'

'*Chocho?*' Arisaka shouted, goaded beyond control. 'Butterfly? Then die, Butterfly!'

He leaped forward, the *katana* rising for a lethal strike at the unarmed foreigner. But then Will's right arm shot forward from beneath his cloak and he stepped forward with his right leg, going into a crouch as he released the saxe knife in an underarm throw.

A spinning pinwheel of light, it flashed towards the charging Arisaka, hitting him above the breastplate of his armour, below his chin, and burying itself in his throat.

The impact of the heavy blade jerked Arisaka's head back. He felt the *katana* drop from his suddenly slack fingers, felt hot blood gushing from the huge wound. Then he felt . . . nothing.

Will straightened from his crouch as Shigeru stepped forward and laid a hand on his shoulder.

'It seems he mistook a butterfly for a wasp,' the Emperor said.

Fifty-three

The farewells had been said, for the most part. Will, Halt, Selethen and the two girls were already on board *Wolfwill*. The ship lay with its bow beached on the sand, at the cove where the Araluan party had originally come ashore. Gundar and his men had spent a relatively comfortable winter on the offshore island, although Gundar had been sorry to hear that he had missed an epic battle. But there had been plenty of fish and shellfish in the cold waters, and a good supply of game onshore. Now, like their passengers, the Skandians were eager to turn the ship towards home waters.

Only Horace remained on the beach, standing facing the Emperor, dwarfing the smaller man. Tears formed in the young warrior's eyes now that the time had come to say goodbye. In the months that had passed, he realised he had come to love this brave and unselfish ruler, to respect his unwavering sense of justice and his unfailing good humour. He knew he would miss Shigeru's deep rumbling chuckle — a sound so massive that he always wondered how it came from such a small frame.

Now, faced with the moment of leaving, there was an enormous lump in his throat, a lump that blocked the many words he wanted to say.

Shigeru stepped forward and embraced him. He knew how much he owed to the young man. He knew how Horace's courage, resolve and loyalty had sustained him and his small band of followers throughout the difficult and dangerous weeks when they were escaping from Arisaka. He remembered how Horace had stepped forward unhesitatingly to take Shukin's place when his cousin had died at Arisaka's hand.

The two Rangers, of course, had done a great service for him with their innovative tactics and battle plans, as had the dark-skinned, hawk-nosed Arridi warrior. And Evanlyn and Alyss, by their courage and initiative, had been the instruments that saved his throne, bringing the mighty Hasanu army to his rescue. He was grateful to them all.

But without *Kurokuma*, none of them would have been here. Without *Kurokuma*, Arisaka would now be Emperor.

'Shigeru . . .' Horace managed one word, then, choked with emotion, he stepped back from the older man's embrace, his head lowered, his cheeks running with tears.

Shigeru patted the muscular arm. 'Parting is hard, *Kurokuma*. But you and I will always be together. Just look into your mind and heart and you'll find me there. I will never forget you. I will never forget that I owe you everything.'

'I . . . I don't . . .' Horace could manage no more, but Shigeru knew what he was trying to say.

'I wish you could stay with us, my son. But your own country and your own king need you.'

Horace nodded, overwhelmed by the sense of conflicting loyalties. Shigeru couldn't have picked a more compelling form of address than to call Horace 'son'. Horace had grown up an orphan, deprived of a father's love and guidance from an early age. Then Shigeru smiled and spoke in a lower voice, so that nobody else could hear.

'And I believe that a certain young princess has need of you too. Take good care of her. She is a jewel beyond price.'

Horace raised his tear-reddened eyes to meet Shigeru's. He managed a faint smile in return. 'She certainly is that,' he agreed.

'We'll see each other again. I know that in my heart. You know you will always be welcome here in Nihon-Ja. You are one of us.'

Horace nodded. 'I will come back one day,' he said. 'That's a definite promise. And maybe you could travel to Araluen.'

Shigeru pursed his lips. 'Yes. But perhaps not for a while. I think I need to stay here until matters are stabilised,' he said. 'But who knows? If there were an important occasion of state — a high-ranking wedding, perhaps?'

He left the thought open and again they shared a conspirators' smile. Then he reached into the wide sleeve of his robe and produced a small scroll, tied with black silk ribbon. He handed it to Horace.

'In the meantime, remember me by this. A token of my friendship.'

Horace took the scroll. He hesitated, then Shigeru gestured for him to open it. It was fine linen paper, and on it, painted in the stylised, deceptively simple strokes that typified fine Nihon-Jan art, was a rendition of a bear, depicted in the act of catching a salmon at a waterfall. It was a fascinating piece, with only the barest of detail inked in. Yet somehow, the viewer's eye was led to provide the missing lines and features, creating a complete and comprehensive illustration. The more Horace looked, the more the bear seemed to become alive. The more he could see the water flowing around him. All accomplished with a few masterly brush strokes on the linen.

'You painted this?' he said, noting the small rendition of three cherries in the bottom left-hand corner.

Shigeru bowed his head in acknowledgement. 'It's a little crude. But it was done with love.'

Horace slowly rolled the linen up, replaced the ribbon, and placed it safely in the breast of his jacket.

'It's a true treasure,' he said. 'I will keep it always.'

'Then I am content,' Shigeru said.

Horace spread his hands in an awkward gesture. He hadn't thought to find a gift for Shigeru.

'I have nothing to give you . . .' he began. But the Emperor held up one graceful forefinger to silence him.

'You gave me my country,' he said simply.

They faced each other for a long moment. There were no more words. From the ship, they heard Halt call, his voice a little apologetic for the intrusion.

'Horace. Gundar says the tide is falling. Or rising. Whatever it's doing, we have to be on our way.'

His tone was gentle. He had watched his young friend and Shigeru and he sensed they had reached the awkward point that comes in all farewells — when there is nothing further to say, yet neither person wants to be the one to make the final move, to break the bond between them. When someone or something needs to give them the impetus to part.

'I've got to go,' Horace said huskily.

Shigeru nodded. 'Yes.'

Briefly, they embraced once more, careful not to crumple the scroll inside Horace's jacket. Then the tall young warrior turned abruptly and ran up the boarding ladder. His feet had barely touched the deck when the crew hauled the ladder aboard and began poling the ship clear of the beach, turning its bow to the open sea. Horace moved to the stern, his hand raised in farewell. On the beach, Shigeru mirrored the gesture.

The ebbing tide took hold of the wolfship, pulling it swiftly away from the beach while the crew hoisted the triangular sail. Then, as the yard was braced around, the sail filled and the rudder began to bite as Gundar set a course to weather the headland. Horace remained in the stern, watching the figure on the shore grow increasingly smaller. After several minutes, Evanlyn moved to stand with him, slipping her arm around his waist.

Impulsively, Will went to join them, intending to add his support and comfort to Evanlyn's. But Alyss caught his arm and stopped him.

'Leave them,' she said quietly.

He frowned, not quite understanding for a second or two, then the message sank in. His mouth formed a silent 'Oh'.

The deck heeled as the wind freshened and the water began to chuckle louder as it slid down the sides of the accelerating wolfship.

Finally, they rounded the point and Horace could no longer see his friend, the Emperor of Nihon-Ja.

Fifty-four

'**B**utterfly?' Will said. 'Why "Butterfly"?'

'I believe it's a term of great respect,' Selethen said gravely. He was very obviously not laughing. Too obviously, Will thought.

'It's all right for you,' he said. 'They called you "Hawk". "Hawk" is an excellent name. It's warlike and noble. But . . . Butterfly?'

Selethen nodded. 'I agree that Hawk is an eminently suitable name. I assume it had to do with my courage and nobility of heart.'

Halt coughed and the Arridi lord looked at him, eyebrows raised.

'I think it referred less to your heart and more to another part of your body,' Halt said mildly. He tapped his finger meaningfully along the side of his nose. It was a gesture he'd always wanted an opportunity to use and this one was too good to miss. Selethen sniffed and turned away, affecting not to notice.

They'd been at sea for five days, which explained Halt's current good spirits. He'd gone through the usual period spent huddled by the lee rail, face white, eyes sunk deep in his head. His friends had tactfully ignored him while he got his sealegs.

Now, with a constant wind over their port quarter and a smooth, even swell, *Wolfwill* was eating up the kilometres on the trip home. In the west, a magnificent sunset was painting the low-lying clouds on the horizon in shades of brilliant gold and orange. The six friends sat in low canvas chairs in a clear space just forward of Gundar's steering position, discussing the names they had been given by the Kikori.

Selethen was named Hawk. Alyss had been given the title of *Tsuru*, or Crane. It was a long-legged, graceful bird and the name was appropriate. Evanlyn was *Kitsuné*, the Nihon-Jan word for fox — a tribute to her speed and agility.

Halt, strangely enough, had been known only as Halto-san. Perhaps this was because, of all of them, his name was the easiest for the Nihon-Jan to enunciate.

But Will had been taken aback in his confrontation with Arisaka to discover that his name — *Chocho* — meant Butterfly. It seemed a highly unwarlike name to him — not at all glamorous. And he was puzzled to know why they had selected it. His friends, of course, delighted in helping him guess the reason.

'I assume it's because you're such a snazzy dresser,' Evanlyn said. 'You Rangers are a riot of colour, after all.'

Will glared at her, and was mortified to hear Alyss snigger at the princess's sally. He'd thought Alyss, at least, might stick up for him.

'I think it might be more to do with the way he raced around the training ground, darting here and there to correct the way a man might be holding his shield, then dashing off to show someone how to put their body weight into their javelin cast,' said Horace, a little more sympathetically. Then he ruined the effect by adding thoughtlessly, 'I must say, your cloak did flutter around like a butterfly's wings.'

'It was neither of those things,' Halt said finally, and they all turned to look at him. 'I asked Shigeru,' he explained. 'He said that they had all noticed how Will's mind and imagination darts from one idea to another at such high speed, backwards, forwards, sideways, in a totally unpredictable pattern – something I've noticed myself. Actually, it's a pretty fair name for you when you think about it.'

Will looked mollified. 'I suppose it's not too bad if you put it that way. It's just it does seem a bit . . . girly.' He sensed the stiffening of attitude from Evanlyn and Alyss and hastened to qualify his words, 'Which I, for one, don't mind a bit. It's a compliment, really. A term of great respect, in fact.'

'I like my name,' Horace said, a little smugly. 'Black Bear. It describes my prodigious strength and my mighty prowess in battle.'

Alyss might have let him get away with it, if it hadn't been for his tactless remark about Will's cloak flapping like a butterfly's wings.

'Not quite,' she said. 'I asked Mikeru where the name came from. He said it described your prodigious appetite and your mighty prowess at the dinner table. It seems that when you were escaping through the mountains, Shigeru and his followers were worried you'd eat all the supplies by yourself.'

There was a general round of laughter. After a few seconds, Horace joined in. Halt, watching him closely, thought to himself how well this young man had turned out. Courageous, loyal and with unsurpassed skill with weapons, he was a credit to Baron Arald's Ward and the Castle Redmont Battleschool. Halt didn't factor in that his own influence and example might have played some role in forming such a strong and likeable character.

'Well,' said Evanlyn, 'we're going to have to find another title for him soon.'

They all looked at her, puzzled by her words. Will, glancing at Horace, noticed that his best friend had gone beet red with embarrassment. Evanlyn, sitting close beside Horace, jogged him gently with her elbow.

'Tell them,' she said, grinning broadly. Horace cleared his throat, humphed and harrumphed several times and finally managed to speak.

'Well, it's just that . . . you see . . . we're sort of . . .' He hesitated, cleared his throat two or three more times, and Evanlyn jogged him again, a little less gently.

'Tell them,' she repeated and the words came in a rush, like water from a collapsing dam.

'LastnightIproposedtoEvanlynandshesaidyes . . .' He managed to slow down and said at a more comprehensible speed, 'so when we get home, we're going to be married and I hope —'

He said more. But nobody heard him in the general whoop of delight and congratulations that erupted from his friends. The Skandians looked up, startled at the sudden commotion. Halt turned to Gundar as Will surged across the deck to embrace first Horace, then Evanlyn, his face alight with joy for the two of them, his heart swelling with happiness.

'Gundar!' Halt cried. 'Break out some of our special provisions, and some wine and ale. We're having a party tonight!'

'I'm for that!' Gundar said, grinning broadly. He'd heard Horace's announcement and he was delighted for the two young people. Word of the engagement flashed along the rowing benches where the crew were relaxing. There was a roar of delight from the forward bench, then the bear-like figure of Nils Ropehander came lumbering down the deck, bellowing congratulations.

'What's that? The General? Engaged? Well, General, here's my hand in congratulations!'

The expression *here's my hand* turned out to be a loose one. Nils scooped Horace up in a massive bearhug of delight. The hug, unlike the expression, was not a loose one. When he released Horace, the young groom-to-be crumpled, moaning breathlessly, to the deck. Nils then turned to Evanlyn. She stood up warily and began to back away. But the sea wolf quickly seized her hand, bowed, and raised it to his lips, delivering a wet, smacking kiss.

'I expect to be a pageboy at the wedding!' he bellowed.

Evanlyn grinned, surreptitiously wiping her wet hand on her jacket.

'I think I'd like to see that,' she said. She looked at Alyss, saw the pleasure in the tall girl's eyes. 'Speaking of official duties, I hope you'll be my bridesmaid?'

'I'll be delighted,' Alyss said. 'And I assume that means I'll finally get to finish a wedding dance with Will.'

There was no question in anyone's mind that Will would be the best man. At Halt's wedding, his dance with Alyss had been interrupted by the unexpected arrival of Svengal, with the news that Erak was being held to ransom.

'I've got a great idea!' Horace said, having recovered most of his breath. He looked around the circle of his closest friends. 'We've got the bridesmaid and best man right here. Why not have the wedding now? Gundar's a ship's captain. They can perform weddings, can't they, Halt? You could marry us, couldn't you, Gundar?'

'I'm not sure that's such a *great* idea . . .' Halt began but Gundar cheerfully overrode him.

'Gorlog's teeth, boy, I don't know if I can or not. But tell me the words and I'll say 'em for you!'

'Um, Horace, darling,' Evanlyn said, choosing her words carefully, 'Gundar isn't so much a ship's captain as a reformed pirate and a heathen.' She looked apologetically at Gundar. 'No offence, Gundar.'

The skirl shrugged cheerfully. 'None taken, little lady. It's a pretty fair description. Not sure about the reformed part,' he added thoughtfully.

'I'm not sure my father would totally approve of us getting married here. I think he might like to know about it first,' Evanlyn continued.

Horace, unabashed, shrugged. 'Fine,' he said. 'It was just an idea. But if you say no, then no it is.'

Halt stepped closer to him and patted him gently on the arm.

'Get used to that,' he said.

Epilogue

They celebrated long into the night. When the others had all retired, Will and Alyss stood together, his arm around her waist, hers around his shoulders, in the bow of the ship. It was a beautiful night and the moon hung low to the horizon, casting a silver path down the dark water towards them.

Astern, they could hear the occasional low murmur of conversation from the crew on watch.

'I'm glad you and Evanlyn are finally friends,' Will said.

Alyss laid her head on his shoulder. 'Me too. She's really quite a girl.'

'She is indeed,' he said. Alyss raised her head to look at him.

'You didn't have to agree quite so readily,' she told him. Then she smiled and put her head back on his shoulder.

'So . . . they're getting married. Horace and Evanlyn. How about that?' Will shook his head in wonder.

'Indeed,' she said, not sure where this conversation was going.

'You know . . .' He paused, seeming to gather his resolve, then continued, 'Maybe you and I should think about doing something like that.'

Her head came off his shoulder. Her arm slipped from around him and she stepped away from him.

'*Maybe you and I should think about doing something like that?*' she repeated, her voice rising with each word. 'Is that your idea of a proposal?'

'Well . . . I . . . er . . .' Will began. But he had no idea where to go, what to say. In any event, Alyss gave him no chance to continue.

'Because if it is, you're going to have to do a whole lot better!'

She turned away and strode off down the deck, taking long, angry paces. Will made an ineffectual gesture after her, then stopped. He sensed he'd got that wrong. Really wrong. He could see her slim back, stiff and upright, radiating total outrage.

What he couldn't see — and what she had no intention of letting him see — was the huge, delighted smile that was lighting up her face.

Acknowledgements

After ten books, it's time to acknowledge the efforts and support of a few people who have been involved with me, and this series, over the years.

For this book in particular, I'd like to thank my friend and fellow author, Simon Higgins, for his suggestions and advice on the comparative merits of European and Japanese weapons and fighting styles. If I've got any of it wrong, be assured the mistakes were all mine and not his.

Thanks, too, to Ryoko and Akiko Sakai, for their gracious permission in allowing me to name the emperor in this book after their late father, Shigeru. Arigato, Ryoko-san and Akiko-san.

It's high time I bowed deeply in the direction of my two editors — Zoe Walton at Random House Australia and Michael Green of Philomel in the United States. They've curbed my excesses and suffered my tantrums over the years. Their guidance and wisdom has been invaluable —

and they've usually managed to make me feel that any changes were my ideas. I'm pleased to count them both as friends as well as professional colleagues. Thanks, guys.

And finally, from the millions who have now read this series, I'd like to single out four. (Can you single out four, or is that a contradiction in terms?)

In Australia, Ginger and Merry Hansen were my first-ever correspondents, sending me fan letters after the publication of *The Ruins of Gorlan*. They've stayed in touch over the years and their approval of each subsequent book has become an ongoing good luck charm for me. Late last year, I finally had the opportunity to meet these charming young ladies face to face. Thanks to both of you.

In the United States early in 2010, I also met with two long-term regular correspondents, and I'm delighted by the fact that their contact with me has led to their becoming good friends. Maddie Jones — effervescent, energetic, enthusiastic, bubbling over with the sheer joy of life — what would I do without you, Maddie? And Shea Megale, a young lady who holds a very special place in my heart and whose courage and dry, sly wit have been a delight to me for the past couple of years.

Thank you all.

John Flanagan

Read on for a preview of book 11

RANGER'S
APPRENTICE

THE
LOST
STORIES

JOHN FLANAGAN

Redman County
The Republic of Aralan States
(formerly the medieval Kingdom of Araluen)
July 1896

Professor Giles MacFarlane groaned softly as he eased his aching back. He was getting too old to remain crouched for long periods like this, gently whisking dust away from the excavated ground before him as he sought to release yet another artefact from the earth that had held it captive for so long.

He and his team had come upon this ruined castle several years ago. They had mapped the outline of its triangular main walls — an unusual shape for a castle. The jagged stump of the ancient keep tower stood in the middle of the space they had cleared. The collapsed tower was barely four metres high now. But even in its ruined state, MacFarlane could see that it had been a formidable building.

Their first digging season had been spent determining the outer limits of the building. The following year, they had begun a series of cross trenches, digging down to discover what lay beneath the build-up of earth and rock and detritus that had collected over twelve hundred years.

Now, in the third season, they were down to the fine work, and beginning to unearth the ancient treasures of the dig. A belt buckle here. An arrowhead there. A knife. A cracked ladle. Jewellery whose design and general appearance dated to around the middle of the seventh century in the Common Era.

On one momentous day, they had unearthed a granite plaque, carved with the likeness of a tusked boar. It was that piece that had identified the castle beyond doubt.

'This was Castle Redmont,' MacFarlane had told his hushed assistants.

Castle Redmont. Contemporary of the fabled Castle Araluen. Seat of Baron Arald, known as one of the legendary King Duncan's staunchest retainers. If Redmont had really existed, then surely all the tales of its people might have a basis in fact. Perhaps, MacFarlane thought, hoping beyond hope, he would find proof that the mysterious Rangers of Araluen had actually existed. It would be a staggeringly significant discovery.

But as this season had progressed and the trenches had been dug deeper still, there had been no find as important as that first one. MacFarlane and his people had to be content with the normal fare of excavations — nondescript metal tools and ornaments, pottery shards and remnants of cooking vessels.

They searched and dug and brushed, hoping every day that they would discover their personal Holy Grail. But as the summer digging season passed, MacFarlane had begun to lose hope. For this year, at least.

'Professor! Professor!'

He stood, rubbing his back again, as he heard his name being called. One of the young volunteers who augmented his paid staff from the university was running through the excavation, waving as she saw him. He frowned. An archaeological dig was no place to be moving so recklessly. A slight misstep could ruin weeks of patient work. Then he recognised her as Audrey, one of his favourites, and his expression softened. She was young. The young were often reckless.

She drew level with him and stood, shoulders heaving, as she recovered her breath.

'Well, Audrey, what is it?' he said, after giving her a little time.

Still panting, she pointed down the hill towards the River Tarb.

'Across the river,' she said. 'Among a tangle of trees and bushes. We've found the outline of an ancient cabin.'

He shrugged, not excited by this revelation. 'There was a village down there,' he said. 'It's not surprising.' But Audrey was shaking her head and grasped his arm to lead him down the hill.

'It's way outside the village limits,' she said. 'It was on its own. You must come and see it!'

MacFarlane hesitated. It would be a long walk downhill, and an even longer one back up. Then he shrugged mentally. Enthusiasm like Audrey's should be encouraged, he thought, not stifled. He allowed the girl to lead him down the rough zigzag path.

They crossed the old bridge that spanned the river. Never one to miss a chance to teach, he indicated to the girl how the supports at either end were older than the middle span.

'The middle section is much newer,' he said. 'These bridges were designed so that the centre span could be removed or destroyed in the event of an attack.'

Normally, Audrey would have hung on his every word. The professor was a personal hero for her. But today she was in a fever of excitement to show him her find.

'Yes, yes,' she said distractedly, urging him on. He smiled indulgently as she tugged at his sleeve, leading him away from the remains of the ancient village. The going became tougher as they entered the forest and had to make their way along a narrow path, through the close-growing large trees and unkempt undergrowth. Finally, Audrey turned off the path and, bending double, forced a way through a tangle of vines and creepers. MacFarlane followed awkwardly, then stood in some amazement as he found himself in a small clearing, surrounded by ancient oaks and more modern dogwood.

'How on earth did you find this?' he asked and Audrey blushed.

'Oh ... I ... er ... needed a little privacy ... you know,' she said awkwardly.

He nodded, waving a hand. 'Say no more.'

She led him forward and, looking where she pointed, his practised eye could see the unmistakable outline of a small hut or cabin. Most of the structure had rotted away, of course. But there were still a few vestiges of the upright columns remaining.

'Oak,' he said. 'It'll last for centuries.'

The outlines of the rooms and dividing walls could still be made out — faint signs imprinted into the ground itself over the centuries, even though the original structure was long gone. And the flattened, level ground of the interior floor was all too obvious.

'There may have been a stable at the rear,' she said, her voice hushed in this ancient place. 'I found a few metal pieces — bits and what might have been harness buckles. And the remains of a bucket.'

MacFarlane turned in a slow circle, studying the dim outline of the building.

'It's a different layout to the village houses,' he said, almost to himself. 'Completely different.'

He took a couple of steps, intent on making a rough measurement of the cabin's dimensions, then stopped suddenly.

'Did you hear that?'

Audrey nodded, eyes wide. 'Your last step. It sounded as if the ground were hollow.'

They dropped to their knees together and scrabbled at the dirt and leaf mould. Audrey rapped her knuckles on the ground and again they heard the sound of a hollow space beneath. MacFarlane never moved anywhere without a small hand spade in his belt. He took it now and began tossing the earth aside. Then the blade thumped against something solid — solid, but with a certain give in it.

Working quickly, testing the ground for that hollow sound continually as he went, he cleared a rectangular space, some forty centimetres by fifty. Audrey leaned forward and brushed the remaining earth from the centre. They found themselves looking at an ancient, desiccated timber panel. A brass ring was set in one side and MacFarlane gently eased the spade under it, lifting it.

The panel came with it, splintering and half disintegrating, to reveal a stone-lined space underneath.

A space that contained an ancient wood and brass chest.

Once more, the professor used the spade to edge the lid of the chest open. Audrey put a hand on his to stop him.

'Should we be doing this?' she asked. She knew MacFarlane would normally never disturb an artefact like this without taking the utmost care to preserve it from damage.

He met her gaze.

'No,' he said. 'But I'm not waiting any longer.'

The lid opened with surprising ease. Brass hinges, he thought. If they had been iron they would have fallen to powdery rust long ago. Gently, barely containing his enthusiasm, he lifted it back and peered inside.

The chest was full of pages of manuscripts — written on parchment or vellum that was now brittle and delicate. Gently, he eased one sheet up. The edges crumbled but the centre remained intact. He leaned forward, craning to read the closely written words on the page. Carefully, he studied other pages, handling the brittle manuscript pages with expert care, making out names, places, events.

Then he gently replaced the sheets and leaned back on his haunches, his eyes glistening with excitement.

'Audrey,' he said, 'do you know what we've found?'

She shook her head. Obviously, from his reaction, this was something major. No, she thought, more than that, something *unprecedented.*

'What is it?' she asked.

MacFarlane threw back his head and laughed, still unwilling to believe it.

'We never knew what had become of them,' he said and, when she cocked her head in an unspoken question, he explained further.

'The Rangers. Halt, Will Treaty and the others. The chronicles and the legends only take us as far as the point where they returned from their voyage to Nihon-Ja. But now, we have these.'

'But what are they, Professor?'

MacFarlane laughed aloud. 'They're the rest of the tale, my girl! We've found the Lost Stories of Araluen!'

A SPECIAL Q & A WITH JOHN FLANAGAN:

Is there a story behind the Rangers' symbol of a silver oak leaf?

I took it from the American military insignia for a major. I just liked the feel of it. It seemed right for people who spent their time in the woods and forests.

Do you think that Will might ever retire?

I shouldn't think so.

Can you give us a hint about what's in store for your new series, Brotherband Chronicles?

Brotherband is set in the same world, about two years before Book 10. The Brotherband concept is a Skandian system wherein sixteen-year-old boys are grouped together in teams of nine or ten and taught weapons craft, seamanship and tactics. The various Brotherbands compete for the title of champion. The central character is Hal, a half-Araluen, half-Skandian boy who, because of his mixed lineage, has spent his childhood as an outcast. He's selected for the rejects Brotherband – the boys nobody wanted.